Praise for Elaine Everest

'A warm tale of friendship and romance'
My Weekly

'Captures the spirit of wartime'
Woman's Weekly

'One of the most iconic stores comes back to life
in this heartwarming tale'
Woman's Own

'Elaine brings the heyday of the iconic high-street
giant to life in her charming novel'
S Magazine

Also by Elaine Everest

The Woolworths Girls
Carols at Woolworths (ebook novella)
Christmas at Woolworths
Wartime at Woolworths
A Gift from Woolworths
Wedding Bells for Woolworths
A Mother Forever

The Butlins Girls

The Teashop Girls
Christmas with the Teashop Girls

The Patchwork Girls

~

Elaine Everest was born and brought up in north-west Kent, where her books are set, and has written widely for women's magazines – both short stories and features – as well as fiction and non-fiction books for the past twenty-four years. Successful in writing competitions, she was shortlisted for the Harry Bowling Prize and was BBC Radio Kent's short-story writer of the year in 2003.

A qualified tutor, she runs The Write Place creative writing school in Hextable, Kent. Elaine lives with her husband, Michael, and their Polish Lowland Sheepdog, Henry, in Swanley, Kent.

You can say hello to Elaine on
Twitter: @ElaineEverest
Facebook: @ElaineEverestAuthor
Instagram: @elaine.everest
Website and blog: www.elaineeverest.com

Elaine Everest

The Patchwork Girls

PAN BOOKS

First published 2021 by Macmillan

This paperback edition first published 2021 by Pan Books
an imprint of Pan Macmillan
The Smithson, 6 Briset Street, London EC1M 5NR
EU representative: Macmillan Publishers Ireland Ltd, 1st Floor,
The Liffey Trust Centre, 117–126 Sheriff Street Upper,
Dublin 1, D01 YC43
Associated companies throughout the world
www.panmacmillan.com

ISBN 978-1-5290-1600-0

1 3 5 7 9 8 6 4 2

A CIP catalogue record for this book is available from the British Library.

Typeset by Palimpsest Book Production Ltd, Falkirk, Stirlingshire
Printed and bound by CPI Group (UK) Ltd, Croydon CR0 4YY

MIX
Paper from
responsible sources
FSC® C116313
www.fsc.org

Visit www.panmacmillan.com to read more about all our books
and to buy them. You will also find features, author interviews and
news of any author events, and you can sign up for e-newsletters
so that you're always first to hear about our new releases.

I dedicate this book to the memory of dog breeders worldwide who fought for the survival of their breeds during World War Two. We are forever in your debt.

Prologue

~

London, October 1939

'I'm sorry, Mrs Wentworth, but you shouldn't be here,' the grey-haired porter said, reaching out gently to take the young woman's arm. He could see she was in shock, her face pale and her body trembling.

Helen looked up at the damaged facade of the Victorian mansion block. The building where she'd started her married life with so many hopes and dreams had fared badly: several window panes were missing and the red brickwork was chipped on the first floor. 'I need to collect a few things,' she pleaded. 'I promise to be careful . . .'

'Okay, missus, but I'll have to accompany you. I would never forgive myself if something 'appened to you after – well, after what went on here yesterday.'

Without a word Helen entered the building, heading towards the ornate iron lift residents used to travel to the upper floors.

'Best we don't use it,' he said, steering her towards the wide staircase. 'It's not been checked out yet and gawd knows what damage has been done.' He scowled. 'I don't know what the world's come to.' He fell into step beside her as they started to climb the winding black-and-white tiled staircase. Already some of the ornate windows had been boarded up, although chinks of light from the midday sun shone through the cracks, illuminating dust motes dancing around them.

'Here we go,' the porter said, pulling open a heavy oak door that led to the upper hallway and the entrance to her home, along with several others. 'You'll find a couple of coppers in there. I did tell them not to hang about, as that ceiling's bound to come down before too long. Who'd have thought this could 'appen here in Cadogan Mansions?' He shook his head. 'I'll come with you to make sure you stay safe. Do you really want to go in there after . . .'

Helen thanked him, but didn't say any more. The porter and his wife liked nothing better than a juicy morsel of gossip to keep them going during their live-in job of caring for the old building. She usually did her best to slip quietly past if either of them was hovering in the entrance lobby. They could chat for England, and what had happened in her apartment would certainly keep them interested for many a day.

A police constable standing at the entrance to her home bowed his head and held the door open for her to enter. She stopped abruptly, and the porter stepped sideways to avoid crashing into her.

'Oh, my goodness; I never thought there would be so much damage! A few broken windows and ruined furnishings, but this . . .' She clasped a hand to her mouth to stifle a sob. The remains of damask curtains flapped in a light breeze coming through the gaps where once there'd been floor-to-ceiling windows. All around the drawing room were scattered pieces of wood and fabric that Helen could only just recognize as her furniture. The desk where John had worked was intact, although scratched by debris, while a large breakfront cabinet had lost its upper doors. Books were everywhere, pages fluttering in the cold air. 'He didn't stand a chance.' Shrugging off the porter's attempt to place an arm round her shoulders, Helen took a deep breath. 'I just need to collect . . .'

'Mrs Wentworth?'

She froze as a tall, fair-haired man in an RAF officer's uniform stepped towards her from where he'd been standing by the remains of a marble fireplace.

'Mrs Wentworth, I'm Inspector Richard Gladstone,' he said, holding out his hand.

Helen looked up at him, confused. His ice-blue eyes grew a little warmer as she shook his hand politely.

'Excuse me, but – why are you here?' she asked uncertainly. 'I wasn't aware a crime had been committed . . .'

'Yes, it's just an unfortunate accident,' the porter echoed from where he stood close behind her. 'I can assure you, Inspector, everyone who lives here in Cadogan Mansions is completely safe. It was an accident.'

Inspector Gladstone did not reply, but swept an eloquent glance around the damaged room. He bent and picked up an overturned chair from beside the mahogany desk, wiping away a layer of brick dust before gesturing for Helen to sit down. As she moved towards it, the shock of seeing the scene of her husband's death finally hit her hard, and she felt her legs buckle.

'Thank you,' she murmured, gripping the chair's leather-covered arms.

'A glass of water for Mrs Wentworth, please, Constable,' the inspector said. The uniformed officer made his way carefully through the broken furniture, fallen lath and plaster from the ceiling towards the kitchen, where they heard him run the tap.

'I didn't realize a gas leak could cause so much damage,' Helen murmured. 'I hope John didn't suffer.'

The three men fell silent as she accepted the glass of water and took a few sips before setting it down on the edge of the desk.

'Would you be able to tell me where you were yesterday?' the inspector asked. 'We had some trouble contacting you.'

Helen took a deep breath. 'I wasn't at work,' she said. 'John suggested I take the afternoon off to do some Christmas shopping. I help my husband in his work and act as his social secretary,' she added, looking at the constable, who had started to take notes. 'He keeps long hours and there never seems to be time for things like shopping – and I like to start early. Then, of course, we have these wretched air-raid sirens interrupting our lives, even though they all seem to be false alarms.' A sudden thought came to her and she put a hand to her mouth. 'Oh – you don't think this could have been a bomb, do you?'

The inspector considered her for a moment before replying. Helen Wentworth looked much younger than her twenty-six years. His notes told him that her deceased husband had been some twenty years her senior. Richard Gladstone wasn't one for sentiment, but it struck him that

4

Helen looked so fragile she might break at any moment, sitting there with her hands tightly clasped in her lap and a smudge of dust across one cheek. She was dressed smartly, as might be expected of the wife of a prominent MP who, according to some, had had the makings of a future prime minister. A smart woollen suit, a felt hat placed jauntily on her head, shining mid-brown curls framing her pale face: she was a true English beauty.

He reined in his thoughts and said: 'No, it wasn't a bomb. Would you be able to tell us where you went shopping and at what time?'

Helen nodded, a couple of loose curls shaking. 'Of course. I had planned to go out around midday to meet a friend, Felicity Davenport, for lunch. As I was about to leave home, she rang to let me know she had a headache. So I lunched at Claridge's and shopped alone, thinking I would drop in to see her later in the afternoon.'

'I can confirm that I put a call through from Miss Davenport,' put in the porter, clearly eager to help with the investigation.

'I have a receipt to show that I shopped at Liberty's in the early afternoon,' Helen added. 'A silk scarf for my mother and a tie for my stepfather.' She picked up her handbag from the tiled floor and searched inside it for the slip of paper. The constable stepped forward and took it from her, noting down the details.

'I'm sure the ladies in the haberdashery department could confirm the time, as we chatted about matching skeins of embroidery silk for my mother-in-law. She's not able to journey to London as often as she would wish, and had asked John if he would remind me to enquire for her. You could verify that with him – oh . . .' She took a shaky breath before continuing. 'They showed me some new stock that had just arrived.' She was clearly trying hard to offer the police any information that might be useful, pushing the horror of the situation aside in order to answer their questions.

'But you didn't come home last night?'

'No. When I went to see Felicity, she was quite poorly – distraught, even. I've never known her to be like that before. I tried ringing to let John know I would be staying the night, but I couldn't get through.'

'The GPO only fixed the line this morning,' the porter said, raising his eyebrows in sympathy. What would his wife think of all this when he told her?

'I rang John's office and left a message,' Helen added. 'I'm sure they can confirm that. It was only this morning that Miss Jones, our office manager, heard about his death and let one of your colleagues know where I was. Your officers came to inform me. I'm certain all of this can be confirmed,' she faltered, pulling a handkerchief from the pocket of her jacket with shaking hands. She managed to unfold it just in time to bury her face in the fine lace as the tears came.

The men fell quiet.

'I'm sorry,' she apologized after a minute or two, blowing her nose and controlling herself with an effort. 'Will you be able to check what I've told you?'

'I'm sure we can,' the inspector replied. 'I think that's all for now. I'm sorry to have bothered you at such a sad time, Mrs Wentworth; please accept my condolences. Can you give us the address of where you'll be staying?'

Helen was thrown for a moment. 'I . . . I suppose I shall have to stay with my mother in Kent. Mrs Hillary Davis, The Maples, close to Biggin Hill.' She reached into her bag again. 'Here are her details. It was my family home as a child,' she added faintly as she handed over her mother's calling card. 'May I collect a few things before I leave?'

'I'm afraid that won't be possible at the moment, Mrs Wentworth. We must investigate a little further before anything can be moved.'

'Investigate? I don't understand. What is there to investigate about a gas explosion?'

'Purely a formality, Mrs Wentworth. Porter, can you arrange for Mrs Wentworth's possessions to be sent on to her once we give permission?'

'Of course, sir.' The porter turned to Helen. 'We can also arrange to put what remains of your furniture into storage, if you wish? Plenty of room in the cellars.'

Helen was beginning to feel overwhelmed. She drew a deep breath. 'Yes, I'd be grateful if you could do that. We have a trunk that you could pack my husband's clothes into, if that's not too much trouble? My suitcases are on top of the wardrobe.' She turned to look at the inspector. 'I wonder – couldn't I possibly take a few of my own clothes now? It seems unlikely they'll be relevant to your investigation. Just a few personal items from the small chest in the bedroom? I don't have anything at my mother's home,' she added as her chin wobbled, tears threatening again.

His heart went out to her. She looked very alone and vulnerable. 'I don't see why not. If you could do it just now, please; and then I'll be sealing off the rooms until our investigation is complete.'

The constable guided Helen back across the devastated drawing room and she hurried into her bedroom, pulling a small leather suitcase from the top of an ornate wardrobe. Opening a drawer, she hastily gathered up lingerie, not stopping to fold any of it or worry about creases. From the wardrobe she pulled out a coat, two day dresses, a skirt and several blouses. Finally she turned to the dressing table, pushing a small jewellery box under the clothing along with a silver-backed hairbrush and hand mirror. Her eyes skimmed over the other items and she picked up a bottle of perfume and a small framed photograph of her late father, adding them to the suitcase. All the time, she was telling herself not to think about how John must have suffered, or about her loss. Snapping shut the brass catches of the case, she took a quick final glance around before rejoining the men.

'I have everything I need. Thank you for allowing that – it means a great deal. If there's nothing else required of me, I'll bid you good day – I'm finding it difficult to be here . . .' Almost before she had finished speaking she was turning away and leaving the apartment, closely followed by the porter.

After a moment, the constable stepped forward and closed the door behind them. 'That one's a bit of a cold fish,' he said to his boss. 'Not exactly the grieving widow, is she?'

'Not everything is as it seems, Constable.'

'If you don't mind me saying, sir, when her husband has just popped his clogs right there on the settee, you would think she'd want to know more about it. Or even get a bit squeamish – what with him dying in an explosion.'

'That's where you're wrong, Constable. John Wentworth MP did not meet his end because of a gas leak, or even the lump of marble from the mantelpiece that hit him squarely on the head.'

'What do you mean? Did something else kill him?'

'Or someone else. Someone handy with a knife, who had no qualms about cutting the throat of a man who could well have been prime minister of this country one day.'

'Cor blimey,' the constable said, rubbing his chin thoughtfully as he looked at the area where the dead man would have been sitting before the explosion. 'I wasn't the first on the scene,' he added apologetically. 'Do you think she did it?'

'At this moment in time, Constable, I cannot ignore any possibility.'

1

Kent, December 1939

'I hate to say this while you are still grieving, my dear, but you really do need to get yourself out into the fresh air. You will feel so much better,' Hillary Davis said as she leant past her daughter and pushed up the sash window. The heavy damask curtains blew inwards, draping round Helen's head.

'For goodness' sake, Mother, please stop fussing,' Helen said as she untangled herself from the curtain. 'Whyever do you want to open the window on such a miserable day? But yes, I'll go for a walk – if only to stop you nagging me,' she added ungraciously.

'Stop talking to your mother like that. I'll not have her spoken to in such a way in my house.'

Helen glared at her stepfather. 'You seem to have forgotten that this is my mother's house. And before that, it was my father's family home. So please don't assume a position you don't have in this household.'

Before he could answer, she flounced out of the room and hurried upstairs to her bedroom. His words floated

11

after her: 'You can get that bloody great trunk out of the hall as well. This house is not somewhere for you to store a dead man's possessions.'

Helen threw herself onto her bed and lay there, trying to control her breathing. She knew she shouldn't let Gavin upset her so much. She'd been able to tolerate him as long as they didn't have to live under the same roof. But now that circumstances had changed – and until she decided what on earth to do with her life next – she would have to make sure she kept away from him if she didn't want to get so upset.

She knew that Gavin had not expected to inherit a daughter when he married. He had made that quite clear with his spiteful comments while she was still young. In a way she was glad she had no siblings, and she was the only child who had been the butt of his taunts and cruel jibes, always just out of her mother's hearing. It was as she'd matured that he'd changed, and even when she rebuffed his cruelty and did her utmost to keep away from him he sought her out, accidentally touching her and forever staring at her growing body. The time could not come quick enough for Helen when she escaped to London and what she thought would be a life away from The Maples. Gavin Davis was a man well worth keeping away from. Even now, after sixteen years, Helen still wondered why her mother had married him. They had been comfortably off after Helen's much-loved father passed away following a short illness; he'd suffered terribly with his chest after serving during the last war, but losing him had still been a shock. At his funeral, ten-year-old Helen had overheard one of his best friends say that Terence Graham would have been better off succumbing to the effects of the mustard gas attack, rather than suffering all these years. Only then had she realized what a perfect father he'd been: always there to help with her homework, always encouraging her to be the best possible version of herself, without letting her see any sign of his illness until the last few months of his life. Their family, albeit small, had been close, with a house full of love and laughter. Helen's mother had changed since marrying Gavin, becoming harder and more belligerent towards her only child.

Helen knew she should never have come back to The Maples after her husband's death. But where else was she to go? When the RAF police inspector had insisted they must have an address for her, it had been the only solution she could think of.

She wiped angry tears from her eyes, sighed deeply and sat up. At this time of year darkness fell early, and if she didn't hurry her walk would be a short one. If she left quietly, she wouldn't be challenged and asked where she was going. The other day, Gavin had followed her out and told her off about the bright beam of her torch; she'd had a job shaking him off, and in the end she had simply turned round and gone home. The way that man acted, she thought irritably – it was as if she ought to be locked up in the Tower of London for attracting the attention of enemy aircraft. Not that anything much had happened yet, even though they'd been at war for three months. She hadn't spotted a single German plane. There again, this house was only half a mile from Biggin Hill airfield; and what with it being a buzz of activity all the time, the Germans would have to be mad to fly over this part of Kent.

Slipping her feet into stout brown leather brogues and lacing them up before reaching for her handbag and gas mask, she headed downstairs. She could hear Gavin through the closed door of the drawing room, talking about a forthcoming trip to play an away match with his bowling club. With luck, she could slip out unheard. Quickly she pulled on her black coat, fastening it tightly around her waist, then tucked a woollen scarf around her neck and stepped out the front door, setting off at a brisk pace.

Biting wind stung her cheeks as she headed down the sloping pavement in the direction of the airfield. She had no real destination in mind, but in her pocket was a letter addressed to her friend Felicity. She felt guilty about not having been in touch for so long. However, Felicity hadn't been in touch either – even though she knew where Helen was staying – so perhaps she was avoiding her? She recalled her mother saying that after Helen's father died, people had crossed the road rather than stop to talk. They hadn't known what to say and then, as time ticked by, it had become harder and harder for them to reach out and be the good friends they once were. Eventually Hillary had become quite brittle towards those who'd ignored her.

The letter Helen had written today was only a brief note, asking after Felicity and suggesting they meet when Helen was next in London – although she had no idea when she would really be up to that kind of trip. Much of the time these days she felt hollow, devoid of feeling. If her mother had allowed it, she could easily have stayed in her bed for days on end – in fact, forever. It was still hard to believe John was really gone, that she would never see him again and their marriage was a thing of the past.

She grabbed at her hat as the wind tried to whip it from her head. It felt as if there was rain in the air now. Up ahead, she could see the small village shop with the postbox outside. Thinking it would be good to get into the warmth for a few minutes, she decided to step in and see whether there were any provisions she could collect for her mother. The news that rationing would begin in January had made Hillary worry about not being able to put a decent meal in front of her husband each night. At the thought of her stepfather, Helen grimaced. She couldn't live alongside Gavin for much longer. Perhaps she should write to her landlord in London to see when – or if – the Cadogan Mansions apartment would be live-able again. But she wasn't very sure she wanted to return to the home where her husband had met his death. Would the atmosphere of what had happened linger, and if so, could she bear it?

She needed to sit down and think seriously about her future. If she did return to London, would there be a job available for her in the government offices John had run so diligently? She'd assisted him and knew the workings of his department inside out, but would that be enough for them to welcome her back? It might be that some staff would be uncomfortable working alongside the wife of a deceased colleague.

Helen knew that for John she had ticked all the boxes as an ideal MP's wife. The difference in their ages and the practical, unromantic nature of their relationship had in some ways made things very straightforward between them. When his polite proposal of marriage had come along she had accepted with alacrity, seeing it as a way to sever her links with Biggin Hill; but even while living and working in London, she had been too shy and unworldly to step completely out onto the path of independence. And she had always been aware that if her mother had been alone, she'd have called on Helen to return home and care for her in her dotage. Hillary persisted in seeing her as a spinster daughter rather than a married woman.

Yes, Helen mourned the passing of her husband because she had enjoyed the feeling of being needed, even if only as a person to stand by his side at official functions and carry out the tasks required of an MP's wife. Often, she had heard people say that John could be prime minister one day, but that idea had put the fear of God in her. Not in a million years could she imagine herself as the wife of a man who ran the country; even so, she was willing to learn and would have supported him. Wasn't that what wives did?

She knew her mother, for the first time in her life, had been proud of her and had enjoyed cutting out snippets from the newspapers along with photographs of John and Helen attending functions together. For Hillary Davis, the main benefit of her daughter's marriage had been that it moved her up the social ladder in her own community. Now she was struggling to accept the death of her son-in-law, seeing it as an affront to her own life. Her status as a woman of note was in danger of being lost.

Approaching the door to the shop, Helen froze with one hand on the handle. Inside she could see one of her mother's friends chatting in an animated way to the shop-keeper. The last thing she wanted was to discuss her grief with Mrs Kennard; that woman took far too much pleasure in dwelling on the gloomier side of life.

Helen turned away, but it was too late: she'd been spotted. Mrs Kennard picked up her straw shopping basket and rushed out the door.

'Oh, Helen, you poor, poor girl. What a coincidence – we were just chatting about you. We've been so concerned for you, what with being widowed at such a young age. You must feel as though your life is over!' She grasped Helen's hand and clung to it. 'How are you, my dear, and what are your plans for the future? I suppose it's too early to think about marriage again, but I'm sure there will be many eligible young men lining up to walk you down the aisle before too long. There are plenty more fish in the sea.'

Helen was shocked. How dare this woman even speak about her remarrying? Why, it was almost disgusting, she thought. The devil in her wanted to reply that she was looking forward to meeting the fish, but out of respect for John she only smiled politely, murmuring her thanks before skirting around Mrs Kennard and entering the shop.

'Don't take any notice of her, ducks. She's a nosy old bat and just thinks of herself most of the time,' the woman behind the counter sympathized. 'She was asking me to put some bacon and a twist of sugar to one side for her in early January. It seems she'll be all right for butter, as she's come to an agreement with a man at the dairy. What a bloody nerve! She'll get a name for herself and no mistake. Would you believe, she reckoned her ration card hadn't arrived? The greedy old so-and-so had completely forgotten she'd already registered with me.' She tutted as she started to wipe down the marble-topped counter. 'No doubt some shopkeepers will fall for her cheek. Her kind are like cockroaches: they'll survive anything. Now, is there anything I can help you with, love?'

'I'm fine, thank you. I came out for a walk and to post a letter. I thought while I was here, I'd see if there was anything my mother would like . . . I'll have a browse, if that's all right with you?' Helen gazed up at the well-stocked shelves behind the counter.

'You might like to have a look at my noticeboard.' The woman indicated the back of the shop door, half covered in posters about fundraising events and hand-written cards advertising items for sale.

Out of politeness, Helen stepped closer to take a look. A postcard caught her eye. She drew nearer to read the small print.

The talkative shopkeeper was still watching her. 'That's the new women's sewing group our vicar's wife is organizing. I'm not one for sewing myself. No good with my hands, and after a day in the shop I don't want to be fiddling with bits of wool and thread. I'm ready to put my feet up and listen to the wireless. Are you one for knitting and making your own clothes? Or do you use a dressmaker, like your mother?' Seeing the surprise on Helen's face, she quickly added: 'We use the same lady; I'm not prying, my dear.'

Helen nodded vaguely, her thoughts turning over. She'd forgotten how nosy people in a small community could be. Before her marriage she had liked to sew, although her knitting wasn't up to much. These days, magazines were calling for women to knit for the men in the services. Perhaps if she joined this group, it would be an escape from the house for a few hours each week. She'd be away from her mother, who was forever chivvying her to do something rather than mope about all day. It would also keep her away from Gavin's staring.

Rummaging in her handbag, she pulled out a pencil and an old envelope and scribbled down the name of the vicar's wife, who was asking for women to make contact if they were interested. There was also a telephone number and, as Helen looked up thoughtfully, a telephone box on the other side of the window caught her eye.

Impulsively she decided to place a call now, before going home, rather than have her mother listening while she used the apparatus in the house. Hillary was so proud of having had a telephone installed that she treated it like a guest, noting every word that came out of the instrument or went back down the line. She would hover nearby, duster in hand, ready to polish the telephone the moment Helen put it down – and consequently she knew just about everything that went on in Helen's life.

'I wonder, would you have some change I could use for the telephone?' she asked, holding out a coin.

'Here you are, love,' the shopkeeper said, handing back a small pile of pennies. 'It'll give you something to do.' She smiled knowingly. It was almost as if she understood what Helen had been thinking.

Helen stepped out of the shop with the woman's words still ringing in her ears. Pulling back the heavy door of the telephone box, she placed her handbag and gas mask on the floor and her coins on the little shelf next to the telephone. Lifting the heavy Bakelite handpiece, she asked the operator to place her call.

A few minutes later, Helen was heading home through a shower of rain with a spring in her step. The vicar's wife had encouraged her to come along to the sewing group at the church hall for one session, with no obligation to return if she didn't enjoy herself. A couple of hours with the group, away from her mother, would surely give her a chance to breathe and think. Even if the other women present were only there to sew and knit, at least she would have some peace and quiet. She just hoped they weren't like the busybody behind the shop counter; otherwise she would flee for her life. She giggled at the thought. At least her mother wouldn't follow her and join in, because – as she often informed Helen – she had people she could pay to do such things for her.

She hardly noticed the weight of the cans and packets she'd purchased after making her telephone call. Her mind had been so full of the sewing group that she'd only just remembered to post her letter. Stopping halfway up the hill, not only to catch her breath but to turn her back on the wind and rain for a moment, she heard the roar of aircraft. She shielded her eyes towards the sky and saw planes flying above her, approaching Biggin Hill airfield.

There seemed to be a lot of activity locally, considering not much had happened so far in this war. The department John had been running before his death was involved in the supply and production of food; Helen had been so focused on helping him that she hadn't taken much notice of other war news. She knew about what they were calling the Phoney War, but little else. It was sad that with his untimely death the nation had lost a hard-working man, dedicated to his work and so knowledgeable about the war. She'd also lost a husband who had generally treated her well. True, there had never been any passion between them; but she had put that down to their age gap and John's commitment to his work. There had been times when they'd disagreed, of course, and times when she'd longed for the kind of all-consuming love you saw at the cinema. But all in all, they'd had a good life.

Moving on again towards home, she wondered, not for the first time, if there was any news on the investigation into the gas explosion. It had now been over two months; surely there should at least have been a letter? John's family lived in Oxfordshire and his elderly mother and sisters had never thought much of his choice of wife, especially as Helen was so much younger. There was also the question of class. Helen's background had been sniffed at, even though she came from a perfectly respectable family. As a result, she had had little contact with the Wentworths since the funeral. John's will had stated that he wished to be buried in the family plot, so she had travelled alone, staying in a small local hotel the night before the service; no invitation to stay at the family home had been forthcoming. She had left as soon as it was over.

Helen had received only a few personal effects from the estate. John's home had been left to a close male relative, with the proviso that his mother could live out her life there as Helen and John had no children of their own. Helen could hardly begin to imagine what the atmosphere would have been like if she'd inherited the house.

21

All in all, she was strangely pleased that their marriage had left her with nothing apart from the trunk that now sat in the hall at her mother's house, a few knick-knacks, and a small annuity from his life insurance policy. At the funeral, she had planned to sit at the back of the small chapel, make her personal goodbyes and leave. It had been a surprise to find she was the chief mourner, as John had dictated in the instructions held by his solicitor. This had meant she was the person her husband's colleagues sought out when paying their respects after the service; she was in the limelight, rather than in the shadows as she'd have preferred. All through it, she could feel the venomous glances from John's mother and sisters.

Once home from the funeral she had placed a call to Felicity, who to her surprise had been terribly upset during the conversation. She seemed far more affected by John's death than Helen had realized. Felicity had eventually ended the call by saying that she needed to lie down. Helen had been miffed at her friend's lack of support, and they hadn't spoken since. At the time, Helen had thought she might not contact Felicity again; they'd only known each other since Helen's move to London, and she knew that friendships of that type didn't always last. However, as the weeks passed she had started to miss their chats and outings, so had written the letter hoping for a friendly reply.

Deep in thought, she approached the house and snapped out of her reverie at the sound of her mother's shrill voice. Was there an emergency of some kind? Had her stepfather been taken ill?

'I thought you'd never come home.' Hillary appeared

22

in the doorway, looking annoyed. 'There's been such a to-do. The girl has arrived home with her children. I won't have it!'

Helen was puzzled until she realized her mother was referring to Effie King, the young woman she had hired as housekeeper last summer. There was really no need to have live-in help, but it was all part of Hillary Davis's determination to maintain her social standing in the community. It irked Helen that her mother called Effie 'the girl', as she was well over thirty years of age.

'I informed her there were to be no children at The Maples. She knew that, and still she has brought them here. She promised they had been evacuated. I've told her it would be best for them to be returned home at once.'

'Oh, Mother, children aren't parcels that can be sent away so easily. Did you ask if there was a problem?'

'The girl's family arrangements are her own affair. She knew my rules when I hired her,' Hillary sniffed. 'Perhaps you can deal with this. It's high time you pulled yourself together and took some responsibility for this household.'

Ignoring this remark, Helen said thoughtfully, 'I don't believe Effie would willingly break her contract.' She'd seen relatively little of the woman, but found her to be quiet and pleasant. It had been Effie who made sure Helen was fed and cared for in her early days of shock and grief, saying little but appearing regularly at her bedroom door with a smile and a hot drink or sandwich, asking how she was feeling. Much as Hillary had wanted Helen to be up and about, she'd never actually taken the trouble to look after her daughter.

'She said something about the elder girl being disobedient, so Effie was summoned to collect them. I've told her she should find somewhere else to send them, as I've made it clear no children are to live under this roof.'

Helen gave her mother a puzzled look.

'There is no need to look at me like that. Children in the house are not an option. They are noisy and will get in the way of my entertaining friends. If she doesn't find them somewhere else to live, she will have to go – I told her that when she came back with them earlier. Where are you going?' she asked, as Helen started down the side of the house towards the rooms Hillary liked to call 'the servants' quarters'. 'There's a man waiting to see you. I've put him in the breakfast room.'

Helen stopped in her tracks. 'A man? To see me?'

'Yes, some chappie in an RAF uniform. He asked for you personally. I hope you're not courting already. What would the neighbours think?' Hillary tutted. 'Why, it's only been two months since you were widowed. What are you thinking of?'

Helen frowned. 'I have no idea who this person could be, but we won't be any the wiser standing out here in the rain,' she said as she changed direction and went into the house. Putting her head round the door to the breakfast room, she began: 'I'm sorry to keep you waiting. I'll just hang up my coat – Oh! it's you.'

Richard Gladstone turned from the window, where he'd been looking out over the garden. His smile of greeting faded as he took in her appearance, and Helen suddenly realized that she must look like a drowned rat.

'If you will excuse me for a minute, I'll change out of

these wet clothes. Let me show you to the drawing room. Goodness knows why Mother put you into the breakfast room. This isn't usually where we entertain guests.'

'I'm quite comfortable here, thank you, Mrs Wentworth . . . Are these your siblings?' he asked, nodding out to where two children, presumably Effie's, were racing round the garden in raincoats.

'No, they are our housekeeper's children,' she murmured, feeling warmth spread over her face as he held her look for a little longer than necessary. Placing a hand to her chest to calm her beating heart, she became aware of her wet blouse clinging to her skin. 'I'm sorry, I'll be as quick as I can,' she said before hurrying out into the scullery. Effie was there, busily chopping vegetables. Helen stopped to lean against the door frame, trying to catch her breath.

'Why, you look as though you've come over all unnecessary,' Effie said, pausing mid-chop with her knife poised. 'Mind you, so would I, with a man like that turning up to see me. He has a look of that actor . . . Johnny Johnson. I get goosebumps all over when I see him in films at the picture house,' she giggled before slapping a hand to her mouth. 'Don't take no notice of me, Mrs Wentworth. There's you recently lost your husband, and me talking nineteen to the dozen about . . . well, about men. I'm sorry for any offence caused.'

Helen laughed. It was clear Effie was a kindly soul who meant no harm. There wasn't a nasty bone in her body, as some would say, and Helen was in dire need of people like that around her at the moment. 'No offence taken, Effie. I must change before I go back in to speak to our guest. Would you put these away in the pantry, please?' She held out the shopping she'd carried home. 'Put them at the back of the shelf with the other things we've saved. Goodness knows what will happen in the months to come, once rationing becomes the norm. Perhaps we'd better not mention them to my mother.'

Effie took the bag. 'Bob's your uncle,' she winked.

'And Fanny's your aunt,' a fair-haired little girl chimed in as she entered by the back door, much to her mother's horror.

'Dorothy, that's no way to speak to your elders and betters. Apologize now or I shall be washing your mouth out with soap, young lady,' Effie scolded, giving Helen an apologetic look. 'I'm sorry. They never used words like that before. It's those other evacuees they stayed with when they got sent off to the country.'

'There's no need to apologize, Effie – children will be children. I just wondered why they've come back? Surely it would have been safer wherever you sent them?'

'I agree with you, and when the people that was looking after them sent me that letter to say come and get them, I didn't know what to do. Someone put them on the train for London and I collected them, and here we are. I've got a feeling I'm going to be packing my bags and going back to the East End before too long. Your mother is a good woman, but she did say no children when she gave me the job, and at the time it wasn't a problem what with the kids being packed off to Somerset. I've been beside myself with worry, I can tell you. I love living here and looking after this nice house and everything. I've even made a couple of friends. Now it looks as though I'll be back in Stepney before Christmas – God knows where we'll live.' To Helen's dismay, Effie's chin started to wobble and her eyes filled with tears.

Helen patted her shoulder. 'Please don't worry about it, Effie. Let me change and see what the RAF man wants, then we can sit down and put our heads together, eh?'

Effie gave a little smile. 'Thank you, Mrs Wentworth. And as for you, young lady, haven't you heard the saying children should be seen and not heard?' Dorothy, suddenly shy, put a finger in her mouth and clung to her mother's skirt.

'Would you be a dear and take a tea tray in for the gentleman while I make myself presentable?' Helen asked.

'Of course, I will, Miss, and I'll make one for you as well. It'll warm you up a bit after the drenching you've had. I made some bread pudding yesterday, so I'll put some on a plate with the tea. He looks like the sort of man who likes his food.'

Helen grinned to herself as she hurried upstairs, unbuttoning the collar of her blouse as she went. How Effie could tell that a man liked his food when she'd just met him, she didn't know, but it looked as though she could be a right laugh; Helen would miss her if she left. I'll do all I can to help keep her here, she thought, already feeling a glow of affection for the woman and her two children. With her head down, she didn't see her stepfather above her on the staircase until they collided.

'Whoa there,' Gavin said, catching her shoulders to steady her as she wobbled on the step.

'I'm fine now, thank you,' she said, pulling away while pressing a hand against her chest to keep the top of her blouse closed.

'What's the hurry?'

'I can't stop,' she said stiffly, aware that he had noticed the disarrangement of her clothing. His gaze drifted down over her breasts. 'There's an officer downstairs who wants to speak to me. If you'll excuse me,' she added.

There was a brief, uncomfortable pause, and finally Helen put out a hand and gave him a firm push. Gavin's hands left her shoulders as he steadied himself with the banister. The staircase was wide enough for her to dart past, but he was still watching her as she hurried up the last flight of stairs and into her room.

Locking the door, she quickly undressed and dried herself with a rough towel hanging on the back of the door. She pulled a lightweight pale-blue woollen dress from her wardrobe and stepped into it, kicking off her shoes as she did so and stepping into her slippers. At once her toes started to warm up after being in the wet shoes for so long. She ran a brush through her hair and watched in the dressing-table mirror as her damp curls bounced back into shape around her shoulders. Clipping them back from her face with two tortoiseshell clasps, she leant in to the mirror and gave her face one final check, then reached for a lipstick, quickly applying a layer of colour. Pursing her lips together and checking her teeth weren't stained, she headed back downstairs, first making sure that her stepfather wasn't loitering on the staircase.

'I'm sorry to have kept you,' she apologized as she joined the inspector, gesturing for him to sit down.

'Shall I be mother?' he asked as he reached for the teapot set out on a silver tray on the occasional table between them. She noticed his strong hands and long fingers as he picked up her mother's best bone china teapot and poured the tea without spilling it.

For a few minutes they made conversation about the weather, and whether Helen had settled in since her move back to Biggin Hill. The inspector asked if she preferred living in the country to the bustle of London and assisting her late husband with his parliamentary work. Although he was perfectly pleasant, it felt a little like she was being examined under a magnifying glass. Helen made polite answers without being overly friendly.

Eventually, as he lifted a plate with a generous slice of Effie's bread pudding, she took the opportunity to ask why he was there. 'I assume you haven't come all the way to Biggin Hill to pass the time of day, Inspector. Do you have any new information about my husband's death? I'm still unsure why the police and the RAF were at my home when it was a simple gas explosion. The loss is devastating enough for me, let alone this idea that's forming in my mind of something else having happened.'

The inspector nodded in acknowledgement. 'My reason for coming here is twofold. Apart from taking tea with you on this abysmal day, I'm reporting for duty at the airfield. I'll be based there for the foreseeable future, along with much of my department.'

Helen was surprised. 'Are you a pilot?'

'No, I'm an RAF police officer,' he said, tapping the badge on his sleeve. 'Just as other services have their police divisions, so does the RAF. I'm an RAF police detective, working for the special investigation branch. It's a job that sees me move from place to place, so you may spot me around the area.'

Helen was thoughtful as she absorbed this information. She still didn't understand why he'd come to The Maples, when he could simply have written to her with any updates on the case. She'd never shown any interest in him as a man; in fact, apart from his brief appearance at John's funeral to pay his respects, their only meeting had been on that awful day at her London home. 'You said there was another reason?'

He put down his plate and cleared his throat. 'I am also here to inform you that your husband's death was not an accident. I will be undertaking further investigations, and I hope that you will be able to help me with my enquiries.'

Helen froze. 'Whatever do you mean, it wasn't an accident? Why, he died in a gas explosion. Are you saying somebody deliberately caused the explosion?'

'I'm not able to give you much information at this time. All I will say is that the explosion was a deliberate attempt to cover up your husband's murder.'

Helen had to pause for a moment to collect her thoughts. 'Would this be because of his work as a Member of Parliament? I can't think why anyone would want to kill John. He was such a dear man – he wouldn't have hurt a soul.' She gripped the arm of her chair, suddenly feeling faint.

He leant forward a little, concerned. 'Helen – Mrs Wentworth – try to take slow, deep breaths. This has come as a shock to you.'

She sat back and closed her eyes. As if it wasn't bad enough to have lost her husband, and her home, she now had to try and understand why someone would have wanted to kill him. 'Of course I'll try to help in any way I can. I should be able to make a list of his acquaintances. I'm afraid his diary was left in our home, otherwise I could give you much more information now. I do have our address book with me, though, and that may help . . .' She took a breath, trying to gather her thoughts. Thank goodness her mother wasn't in the room – she would only be making a fuss about what the neighbours would think. A murder in the family was not something one chatted about at social events, after all, and Hillary Davis would be desperate to brush it under the carpet. Skeletons in the family cupboard might be amusing when they were centuries-old anecdotes for a cocktail party; but something like this was much too close to home. Helen knew her mother would take to her bed rather than face what was happening.

'I'll do all I can to assist you,' she assured the inspector again. 'Have you any idea at all who could have done this monstrous thing?'

He cleared his throat, looking a little embarrassed. He badly wanted to believe that the woman in front of him was genuinely concerned over the death of her husband, but . . . 'At the moment we have no clear suspects, and that is why I'm interviewing everyone who was known to your husband.'

It was only then that Helen realized he had not come to give her an update, but to tell her that she was a suspect on his list of potential murderers.

2

The next half hour passed in a blur. Helen went through the motions of finishing her conversation with the inspector and agreed to be interviewed formally by him the next day. It was clear to him that she was in no state to continue now; she was actually starting to shiver. Whether this was because of the recent rain shower or the news of how her husband had lost his life, he couldn't say.

Later, with her mother and stepfather off to the golf club, Helen found herself alone in the house, Hillary's words still ringing in her ears: 'Sort out that woman's children, or I'll send them all packing.' Hillary had not asked why Richard Gladstone had visited the house, still assuming he was Helen's gentleman caller – not that she'd ever had a visitor of the opposite sex even step over the threshold before. If she hadn't moved to London to work, she might well have still been a spinster.

At least now she could chat with Effie, she decided, carrying the tea tray through to the kitchen, where she found the housekeeper peeling potatoes for their evening meal.

'Let me take that, Miss Helen. I could've come in for it. You only had to ring the bell.'

Helen shook her head. Hell would have to freeze over before she used one of the strategically placed bells her mother had installed throughout the house to summon Effie. 'No, I'm fine. I'll rinse these and leave them on the drainer. I don't want to hold you up when you're so busy.'

Effie used the back of her hand to brush away a few stray hairs from her flushed face. Although she wore a voluminous white apron supplied by her mistress, she always appeared dishevelled as she dashed from one job to another. Now, with her two children to worry about as well, she seemed even more stressed. 'There's fresh tea in the pot if you'd like a cup – that's if you don't mind pouring it yourself,' she said, stabbing a knife into the potato she held to remove a stubborn eye.

Helen reached for two earthenware mugs from the dresser and poured the amber liquid, adding a dash of milk to both. 'Here you are,' she said, placing the mug close to where Effie was working. She sat down at the other side of the large wooden table. 'I enjoy cooking myself, you know. With so much spare time on my hands, perhaps I could help out here – that's if you don't mind?' She smiled.

Effie looked worried. 'I don't know about that, Miss Helen. Your mother will have my guts for garters if she thinks for one minute I'm slacking in my work, and you having to help me, like . . .'

'But you wouldn't be. I'd make it clear to my mother that I wanted to help out.'

Effie nodded, but she didn't look convinced. 'I hope

you don't mind me asking – had you thought much about finding yourself a job? There's talk of young women taking on more work for the war effort. After you worked so hard for that husband of yours, you'd be snapped up like a shot. I overheard your mother telling someone when they came to tea. She was singing your praises, and your late husband's too. You don't want to be stuck here in this house wasting your life away, after all you've done.'

Helen noted the wistful look on Effie's face. 'But what about you, Effie – have you not thought of doing something yourself, other than waiting on my family hand and foot? So many women are leaving domestic service nowadays, and earning much more than what my mother must be paying.'

'It's good of you to think of me, Miss, but with my two kids back here there's not much I can do. Not many people will want to take me on with two children in tow. Like your mother.' Effie shook her head. 'I don't think she likes children.'

Helen felt Effie had summed up her mother perfectly. Although she had been very well cared for as a little girl, it had really been her late father who showed her love, much more than her mother. Hillary had seemed unable to cope with a child: she spoke to Helen as an adult and expected her to reply in the same manner. Helen's younger years were spent minding her manners, making sure that her ribbon bows stayed neatly in her hair and that she didn't speak or play with the rougher kids in the school playground. At the age of eleven she had been moved to a boarding school and out of her mother's house, which had suited Helen admirably as she'd started to enjoy being a typical little girl and having friends. 'Yes, I must admit The Maples isn't an ideal place to live with children, given my mother's feelings on the matter.' She decided there and then that she would do her utmost to be a friend to Effie.

'I did think of going back home to Stepney, but that's not possible at the moment. The landlord has let out the house, so it would mean staying at my mum's place. You think you've got problems, well, you should meet my mum,' Effie grinned.

Helen chuckled. 'Goodness, is she that bad?'

Effie only laughed in reply as she cut the potato into four pieces and dropped them into a pan of cold water. 'You must miss your home,' she said, changing the subject. 'And your husband. How bad was the damage to your flat?'

Helen looked at Effie and could tell the question was thoughtful, not just a passing enquiry. To her surprise, she felt a tear fall onto her cheek and she coughed, trying to clear the lump that had suddenly formed in her throat. She wasn't used to kind comments in this house. 'It's not so much the damage to my home, it's more that . . .' She couldn't speak.

'Aw, Miss, I do understand – you can't live there now your husband's passed on. Mum was the same after Dad died, so she went to live with my Aunt May in Southend for a while. Now she's back and as right as rain. Give it a while, eh?'

'No . . . I'm not worried about living in the home that I shared with John. But the RAF police detective who visited earlier is investigating his death.'

'Investigating?' Effie dropped a large potato into the

water, causing it to slop over onto the table. Helen helped her wipe it up and apologized for startling her.

'It was a shock for me as well. He's coming back here to interview me tomorrow.'

'Well, that RAF copper better not upset you, or he won't be getting any more of my cake,' Effie huffed.

Helen smiled at her new friend. 'RAF copper' didn't sound quite as important as the role she knew Richard Gladstone held. She understood that he was equal to a detective inspector and also held an important rank in the RAF. What she didn't know was why he was leading this investigation into John's death, and not someone from the Metropolitan Police. John had been a high-profile MP – so surely Scotland Yard should have been involved?

There must be a reason, she thought, but she shrugged as she answered Effie. 'Maybe we'll know more once he interviews me tomorrow. He will have to see I have nothing to add to what I've told him already. Oh, my goodness,' she added, clapping her hands to her mouth. 'I forgot – I'm supposed to be somewhere else tomorrow. I'll hardly make it home before he arrives.' Noticing Effie's surprise, as Helen had hardly left the house since moving home, she felt she should explain. 'I saw a card in the shop window: some of the local women have formed a sewing circle. It's meeting tomorrow in the church hall. I've spoken to the vicar's wife about it, so it will seem rude if I don't attend. I did explain that I'm not much of a dressmaker, but she says there will be other projects to try my hand at, and people there only too willing to teach me.' She gave a sigh. 'Look at me – reduced to attending a sewing circle. My life used to be so busy . . .'

Effie leant across the table and patted her hand. 'I'd heard about that group. I wish I could find time to go along myself, but being so busy with the house – and now the kids being here – it's out of the question. You must go, if only to take your mind off your problems. If that copper arrives before you get home, I'll fill him up with tea and cake to buy you some time. On the condition you tell me all about the group.'

Helen's face twitched as she tried not to laugh. Hadn't Effie not long said she'd never give Richard Gladstone another slice of cake? 'That's very kind of you. I intend to dust off my bicycle; that should get me home a little quicker. I wonder what I'll find at the group?' she said, feeling a little thread of excitement at the thought of doing something different with her day. Which reminded her . . . 'Effie, would you give me a hand taking my husband's trunk up to my room? Mother keeps reminding me the hall is not the place to store it, and now my step-father is moaning too. At least then I can unpack it in private and decide what to do with the contents. I don't know exactly what the porter has packed, and I'm not looking forward to it; but I do need to get it done.'

'Of course I will, Miss Helen. You really have no idea what's inside?'

Helen shrugged, shaking her head. 'I suppose it must be clothing from the wardrobe and other personal effects. John's mother asked at the funeral about a few family heirlooms that were on his desk, so I wrote to the porter asking for them to be boxed up and sent to her. I've not heard any more, so I assume that's been done. But really, that's enough about me. Before we go and deal with the trunk, why don't you tell me something about your life before you arrived here to work for us?'

'There's not much to tell really, Miss. I was born and brought up in the Edmonton area. That's over North London way,' she added, seeing Helen's questioning look. 'Later I moved to Stepney, when I got married. We was quite happy there, but after my old man went off to do his bit in the army and the girls' school told us mums we should be considering sending the kiddies away from London for their safety – well, it made me start thinking about our future. I don't know; do you think it's wrong of me to hope for a bit more out of life?'

'No, of course not. We should all keep looking ahead, especially now that we have this horrible war to contend with. Why, parents should never lose sight of what's best for their children.'

'Thank you, Miss. It seems like more than six months ago I packed their little cases and walked them to the school to join their classmates. Do you know they was all labelled? It reminded me of the butcher when he labels the weight of the chickens for Christmas.' She giggled. 'Silly of me, eh?'

Helen smiled. 'It must have been a sight to behold, all those children waiting to set off on their adventures. I did see photographs in the papers at the time and I believe there was something on Pathé News about it at the cinema. It made me thankful I didn't have any children myself to say goodbye to.'

'You were never blessed then, Miss? I mean, you and your husband didn't . . .'

Helen blushed slightly. 'No, you could say we weren't

blessed; but then, we were only married a couple of years. Who knows what might have happened in the future? Tell me what happened next,' she said, bringing the subject back to Effie's children.

'Well, Miss, I received a letter from the kids to say they'd arrived. They wrote the name of the town – it was somewhere called Chard. Have you heard of it?'

'I know of the area, but I've never visited. I'm led to believe Somerset is a beautiful county.'

'Yes, Miss, in the short time that it was hinted where the children would go, I took myself off to the lending library and looked in an encyclopaedia. It was the lovely countryside and the threats of bombing back in London that had me decide to move away and find myself a job in the country as well. Knowing the girls would be away for a while, as would my husband, my plan was to find a little home to rent and make cosy for when my family returned to me. Now, well, I don't know what to do. I feel such a failure.'

Helen admired Effie's plans for her family's future, although she did wonder why the woman had chosen to settle down so close to an airfield. When John was alive, he'd remarked that he thought it reckless of Helen's mother to stay in the Biggin Hill area as 'anything could happen' with the airfield being so nearby. The memory of those words caused a shiver to run through her, but she pulled herself together and tried to focus on Effie's dilemma. 'Please don't feel you have failed. After all, you have Dorothy and Jane living here with you, so you know they're safe. That's the most important job you have. It wasn't your fault they were sent back. I'm sure we can come up with something, if we put our heads together.'

'That's good of you, Miss; but what about your mother? I'm not sure your father will want youngsters under his feet, either.'

'He's not my father,' Helen snapped back before apologizing. 'I'm sorry – it's just that he doesn't feel like a father to me. He married my mother when I was eleven years old. I was sent away to boarding school and I've not had much to do with him since then.' She glanced down into her lap. 'When I finished school I took a secretarial course, then went to work in London.'

Effie nodded. 'At least in a house this size, you don't have to live in each other's pockets. Where I come from, we had no choice. The house we rented was a two-up, two-down with a lavvie out the back that we shared with next door. Oh, it was clean,' she was quick to add. 'I was always on my knees with a scrubbing brush. But it wasn't what I wanted for my children.' She looked out the window to where the girls were throwing a ball back and forth. 'I need to make some decisions,' she said, wringing her hands together. 'If only I knew more people in the area, I could ask about places to rent.'

Helen's mind went to the village shop and the post-cards on the noticeboard. 'I have an idea. Why don't we write a card and put it in the shop? People do stop to read them. In fact, that's how I found out about the sewing group.'

Effie didn't look convinced. 'I'm not sure anyone will want to rent a place to a woman with two kids and no husband at home. Landlords can be funny about such things. Perhaps I'll have to look for new live-in work, instead of just a house to rent?'

'Oh no, don't say that,' Helen said. 'I'm sure we can sort something out. Why don't you come along with me to the sewing group tomorrow afternoon? There may be someone there who can help you. To be honest, I'm a bit nervous about walking into the hall on my own. I'm only going so as to get out of the house a little more.'

Effie raised her eyebrows. Anyone would find it hard living under the same roof as Mrs Davis, she thought. 'If you think it would help, then I'll come along. The children will be going to the local school for the first time tomorrow, but after Christmas it's closing down and moving lock, stock and barrel to Wales. That's another problem for me to solve,' she said, looking glum. 'But at least I can fit in joining you for a while – as long as your mother doesn't notice. She might well think I'm moving above my station in life, going out with you.'

'Don't worry about my mother. I'll tell her you are helping me for the afternoon. She won't argue if she knows I'll be out from under her feet. She likes her peace and quiet and an orderly life. A widowed daughter was not part of her plan to climb the social ladder,' Helen grimaced.

Effie smiled. She liked Helen, and wondered why a young woman like her had decided to marry a man so much older. There again, perhaps it had been better than putting up with her waspish mother.

'That's a plan, then. In the meantime, let's not give your mum any cause for complaint. Drink up your tea and we'll get that trunk dragged upstairs and stowed in your bedroom. Do you want me to help you unpack it?'

'No, it can sit in the corner out of the way until I can bring myself to go through John's things.' Helen glanced into the hall, where the trunk sat close to the kitchen doorway. Apart from her memories, it contained all the remaining links to her life in London. Did she even wish to revisit it?

3

'Should we have brought something with us, do you think?' Helen asked, as they watched a woman laden with bags struggling up the path to the church hall. Without waiting for an answer, she hurried after the woman. 'Here, let me help you,' she said, taking one of the bags while Effie took another.

'Are you here to join our little group?' the red-faced woman asked as she put her remaining bags down on a step, pulling a bunch of keys from her pocket. 'Let's get inside out of this awful weather, shall we?' She ushered them into the gloomy hall. 'The light switch is on the left,' she instructed Effie, who'd taken a few steps ahead and then halted, not knowing where to go in the semi-darkness. 'Dearie me, the caretaker is supposed to open the blackout curtains each morning.' She tutted as she pulled the drapes aside. Grey mid-morning December light filtered through the criss-cross of blast tape, casting triangles onto the wooden floor.

Helen looked around, not feeling particularly inspired by their surroundings. She had imagined a busy sewing bee with tables heaped with coloured fabric and wool into which she could delve to start a project – to make what, she wasn't yet sure. But perhaps the atmosphere would brighten up once more people arrived.

'I'm Letitia Green, but you can call me Tish,' the woman said, holding out her hand to Helen and Effie, who in turn introduced themselves. 'It will be good to have fresh blood in our little circle. We certainly need it,' she grimaced.

'I thought this was a new group?' Helen said, hoping she wasn't going to experience being ignored by an established clique, as she had when she'd first married John and been introduced to his colleagues' wives. She had spent most of her time watching the clock and waiting for the earliest possible opportunity to make her excuses and leave their little soirées. She'd only been really happy while working alongside John in his office, arranging his social appointments.

'Yes, this is our first official meeting of the group here in the church hall. I've had a few get-togethers at home, but I wanted to do something more worthwhile. Not just for the war effort, but to boost the morale of the women who live in the area,' Tish added, looking pleased with herself.

'I'm really not sure sitting in a draughty church hall knitting socks for the troops is going to boost anyone's morale,' Effie huffed, obviously not much taken with her first impression of Tish. 'Do you want me to sort the kitchen out and get the kettle on?' she added, peering through an open doorway. Beyond it was a long room that ran the length of the side of the hall and contained a sink, a large gas stove and a table.

'Here, take this bag – you should find everything you

require. I plan to carry everything for our tea breaks rather than leave it in the kitchen cupboard; the Boy Scouts pinch anything that's not nailed down. I dare not leave the biscuit tin here, either, because the verger's partial to a nibble.'

Helen couldn't help but giggle. 'You seem to know the ins and outs of the people who use this hall,' she said, taking a heavy bag from Tish and passing it to Effie.

'So true,' the woman said. 'I'm married to the job.'

Helen looked at her, confused.

'My husband is the vicar,' Tish said, with an expression that suggested this should have been obvious.

'Oh, I'm sorry – I ought to have remembered your name after our conversation yesterday,' Helen apologized. 'I'm Helen Wentworth, and the lady out there sorting out the kitchen is Effie King, my mother's housekeeper.'

'Oh, so you're the lady who made the telephone call yesterday? I'm sorry I couldn't speak for long. We had representatives from the Mothers' Union visiting with my husband and things were getting quite fraught. You have no idea how territorial some of these ladies can be over the preparation of the church flowers.'

Helen wasn't sure what to make of Tish. In the few minutes she'd known her, she'd got the impression that the vicar's wife was someone who called a spade a spade. 'I'm not sure how much use I'll be. It would take me so long to knit a pair of socks, the war would be over by the time I'd cast off. As for my sewing skills – well, I can just about manage to turn up a hem on a frock and replace a loose button. However, I look forward to coming to the meetings, if only to get out of the house,' she smiled.

'I've heard about you, of course; you're the MP's widow. It must have been a terrible shock to you to lose your husband like that,' Tish said, patting her hand. 'I'm pleased you've come back to live with your mother. If we haven't got family at times like this, what do we have?'

Helen only smiled, unable to think of a reply. There was a glint in Tish's eye that might have been irony, and it made her wonder if the woman might have crossed paths with Hillary at some point.

'And don't worry about your sewing skills today. This is a "let's get to know each other" meeting – and we have a special guest.'

'That does sound interesting,' Helen said, wondering what she'd let herself in for.

'Oh, yes. Our speaker is Elizabeth Donnington, and she's going to tell us all about her quilts.'

Helen groaned inwardly. As far as she was concerned, a quilt was something to hide under when she was feeling miserable, and she had done a lot of that lately. She wished she was at home right now, snuggled in with a good book and a cup of cocoa. Thoughts of home reminded her that Inspector Gladstone would be there to interview her later, so at least she had an excuse to hurry away if things became too boring here. 'Wonderful. Now, is there anything I can do to help?'

Tish looked at her watch. 'Good grief, the hordes will be descending on us within ten minutes and the seats haven't been put out. Would you be a dear . . . ? I'll have a quick word with Effie about using the right cups and saucers.'

Helen was only too happy to have something to do,

and she set to pulling stacks of metal chairs from behind a curtain next to the stage at one end of the hall. 'Er – Tish, will your speaker be up on the stage?' she called out.

'Yes; just two chairs behind the small table, please. She's going to work near the audience so we can have a close look at her quilts.'

Helen set up a couple of wooden trestle tables before laying out three rows of chairs.

'That looks splendid. I can see you're going to be a great asset to the group,' Tish remarked as she shook out a large white sheet to cover the tables. 'Perfect,' she announced, stepping back to check it was straight.

Helen wondered if the praise was because the vicar's wife had found someone young enough to do the heavy work involved in setting up a group meeting.

The doors opened and a horde of women and excited children entered, filling the empty hall with noisy chit-chat. Effie emerged from the kitchen, looking round the newly busy space before coming over to join Helen. 'I don't think I'm needed; a couple of other women have taken over,' she said, looking slightly downcast.

'I hope they didn't say anything rude to you?' Helen was ready to be offended on her behalf.

'No, not at all. It's just . . . I'm not good with strangers and I didn't want to step on anyone's toes, so I slid out after saying hello.'

Helen understood how she felt. It was better sometimes to slide away than stay and be ignored, or spoken to dismissively. There were times she could put on a brave face, but there were plenty of other times when it didn't work. 'Oh look, Effie,' she said as one of the women came out of the kitchen, scanned the room and approached them.

'There you are! I wanted to say thank you, but you vanished. It's not often we arrive to a clean and tidy kitchen, I can tell you. It saves so much time, especially when I'm running late. I'm Jean Carter, I knit and do kitchen duties – I make a mean cake, too. My cohort is Ivy Brown, she's our expert on rag rugs and tea-making. That's why Tish delegated us to kitchen duties, bless her,' she grinned.

The women shook hands with Jean. 'What's a rag rug?' Helen asked.

'That question shows how posh you are,' Effie chuckled. 'We had a couple made by my mum, but I left them behind when we left the East End. Mum made ours out of old rags, and they last for years and cost hardly anything to make. I'd love to try again, especially if I need to provide a home for me and the kids.'

'I'm intrigued,' Helen said, ignoring the comment about being posh. She had never thought of herself that way, although anyone who'd met her mother might see it differently.

Jean slipped her arm through Effie's. 'You must come and meet Ivy properly. She can help furnish your home, as she's a dab hand with rags. If you don't mind being a third pair of hands in the kitchen, it would be wonderful. We're expecting quite a few people today as we have a speaker and there's been a lot of interest about Tish's new group. Let's face it, it's a good way to kill a few hours – even if some women ignore the orders to leave their children at home.' She winked. 'Would you like to join us?' she asked Helen.

'No, I'll stay here and help Tish with the seats. If there are more coming along, we might need to pull out extra chairs.' Helen smiled, hoping that was the case and she didn't stand there on her own looking like a lemon.

She needn't have worried, because at that moment a striking woman dressed in a smart green woollen suit with a matching hat entered the hall, followed by two men carrying large suitcases. 'You can leave them here, thank you,' she said, indicating a space next to the trestle tables. Helen couldn't quite place her accent. Was she American?

'Helen, dear, come over and meet Elizabeth. She may need a hand displaying her quilts,' Tish called to her, in an affected tone of voice quite unlike the one she had used earlier. After introducing the two women, she bustled off.

'These are beautiful,' Helen said, as Elizabeth passed her the quilts so that she could drape them over the tables. 'The colours and patterns are stunning.' She ran her fingers over one particularly eye-catching example in which all the colours of the rainbow were pieced together, and felt a stirring of interest that had deserted her since John's death. 'I really wouldn't know where to start making one, but I'd love to try. You are so talented, Elizabeth.'

Elizabeth stood up and straightened her skirt after sliding the last of the suitcases behind the table. She reached for a large shopping bag, pulling out books and leaflets. 'Please, you must call me Lizzie. Most people do,' she said. She stood inches taller than Helen, and with her hat and smart heeled shoes, seemed to tower over her. 'As for where to start – just start at the beginning.' She smiled gently.

'With my limited sewing skills, I can only dream of creating something so beautiful,' Helen replied, looking wistful.

Lizzie took a closer look at her, taking in the shadows under her eyes and her pale skin. 'It's not so hard, you know. You might think I'm joking by saying start at the beginning, but it's quite easy. Let's have a chat after I've given my talk, when you understand a little more about the process and the history.'

'History? How long have you been making them?'

'You wait and see,' Lizzie said mysteriously. 'All will be revealed.'

Both of them jumped as Tish materialized on the stage behind them and clapped her hands for attention. 'Ladies, will you please take your seats? The talk will start soon, once I've made a few announcements and introduced our guest.'

The sound of shuffling feet increased as the women who had been standing about chatting sorted out the best places to sit while calling out to their offspring to sit cross-legged on the wooden floor and behave. With eager eyes they all looked up to the stage as Tish sat next to another woman, who peered down at the audience. She began to talk about membership fees and the money held in the group's post office account. Helen's mind wandered. Why was it, she thought, that all public halls smelt the same? It was as if the dust of years past had stayed behind long after the people had left, and whatever events were held in the hall remained just a whisper of times gone by.

Her eyes drifted to the quilts, only a few feet away from her seat in the front row. She longed to reach out and run her fingers over their intricate, multi-coloured patterns; she wondered what they smelt of. Some looked new, while others carried their age with a faded grace. Perhaps Lizzie hadn't long created the brighter-coloured coverings? She imagined the scent of the fabric to be similar to a new cotton frock worn for the first time after purchasing from a shop. Was there anything more delicious? She was dragged back to the present as Tish began to talk again, welcoming everybody to the inaugural meeting of the ladies' crafting group.

'We have a special raffle competition today. The prize will be a sewing box, complete with needles and thread. It even contains some pretty fabric that the winner can use to sew a patchwork pot-holder. I urge you all to spare a few coppers and buy a ticket. Now, I would like to introduce a very special guest who has come to us all the way from Canada . . .' She turned to Lizzie, smiling proudly. 'Please give a hearty welcome to Mrs Elizabeth Donnington, who will enlighten us with the history of her collection of beautiful quilts. And furthermore, she will tell us about the quilts she has made herself. We hope Elizabeth will be a regular visitor to our little circle. Welcome, Elizabeth,' she finished, clapping enthusiastically, which prompted everyone else to join in.

The room fell silent as Lizzie stood up and looked out over the audience with a broad smile. 'It is such an honour to be here. I'm already aware that one member of this audience is keen to know how I make my own quilts; but first, let me tell you something about myself and why I am here in your beautiful country.

'Even in a time of war, there is no place like England. You may have noticed my accent, and yes, I hail from Canada. Thank you,' she added, as polite applause rippled through the room. 'My love of quilts started in childhood, when my late and much-missed grandmother would tuck me up in bed under one of her own homemade quilts. I can see it now: it was pink and green, made up with different patterned fabrics, my favourite being the rosebud material scattered in each corner. There was just one blue square, with a small heart embroidered in the middle. I loved to hear the stories about the different fabrics, and Grandma would tell me that the quilters of old would always add a small fault, often a mismatched square, into their quilts to show that only God was perfect. Like some of you,' she said, as a murmur of laughter was heard in the room, 'I wasn't so sure about this, but as I started to collect quilts and speak to the women who made them I heard this often, so who knows – perhaps there is some truth in it. I would like to believe so, wouldn't you? However, I digress. As a teenager, I showed no interest in sewing, but upon my first marriage – oh yes, ladies, I've been married more than once. How shocking,' she said, a tinkle of laughter coming from her voice as she raised her eyes to heaven. 'Yes, upon my first marriage, my grandmother presented me with my own quilt. It was made in a different design to any I'd seen before. It was common at one time to present a bride-to-be with her own quilt before her wedding. Women in the family would sit together, piecing the fabric and quilting the completed bedcover, ready for the bride's nuptials. Sometimes the quilt would go into the bride's bottom drawer, but it was always made and given with love. So yes, my very first quilt was a gift from my grandma and her friends.'

Turning to the table, she lifted up one of the folded quilts, shaking it out so the full glory of its colours could be seen. 'Would you give me a hand, please?' she asked Helen, who went to the other end of the quilt and held it up at the same height. Gasps of admiration could be heard as its autumnal colours brightened the room. 'I was married in the fall, and Grandma chose the colours to represent that time of year. I was only married for five years before my husband passed away, but this quilt is very special to me. It represents young love, happy thoughts and the promise of what would come. The quilt pattern is called The Wheel of Life.'

Helen helped Lizzie to fold the quilt amidst sympathetic murmurs, then returned to her seat. As Lizzie held up further folded quilts, not attempting to open them, she explained, 'These are my inheritance. The cream and blue patterned was my mother's quilt, made for her by her own mother. The design is called Flying Geese. And this one,' she said, running her fingers over a rainbow of colours, 'was another quilt from my first marriage, given to me by my mother-in-law. Grandma was none too pleased that another woman had made me a quilt. In fact, she was so miffed to have competition as the "maker" in our family that, when I met and married my present husband two years after I was widowed, she announced that one wedding was enough for anyone and there would not be another quilt. She was a firm believer in one marriage being enough for any woman. I was disappointed, because I didn't feel that a quilt from my first marriage should go on the bed I shared with my new husband. Call me superstitious, but I've never put this quilt on a bed since then. So, what was I to do? If I wanted a wedding quilt for my second marriage, I would have to make it myself. Yes – me, who couldn't even sew a button on a shirt.' She smiled towards Helen. 'I planned to make the most beautiful quilt possible. I'd show them! By then I'd learnt that the tradition of making quilts went back hundreds of years. I needed to investigate more about the patterns and traditions of quilt-making. At that time I had a small daughter from my first marriage, so could only spare a little time on the project. I stole time wherever I could, shirking on housekeeping and working through the night while my child slept. Verity would nap at the library while I found out all I could from books and archives, and this became the start of my love affair with patchwork and quilting. I started to collect fabric to cut and piece by hand, late at night, when my then-fiancé was on duty. And I did manage to make my quilt by the time we were married.

'It was my husband's job that brought us to England, and although he suggested I put my quilts and many books into storage, I couldn't resist bringing a few of them with me, the ones I have the fondest memories of. However, my grandma had relented and, unbeknown to me, she had made me a second quilt. She told me it was for me alone and not for any of my weddings. For some reason, she had the idea I intended to collect husbands. This is the very same quilt,' she said, asking Helen to again help her hold up an exquisite patchwork quilt of different shades of blue and cream. 'It is called Friendship, which I feel is very apt – wouldn't you all agree?' The audience most certainly did, going by the sighs that echoed from the front to the back of the hall.

'I know there are women who simply make quilts for no particular reason other than they like a certain fabric or the design of the patchwork. But for me, my quilts need to hold memories.' She turned back to the table, leaving Helen to fold the Friendship quilt, and picked up a smaller quilt. 'This was made for my daughter's bed. You will see it is made completely of cream silk, and you may think that is boring, but when you come to the table and look closer you will find that I have pieced together different shapes and quilted over them with the names of my female ancestors. I like to think that when she slept beneath the quilt, they were looking over her and keeping her safe. The fabric came from the wedding gown from my first marriage. I was expecting Verity when her daddy died, and I wanted to make good use of the gown.'

One member of the audience raised a hand to ask why she hadn't kept the gown for her daughter to wear, as was often the tradition.

Lizzie thought for a moment. 'You are not the first person to ask that question. My mother scolded me for spoiling the gown. I have kept the remains of the fabric, so perhaps when the time comes for Verity to marry, she may wish to incorporate them into her own design. However, she has a stepfather she adores and there is a second wedding gown hanging in my closet back in Canada, so perhaps she will make use of that instead?'

Another hand went up. 'What colour is the quilt you made for your second marriage?'

Lizzie burst out laughing. 'Some of my grandma's friends were rather shocked that I'd married so quickly, and it was hinted that I was a scarlet woman for not spending longer as a grieving widow, so the colour choice was easy. It is made up of many different patterned fabrics, but the colourway is red.' Many of the ladies laughed out loud and several applauded her, Helen joining in.

Lizzie went on to briefly outline the different stages of making a quilt, and then Tish stood up from behind the table on stage. 'I hear that tea has been made, and there is cake for everybody. I'm sure that Lizzie especially could do with a cup of tea, and then perhaps we could all take a closer look at the quilts she has brought along today and ask more questions. I'll be going around with the raffle ticket book, so please get your money ready, ladies. We have lots of lovely Christmas gifts to be won, as well as the special prize – all donated by local businesses to raise funds for the children's home.'

Seeing that Lizzie was busy talking with the women huddled around her table, Helen went off to the serving hatch by the kitchen and collected two cups of tea and slices of Christmas cake, dropping a few coppers into a saucer before returning to the front of the hall and carefully placing the refreshments on the edge of the stage away from the quilts. God forbid if anything was spilt on them, I would never forgive myself, she thought with horror.

'I've never been so popular, although I've had to ask a few of the mothers not to let their children touch the older quilts.' Lizzie smiled as she accepted the tea and picked at the icing on the cake. 'Do you know, four people asked if I took commissions to make quilts? Perhaps I should consider setting up a business,' she grinned.

'They are beautiful, but the patterns are so complicated. I could never do something like that,' Helen said.

Lizzie put down her cup and saucer and bent beneath the table, pulling out a small box. She opened it and tipped out a small pile of coloured pieces of fabric. 'This is how you start,' she said, picking up a few pieces and laying them side by side. 'You add one to the other, and you continue until it is large enough to cover a bed.'

Helen moved closer to the table, picking out certain colours and making a pattern as she did so.

'You certainly have an eye for shapes and colours,' Lizzie said approvingly. 'Why don't you make it your project? I assume you will be attending the group regularly?'

'I really don't know. For me, it would have to be something I could stick at. Perhaps something that had meaning to me,' Helen mused, running her fingers over the soft satin of the bedcover Lizzie had made for her daughter.

'I wonder, have you lost a relative? Could you use something from a loved one's clothing, perhaps make a cushion from a couple of frocks or a skirt?'

Helen was thoughtful. 'I don't have anything like that from a female relative. My mother is still with me, and it's been many years since my grandmother passed away. I did lose my husband recently,' she added.

'Oh, my dear, I'm so sorry. You're no age at all to be losing your husband. Was it sudden? I only ask as my own first husband died quickly and I still think back to the shock I carried with me for years, even after I remarried. Thank goodness I married an understanding man.'

'Yes, it was in London where we lived. There was a gas explosion. I wasn't home at the time.'

Lizzie frowned. 'Was your husband a Member of Parliament?'

News always travels fast in small communities, and no doubt in this case it was also fuelled by her mother seeking attention. Most people in the area knew about Helen's loss. 'Yes. I've come home for the time being. I'm staying with my mother, Mrs Hillary Davis, at The Maples. In time I will find some form of work; however, for now I need something to take me away from the house and distract me from my thoughts. That's why I came along today.'

Lizzie patted her arm. 'I know just how you feel. I've been in the same boat myself and can sympathize. Why don't you put some thought into doing a patchwork project? We can think about quilting it later. For now, let's put some pieces together and see what happens?'

Helen smiled wryly. 'You could be talking about my life. I need to put the pieces together and see how it grows. I feel rather like a piece of patchwork myself.'

'Well, I'm going to be attending the group each week, so I'll be here to help you with your project. What about fabric . . . ? I have an idea; do you perhaps have a couple of shirts that belonged to your husband? You could make a memory piece of the man you loved.'

Helen hesitated. Had she loved John? He had been good company, but surely marrying him had simply been a reason to move away from her former life. She didn't wish to have to explain this to Lizzie – these were private thoughts – but for now she would go ahead with the suggestion.

'I have a trunk at home that contains some of my husband's possessions and clothing. I've not opened it yet, but I'm sure there will be some things I can use. Perhaps I could make a cushion or quilt to send to his mother?' she added, wondering if her mother-in-law would appreciate such an item. Probably not, but it would keep Helen busy for the time being.

Lizzie watched the younger woman. She could almost see the thoughts flickering across her face before she came to some kind of decision. Perhaps Helen could be her new project? She'd love to help this sad young widow.

'Helen, here: take this book home with you. It gives the basics of patchworking as well as other sewing projects. Read it at your leisure and see what you think. I don't believe the group is meeting again until the new year, as Tish said something about the hall being needed for church events. I wonder, would you like to come to my house for coffee? If we make it the end of this week, you would have had the opportunity to look at the book and go through your husband's trunk. Bring along your thoughts and we can get you started.' She took a card with her address and telephone number from her handbag and passed it to Helen, who accepted it gratefully, and they agreed on a time for the visit.

'Excuse me, Miss Helen – I was to remind you that you have an appointment shortly.' Effie said as she appeared in front of the women. 'You might want to check the prizes on the raffle table, too, as the draw has been completed.'

'Oh my goodness, I'd completely forgotten. I've been

having such a pleasant time,' Helen said. 'I mustn't be late, though.' She made her apologies to Lizzie before heading to the trestle table, which was laden with prizes. Presenting her ticket, she was delighted to find she'd won the sewing basket. She would start to tackle the pot-holder project once she'd finished her afternoon tasks.

After seeking out Tish to give her thanks, she found Effie waiting by the door. 'Did you enjoy yourself, Effie? I'm sorry you ended up in the kitchen. It must have been like a busman's holiday.' Seeing Effie's puzzled look, she explained, 'I mean, you did the same as you would have done in your work.'

Effie looked surprised. 'But I enjoy being in a kitchen. Looking after people and feeding them is what I'm good at. You can't beat pouring out fifty cups of tea into green Beryls.'

'Green Beryls?' Helen looked confused.

'It's what they call the cups that are often used in church halls. Cheap cups and saucers,' Effie explained. 'If you turn them upside down, you'll see the word "Beryl" on the bottom. But don't do it while the cup's full,' she added with a grin.

'Well, that's something else I've learnt today. I hope you got more out of the group than just serving tea. You seemed to get on well with Jean and Ivy.'

'They're nice ladies. I'm joining their circle and learning how to make a rag rug. It should come in handy, and it's something the girls could learn as well. Oh, bugger!' she exclaimed before clamping a hand to her mouth and apologizing for her rudeness. 'I forgot to ask if anyone knew of a place I could rent.'

'Don't worry, I'm sure we can work something out. With Christmas coming up, it's probably not the right time to be moving home, especially in this awful weather.' Helen shivered, pulling her coat collar up round her neck. 'Let's hurry, shall we? I swear I can feel snow in the air.'

There again, she thought, it might just be my nerves about seeing Richard Gladstone and wondering what he'll say about John's death. As they set off, she could feel the butterflies in her stomach beginning to flutter.

4

As Helen approached the house she could see her mother standing on the top step, waving her arms and bellowing at an elderly man who had just dumped a pile of holly at her feet. He stood holding a bunch of mistletoe, offering it out to her. 'Don't wave that at me,' she shouted, at which point he placed it on top of the holly and walked back to his horse and cart.

'Is there a problem?' Helen asked him, ignoring her mother for a moment as she and Effie drew near.

'I can't rightly say, Miss. I was just told to deliver it here. This is The Maples, isn't it?'

'Yes, it is – thank you for your time,' she said, reaching into her pocket and pulling out a thruppenny bit to hand to him.

'What are you doing, Helen? We can't have all this left here.' Her mother gesticulated madly. 'What will people say?'

'Mother, people will say that Hillary Davis knows how to celebrate Christmas well,' she smiled, wondering if her mother realized she'd all but copied a quote from *A Christmas Carol*. 'They'll know we are about to decorate the house for Christmas and will think we are a happy family.' She smiled benignly. 'Let me change into my old clothes and I'll get started.'

'But we haven't done this for years,' Hillary said, wringing her hands in agitation.

'I thought it would brighten our Christmas. God only knows what next year will bring. Besides, whether you like it or not, we'll have two children in the house for the festivities – so let us spread a little cheer, shall we?' Turning to Effie, she asked, 'Would you like to help me with this? That's if you don't have to dash off to collect the children?'

'I've got an hour yet, Miss Helen, so I can lend a hand. It's so good of you to do this, the girls will be thrilled. When we lived at our own house we always put up some paper chains and bits. They were so old I believe one of the Chinese lanterns was my nan's, but it made Christmas feel special.'

'It will be even more special when the Christmas trees arrive. A large one to be placed in the bay window, just as we did when I was a small child, and a smaller one for the kitchen. Perhaps the girls would like to decorate that? I'll need to get up into the attic where the decorations are stored. Ours too are years old – we had them when my father was alive. He loved Christmas.' Helen bit her lip, but forced herself to remain cheerful. 'Those old decorations that hold memories are a big part of Christmas; don't you think?'

'They are indeed,' Effie agreed. 'I'll go and get into my working clothes.' She hurried away along the side of the house.

In a few minutes they were both back outside. 'That's the rain off, thank goodness, although there's still quite a nip in the air.'

With scissors and wearing gardening gloves, Helen snipped at the heap of holly branches, turning them into small bundles tied up with twine. 'I'm going to tie these to the banisters; it will make a lovely display for anyone coming into the house. There are so many red berries this year.'

'That's a sign of a bad winter,' Effie said with a grimace.

'Oh, I don't take any notice of old wives' tales,' Helen said. 'I feel life is bad enough right now,' she added, trying to ignore a looming sense of despair about her future. 'Would you like to arrange some of this into a display we can put in a vase on the hall table? Perhaps we could add some of the mistletoe as well.'

Effie giggled. 'That depends if you want to be kissed,' she said, giving Helen a nudge as a polite cough was heard just behind them.

'Have I called at an inopportune time?' Richard Gladstone asked.

'I'm sorry, Inspector – I hadn't forgotten you were calling.' Helen straightened up to greet him with a polite smile. 'We've just been caught up in sorting all of this out,' she added, as three men appeared in front of the house carrying a large Christmas tree. Behind them was a younger man carrying a smaller one.

'Where do you want these, Miss?'

'Oh my goodness,' she said, frozen in uncertainty for a moment as she looked between the heap of holly, the two trees, and the RAF police inspector waiting to interview her about John's death.

He had no doubt expected a conventionally grieving widow, but instead he was faced with a dishevelled woman laughing as she decorated her house for Christmas. She wasn't giving the right impression; but then, she'd never been a widow before and wasn't sure how she should act. Well, it was too late now. She would just have to carry on, and be blowed what he thought.

As for her mother, who seemed to be in a state of hysteria about the 'mess' in the house, she would have to be ignored for now. Once the decorating was finished Hillary would almost certainly be showing it off to her friends. A thought crossed Helen's mind about a magazine advertisement she'd seen for a nerve tonic. Yes, perhaps she should purchase a bottle of Sanatogen. If her mother knew it had been advertised in *The Lady* she'd be sure to take it. She smiled to herself at the thought.

'Here, let me lend a hand,' Richard said, taking the heavy end of the larger tree. 'Would you like to lead the way?' he asked Helen. She showed him through to the front room while Effie buzzed around them, moving an armchair and a side table to make room for the tree. Handing some coins to the delivery men, Helen thanked them for their help.

Effie looked at the bare roots of the tree. 'What should we put it in?' she asked.

'There's a large tub in the garden shed; I thought we could use that.'

'I'll go and get it,' Effie said, eager to see the trees in place.

'Allow me, that's no work for a young lady. Lead the way, please,' Richard offered.

Helen shook her head as she watched Effie almost melt

in front of the man. Granted he was tall and handsome, just like the men the housekeeper read about in the magazines she devoured. Helen had seen her with them more than once in the kitchen, sighing over the latest romantic story.

'I'll take the small tree through to the kitchen and the children can help with it when they come home,' Helen called after them.

By the time Effie and Richard returned with the wooden tub, not only had she put the smaller tree in the kitchen, but she'd run a brush through her hair and checked her lipstick before returning to the heap of holly and mistletoe branches in the drive. Deftly breaking them into small, manageable bunches and tying them with garden twine, she carried them indoors. Her mother was hovering in the hallway, still looking distressed as she surveyed the chaos.

'Please don't worry, Mother. Why don't you go into the drawing room? I'm sure Effie will bring tea to you shortly. It won't take long for me to clean up here.'

Her mother sniffed and walked away. 'I don't know what your stepfather will say about this mess, I really don't.'

Helen was thankful Richard Gladstone was there to lend a hand; it would have taken the rest of the day left to herself and Effie. They stepped back to admire their handiwork once the tree was in place and all agreed it was just the right size, sitting in the large bay window with its top almost touching the high ceiling.

'It will look super once decorated,' Helen said. 'I've not seen one as beautiful as this since . . . since my father was alive.' Her voice broke, and she controlled herself with an effort. 'I must thank you for your help,' she said to Richard. 'Please, let me take your coat.'

'Or you'll not get the benefit when you go out, it's getting so cold out there.' Effie shivered to add effect to her words.

Helen had to admit Richard looked smart out of uniform as she watched him open his heavy brown tweed coat. She admired his smart knitted pullover and matching woollen scarf, which he pulled off and tucked into one of the coat pockets with a nod of thanks to Effie before crossing over to rub his hands at the open fire.

'I'll bring in a tray shortly, I'll just see to your mother,' Effie said as she left with Richard's coat. Helen smiled at her gratefully.

'Please take a seat,' she said, indicating the armchair by the fire. 'I can't thank you enough for your help, when all you intended to do was to come here to interview me. Are you not on duty? Surely you aren't here in your own time? I'd feel guilty if you were.'

He looked slightly sheepish. 'I didn't have much on, as I'm new in the area, so I thought I might as well carry on with my enquiries.'

Helen nodded seriously as she took the chair opposite his. It was time for the conversation she had been dreading.

'What you told me yesterday about John's death was a terrible shock,' she began. 'I had no idea . . .' She closed her eyes briefly, then took a deep breath. 'As you can see, I've been keeping myself busy here with other things. But I'm sure Effie will bring in the tea shortly and then, of course, I'm ready to answer any questions you have.'

As she spoke, the door was pushed open and Effie edged

in backwards, bumping it wider with her backside as she struggled with a heavy tray.

'Looking at the time, I thought it was worth bringing in tea straight away. I'm sure you could both do with this, after all the work you've done. My goodness – whatever has happened?' she asked, seeing their serious faces.

Richard got to his feet to take the tray, which was wobbling dangerously. 'Here, let me take that.'

'Thank you, Effie. It's all right. The inspector was just about to begin interviewing me about . . .' Helen saw Effie's eyes widen in recollection of their conversation in the kitchen the previous night.

Apologizing profusely, Effie made to leave the room.

'No, please stay for a moment, Effie – I want you to hear.' Helen glanced at Richard. 'The police have now confirmed that my husband was killed.'

'But you already knew that, Miss Helen . . .'

'No – what I mean is, he was deliberately murdered. Who would do such a thing?' she asked, shaking her head in bewilderment. 'John was a dear man who wouldn't have hurt a living soul. He worked hard for this country. He didn't deserve to die.'

Richard frowned. 'Well, that is why I'm here.'

Effie began pouring the tea, adding an extra spoonful of sugar to Helen's cup. 'You'll feel better when you've had some hot tea, Miss,' she said as she passed it over. Turning to Richard, she added impulsively: 'Surely you don't think Miss Helen did it, do you?' Her ruddy cheeks flushed even redder than usual.

'I'm making enquiries at this stage,' he replied, keeping his tone carefully neutral as he accepted a cup.

'But how do you know he was murdered?' Effie persisted, giving Helen an apologetic look. 'Could you be mistaken?'

'I don't think a paper knife stab to the throat is a mistake, do you?' He watched Helen closely to see how she reacted to his words.

'Please don't say it was the paper knife I gave him, with his name engraved on it?' Helen asked, looking horrified.

'*To John, with love from Helen,*' Richard said thoughtfully, looking at both women. 'Please be assured that we will leave no stone unturned to find the murderer.'

'Well, you can't think Miss Helen would do such a thing,' Effie said firmly. 'She gave him that gift out of love, and she's no cold-blooded killer. Could it have been a spy, or the enemy? Perhaps the Germans are bumping off all our MPs? I've read about that kind of thing.'

Helen shook her head. 'This is real life, Effie, not a novel.'

Richard cleared his throat. 'At this point, I'm speaking to everyone known to your husband.'

'Well, I have nothing to hide,' Helen said quietly. 'I'll tell you anything you want to know.'

'And I never met him,' Effie added.

The conversation that followed felt to Helen like a bad dream. Effie excused herself to go and collect her children after pressing sandwiches on them, insisting Helen ate something and reminding them they should not be wasting food with rationing on the horizon.

Helen nibbled at one sandwich but really didn't have the stomach for it, whereas Richard not only had four sandwiches but also a slice of Effie's Victoria sponge washed down with a second cup of tea, which he poured after taking Helen's plate from her.

Once he'd brushed crumbs from his jumper and drained the last of the tea from his cup, he looked at Helen. 'Would you please remind me where you were on the day of your husband's death, so I can be sure I have all the facts?'

Helen clasped her hands in her lap. 'As I told you that day at the apartment, I had stayed the night before with my friend, Felicity Davenport. We'd planned to have lunch but she was unwell, so I decided to stay and keep an eye on her. I rang to let my husband know, but there was no answer from the flat. Assuming the line was down, I left a message at his office – he always checked in last thing. It was only the next morning that I was informed of the explosion and hurried back, after going to the hospital. I was foolish in thinking I could see . . . I could see John . . . I was hoping there'd been some kind of mistake, a mix-up. If you recall, you were already at the flat when I arrived. I'm not sure what else I can tell you.'

'What state of mind was your husband in the last time you saw him?'

'Why do you ask? You can't honestly think he stabbed himself in the neck?'

'If only it were that simple,' he replied, keeping eye contact with her. 'Is it true that you had an argument with your husband before you left the building?'

Helen flinched at his words. 'It was nothing,' she said after a moment's hesitation. 'Really, it was nothing at all.'

'The porter seems to think it was more than that.'

'Then he is lying. How could he have heard us from his desk, two floors below?'

'He was on your floor, taking a parcel from one of your neighbours. In fact, if you recall, he took the lift down with you to the ground floor and left the building at the same time as you, to go to the post office.'

Helen thought for a moment. 'Yes, you're right. He did leave the building with me.'

'Why did you argue with your husband, Mrs Wentworth?'

'It was nothing at all. All husbands and wives argue sometimes. Don't you find that?'

'I'm not married,' he replied, his eyes still not leaving her face. 'Can you tell me what you argued about?'

Helen sighed and sat back in her chair, gathering her thoughts before replying. 'John was much older than me. He lived for his work, and would only socialize when it was work-related. There were times when I wanted to go out and meet Felicity, but he didn't like her very much, and on this occasion he actually forbade me to meet her. I refused, and we argued. It seems rather childish now that I think back on it, but . . . I stormed out of the flat after telling him that I wanted a divorce.'

'And did you want a divorce?' Richard asked quietly.

'It was just a foolish thing, said in the heat of the moment.'

'And your friend Felicity . . . ?'

'Felicity?'

'Yes – was there any particular reason he shouldn't like her? How do you know her?'

'Felicity and I worked together before I married. I met John when I was moved from our office to be his secretary, but I kept in touch with Felicity. She is rather a social butterfly, nothing gets her down; or at least, I never thought it did . . . She enjoys men's company and she loves going to parties.'

'And are you a social butterfly?'

Helen let out a harsh laugh. 'No, not by any means. I did accompany Felicity to the odd party, and I enjoy trips to the theatre. But I was very much the country-bumpkin friend who stayed at home and washed her hair, while Felicity had men throwing themselves at her feet. She reminds me rather of a Hollywood actress; she is a real beauty. We only became friends because we both needed somewhere to live. I suppose you might say we were like chalk and cheese, it's as simple as that.'

Richard asked a few more questions about Helen's routine while John was alive, but steered clear of further questions about their relationship. Eventually he rose and thanked her for her time. Helen showed him to the door, promising that if anything relevant came to mind she would be in touch. They agreed that he would make an appointment to speak to her again at a later date.

Closing the front door on his departing figure, she went back into the front room and watched from the window as he walked down the road and climbed into his motor car. Further down the road, she spotted Effie holding hands with her little girls. They were skipping excitedly at either side of her. No doubt she had told them about the Christmas tree.

It was starting to get dark, and fast-moving clouds scudded across the sky. Helen could hear the wind whistling through the trees. The rain had returned as an icy drizzle competing with the wind. It looked as cold outside as the ice that had crept into her heart.

Had she been right to hold back and not tell Richard Gladstone everything? He'd only have thought worse of her, and for some reason that idea made her sad.

She reached out and pulled the heavy curtains closed, shutting out the world at least for that day. If only she could roll back time.

Her thoughts went to the trunk, now deposited in her bedroom. It was time to open it and face her past. Then, hopefully, she'd be able to move forward – if that was possible. Switching on the light, she took a deep breath and headed for the stairs.

5

Helen sat on the edge of her bed, looking at the scuffed brown leather of the trunk. John had told her that he'd travelled back and forth to boarding school, and later to university, with this same trunk by his side. Once it had been emptied, she would return it to his family; they could no doubt make better use of it than she could, and it would be a memento of John's childhood.

But first she had to open it, and so far she had got no further than flicking the two brass catches and undoing the leather straps. Why was she so nervous? After all, it only held memories of someone she was fond of; there was nothing to fear.

As she leant forward, taking a deep breath, ready to pull back the lid, she jumped as the bedroom door opened. Please don't let it be my mother, she thought fleetingly – she couldn't cope with Hillary crying about Helen's lost opportunities now she was no longer the wife of an MP. Thankfully it was Effie, carrying a small tray.

'I hope you don't mind, Miss Helen; I brought up a cup of tea, and one for myself while we get stuck in. You still want me to help out, don't you?'

Helen smiled. Effie's cheerful company was exactly what she needed. If Effie did ask questions or make comments, they would be innocent and well-intentioned, unlike her mother's incessant digging and whining.

'Come in, Effie. I'll be grateful for some company and that cup of tea.'

'Why, Miss Helen, you've not even started yet.'

'I'm finding it difficult. I didn't think it would be, but . . .'

Effie put down the tray and hurried over to give Helen a hug. 'Oh, Miss Helen, of course it's going to be difficult; it's a bit like digging up memories and yours must be so raw, why it's only been a few months since he . . .'

'Was murdered?'

'What a horrible word that is. I do hope they've made a mistake. It's a nasty way to meet your end. And then to set up the gas explosion soon afterwards. Though . . . if they'd wanted to make it look like an accident, they shouldn't have used a knife, surely?'

Helen frowned; Effie had a point. Whatever the reason, it was a horrible way for him to die.

Effie rubbed her hands together. 'Let's get cracking, Miss Helen. It might just take your mind off things for a while.'

'Please, Effie, can you stop calling me Miss Helen? Helen is fine.'

'But your mother wouldn't like it.'

Helen sighed; her mother had a lot to answer for. 'In that case, just call me Helen when we are alone. When Mother's about, you can call me whatever you wish. Do you agree?'

'That sounds good to me, Mi— Helen.'

She couldn't help but chuckle as Effie corrected herself. 'I must say, I do like your name. Effie isn't a name I've come across before. Is it a family name?'

Effie pulled a face. 'You could say that. I'm named after my dad's maiden aunt. She'd promised to leave him something in her will, so when I came along, I was christened Euphemia, would you believe? She popped her clogs a couple of months later and my parents, who could never get their tongue around the name, quickly started calling me Effie, thank the Lord.'

Helen snorted with laughter. 'I hope your parents did well out of the lady.'

'A pottery dog with a crack in one ear and a mourning brooch. You can see why I never passed the name on to either of my girls. Even my Frank refused to say my full name when we married. He said he almost left me at the altar until the vicar told him Effie would be sufficient. I had my doubts whether the old boy could say it, either,' she laughed.

'Oh my,' Helen said as she dabbed away tears of laughter. Effie was such a lovely person, she couldn't help but like her. 'You are a tonic.'

'Come on, open the trunk. Let's get started and then we can drink our tea. I put a couple of slices of fruit cake on a plate as well. I wonder if we'll still be able to have that, once the rationing starts? It's a bloody liberty, that's what it is. Someone ought to complain. Gawd knows what I'll do when I can't put one of my cakes in front of Mrs Davis.' Effie seemed to have momentarily forgotten that Hillary had all but given her marching orders. 'A bloody liberty!'

'The man you need to complain to is Mr Hitler, Effie. He's at the bottom of the world's problems,' Helen said as she pulled back the lid of the trunk. Straight away, she could identify the familiar smell of John's cigarettes and Old Spice cologne; if she closed her eyes, she could imagine him standing there. She gave herself a mental shake. This wouldn't get things done.

'He was a snappy dresser,' Effie said, lifting out a smart grey woollen suit and hanging it from the picture rail. 'Crikey, there's another,' she added, pulling out a navy-blue one. 'Fancy him having more than one suit. All the men I knew just had one for Sunday best. But then, I suppose someone like your husband would've worn them all the time, wouldn't he . . . What's this?'

She put her hand into the pocket of the grey suit.

'Oh, look,' she went on, pulling out a woman's silk scarf. 'It's like one the Queen would wear. They must have packed your scarf in here by mistake, instead of putting it in your suitcases.'

Helen was about to say that the scarf wasn't hers, but then she stopped speaking and took it from Effie, lifting it to her face. She recognized it – and the lingering scent it carried of the Schiaparelli perfume, Shocking. The only person she knew who wore that was Felicity.

But what was Felicity's scarf doing in John's pocket? They'd hated each other. John was forever telling Helen that he did not approve of her friends; and hadn't Felicity told her only the night before John's death that she should consider leaving him?

She pushed the unanswered questions to the back of her mind. I'll get this trunk cleared and then I will think about the scarf later, she told herself. As much as she liked Effie, it didn't seem right to burden her with all of these troubles. Not at the moment, anyway.

In all there were six business suits, a formal dress suit and several pairs of casual trousers, including tweeds that Helen knew were normally kept at John's parents' home in the country. He must have worn them back to London at some time when he'd visited. He had liked to go up there to shoot or ride, while she'd preferred to remain in London.

'Look at all these ties,' Effie exclaimed. 'Are they silk?'

'Yes, I believe they are,' Helen answered as she added several bow ties and black cummerbunds to the pile Effie had placed on the bed.

'And a red shirt – no, it's a blouse,' Effie said as she passed a garment to Helen. 'Another of yours packed by mistake.'

Helen couldn't believe her eyes. Something else belonging to Felicity? She'd know this blouse anywhere, having been with her friend when it was purchased. A dull pain pierced her heart as she held the proof in her hand that her husband had been unfaithful. Why else would the blouse and the scarf be mixed up with his own clothing? How had they gotten there? Again, she pushed the thought from her mind and carried on with the job at hand. Next came shirts: pure cotton, pale pinstripes, small checks, and several casual shirts that she remembered John wearing when he wasn't at the office. She laid them out on her bed.

'All this is so beautiful. You'd not think such material was used to make men's clothing,' Effie remarked, holding up a paisley silk smoking jacket to admire its red lapels and elegant design. 'How posh, and what's this, a dressing gown . . . ? And look at these pyjamas – just to wear in bed. Who would've thought it?'

'John did like to dress well,' Helen said, feeling slightly embarrassed that her husband had owned so much fine clothing. She quickly lifted out a pile of underclothes and put them to one side.

'We still haven't reached the bottom of the trunk . . .' Effie gasped and picked up a case containing a shaving kit, silver-backed brush and several bottles of cologne. 'He obviously liked to look after himself. I wish I'd met him. He makes my old man look downright scruffy. A bar of carbolic soap and a jar of Brylcreem along with his ciggies is all he ever needs. But I suppose when we had to drag in the old tin bath from the backyard just to have a scrub down, we couldn't afford to be fussy.'

There was such a large divide, thought Helen, between her late husband and Effie's husband – they were classes apart.

'If it's any consolation, my husband had more clothes than I did,' she smiled. 'In his job he had to be seen to dress well. He was always encouraging me to buy more frocks, but I wasn't one for dressing up. A few good pieces were all I required.' She recalled the designer pieces she had worn to important events, although they hadn't brought her much enjoyment. That lifestyle had never reflected who she really was – more what John had wished her to be.

'Oh, look at these socks! Surely they're not silk too?' Effie said, reaching out to pick up several black pairs. 'The woollen ones are so soft,' she sighed, holding them to her face.

'I have no need of them, so would you like to take them for your husband? I'm sure he could make good use of them.'

'I'll take the wool ones, if you don't mind,' Effie said gratefully. 'My old man wouldn't have much use for silk socks while he's in the service. Oh, there's something else here,' she added, reaching in and pulling out a flat gift box with the name of a well-known department store embossed in one corner.

Helen had no idea what might be inside. 'Go ahead and open it,' she suggested.

'Oh, Miss Helen,' Effie said, forgetting she'd promised not to use the title. 'Do you think your husband bought it for you as a gift before he died?' She lifted the thin straps of an elegant cream satin negligee, draping it against herself before handing it over to Helen with an envious look on her face.

Helen didn't like to say that there had been no reason for John to buy her a present, as her birthday had been back in April. Nor was he the type of person to shop early for Christmas, and considering he'd died in October, she was certain that wasn't the answer. She ran her fingers over the delicate cream lace on the bodice. It matched the trim on the hem of the flowing, almost diaphanous skirt. No, this was not a gift for his wife. A quick glance at the discreet size label showed it was meant for a more voluptuous woman than Helen – a woman like Felicity.

'Oh look, there's a card,' Effie said, handing over the vellum envelope.

Helen pulled a small notecard from inside and read the few words before putting it back and sliding it into the drawer of her bedside table. 'I'll read it properly later,' she smiled. 'Let's have that cake, shall we?' The writing on the card was familiar to her, but was not John's handwriting. *For our eyes only* was not something he would ever have said to her, let alone written.

Effie, more than pleased with the bundle of underwear and socks she'd been given, went to check on her girls, who were colouring paper shapes to hang on the small Christmas tree. Helen sat on the edge of the bed, deep in thought. She'd overheard on more than one occasion the wives of her husband's colleagues whispering about him having a fondness for the ladies. Helen had shrugged it off at the time; she'd only known him to be a hard worker and a man who seemed to care for her. They'd planned to spend their lives together, and to have a family; that was the usual expectation for any respectable politician.

John had laughed it off when, early in their marriage, one particularly spiteful comment had been meant for Helen to overhear. She'd held herself together until they were in a taxicab travelling home, when her worries had spilt out. Seeing how upset she was, he had reassured her that none of it was true. He'd explained that some wives of MPs fought between themselves to make their husbands stand out more in the newspapers by tearing others to pieces. He'd said it was a competition of sorts, and she would need to accept it – either that, or stay at home and not attend events where she might be belittled or put down. He'd pulled a newspaper from his pocket and opened it to the society pages, pointing out that the women she'd mentioned were prominently featured at different social events. 'This is what you should be doing,' he'd said, 'rather than feeling sorry for yourself. When you married me, you took on more than a husband – you took on an essential job.'

Helen had accepted all of this and worked hard to live up to his expectations, visiting couture houses to be fitted for the right sort of gowns and smiling her way through high-profile gatherings. She'd hated every minute of these affairs and generally preferred to busy herself working with John's social diary, representing him at charity meetings and accompanying him to meet constituents. The same society pages he'd pointed out to her now featured Helen as a hard-working, smartly dressed wife, chatting to housewives about the price of food and consoling those whose husbands were away serving their country. She did her best to steer clear of her fellow political wives, whom she now thought of as a witches' coven.

They'd fallen into a routine which seemed, for the most part, to suit them both. If they were invited to evening affairs, he never pressed her to accompany him. She made a point of not listening to gossip, and was able to ignore anything that was being said. Occasionally Helen did wish their relationship was more passionate, but she always pushed that longing to the back of her mind. John wasn't one for romance and she had known that when she'd agreed to be his wife. She'd made herself useful to him – that was what mattered.

She wondered what those other women were saying now.

Reaching into her handbag for a handkerchief, she came across the card Lizzie had given her earlier in the day and remembered the older woman's invitation to visit. Helen would have loved to make a quilt using pieces of fabric representing precious memories. How unfortunate that her immediate memory just now was of a horribly murdered husband who had likely been unfaithful.

A thought came to her as she stared at the suits and shirts, the silk ties and the flat gift box. Opening her wardrobe, she took out the sewing box she'd won in the raffle and removed a pair of scissors before turning to the grey suit and swiftly cutting off one of the trouser legs. With a sigh of satisfaction, she set to cutting pieces of fabric from every one of her husband's garments. He had obviously been keeping secrets, and she didn't like secrets . . .

She placed all the pieces into a canvas bag, then tipped the contents of the gift box in as well. Going to her wardrobe again, she took out a full-length eau-de-nil taffeta gown, cutting the full skirt straight across the waistline and separating it from the bodice. As she shook it out before folding it to place in the bag, the shot silk lining fell to her feet. She picked it up, admiring the colour.

'I think I have myself a project,' she smiled to herself, before standing back to look at her handiwork. Then she opened the sewing basket to examine the rest of its contents. Her life was starting to become interesting.

Helen's chin almost hit the ground as she turned the corner and looked up the lane towards Lizzie's house. Pulling to a halt on her bicycle, she called out to a man working in a nearby garden. 'Excuse me – can you tell me if that property up ahead is Dalton Court?'

He tapped the brim of his cap in greeting. 'Yes, it is, and all the land round here. It's just my cottage and garden that don't belong to them.'

Helen thanked him and cycled on her way, feeling the heavy weight of the fabric packed into the canvas bag, which she'd strapped to her bicycle basket. She was careful not to wobble on the bike whenever she thought of how she'd attacked John's clothing. She felt rather sick. What had she done? Then she thought of the silk scarf, the heady perfume that still clung to the fabric and stirred memories. As for the negligee . . . She felt her fury return as she pedalled hard up the lane, anger spurring her on to reach the large house at the end of the drive bordered by mature oak trees.

Feeling as though she should be parking her bicycle around the back of the house by the servants' entrance, Helen instead leant it against one of the ornate pillars close to the house's large double front doors, and unstrapped her bag of fabric. As she was raising her hand to knock on the door it suddenly swung open and Lizzie stood there, immaculately made up and with not a hair out of place, wearing a bright floral tea dress.

'I'm sorry about . . .' Helen started to say.

'Oh, my dear, don't worry about that. Mine is usually propped up against one of the trees. Come along in – I think the time is about right for drinks, don't you?'

Helen followed, not sure three o'clock was quite right for drinks, unless of course Lizzie meant tea or coffee. Stepping into the large hall, she was faced with a wide staircase that split at the top, turning left and right. The pillars supporting the entrance to the front door were also visible in the hall, reaching up to the high ceiling. The floor was a mosaic pattern of black and white marble.

'You have a beautiful home,' was all she could think of to say. Her mother would have been so envious of Lizzie's lifestyle: in her world, the size of one's house was a direct reflection of one's social position. By that measure, Lizzie's social standing was up in the clouds somewhere.

'We don't own the property, just rent. I thought coming over to England to live, we should try to live like country folk. It's such fun – we even have a butler,' Lizzie whispered as she led Helen into a drawing room. 'Sit yourself down, you must be exhausted after that ride. I cycle up and down the drive to keep fit, as I don't ride a horse. It keeps me slim,' she said, slapping the sides of her legs. 'What do you fancy?' She went over to a cocktail cabinet. 'A Sidecar perhaps, or a Mary Pickford? I make a mean Torpedo.' She winked. 'We have an hour before tea is served. I told Doreen four o'clock to give us time to have a chat, and for me to show you more of my quilts. I've set up a sewing room in one of the spare bedrooms.' She added with a chuckle, 'And there are plenty of spare rooms in this house.'

Helen was completely thrown. She suddenly couldn't think of the name of a single cocktail, even though she'd been served them plenty of times in London. 'Oh, I don't know – surprise me,' she said, trying to sound like a confident woman of the world, although inside she was quaking. She'd expected Lizzie's home to be a nice little cottage where she sat and worked on her patchwork quilts. This grand house had thrown her completely. 'What does your husband do that affords you such an impressive house?' she asked, then stopped to apologize. 'I'm so sorry – that does sound rather nosy of me.'

Lizzie laughed as she finished mixing the drinks and brought them over, handing one to Helen. 'Here, try this, it's a Shirley Temple. I'm rather partial to them – at this time of day I seldom touch alcohol. If you don't like the taste, I'll make something stronger.' She sat down. 'My husband, Gerald, is a major in the Canadian air force. He's over here on top secret business. God knows what it is: he doesn't tell me a thing. Oh dear, perhaps I shouldn't have told you. You could be a spy,' she chuckled.

'I'm trustworthy,' Helen grinned back as she sipped her drink, which she found remarkably tasty. Thank goodness there was no alcohol in it, or she'd never be able to cycle in a straight line going home. 'My husband was a Member of Parliament, after all. In fact, if you got me tipsy, I might spill the beans on some top secret developments at the Ministry of Food, and then the pair of us would be locked up in the Tower,' she added, looking serious.

'Oh my goodness,' Lizzie said, looking alarmed until she saw Helen's mouth twitch into a smile. 'I fall for anything . . . I'm sorry, I shouldn't joke, especially not with you having lost your husband recently. You must be devastated.'

'I'm sad that anyone should die like that.'

'It was a gas explosion, wasn't it?'

'Yes, there was a gas explosion. But you may as well hear from me, as no doubt it will be in the newspapers soon: John was dead before the explosion.'

'Oh, my goodness,' Lizzie said, reaching out and taking her hand in sympathy. 'Was it his heart? I understand he was older than you.'

Helen shook her head and looked down into her lap. 'If only it had been something as simple as a heart attack; if heart attacks are simple. I'm afraid it is much worse. I can't help thinking that if I'd been there, his death might not have happened.'

Lizzie looked confused. Taking Helen's empty glass, she returned to the cocktail cabinet and slowly filled two clean glasses. 'I get the feeling that more has happened than just what people are saying. If you want to confide in me, you'll find me a good friend, but if you prefer not to, then just tell me to mind my own business.'

Helen took comfort in Lizzie's words. Her mother was tied up in her own thoughts most of the time, as well as her regret that Helen would never be the wife of a prime minister. She was not the kind of woman one confided in at the best of times; she never had been. Effie was a kind soul, but she had her own worries, with a husband serving God only knew where and two children who needed a place they could call home. As for Felicity, she'd not seen hide nor hair of her in a long time – not that it looked as though she was much of a real friend before then, she thought, glancing at the bag by her side.

She gave Lizzie a grateful smile. 'I know we haven't known each other very long at all, but I truly do feel I can talk to you; that's if you don't think too badly of me,' she said sadly.

'My poor love,' Lizzie said as she left the drinks by the cocktail cabinet and went to sit next to Helen, placing an arm round her shoulder. 'Come on, you can tell Auntie Lizzie. I promise I'll not judge you.'

'After the women's group yesterday, I had a meeting with a policeman. He's one of those police who work for the RAF.'

'Oh yes, I know what you mean – my husband often has dealings with them. Most of the services have their own versions of a police force. What did he say to you to make you look so upset? Was it something about the way your husband died?'

'John was murdered. And the way I was interviewed gave me the impression that he believes I might have done it. Oh, I told him everything I knew, as well as a little about my relationship with my husband; after all, I had nothing to hide. I was staying with a friend the night he was murdered. We'd had a row, you see . . .'

'Oh dear, that doesn't sound good. But at least your friend can vouch for you,' Lizzie said consolingly.

'The thing is . . . the thing is, I don't know if I can trust her.'

'Why do you say that? Surely you can trust a friend?'

Helen bent over and picked up her bag. 'No, I don't feel I can. And I think my husband was lying to me, too,' she said as she picked up the edge of the bag and tipped its contents onto the Persian rug at her feet, displaying pieces of men's clothing in amongst the satin nightgown. She tugged at the edge of the scarf and pulled it out of the pile. Both women caught a waft of heady perfume as the scarf floated for a moment before settling.

'That's a Schiaparelli perfume, I recognize it. Gerald gave me a bottle once as a present, but it just didn't suit me, so I passed it on to my daughter. It is rather expensive.'

'It's not one I favour either,' Helen said. 'But Felicity – my friend – uses it all the time.'

Lizzie frowned at Helen's words. 'Where did you find the scarf?'

'It was in the pocket of John's suit jacket,' she said.

Lizzie reached for a piece of the fine grey woollen suiting and lifted up the left leg of what had been a perfectly pressed pair of trousers. 'Did you . . . ?'

'If you mean did I cut up all his clothing, yes, I did. As for that—' She kicked at the silk negligee, then went on to explain that she'd found the box in the trunk full of John's clothes. 'I was so angry to think that my husband had secrets that he's taken to his grave and my so-called friend must have been party to some of them.'

'It's not that I don't believe you, Helen, but . . . surely more women than just your friend wear this perfume?'

'The scarf comes from a limited design, and I purchased the very same one for her birthday last year. It would be such a coincidence if it belonged to somebody else and was covered in the perfume she always wears. As for the negligee – well, it's not to my taste, and it wasn't purchased for me as it's not my size. For all his faults, he did know my size in clothing.' Helen choked on the last few words before shuddering sobs wracked her body.

Lizzie enveloped Helen in her arms and rocked her gently, making soothing noises, until Helen's breathing became calmer and the tears subsided. She didn't feel she should say what was on her mind, but she feared Helen had made any case against herself much worse by damaging her husband's clothing. However, she would stand by her side and be the friend Helen needed at the moment, regardless of the outcome. If truth be known, Lizzie too needed a friend; since coming to England and leaving her daughters behind with their families, she had been lonely. Living in a grand house and coming from a foreign land didn't always make it easy to form friendships in a community like theirs.

'Do you know what, Helen? We two should stick together. We are both oddballs in this village and we could both do with a good friend. What do you say – do you want to be mates with a woman nearly old enough to be your mother?'

Helen sniffed into a handkerchief. 'I'd be very grateful, thank you. Oh, and believe me, you are nothing like my mother, and I don't think you're that old at all,' she said, giving a watery smile.

'I accept the compliment gratefully, although I'm old enough to have grown-up daughters. Now, how about we knock back these cocktails I started to prepare, and I'll show you my workroom? I also have an idea,' she said as she carefully placed the pieces of fabric back into the bag. She got up to finish mixing the drinks, a worried expression crossing her face as she turned away from Helen.

'Oh, what a glorious room,' Helen exclaimed as Lizzie led her into a large bedroom at the front of the house. 'How can you get any work done with such a marvellous view?' She walked over to one of the three floor-to-ceiling windows.

'It is rather special, isn't it?' Lizzie came to stand beside her. 'It's amazing the wildlife I see while I sit here sewing. That's why my sewing table faces the window, so I don't miss a thing. The deer have no idea they are being observed. It's not quite the same as the bear I once spotted in our garden back home, but all wildlife is a treat to observe in its natural habitat, don't you agree?'

'Oh, I do. I missed it so much while living in London. As cheeky as the little sparrows were, I missed the countryside.'

'What made you go to work in London?' Lizzie asked as she took the pieces of garment from the bag she'd carried upstairs, placing them carefully side by side on a large cutting table. 'Take a pew,' she invited, pulling up two chairs.

'Once I finished at school, I took a secretarial course. I'd decided I'd rather be away from home and London seemed the obvious choice. To begin with I lived in a hostel for young professional women while I settled into work. I met Felicity when she placed a card on our staff noticeboard looking for someone to share a flat with. It seemed a perfect idea. I had company, had halved my living costs and for the first time I started to go out and enjoy myself. Working for the civil service might sound impressive, but we secretaries didn't earn very well.'

'And this Felicity is the same woman you now suspect of having an affair with your husband?'

Helen grimaced. To hear someone saying the words out loud made her feel sick to her stomach. 'Yes. She was a close friend, so of course I always knew she enjoyed being entertained by men – but all the same, I honestly thought she was a decent sort who wouldn't for one moment look at a married man. Let alone a friend's husband.'

Lizzie reached for the satin garment, running it between

her fingers thoughtfully. 'Are there any other signs that they were seeing each other?'

Helen thought for a moment before replying. 'My friendship with Felicity, once I was married, drifted. John's social circle was different to mine; Felicity wouldn't have fitted in amongst his friends and their wives. Yes, she knew some of the men from work – but outside work was completely different. I hardly fitted in as it was, and tried to avoid socializing as much as possible. The times I thought to speak to Felicity, suggesting an outing of some kind, she always seemed to be busy. I simply thought that it was a case of someone I knew in my single days drifting away once I was married.'

'Do you know if your husband had any form of contact with Felicity while at work?'

'Oh yes, she was promoted several times. The last I heard, she worked in a parliamentary under-secretary's office. She would have bumped into John quite often, I should think. He told me he'd prefer that I no longer mix with her. I took that to mean he wanted me to concentrate on his social circle.'

Lizzie raised her eyebrows, somewhat surprised at what Helen had told her. 'You should distance yourself as much as possible – get involved with new people and make a new life for yourself. That's what I decided to do when we first moved here, just six months ago. What about your mother and father?'

Helen felt a pang of sadness at the mention of her father. 'He died when I was young. Mother remarried within a year – I felt it was in haste, but she is the kind of woman who needs a man to support her, or she only feels half a person. She sees having a husband as giving her social standing in life. That's why she adored my husband, because she was the mother-in-law to a Member of Parliament. Now . . . well, now she's just the mother of a young widow who sits around her house, moping.'

'What about your stepfather? He must be more like a father to you, if you've known him since you were young?'

Helen tensed. 'If you don't mind, I'd rather not talk about him,' she said, turning towards a bookcase that covered almost an entire wall. 'You do have a lot of books; are they all about sewing?' she asked as she moved closer to the shelves to browse.

Lizzie watched the girl, feeling troubled. What was it about the stepfather? Was he the reason Helen had gone scurrying off to work in London as soon as she was able?

6

Lizzie looked thoughtful as she moved pieces of fabric around on her large worktable before giving a sigh of satisfaction. 'Come and look at these,' she said as she led Helen over to a cupboard fitted into one of the alcoves next to a marbled fireplace. Pulling open the wide drawers, she placed quilt after quilt into Helen's arms.

'You said you've been here six months. You can't have made this many quilts in that time. Did you bring these with you?' Helen asked in astonishment.

'We spent a year up in Yorkshire before Gerald was moved south. A few of these came with me, just as I said at my talk. I couldn't leave all my family heirlooms indefinitely, so once we knew we wouldn't be returning to Canada any time soon, I asked my daughter to ship them over. I'd never have forgiven myself if something awful happened to them.'

'They're beautiful,' Helen said as she carried them over to the worktable. Lizzie followed with another armful of the brightly coloured bedcovers.

Lizzie arranged the quilts across one end of the table, and also over the backs of two large armchairs set each side of the fireplace. She bent down and lit a taper, holding it to the grate, where a fire had been prepared. 'We may as well be cosy while we're here. I'll have tea sent up shortly, then we won't be disturbed. Now, tell me which quilts you prefer.'

Helen moved from one to another, running her hands over the fabric and shaking out a few so she could see their full beauty. 'It's so hard to choose. Can you tell me more about them? Which ones did you make, and which did you inherit? I'm veering towards this one,' she said, indicating a pattern in which strips of fabric were sewn around a square of cotton in the centre of the quilt, with each coloured strip getting longer as they moved towards the outside border.

'That design is called Barn Raising; it's quite an old style. Here, look at this one,' Lizzie said, pulling out a quilt made of different shades of green and brown floral cotton. 'Can you see how it's the same design? Instead of working as one piece, here the design has been made in six equal sizes and then sewn together – but it's still the basic Barn Raising design.'

Helen looked between the two. 'I see what you mean, yes; a simple design, but they're so different.'

'I made them both quite recently. I do like to play around with colours and fabrics. Of course, with sewing material becoming scarce we are going to have to reuse old fabric. This is why I'm so interested in the pieces you brought along today. This one' – she shook out a third quilt – 'has been made from unwanted clothing. I purchased it at a house sale. I recognized it as a Barn Raising quilt and just had to have it, not only to drool over but also to copy the design.'

'What about this one?' Helen said, unfolding a smaller quilt made up of pink and pale-blue floral fabric. 'It seems to have been hand sewn and must have taken forever. I see there's one piece in the design different to the rest. Is this what you referred to in your talk about no quilt ever being perfect? What was it you said the quilters say – "only God is perfect"? I find the whole tradition of quilting fascinating.'

Lizzie chuckled. 'It's just a bit of superstition, but it's nice to continue all the same. If you feel this one,' she said, pulling out yet another quilt and laying it on top of the others across the armchair, 'touch the pieces and tell me what you notice?'

Helen ran her hands over the small shapes intricately pieced together. She observed the bottom of the quilt was a rich mix of brown fabrics, above it blue, and in one corner the golden rays of the sun. 'Oh, my goodness, this is so beautiful; it looks like the sun shining down on a freshly ploughed field. But hold on a moment . . .' she said as she touched a piece of golden-yellow cotton. 'This feels different . . . why, someone has left what feels like a piece of paper inside it. I can feel it between the top layer and the backing fabric. Did someone forget to take it out? I recall you telling us how many quilts are pieced together using paper templates. Fancy the quilter leaving one in.'

'Again, it is superstition. It was left there on purpose.'

'Well, I never,' Helen said, shaking her head in wonder. 'There's quite a lot involved with this quilt-making. I thought people just stitched bits of fabric together, and that was it. I had no idea until your talk that you also add a wadding and backing, and then you hand-stitch a pattern over the patchwork, creating even more designs.' She ran her fingers along the line of quilting. 'So much time goes into making a quilt this size; no wonder they become family heirlooms. If I'd made such beautiful quilts and then travelled across the world to a new country, I too would want to take them with me. But what did you mean about your idea for my fabrics?'

'Look at this one,' Lizzie said, reaching for yet another quilt, a smaller one this time. It looked like something a person might lay across their lap. 'I made it for my mother. What do you think the fabric is from?'

Helen picked it up and hugged it to her. 'There is something about quilts that makes you just want to snuggle up and snooze in front of a fire on a cold afternoon. It's quite simple in design, and the colours aren't quite as vibrant as some of the others . . . but what is this?' she said as she held it to her nose and inhaled with her eyes closed. 'There's something familiar. It reminds me of . . . No, it can't be; yes, it smells of tobacco.' She sniffed other parts of the piece until she reached a corner that was slightly thicker, and again there was a perfume of some kind. She looked at Lizzie and smiled. 'This quilt is telling a story, not just with the fabric but also with scent. Please, tell me the story?'

Lizzie took the quilt from her. 'I made this throw for my mother after my dad died. Mum was ready to put his clothes into a thrift shop; that's what we call charity shops. She wanted them to do some good for somebody living, rather than keep them tucked away where they'd do nothing apart from perhaps feed the moths. I persuaded her to let me have Dad's shirts: his old work shirts, even his gardening shirt. But as I stitched the pieces together, there was something not quite right. It was Dad that was missing, if you know what I mean? I was missing the essence of him. So in here' – she pointed to where Helen had smelt tobacco – 'I inserted a small pouch of Old Holborn, his favourite pipe tobacco, and up here I stitched in a wad of fabric soaked in the shaving soap he used every day. It's very special to me, just as it was to my mum until she passed away.'

Helen was touched by the story. 'That's wonderful,' she said. 'I'm surprised the scents have stayed so strong.'

Lizzie gave her a knowing smile. 'I have to confess to having unstitched the quilt in certain places and reinserted patches from time to time. It's a small cheat, but the memory is still there, and when I'm feeling particularly sad I take it out and feel as though Dad is here with me again.'

Helen sighed, almost overcome with the sentiment of the piece. 'I wish I'd had something like this to console me when my dad passed away.' She had a sudden memory of her mother burning his clothes in the back garden, erasing everything to do with her husband as she was so angry that he'd fallen ill and left her.

'I'm so pleased you understand what this quilt means to me. It's what I want you to do with your pieces – make a quilt of memories. Try and rescue the good memories from the bad. I'm sure you have enough fabric here, and if not, I would think you have the other parts of the garments at home?'

Helen was taken aback. Yes, she had the other pieces of the garments stuffed back in the trunk; but to make something as beautiful as what Lizzie had made from her own father's shirts? She wasn't sure about that. 'There is a problem with that,' she said quietly.

'If you're worried about the sewing, don't be; I can help you. It could be done on a sewing machine. If you don't have one, I have a spare. Or you're welcome to come here and work. I could do with the company.'

'That's very generous of you, and whatever I decide to sew, I'll be grateful for your help and your company. However, there is one difference between your quilt and your idea for mine.' Her voice faltered as she said, 'You loved your dad dearly, whereas I can honestly say I never really loved my husband. And after discovering this' – she pointed to the satin negligee – 'I'm inclined to hate him. I married John for security and friendship, nothing more. There was nothing left for me back at home. Mother had never shown me much warmth or love, and after she married Gavin it was worse. I was comfortable in John's company, and I was never a bad wife. However, there was no passion or undying love. I suited what he wanted for a wife, but at times I feared for the future and what it held for me. All I could see was an empty void without love. To know now that he must have been unfaithful is more than I can bear ... so you see, I'm not sure I can make this piece, as the fabrics in that pile remind me of painful aspects of my marriage. Don't get me wrong, I never wished him dead – I just wanted more. Instead, all I'm left with is a pile of fabrics suitable only for patchwork pieces.'

Lizzie put her arms around the young woman and hugged her tight. 'Oh, my poor love, what a dreadful time you've had. I will make it my mission to see you happy once more, my patchwork girl.'

She settled Helen in one of the armchairs and wrapped a quilt around her. 'It's what they're meant for,' she tutted, as Helen objected and tried to push the quilt away. 'Don't be silly. This is where the warmth and comfort comes into its own. Why, you're trembling; stay there for a while and calm yourself.' She moved to a small cupboard set above the drawers where she kept her quilts. Opening a door, she lifted out a bottle of brandy and two small glasses. 'I keep this here for emergencies,' she winked, pouring out two generous measures and handing one to Helen. Pushing the quilts aside and sitting in the other armchair, she cupped her glass in her hands and sipped the warming liquid. 'That hit the spot,' she said before reaching for a telephone on a side table. 'Will you bring tea now, please, Doreen? Make sure there's plenty of it, as I'm starving,' she added, before thanking her servant and replacing the receiver. 'I've got used to English afternoon tea since living here. I could simply forgo dinner and enjoy sandwiches and cakes instead, don't you agree?'

Helen, coughing as the brandy caught in her throat, spoke as soon as she was able. 'Oh yes, it reminds me so much of parties when I was a child. Especially if there was jelly and ice cream as well.'

'Hold on to those memories, Helen. You know, it could be rather cathartic to face your fears and worries. I find there's nothing better than to stick pins into a problem . . . think how many times you would have to stick a pin into all that fabric in order to create something beautiful . . .'

A frown creased Helen's forehead as she looked between Lizzie and the table where the offcuts of John's clothing were laid out. She took a rather large gulp of the remaining brandy and swallowed, her eyes shooting wide open. 'My goodness, I never get used to drinking this stuff, but it's warming me up nicely. I rather like the idea of sticking pins into John, even though he can no longer feel the pain. Perhaps I should do it – make the quilt, I mean – but then give it away, so that it has some use.'

'That's a splendid idea. And hang on to all the offcuts as well.'

Helen, who was keen to emulate her mother and burn the remains of the clothing, was puzzled. 'Why?'

'For the ladies in the rag rug circle. Your late husband's clothing could be warming a few cold floors before too long. Imagine people walking all over his precious suits.' Lizzie wasn't really a vengeful person herself, but she knew she had to fire up Helen's enthusiasm in order to get her out of this melancholy state. It was beginning to work, as Helen burst out laughing; but that was possibly more to do with the influence of the brandy. 'Let's enjoy our tea and then start to plan your quilt. I have pencils and a notepad. Would you like to work here on the project, or take it home with you?'

Helen imagined the look of horror that would cross her mother's face if she found out what her daughter was doing. The recriminations would never end, as in Hillary Davis's eyes John Wentworth had been a man without fault – even more so since he died.

'Why is it that when people die, they are put up on

pedestals as perfect human beings?' she wondered aloud.

'I beg your pardon?'

'I'm sorry; I was thinking out loud. If you don't mind, I would love to work here, but you must tell me if I'm getting under your feet. My mother wouldn't understand why I'd taken a pair of scissors to John's clothing, so sewing at home is out of the question. I'd never hear the end of it,' she said with a grimace.

Lizzie chuckled, pleased that Helen was starting to see sense. She couldn't guess what the outcome would be of the investigation into John's death; she prayed that Helen had nothing to do with it, and her gut told her the girl was innocent. However, in the weeks to come, at least sewing would provide a distraction.

'There's nowt queerer than folk,' she said in a perfect Yorkshire accent, and then beamed at Helen. 'I learnt that living up north. Oh, good – here's our tea. I've had another idea I want to discuss with you while we eat. And you needn't look at me like that, I'm not planning on turning anyone else's clothing into quilts,' she added, as the maid wheeled in a trolley laden with enough food to feed an army. 'However did you get that trolley upstairs on your own, Doreen?'

'It's all right, ma'am, George is back with the car. He helped carry it up for me, as the dumbwaiter is stuck again. He said he'd take a look at it later.'

'Bless the man, he thought he was coming here as a driver but he's turned into a jack of all trades. I don't know what we'll do without him. When he joins up, which I understand will be early in the new year, we will be lost. This war does disrupt life so much – but there again, without it, I wouldn't be living here in England. And I wouldn't have met you.'

Helen raised her empty glass. 'That is certainly something worth toasting.'

'Gosh, I don't think I can move, let alone work,' Helen said, sinking back in her seat with a hand on her stomach. 'That was completely delicious. I might just move into your house to be fed and cosseted for the duration.'

'You would be more than welcome. I've got plenty of room, that's until my husband moves in the lodgers.'

'Lodgers?'

'Yes, Canadian pilots and officers. It seems they're going to need billeting once they're over here. They are on special duties. All terribly hush-hush and all that.' She shrugged. 'I'm sure it'll be fine, as long as they don't take to keeping me up most of the night with drinking and what have you. Perhaps I'll throw them in the barn behind the old stables, that should keep them far enough away,' she chuckled. 'Now, are you ready to decide on a design for your special quilt?'

'Yes, let's get cracking. The sooner the fabric doesn't look like the legs of my husband's trousers, the better I will feel. I can't help thinking, though, that it will be rather bland,' Helen said, looking at the fine woollen suiting.

'There's a lot of colour, actually. Look at that beautiful silk cummerbund, and the ties. For starters, I want you to unpick and open out all the ties – the silks will look glorious with what I have in mind.'

'Perhaps I should just start afresh with new fabric?'

'Don't be a defeatist,' Lizzie chided her. 'Here, come and look at some of these books. You were eyeing them earlier.' They got up and went over to the large bookcase, where she ran her fingers along a shelf before pulling out several volumes and taking them to the table. 'Here you are: what about one of these old designs?' She used strips of fabric to mark several pages in each book. 'Of course, some of the picture plates are black and white, but you still get the idea, don't you? Let me just ring for Doreen to come and collect the tea things and I'll come back and see what you've chosen.'

Helen flicked backwards and forwards, pulling out the fabric markers as she discounted certain designs. She burst out laughing. 'I've chosen my project.'

'Do show me,' Lizzie said, returning to her side. 'Oh my, it is perfect – and it suits your situation, doesn't it? The double wedding ring quilt is a very old design and would make the perfect project for you.'

'You don't think it's too complicated for me? Look at all those circles, and the way the colour picks out the ring shapes.'

'Never you fear, I'm here to guide you. I wouldn't let you start a project if I didn't feel you were up to the challenge. I do see one problem, though,' Lizzie said, moving some of the pieces of Helen's fabric together and tipping her head to one side.

'Tell me,' Helen urged her.

Lizzie fiddled with the pieces of fabric, twisting them this way and that, putting colours next to each other and then moving them. 'I think, as the quilt is to commemorate your marriage . . . however sadly it turned out, with your husband's possible infidelity . . . I feel there should be part of you in the quilt as well; do you agree?'

'Yes, you're right. But what do you suggest?'

'How would you feel about using the outfit you were married in? Or perhaps a gown you wore while you were together?'

Helen agreed. 'I married in church and wore a traditional white satin gown. The dress is packed away in tissue and stored in a box on top of my wardrobe. It's of no use to me, so I'll donate it to the project . . . And I happen to have a rose-pink satin dress worn by one of my bridesmaids, too. It was left behind when they went home to Scotland after the nuptials. Do you think that will do? I also have an eau-de-nil fabric from a gown John insisted I wear . . .'

'If you're sure. I know that would be perfect!'

'I'm more than sure,' Helen said. 'I'm not one for sentiment. Especially now,' she added, glancing at the red blouse. It was like a splash of blood amongst the more subdued colours.

'That's excellent. I can imagine how it will light up the duller colours, with the silk from the colourful ties picking out some of the rings like jewels. It will be a striking memory piece.'

'Yes, although I shan't keep it for myself. Perhaps I'll send it to John's mother and tell her I made it especially for her. Then it will be out of my house – and out of my life.' She didn't add that the addition of two pieces of fabric from Felicity's garments would display John's infidelity without her mother-in-law knowing explicitly that her son had not been perfect. But it would help Helen put this ordeal behind her, once and for all.

'I'm really rather excited for you,' Lizzie said. 'It will be something to keep your mind occupied while you work through the grieving – and anger – process. It's a shame we're not returning to the sewing group until the new year; otherwise you could have got to know more people from the area while you sat amongst them, hand-stitching some of the pieces together. Oh well, we can get on quite well between the pair of us. Now, let me sketch out the shape you're going to make for each block before we prepare templates and decide which colours you'd like to go where.'

Lizzie was just finishing the pencil sketch, writing numbers down the side of the page to denote the colours, when there was a tap at the door and Doreen entered. 'Excuse me, ma'am, but Mrs Green the vicar's wife is on the telephone, and she seems quite flustered. I did tell her you were busy, but she insisted on speaking to you now.'

Lizzie thanked her and asked her to bring them more tea. Leaving Helen alone to carry on, she crossed the room, sat in the armchair and lifted the receiver to her ear.

'Good afternoon, Tish. How are you, my dear?' There was a pause while Tish spoke at length, with Lizzie making sympathetic noises and occasionally adding an 'Oh dear'. Eventually, after promising to visit the vicarage the following morning, she replaced the receiver and turned to Helen. 'You'll never guess what's happened! There's been a fire at the village hall. It's going to be out of commission for at least four months. Some of the events due to be held there can be moved into the church, but

Tish's husband, the vicar, has refused point-blank to, in his words, have "a gaggle of cackling women" chatting and sewing in the house of God. She is at her wits' end. Understandably she wishes the sewing circle to go ahead, as it will benefit the women of the area.'

'Oh dear, that is a shame,' Helen sympathized. 'I was so looking forward to it and I know Effie was as well. Is there not another venue we could use?'

Lizzie walked to one of the windows and gazed out. 'There must be something . . . Oh, what a fool I am,' she said, slapping her head with the palm of her hand, dislodging one of the tortoiseshell clips that pinned her hair back from her face. 'They can all come here. I have plenty of room. Why didn't I think of that straight away?'

Helen thought back to the meeting at the church hall. There had been so much noise. Some women had brought along children who seemed never to sit still. Plus, copious amounts of tea and cake had been consumed. Would Lizzie be able to cope? 'But think of the mess, the noise and the people here in your beautiful rooms with all this delicate furniture. Some of them will even bring children with them,' she exclaimed, much to Lizzie's amusement.

'It just needs careful planning,' Lizzie said thoughtfully. 'Perhaps we could arrange to keep the children occupied out in the barn?'

'That seems rather drastic,' Helen said, shocked. 'At this time of year?'

Lizzie chuckled. 'The barn is very cosy – there's even a log burner in one corner. Gerald had it kitted out for my sewing before I decided I preferred this room. I'm sure I could hire somebody to look after the children. I must admit, I was quite surprised at how many children were still about, considering evacuation procedures are in place.'

'If the children are anything like Effie's, they probably wanted to come home, and many of the parents feel the same, since nothing has really happened. Not in this country, anyway,' Helen amended. 'We've had the odd scare, but it's fairly quiet; no wonder they're calling it the Phoney War. I expect we'll see many more children coming back before too long, especially this close to Christmas. They'll be homesick.'

'Then we will prepare accordingly,' Lizzie said with determination.

'We?'

'You will help me, won't you, Helen? I really do need your help. There are three more large bedrooms in this wing. We could have the furniture taken out and chairs and tables moved in, and perhaps have a project for each room,' she said, getting more excited by the minute. 'There could be an embroidery room, a room for the women making rag rugs, and a room where we could teach women how to alter and repair clothing. This would remain as the patchwork quilt room. I really think we should encourage women to learn how to quilt. Why, in the first war, the president of the United States announced it was a woman's duty to make patchwork quilts from scraps of fabric, thereby freeing up other blankets for the men at the front.'

'Very well, I'll help you organize things. As long as it's not in the barn with the children or repairing clothes, as I'd have no idea what to do. I suggest you have some sort of duty rota for women to make refreshments – it wouldn't be fair to make Doreen and your staff take on all of that. And they should also pay some kind of subscription, at least for a cup of tea, just as they would have done at the church hall.'

'Of course, you're right,' Lizzie said, reaching for a notepad she'd left by the telephone. 'We need to make notes. Let's stop thinking about quilts and turn our minds to the problem at hand. If I can pull some information together, I'll pop in to see Tish and hand her all the plans on a plate. She must have enough to do, what with church duties and arranging repairs to the hall.'

They sat by the fireside making plans until Doreen came back. 'Excuse me, Mrs Donnington, but I must sort out the blackout before it gets too dark,' she said, going to the windows to unhook the sashes, holding back the heavy drapes and pulling them closed. 'You might like to know that the master is home. He's brought someone with him for dinner.'

'Goodness, look at the time,' Helen exclaimed, glancing at the ornate clock on the mantelpiece. 'I really should be going. I'll be cycling in the dark at this rate.'

'Nonsense, stay to dinner. I'll have you driven home afterwards. In fact, tomorrow I'll collect you in my motor car and we can both go and see Tish together. Afterwards, if you have nothing arranged, you could come back here to get cracking on our plans.'

Helen smiled. Lizzie was a force to be reckoned with. 'Yes, I'd like that – and in fact it will make it easier for me to bring the rest of the fabric, rather than try to struggle on my bicycle. Will it be all right to leave it here?'

109

'Of course, it won't be a problem at all. I tell you what, why don't we go down and see Gerald now, and meet whomever he has brought home for dinner. It's sure to be one of those boring RAF types, sadly.'

As they headed towards the staircase, Lizzie pointed out several of the rooms she planned to use for the women's groups. When they reached the drawing room, Lizzie started to introduce her husband, but Helen stepped back in shock at the sight of his guest. It was none other than Richard Gladstone. Whyever was he here?

7

Helen accepted the glass of sherry handed to her by Gerald, who'd greeted her with open arms. He and Lizzie made a perfect pair, with Gerald being as welcoming as his wife. He chatted knowledgeably about the area and how he hoped to fit into local life.

'But I've been remiss in not introducing you to our guest,' he said, turning to Richard Gladstone, who stood watching Helen as introductions were made.

They shook hands solemnly. 'We've met before,' Richard said, without going any further into detail.

'Indeed we have, although it wasn't on a social footing. I understand you are here to work at the airfield. How is it you know Major Donnington?'

It was Lizzie who replied, with a smile, 'Richard knows many people. His role is the equivalent of being a police detective in civvy street. That's how he knows my husband – although as far as I know, Gerald hasn't broken the law.' Gerald chuckled as he topped up the sherry glasses, commenting amiably about enjoying certain English customs.

'I believe you mean British, my dear. You must get these

things right or you'll end up offending people. Ah – here is Doreen with the first course. Shall we take our seats?'

Helen sat down, thanking Richard as he held her chair for her. She busied herself straightening the napkin on her lap, avoiding his look.

'Do you plan to be in the area long, Richard?' Lizzie asked, 'or are you not allowed to say?'

Richard laughed. 'Although some of my investigations are not for public knowledge, I can say I'll be based here for the foreseeable future, Mrs Donnington.'

'Oh please, do call me Lizzie, everybody does. Then you mustn't be a stranger. Feel free to visit as often as you like.'

Gerald coughed politely and gave his wife an apologetic look. 'You will be seeing Richard more than occasionally, my dear. I've invited him to be one of our guests. It makes sense for someone in his line of work not to be billeted too close to the men. I did inform you, did I not?'

Without batting an eyelid, Lizzie smiled at her husband. 'Of course you did, my love, just as I told you I'm taking over the top floor of the west wing for the sewing group. The church hall had a fire last night, so we've lost our meeting place.'

Helen noticed a look pass between the couple that showed how close they were, each respecting the other's work. She had never had such closeness with her own husband. Of course, they'd often had discussions, but it had been John's opinion that counted. Helen had decided early on that it was easier to agree than to share her point of view on something when she would only be ignored.

'Actually, my dear,' Lizzie went on as she dabbed at the

corner of her mouth with her napkin, 'it might be very good for public relations if you organized some kind of rescue effort for the hall. It doesn't hurt for you to reach out to the locals; after all, we've invaded their territory. I know you are working with the British, but you and a few colleagues who travelled with us to this delightful country are regarded as cuckoos in the nest. Don't look at me like that; you know darn well many people assume we are American rather than kindly Canadians. Don't you agree, Helen and Richard?'

Helen looked at Richard, hoping he would comment, but he only laughed. She joined in, and thankfully Lizzie didn't insist on an answer to her question.

Doreen came in to collect the soup plates and load them onto a tray. Helen thought to herself that she'd never seen Doreen without a tray in her hand. What a hard worker she was.

'Mrs Donnington, I thought I ought to inform you I've packed George off to bed. He seems to have caught a cold, and I thought an early night would do him no harm.'

'Thank you for letting me know, Doreen. I can drive Mrs Wentworth home myself after dinner.'

'Oh no, please don't put yourself out. I have my bicycle,' Helen said, knowing that she would dread the journey home in the dark. The dynamo fitted to her bike only just gave off a dim, flickering light, even when she cycled fast.

'I won't hear of either of you two ladies driving or cycling late at night. I can take Helen . . . Mrs Wentworth home in my staff car. It's not far out of my way,' Richard said, the tone of his voice showing he did not expect an argument.

The rest of the meal passed pleasantly, with both men asking questions about the sewing group and Lizzie's plans to move furniture from the spare bedrooms in order to accommodate the ladies and their craft materials. Gerald did blanch when she mentioned that the converted barn would be used to care for any children who accompanied their mothers. 'I was thinking that with the village school evacuated further into the countryside, we might even be able to run a few classes for them after the Christmas holidays – what do you think, Helen?'

'That's an excellent idea, and will be a weight off the minds of the parents. I do wonder, though, about finding a suitable teacher. The education authorities would not be impressed if just anybody took over the education of the youngsters.'

'We can ask amongst the women when we have our first meeting. I thought a delightful way to get to know everybody would be to invite them all here for afternoon tea before Christmas. Won't that be fun, Gerald?'

'You may do as you wish, my dear. As long as my guests are not involved,' her husband said, knowing all too well that Lizzie was liable to rope in anyone who happened to be nearby while she was engrossed in one of her schemes.

An hour later, Helen was keeping her eyes pinned to the road as she sat in the passenger seat of Richard's car. With the moon hiding behind clouds and appearing intermittently, the only light came from his shielded headlamps. Apart from the hoot of an owl, there was pure silence, making Helen even more aware that they hadn't said a word to one another since leaving Lizzie's home. She searched for something to say, but could only thank him.

'It's very good of you to drive me home. I hate to put you out, though. I could easily have used my bicycle.'

All evening Richard had watched her across the dinner table, fascinated by her smile and natural chatter. She was so different from other women he knew. He was alarmed by the intensity of his feelings for her after such a short time. This couldn't go on, he thought to himself. Not only was she recently widowed, but he was actively investigating the murder of her husband, for God's sake.

'And have you fall and break your neck in the blackout? Don't be silly, Mrs Wentworth,' he said, not taking his eyes off the road.

Helen felt a flare of irritation. She hated to be patronized, and the way he'd spoken reminded her of her stepfather. 'You forget that I'm a local. I'm used to the roads around here,' she replied a little too sharply. 'I'm not a stranger like you.'

He turned his head fleetingly to glance at her. His fingers tapped hard on the steering wheel. 'I understood, Mrs Wentworth, that you lived in London, and I believe you spent much of your early life at boarding school before heading to the capital. Are you saying that in spite of all that, you've cycled these roads so much they are etched on your mind?'

She was surprised by how angry this made her. 'Please don't be pedantic. I certainly know the roads better than you. You've been here only a few weeks.'

He gave a hard laugh, almost a snarl. 'Well, we're relatively protected in this vehicle, whereas you would only have had two wheels beneath you. Be sensible. Don't spoil what has been a pleasant evening.'

Helen was livid. For her, the evening had been not so much a pleasure as an exercise in good manners. She'd enjoyed Lizzie and Gerald's company, but she had also been aware all the while they sat at the dining table that the man opposite her was investigating the murder of her husband. Try as she might, she couldn't shake off the feeling that he thought she had committed the crime.

She drew a deep breath in an effort to calm herself. She would have to tread carefully and mind what she said in future. It was important that she stay on Richard's good side; he could make life hell for her, as she was on his list of suspects. She tried to think of a conciliatory remark to break the awkward silence, but he spoke before she came up with one.

'How did you come to meet the Donningtons? Did you know them before you moved from London?'

'Lizzie was the speaker at the new women's group in the church hall. I showed an interest in her patchwork and quilting, and she invited me over to see her collection and talk about my own patchwork project. I like her very much, and she seems to be taking me under her wing.' Helen managed a smile. 'I'm looking forward to helping her now that she's moved the women's sewing group to Dalton Court. It will give me something to think about while I decide on my future.'

'I didn't take you for a woman who liked to sit at home sewing,' he said, with a touch of sarcasm in his voice.

'I'm going to make a patchwork quilt.' Helen jutted her chin out defiantly.

He snorted. 'I would have thought you had better things to do than stitch pieces of fabric together.'

Helen knew he was goading her. The tension in the darkened vehicle was palpable as she fought the urge to put him in his place. She didn't succeed. 'You know very little about patchwork quilts, then. Each one is skilfully pieced together following a traditional pattern, and the fabric holds memories; you really ought to do your homework before you dismiss them, you know. My quilt is based on a double wedding band design and represents my short marriage. Each piece will represent a memory, as the fabric comes from the years I was married to John.'

Richard fell silent as he digested her words. The damned woman had completely thrown him. He'd spent the afternoon going over the notes he'd made after her interview, and the picture he'd drawn of Helen Wentworth was nothing like the woman sitting next to him now. This was a woman with a softer side, one who wasn't at all enamoured with life in London – or, from what he could make out, with being the wife of a prominent Member of Parliament. Again, they fell into silence.

'And how do you know the major? You must know him well, to be invited to stay in his home?'

He was grateful to move on from the subject of her marriage and the preposterous patchwork project. 'I met Major Donnington knowing I would be working with him when I came down to Biggin Hill. The subject of him billeting officers came up during the meeting and he generously offered me a room. With you helping Lizzie Donnington, we will be seeing quite a lot of each other.'

The thought made him smile to himself, despite his earlier resolution to distance himself socially from Helen.

As the car approached the lane leading to her mother's home, Helen breathed a sigh of relief. What was it about this man that irked her so much? He seemed to get under her skin every time he spoke. They hadn't started out like this; was it because he had probed into her private life? No one had ever done that before. The thought that she might see him often in the coming days caused an uncomfortable heat to spread across her chest and up to her face. Gathering herself to get out of the vehicle, she was grateful for the darkness that surrounded them.

She had only just stepped into the house when her mother began to scold her. 'For heaven's sake, Helen, you could at least have told us that you were coming home this late. I've been worried out of my mind. Anything could have happened with us so close to the airfield. You should have more sense about you at your age. I shouldn't have to worry about you. Have some care in future and let me know where you are.' Hillary Davis shook her head in despair.

'Mother, I used Lizzie's telephone and rang hours ago! I spoke to Gavin. You mean to say you never told her?' Helen called to her stepfather, whom she could see through the open door to the sitting room. He was reading a newspaper in his favourite armchair and just looked back at her, shaking his head before speaking.

'I didn't know you would be this late,' he muttered. 'Decent young women do not walk the streets at this time of night, especially during a blackout. There's a name for women who do that,' he added, keeping his nose buried in the local pages.

'Excuse me, Miss Helen – I noted down what you told me before I called Mr Davis to the telephone,' Effie said, continuing to dry her hands on a tea towel she was holding.

Hillary looked between Helen and her husband and shook her head in exasperation. 'In future just tell me, Effie, don't leave notes lying about,' she barked at the housekeeper. 'If you want a bath, you're too late. There's no hot water,' she snapped at Helen before returning to the sitting room and pushing the door closed behind her.

'I'm sorry, Helen. I hope your mother forgives you soon.'

Helen gave Effie a gentle smile. 'I'm not worried about my mother, and you did more than enough to leave my message to be seen, Effie. Please don't worry yourself about it. I'm not,' she said.

'Did your visit go well, Miss . . . I mean, Helen?'

'More than all right. Would there be a chance of a hot drink? I'll tell you all about it, that's if I'm not keeping you from your bed?'

'I've just put the kettle on for my own night-time cocoa. If you'd like to join me in the kitchen, it's nice and warm in there.'

'Lead the way,' Helen said. 'I have a lot to tell you, and so much of it is exciting.' For now, she decided to simply wipe the car journey from her mind. She didn't trust Richard Gladstone; he was asking far too many questions. Yes, that was his job, but his presence unnerved her. She'd have to be careful of what she said if they were to be under the same roof as much as he suggested.

'I'm so excited,' Effie said delightedly when Helen had filled her in. 'To think we'll all be attending our groups at that posh house, Miss ... oh blast, I really can't get used to using your first name. It doesn't seem right somehow, me being a servant and all.'

Helen scolded Effie. 'Never, ever think of yourself as our servant. I hate that word. You do us a good service by being here. Your skills in this house far surpass what Mother or I can do – and as for that stepfather of mine, well ...'

Effie gave Helen a shy smile. 'It's very good of you to say so ... Helen. I try to do my best all the time. I do have a question, though. How can I take part in groups at Dalton Court, when I'm supposed to be doing my housekeeping duties here? You mentioned a school for the children and that would be perfect for me; and of course I still have to look for somewhere to live, and we have Christmas in just a week or two. Your mother still hasn't given me any instructions. I think she expects me to conjure up a meal out of thin air. Then there's the rationing coming soon ... Oh my,' she said, suddenly looking as though she had the problems of the world on her shoulders.

Helen shook her head in sympathy. She knew how exasperating her mother could be. 'I think it would be best if I took over the Christmas planning, and between us we can work out what to do. I know quite a bit about how rationing will work, what we need to do with our ration cards and so forth – so you can leave all that side of it to me. It was part of my work helping my husband. Don't you worry about a thing.'

'Oh Helen, thank goodness you're here. That just leaves me to worry about the children and putting a roof over their heads,' Effie said, biting her lip.

'Don't even worry about that, as I have an idea,' Helen said. 'Where is that cocoa? Once we've had our chat, I'm off to my bed – I'd like to sew a little more of my pot-holder. I'm becoming addicted to stitching; it's so soothing.'

Helen stood at the edge of the curb outside The Maples, waiting for Lizzie's chauffeur to arrive. Beside her were Effie and her daughters, Dorothy and Jane, wearing their Sunday best.

It didn't seem like a week since Lizzie had convinced the vicar's wife that she would take over the reins of organizing the sewing group, but today was the big get-together at Dalton Court. It would also be a Christmas tea party for the children, and the chance to meet their new teacher. Helen smiled as she listened to Effie instructing the children about their manners and warning them not to show her up.

'Only speak when you are spoken to, remember to say thank you, and for heaven's sake, Dorothy, remember to use your handkerchief. I don't want to hear either of you squabbling, either, or I'll have you evacuated straight after Christmas. And there will be no presents,' she added for good measure, as a large Daimler pulled up beside them. George, the chauffeur, greeted Helen politely and took their bags and boxes, putting them into the rear of the vehicle before holding the door open for the ladies to climb on board.

'We have to pick up the vicar's wife, and Mrs Binks. I hope there won't be too much of a tight squeeze?'

'Oh no, there's plenty of room,' Helen said quickly. 'We're just grateful that you could collect us.' She wondered how Lizzie got around the petrol rationing. Presumably the vehicle was used for her husband's work; he was a major, after all. Perhaps petrol wasn't such a problem for the Canadian air force? It struck Helen that perhaps, if John had still been alive, they too would have been free from worry about such things. The thought made her feel guilty, as John had always been an honour-able man – at least in that respect. That was why the heartache caused by his infidelity was all the harder to bear.

In the days since her first visit to Lizzie's house, she'd made the decision to travel to London to do some Christmas shopping. Well, that was the excuse she was giving to her mother; only Lizzie knew otherwise. In fact, Helen was going to pay a visit to Felicity – although whether she would actually have the courage to ques-tion her former friend, she wasn't sure. She'd booked herself into a small hotel in Bloomsbury for the night so that she could relax before travelling home the next afternoon. Deep in thought about her forthcoming trip, she was surprised when the car pulled up outside the vicarage.

Effie had her younger daughter sit on her lap to make space for the older women. Once everyone was comfort-able, Tish introduced her friends to Mrs Rita Binks, the teacher. She smiled sweetly at everyone before speaking to the two children. 'I hope you are going to attend my little school? It will be such fun.'

The girls eyed her warily before looking at their mother. 'Yes, both Jane and Dorothy have been fortunate enough to be given places,' Effie said. 'It is so generous of Mrs Donnington to arrange this, what with the school being evacuated and me not being able to take them back to their original school where we used to live. Where did you used to teach?'

'Oh, my goodness – it was over thirty years ago, in a little village down on the Kent coast. I retired here to live with my daughter-in-law; you are bound to meet her at some point. She would have come along today to meet everyone, but sadly she has gone down with a chill. She is very prone to them,' Mrs Binks added, raising her eyebrows at Helen and Effie, 'whereas I'm as fit as a fiddle. It's all down to a strong constitution and wearing warm undergarments.'

Effie gave her children a hard stare, daring them not to giggle.

The women chatted about the day ahead and Rita Binks told them that she was arranging a bingo game to entertain everyone while they had tea. Helen looked out of the window at the bleak December afternoon. At least it wasn't raining, but the chill in the air had her snuggled warmly in her navy-blue woollen coat with matching scarf, her hat pulled around her ears. She would have liked to wear her red coat, but as everyone knew her to be a widow, it didn't seem quite right somehow. The thought made her feel quite melancholy.

'Is your mother not joining us, Helen?' the vicar's wife asked.

'No, she has something on at the golf club. I'm afraid it takes up a lot of her time, what with her sitting on the committee,' Helen replied politely, thankful that she could keep her distance from her parent.

'Of course, this is all temporary,' Tish explained to Rita. 'We hope to be back in the church hall in a month or so, and then Mrs Donnington can have her beautiful home to herself.'

Helen privately thought this was unlikely to happen once all the women from the surrounding area saw what was laid on for them at Dalton Court. There'd be no reason to vote to return to the draughty church hall.

'It's so much easier to get to the church hall,' Tish declared.

Before Helen was able to answer, a local bus overtook them on the lane leading to the house.

'Lizzie had a word at the bus depot, and they kindly agreed to make an extra stop for the days when we have our sewing groups and when school commences,' Helen explained with a smile, leaving Tish looking quite disgruntled.

'Well, in future we can all travel on the bus service,' Miss Binks said. 'We don't want to be putting this young man out, do we?'

Helen spotted a smile cross the chauffeur's face, even though the glass screen between him and the passengers was half closed. She could see it was going to be a battle of wills between the vicar's wife and anyone who chose not to return to the village hall when spring came. This could be fun, she thought, suppressing a smile by chewing the inside of her cheek.

As soon as they arrived, Helen found herself in demand. Lizzie waved frantically to her and she pushed her way through the groups of excited women, along with a gaggle of children, to be given her duties. She'd put her sewing project into her bag, but chances looked slim that she'd manage even one stitch.

'It's quite simple really, Helen. I have a list here headed with each of the sewing groups. As each woman enters the hall, I would like her to add her name to one of the lists before she is directed upstairs. At the top, Doreen will point out which room to go to. I've called in my staff to help provide refreshments . . . Do you think you could take this clipboard and stand at the bottom of the staircase, ensuring that every person's name is added to the lists?'

If only it were that easy. For some reason, most of the women wanted to take their children upstairs with them. 'I'd rather not have them running amok through my rooms,' Lizzie said doubtfully when this became clear. 'The barn has been set up for the children to play in. I thought Mrs Binks along with the vicar's wife could take control of them. What do you think?'

Helen frowned. 'I'm sure Rita will be in her element, and I do think she needs an assistant because of her age; however, from what I gathered in the car travelling here, Tish seems to think she will be in charge today. She isn't going to like being moved into the barn.'

'Oh dear, I did wonder if that would be a problem. How do we delegate, if she expects to run the whole show?'

'I have an idea,' Helen said, making sure they weren't overheard. 'Follow me.'

Pushing through the crowd of women, stopping to say hello to those they knew, they reached Tish, who was beaming from ear to ear while welcoming latecomers with a regal air. Lizzie welcomed them to her home before Helen spoke.

'We really do need your help, Tish, as you seem to know everybody here. Lizzie – I mean Mrs Donnington – wondered if you would take charge of . . .'

Tish snatched the clipboard. 'It goes without saying, my dear. After all, this is my project, even if we've moved venues.'

Helen drew in a breath. This was going to be harder than she'd thought. 'Well, Lizzie has allocated separate rooms for each group. As you can appreciate, we don't have the space for everyone to sit together, even in this grand house, and the problem is we don't know many of the ladies here. We thought, as you have the clipboard in your hand with the four lists, you could check each woman off at the bottom of the stairs?'

Before Tish could reply, Lizzie took over, effusively praising her skill in managing people. Helen watched as Lizzie won the woman over, and Tish then said that she would be only too pleased to take on the important task.

Leading her into position at the base of the grand staircase, Lizzie took the chance to ask Tish if she would head the embroidery circle, leaving her to organize the patchwork and quilting group.

The rug makers would have a room, as would the dressmakers; that would also incorporate the repairs of clothing, which they all agreed could become very important if the war was to continue for long.

'Well, as I told my husband, we really did think it would be over by Christmas, but he reminded me the same was said during the Great War – and look how long that lasted. Yes, I will check your plans, but you seem to have done admirably, my dear. Well done.'

'We do have another problem, in that we need at least one more person to help Mrs Binks with the children. Do you have any suggestions?' Lizzie asked. 'Even though there aren't classes until the new year, it would be rather nice for the children to get to know who will be looking after them. I've arranged a surprise,' she said, giving the woman a conspiratorial wink. 'I will tell you more about it later. Perhaps you can give some thought as to who could help out with the children as well? I know you are the ideal person for this job.' Leaving the vicar's wife at the bottom of the stairs glowing with importance, Lizzie and Helen headed for the top floor, looking into all the rooms to greet the women, who were already sipping tea provided by Lizzie's willing staff.

'You've been ever so generous,' Helen said. 'It seems rather an imposition.'

'Nonsense; I've had Gerald foot the bill. The Canadian air force can be very generous at times. They want to be seen as friendly, rather than foreigners over here taking over. My husband is one of the first to be stationed here working in joint operations. I don't think it will be long before you see many more of us here, so it's imperative the locals aren't worried by the sight of so many foreigners invading your country.'

Helen listened carefully before agreeing that she could see no problem with anyone wanting to come here to help fight the enemy. 'Better the Canadians and any other allies than the dreaded Germans,' she agreed. 'The sooner we defeat Hitler, the better – and then we can enjoy peace once more. And until then we can be busy using our hands to help people make something from nothing, and feel as though we are doing something worthwhile.'

Lizzie clapped her hand to her mouth. 'Oh, blast – I forgot about the knitting circle. Wherever shall I put them? There are quite a few of them. I spotted them with their needles clicking away while I was doing my talk at the church hall; to be honest it was quite off-putting.'

Helen thought for a moment as she looked around her. 'Why not have them work out here in the hall? It's so large, it's almost a room on its own. Why, with a few seats they could be quite comfortable, and when Doreen and your staff bring refreshments they would not only be first in the queue, but could help out. We could even ask them to direct women to the right rooms.'

Lizzie slapped her on the back. 'Well done, that woman! I can see you are going to be a valuable asset to this project.'

Helen thanked her for having the confidence in such a novice handywoman.

'No, it's your skills in organizing people that I need. You must have learnt so much when assisting your husband? Now you can use those skills to help the locals in the war effort.'

'I'll do what I can to help you, but at some point I'm

going to have to find myself a job. It doesn't seem right that I haven't, when so many women are already turning towards war work or joining the services. When I travel up to London to see Felicity, I'm going to visit my husband's former colleagues and find out whether they might have a use for me.'

Lizzie nodded politely, although she wasn't at all sure that venturing back to her old department would be the right thing for Helen to do.

For Helen, the afternoon sped by. Even after stopping to enjoy the dainty sandwiches and cakes (which she secretly nicknamed Canadian Food Aid), she still had plenty of time to plan more of her patchwork quilt. Lizzie had convinced her that the easiest way to work on her first quilt was not to cut paper shapes to attach to the squares of fabric, but instead to simply stitch each piece together using a sewing machine. Again, Lizzie offered the use of the sewing machine in her workroom, which Helen gratefully accepted. There was a machine at home that she intended to clean up and move into her bedroom. That way, she could work alone and not have to join her mother and stepfather for long evenings in the living room.

After their break, Lizzie invited the women to join her in the barn to watch the surprise for the children. Once everybody was present, she went to a side door and beckoned to none other than Father Christmas, who walked in with a jolly 'Ho-ho-ho!', cheerfully waving to the excited children. He stopped by a Christmas tree in the corner of the barn and put down his sack before sitting down in a large armchair. Lizzie went to join him. 'On behalf of myself, my husband and the officers billeted here at the moment, we would like to wish you all a very merry Christmas. This holiday is going to be a tough one, with so many loved ones being away from home and some overseas. You may even be separated from your children. With that in mind, we have a gift for each child, as well as parcels for parents to send to the children who have been evacuated. There is also a little stocking for every adult in the room.' As she spoke, a group of six servicemen entered, carrying more sacks, and began to distribute the gifts among the adults. The children formed an orderly queue supervised by Rita Binks, each having the chance to speak privately to Father Christmas before accepting a wrapped gift.

'And here is something special from me to you,' Lizzie said as she handed a square box to Helen. 'I thought it might come in useful. Please do open it now.'

Helen knew that whatever the box contained, her own gift to Lizzie – a simple silk headscarf and perfumed hand lotion – would not be enough to thank her new friend for her many kindnesses. She was right, as she pulled back the flaps to find a book, *The Encyclopaedia of Patchwork and Quilting*.

'Oh my, I don't know what to say. This is far too generous, thank you so much.'

'If you are going to be working on this quilt, you seriously need the equipment. At least then there'll be no excuse not to carry on when you're working alone at home.' Leaving Helen, she went to speak to a few of the mothers who were waiting to thank her for her generosity.

Effie hurried over to her. 'I'm right gobsmacked, Miss

Helen,' she said, once again forgetting to drop the 'Miss'. 'My gift is a cotton nightdress and the girls both each have a golly, and they love them,' she exclaimed, as excited as many of the children in the room.

'Lizzie has been so generous,' Helen said as she showed Effie her book. 'Have you enjoyed your rag rug group?'

'Oh, yes. I reckon by the time I find somewhere else to live, I'll have made a couple of rugs for the girls to have by their beds. That is, as long as I can find enough scraps of material.'

'Don't forget, I'll be able to give you anything I don't use from my husband's clothes,' Helen reminded her. Seeing the doubtful look cross Effie's face, she added, 'They may as well do you some good, because he no longer has any use for them.'

Effie wriggled, looking uncomfortable. 'It's still a bit like stepping into a dead man's shoes,' she muttered as she turned to walk away, then stopped to add: 'Oh, I almost forgot that Father Christmas wants a word with you.' She pointed to where the man was readjusting a pillow that had shifted underneath his red jacket.

Helen threaded her way through to where Father Christmas sat in his armchair beside the Christmas tree. 'I understand you wished to speak to me?' she asked, wondering if perhaps he had a parcel for her, although she could see no such thing under the tree.

'I hear you're travelling to London tomorrow,' a familiar voice said from beneath the fluffy false beard, which looked very much like cotton wool.

Helen frowned. 'Who . . .' she began, then reached out and tugged at the beard just a fraction, glancing round first to make sure no children were watching. As she'd suspected, the face she glimpsed underneath was Richard Gladstone's. 'Oh, it's you,' she said flatly, letting go of the elastic so that it pinged back and made him yelp. 'What does it have to do with you if I am travelling to London?' She straightened her shoulders and glared at him. 'I had no idea I was under surveillance.'

Richard stood up and took her elbow, leading her out of the barn. Once they were safely round the corner he removed the beard, running a hand across his chin. 'Actually, I only asked because Lizzie mentioned you were going, and I wondered if you'd like me to travel with you.'

Helen frowned. Am I some kind of prime suspect now? she thought. 'If it's all the same to you,' she said firmly, 'I intend to travel by train into London. I applied for a pass through my late husband's office, as I have some of his affairs to put in order. As for the rest of what I'm doing, and when I'm travelling back – that is my own business, and I prefer to keep it to myself. So thank you for the offer, but I shall make my own way.' And with a haughty look, she turned and walked away.

8

Helen was grateful there was no rain as she walked briskly towards the station the next morning, although the air was so crisp that it almost hurt when she took each breath. She was dressed in her best coat of pale-blue wool, with cuffs and collars of black velvet. Having accompanied her husband on numerous official engagements, she was thankful now for her smart clothes, which had been delivered to The Maples where she could make use of them. On her head she wore a petite black hat with a net veil just covering her forehead. In matching black leather shoes, gloves and bag, she felt ready to face whatever the day brought. A porter helped her into the train and lifted her overnight bag onto the rack above her head.

Deciding to make use of the journey, she removed her gloves and reached into her handbag for several pieces of patchwork, a needle and thread. Although Lizzie had said she would be able to stitch her quilt with a sewing machine, she preferred to attempt to stitch at least the intricate wedding ring design by hand. She'd sat up late finishing the pot-holder in order to start this larger project. Before beginning, she used a handkerchief to wipe the yellowing grime from the inside of the carriage window, so that at least she'd be able to see some of the country-side before the train reached the suburbs.

Concentrating on the first few stitches, she was only slightly aware of one last passenger entering the carriage before the guard blew his whistle and the train pulled away.

'What a coincidence,' said a familiar voice.

Helen looked up and swore under her breath. Richard placed a small suitcase on the rack next to her bag before sitting down next to her. He apologized to the other passengers, who had to pull in their feet in order to let him reach the only available seat.

She looked at him coldly. 'I wouldn't call it a coincidence, especially after our conversation yesterday,' she hissed, almost stabbing her finger with the needle. 'I thought you intended to drive to London?'

He smiled benignly. 'I didn't actually say that, Mrs Wentworth. I simply asked if you would like a travelling companion,' he replied before taking his newspaper out of his pocket and opening it.

'Even so, it's remarkable to see you, considering the number of trains that travel into London,' she spat back, keeping her voice low so other travellers didn't hear.

'Like you, I wanted to make an early start,' he said mildly. 'Is this part of the quilting project I heard about? The fabric looks rather drab for something so special. Isn't it to commemorate your marriage to your late husband?'

Helen sighed before turning the fabric over, at the same time pulling several more pieces from her bag. 'The navy is from the suit my husband wore for his maiden speech in Parliament. This' – she pointed to a small blue paisley printed silk – 'is cut from the tie he wore at our wedding.' She saw Richard's cheeks turn pink and was pleased she'd embarrassed him but continued, picking up a pale-pink square. 'This was part of my trousseau from our honeymoon in Venice, and this piece,' she said through gritted teeth, 'is cut from a woman's blouse that I found among my husband's possessions after he died. I intend to visit her today to ask for an explanation. So you see, Mr Gladstone, this patchwork quilt will be very personal to me and my late husband and will tell the story of the few years of . . . of . . . my marriage.' So far she had kept her emotions in check, but it was a losing battle. Pulling a handkerchief from her pocket, she quickly dabbed at her eyes.

'Here, let me help you,' he said, taking the handkerchief from her and passing her his own.

'I'm perfectly able to wipe my own eyes,' she sniffed, conscious of some interest from their fellow passengers.

'Will you at least allow me to wipe the black smudges from your face?' he asked.

With a gasp, Helen reached for her powder compact and clicked it open to check her face in the small mirror. She was horrified to see a grimy patch under each eye, and suddenly realized she had used the same handkerchief that she'd earlier used to clean the grimy windows. 'Thank you,' she muttered, wiping away the marks before dabbing at her cheeks with fresh powder.

'I didn't mean to upset you,' he murmured once she had put away her sewing and leant back in the seat, averting her eyes.

'You haven't upset me,' she said. 'It's just that you seem

135

to be everywhere that I am, and it feels as though you're following me.'

'I can assure you it is pure coincidence, although I would have enjoyed your company travelling to London. And perhaps I should have driven? At least then you wouldn't have dirtied your handkerchief,' he smiled.

'Maybe,' she replied, before looking away from him again and staring out of the window for the remainder of the journey.

As the train pulled in, Richard reached for her overnight bag as well as his suitcase before taking her hand to help her down to the platform. 'Thank you,' Helen said, pulling on her gloves and taking the suitcase from him. 'I hope you have a pleasant day,' she added, and set off at a brisk pace towards the exit of the busy station. She was aware of him not far behind her as she approached the taxi rank. 'The Dalglish Hotel, Bloomsbury, please,' she said to the driver before opening the door.

'Here, let me help you,' Richard said as he caught up with her. 'We may as well share, as I'm heading in that direction too.'

'I don't believe it,' she muttered. Would she ever shake this man off?

'What did you think I was about to do? Go to Westminster and murder another MP?' she hissed, noticing the driver's alarmed expression.

'I'm simply going in your direction,' he smiled.

'How fortuitous for you,' she said, glaring at him. 'Of all the hotels in London, you happen to be heading towards mine!' The only person who had known of her plans, apart from Effie, was Lizzie. Had her new friend been talking behind her back? Helen wondered as the black taxi sped through the streets.

Everywhere, windows were covered in blast tape and sandbags stacked in front of buildings. There seemed to be more people than ever in uniform, and even more signs pointing to public air-raid shelters. She'd heard early on, courtesy of John's position, the safety plans for the city, and gave a small shudder at the signs that some of this was already in place.

'Are you cold?' he asked.

'No, just someone walking over my grave,' she replied, using one of Effie's favourite sayings.

He frowned. 'I don't understand.'

'It's an expression. An involuntary shudder, not caused by cold or fear, but by a portentous thought – if you know what that means?' she snapped back.

'I know exactly what it means. I just wondered what had caused it?'

'A private thought; nothing for you to worry about. I wasn't planning grievous bodily harm, if that's what you're thinking.'

He had the good grace to laugh. 'Good grief, woman, do you think that I'm following you and stalking your every movement? Please believe me when I say it is pure coincidence that we are travelling in the same direction today. However, what concerns me most is what you told me about your friend, and your belief that she was more than friendly with your late husband. You could be putting yourself in danger by visiting someone who may know something about his death.'

'It's not that I plan to say anything to her. After all,

even if they did have an affair, it's all in the past,' Helen replied. 'We worked together for a few years, and at one time I shared a flat with her before I married. I just want to catch up on news and go for lunch,' she said, checking her watch. 'I may not say anything to her,' she said again, even though she intended to do just that. *Besides, she might not even be home, although I'd prefer to talk there than publicly*, she thought.

He nodded thoughtfully. 'Are you late for your appointment? I could hold on to the taxi and drop you off there, once you've left your bags?'

That was the last thing she wanted. Helen kept her expression neutral. 'I have plenty of time and would like to freshen up in my room before I go out. But thank you for your kind offer.'

'Any time,' he said, looking ahead. 'I do believe this is our hotel at the end of the road.'

Helen took her purse from her handbag.

'No, I insist on paying,' he said, but noticed her horrified look. 'Call it a perk of my job.'

'Then thank you, that is most generous,' she said before alighting from the taxi, picking up her bag and walking into the foyer of the hotel without waiting for him. As quickly as she could she gave her name and details at the desk, collected her key and hurried to the lift, where she travelled to the third floor, all the time looking over her shoulder. Thank goodness she was finally alone. Tipping the porter who'd carried her bag, she closed the door firmly behind him and sank onto the bed. Kicking off her shoes, she lay back and stared at the ceiling, controlling her breath until she felt calm.

What was happening here; why was he following her? Why was he now living at Lizzie's house, when his job was to investigate John's death? She couldn't shake off the feeling that he was watching and waiting for her to make a mistake . . .

After freshening up and reapplying her make-up, she tucked her room key into her handbag and headed down to the foyer, intending to ask the receptionist to book her a cab to Felicity's address. Then she spotted Richard sitting in an armchair reading his newspaper, close to the hotel reception desk. Changing direction without missing a beat, she walked briskly out of the revolving doors and marched down the street, checking over her shoulder several times. Noticing an approaching taxi, she hailed the driver, who pulled in smartly to the kerb. She leant closely through the window to give the address, hoping no one nearby could hear. Once in the cab she sat back and gave a sigh of relief as the driver turned in the traffic and headed back down the road past the hotel. Watching from the window, she spotted Richard standing on the pavement in front of the hotel, searching left and right; thankfully, she'd given him the slip. Finally Helen was able to relax a little as the taxi headed towards Kensington. By the time it pulled up in front of the block of flats, she felt calm and in control once more.

Using the key she'd meant to return after moving out, she was able to let herself into the main entrance and head towards the staircase. Felicity's flat was on the second floor. Helen ran up the wide stairs as quickly as she could in case somebody challenged her now that she didn't live in the building.

139

The key they'd always kept under the doormat was still there. She pushed open the door and called, 'It's only me,' doing her utmost to keep a friendly note to her voice.

'Bloody hell, what's going on here?' a young man shouted as he reached for a towel and wrapped it round his naked torso.

Helen whirled away, covering her eyes with one hand. 'I'm so terribly sorry! I thought my friend lived here . . . Perhaps she still does? Felicity Davenport . . . ?'

'It's all right, you can turn round now,' he chuckled. 'I'm afraid your friend moved out two weeks ago. I took over the lease. As you can see, I'm still moving in.' He waved a hand around the room, indicating piles of boxes yet to be unpacked.

'Oh, dear. I'm so sorry for the intrusion. I used to live here with Felicity and took a chance there was still a hidden key. I'm surprised she didn't let me know she was giving up the flat, but then, we've not spoken much lately . . . Did she happen to leave a forwarding address?'

'She left in rather a hurry. All I know is that she suffered some kind of bereavement and decided to make a fresh start. Here,' he said, rummaging in a fruit bowl on a sideboard for a piece of paper. 'This is her new address. She left it in case I needed to forward any post.'

'Thank you.' Helen scribbled down the details in a small diary she kept in her bag. 'I didn't know she'd had a bereavement.'

'Apparently she moved departments in her workplace as well; the porter mentioned it. I'd hoped to send her some flowers to say thank you for leaving a few sticks of furniture behind. I've come here with very little.'

It was only then that Helen looked around properly and realized the room was furnished in very much the same way it had been when she lived there.

'May I offer you a drink?'

'Thank you, but I must be getting on,' she demurred. 'And thank you also for not screaming blue murder when I broke in just now.' She smiled.

'It's been my pleasure,' he grinned back.

Hailing yet another taxi, this time Helen headed towards Westminster. She wasn't sure whether the gurgling sensation in her stomach was simply a result of missing lunch, or whether she was nervous about visiting the offices she'd once known so well. She wondered which office Felicity had moved to, but knew that the long-term staff still working there would be able to tell her.

It took a while for her to reach the offices, as every person in the building who recognized her wanted to offer condolences and ask about a memorial service for her husband. John had always cared for his staff, and would often stop to speak to them, remembering little snippets about their family lives and connecting with them on a personal level. In some ways, Helen thought, he really would have made the perfect prime minister, as he had time for everybody – everybody except her. She had her role to play in his life, and that was it. Still, the queries about a memorial service reminded her that she ought to ask his office manager about it while she was here. Very few staff members had managed to travel to Oxfordshire for the funeral, and it was important that those who'd known John had the chance to pay their respects.

News of her presence in the building had quickly

spread. As she headed down a corridor towards the staircase to her old office, a door opened and one of John's fellow MPs came out to greet her.

'My dear Helen. How are you? If only you'd let us know you were coming, we could have had lunch – and Deirdre would have been able to join us,' he said. Deirdre, his wife, was one of the women who'd made life hell for Helen and whom she'd thought of as a member of the coven.

'I'm very well, thank you, Jeremy. But I don't want to stay for long. This is my first journey into town since . . . since we lost John. I don't want a big fuss made. I only wanted to pop in and ask if there was any news about the memorial service, and if I needed to do anything to help? I also thought I'd say hello to the staff, if that's all right. I promise not to be long. I'll avert my eyes from any important documents,' she smiled.

'The ladies will be so pleased to see you,' he said. 'Why don't you go along there now, and I'll arrange for tea when you come back? I'll have some paperwork pulled together so that you can see what is planned for the service.' He gave her a quick peck on the cheek.

Helen had always liked Jeremy; he was an affable enough man. It was just his wife she detested. Thankfully, the days of meeting Deirdre and the rest of the coven were over. That was one part of her old life she wouldn't miss.

'Give me ten minutes,' she said as she turned to the staircase and went to the upper floor, where she knew much of the most important work was undertaken. There were exclamations of joy as the older women spotted Helen. Tears, hugs and kisses ensued before the women settled down to talk, and the conversation turned to everyday life and what had gone on in the office since her departure.

'My goodness, so much news of babies and weddings,' she smiled. 'You must make me a list so I can write my congratulations, if you don't mind, Bella?' she said to the office manager. 'Please, would you keep me up to date with any news? I'll give you my new address.' She knew how surprised they'd be at all the changes in her life. 'Even if I'm a widow now, I'm still part of this place and I do want to keep in touch with everyone. I've missed you all so much. Speaking of which . . . what has happened to Felicity?'

A few of the women looked awkwardly at each other and then at Bella, waiting for her to explain.

'Why don't we sit down?' Bella said, taking Helen's arm and leading her to the corner of the room where her desk was situated. 'Back to work, ladies,' she called out. 'I'm sure Helen will speak to you all again before she leaves.'

Helen raised her eyebrows. 'I take it something has happened, if Felicity has moved on?' She explained how she'd tried to call on Felicity at home, only to be greeted by a man dressed in a towel.

Bella laughed before becoming serious. 'I'm afraid something came to light after John's death. We discovered . . . well, I don't really know how to explain this, Helen, it's just that . . .'

Helen took a deep breath before reaching out to hold Bella's hand. 'It's all right, I think I know. Felicity was having an affair with my husband, wasn't she?'

Bella gripped Helen's hand tightly. 'When I found out,

I was torn. I felt it was your right to know – after all, you two were friends. I was shocked that she would do such a thing, but then, even though I don't want to speak ill of the dead, John was as much to blame. To think all this was going on behind your back. And then he died so tragically in that accident . . . Regardless of his philandering, it was such a loss.'

Helen had to make a mental adjustment; of course, no one here knew that John had been murdered. They all still thought it was a gas explosion. She must try to remember not to let anything slip out.

'Felicity was always rather dramatic. I take it she fell to pieces in the office?'

'Oh, yes.' Bella gave her a significant look. 'We had the weeping, the wailing and the hysterics. I was sick to death of her. Of course, some of the girls thought it was boyfriend problems; only a few of us were in the know, and the more she carried on, the harder it got to work with her. How could we sympathize, when we knew she'd tried to steal your husband? In the end, I made it my job to have her moved to another department and gave her a good talking-to. I told her I knew what she'd done and she had to pull herself together, before I reported her and she was removed from the building. How did you guess?'

Helen opened her handbag and pulled out the scarf from where she'd tucked it away. 'You might recognize this? I found it in John's pocket. She also left a blouse behind that came to light when our porter hastily packed all of John's clothing into a trunk and sent it down to Biggin Hill, where I am staying with my mother.'

'I take it you want me to keep this quiet?' Bella said,

looking angry. 'By rights she should be given her marching orders.'

'For now, yes, please do keep it quiet,' Helen replied, deciding not to mention the negligee John had no doubt planned to give to Felicity. Unless, of course, that was for another of his lady loves . . .

'Do you want to have a word with her?'

'Yes, I do. In fact, that was my main reason for coming to London.' Helen smiled, giving Bella a wink. 'Just point the way, will you?'

Helen followed Bella out into the wide corridor and up two flights of stairs, until they were faced with a door leading to a large office not unlike the one she'd just left. Bella spoke quietly to the woman at the largest desk in the room, who directed them to a side door. They went through it to find Felicity and three other women working at their desks.

Felicity glanced up, and a look of astonishment crossed her face as she recognized Helen. Getting to her feet, she rushed over, arms outstretched. 'Why, Helen, what a lovely surprise!' she said, although there was a wary look in her eyes.

Helen turned aside to avoid her embrace. 'I haven't come here to exchange pleasantries, Felicity,' she said coolly. The sight of her former friend brought with it a rush of memories of happier times, but she pushed them aside with an effort.

Felicity halted and blinked for a moment, her cheeks turning pink. 'Oh . . . then why have you come?' she asked, trying to appear normal in front of the other women in the room. 'Perhaps we should speak alone,' she added, noticing her colleagues watching with interest from their desks.

Helen gave her a stern look and started to open her handbag. 'I have a feeling most of your colleagues already know about what I want to discuss. In fact, I was probably the last person to find out,' she said, pulling out the square of fabric cut from Felicity's blouse.

'What have you done? And where is the rest of this? It wasn't cheap, you know,' Felicity exclaimed, reaching for the fabric as Helen snatched it away. 'I take it you picked it up by accident when you last stayed with me,' she added, giving the most charming of smiles, glancing to left and right in hope that their audience would hear and believe her words.

'Oh, no. I had no idea about this until I unpacked the trunk containing my husband's possessions and found it tucked in amongst his clothing.'

Felicity gave a high-pitched laugh and waved a hand in the air. 'Oh well,' she said, 'I suppose these things happen. It must have been picked up somewhere – I have no idea why, or where.'

'Then perhaps you can explain this,' Helen said, pulling out the silk scarf. 'Do you think I picked it up at the same time I left your flat, with your blouse? Strangely enough, it was found in the pocket of my husband's best suit.'

There was an audible gasp in the room, and the smile dropped from Felicity's face.

'We wondered how long it would be before you found out,' she said after a moment. 'If you'd had any guts, you'd have realized you were in a loveless marriage. John should have left you long ago – and if he had, he might still be with us. Why he married a little dormouse like you, I'll never know; perhaps it was so that you could keep house for him, be the perfect wife, and have his babies one day. But by all accounts, the pair of you weren't compatible.'

Helen felt her stomach churn. Had it been obvious to the whole world that there was no real love between her and her late husband? She'd thought she was like most of the other wives of older MPs: part wife, part social secretary and part homemaker. Would he have left her, if she hadn't died?

She kept her voice steady, looking Felicity in the eye. 'So, I take it you intended to usurp my position and steal my husband?'

Felicity looked angry. 'The fool was too cowardly to be rid of you. I'd given him an ultimatum . . .'

Helen frowned. Could this mean Felicity had had a hand in John's death? 'I thought you were a friend. You were my bridesmaid, for heaven's sake. What kind of harlot tries to steal a woman's husband behind her back?'

'Someone who had more to offer than you,' Felicity sneered, reaching out to take the scarf.

'Oh, no you don't,' Helen snapped, pushing the scarf and fabric back into her bag. 'Let's consider this evidence, shall we?'

Felicity's colleagues gasped again as Bella put her hand on Helen's shoulder and murmured a suggestion that they leave.

Helen turned to follow, but on impulse she spun back round and slapped Felicity hard across the cheek. 'That's just for starters,' she said, holding her head high as she walked away.

After refusing tea or a seat so she could calm down while Bella called for someone to sort out transport for her, Helen left, promising to stay in touch. A policeman standing guard outside the building hailed a taxi for her. Giving the name of her hotel, she sank back against the seat, hardly able to think about what had just happened and still numb from the shock of her former friend's words. Rubbing her stinging hand, she noticed how red it still was. At least she'd have left a reminder of her visit on Felicity's cheek. Who was the dormouse now?

'My God, has that man been hanging around waiting for me to return?' Helen murmured as she walked through the revolving doors of the hotel and marched up to Richard. 'Fancy seeing you here,' she said drily. 'And before you ask what I've been up to, or why I'm back so early, I may have some information for you. I have reason to believe I've discovered the potential murderer. So you can stop following me, as I did not kill my husband. I do have a name for you to add to your shortlist.' Suddenly she faltered and grabbed the back of a nearby chair, feeling as if she might faint.

Without a word, Richard put an arm around her and led her over to a secluded corner of the reception area, helping her to sit on a leather-covered chesterfield settee. Sitting beside her and waving to a passing waiter, he ordered sandwiches, coffee and a double brandy. Helen sat rigidly, clutching her handbag tightly to her chest. He gently took it from her, placing it on the carpeted floor.

'Just relax,' he instructed her, taking her hand and

rubbing it gently between his. 'I had a feeling you'd come to London to do more than just drink tea and chat with your friends. If you want to talk, you'll find me a good listener – and everything will be off the record – but I don't want to hear a thing until you've rested for a few minutes, do you hear me?'

Helen whispered her thanks. She didn't say another word until the waiter appeared, placing a tray on a small table in front of them. Richard handed her the brandy and held her hands as she raised the glass to her lips. 'Take a sip,' he instructed, which she did and grimaced before taking another. The fiery liquid stung her throat, then warmed as it went down. Pushing the glass away, she thanked him.

'I'm sorry, I don't know what came over me. I couldn't face breakfast and it's been rather a long day. I want to tell you what happened . . .'

'No talking until you've eaten something. I'm a great believer in lining your stomach before you venture out on a quest, and I have the feeling that's what you've been doing today,' he said as he took two finger sandwiches from the large plate and handed them to her. 'Come on, I can't eat alone, and these look delicious,' he said, placing four on his own plate. 'Egg and cress, my favourite; and I do believe I can spy smoked salmon. Who knew such things could be found during wartime?' he said, giving her a cheeky grin.

Helen agreed and tucked into the food in front of her, realizing that she was really hungry. No wonder she'd felt so wobbly. 'Egg and cress reminds me of my boarding school days,' she said as she finished the second sandwich, 'whereas smoked salmon is something my mother only produces to impress important guests. I can't stomach it because of that.'

'In that case, I insist you have another egg and cress while I relieve you of the salmon,' he said as he distributed the remaining sandwiches between them. 'Shall I pour?'

'No, let me. I'm starting to feel much better.'

'It'll be the brandy.'

'No, it was the sandwiches. I was famished. In fact, you finish the brandy,' she said, sliding the glass towards him before pouring their tea.

'Don't tell me you're one of those women who abstains from alcohol,' he joshed, thinking of how she'd grimaced at the first sip.

'Good gracious, you forget I worked in London for a few years. I enjoyed nothing better than taking in the occasional show, going dancing and enjoying a drink or two. I was quite a modern young woman in my time, until I married and turned into a dutiful wife. I thought I might have been able to take in the sights of the city today, if the outcome of my conversation with Felicity had been different. Oh well, a quiet night with a book and my sewing is what I have to look forward to. A little shopping, and then an early start home in the morning. I packed my best dress for nothing. I had hoped to dine out with one of my old colleagues.'

'May I suggest you join me this evening – that's if you don't wish to spend the evening sewing? We could meet down here for dinner before we go out, and there might even be the chance of a cocktail or two in the bar of the theatre. I should be able to get two tickets for *Under Your*

Hat with Jack Hulbert and Cicely Courtneidge. That's if you can put up with my company?' He grinned. 'I know I can be infuriating at times. It goes with the job.'

'Is it allowed, what with you investigating John's death?'

Richard knew he was walking on thin ice by associating with the deceased's wife, and he did plan to talk to his superiors about passing the case to a colleague. 'I'm only offering dinner; what harm would it do?'

She had so wanted to see that show when she read about it. 'On one condition,' she replied.

'Please don't say you're a modern woman and you want to pay your own way – I shan't hear a word of it. I just want your company for the evening, and I know you could do with cheering up.'

'I'm certainly not a modern woman. Until recently, I was a settled, married woman looking to the future with a husband and thoughts of a family. That's not very modern, is it?' she said, raising her hand as he went to speak. 'No – I want to tell you everything that happened to me this afternoon. I feel it might have some bearing on John's death. If it isn't relevant, I apologize for wasting your time. But I need to get it all out now, before I can have any hope of enjoying this evening.'

Richard picked up his cup and saucer. 'Go ahead,' he said. 'I'm listening.'

9

Helen checked herself in the dressing-table mirror. The sandwiches and sip of brandy had perked her up. She wouldn't necessarily have accepted Richard's invitation to a show on any other day; but then, she thought, it would at least end a horrid day with a smile.

Her freshly washed hair shone brightly as she ran a brush through it, reapplying her make-up, touching up her pale cheeks with a little rouge and checking in a mirror. 'Considering the tears and the disappointment you've scrubbed up quite well, Mrs Wentworth,' she said to her reflection. Her black crêpe de chine dress was perfect for the evening, elegant and in keeping with her recent loss. Opening a velvet-lined box, she took out a single string of pearls, a wedding gift from her mother, and dabbed a little Chanel No 5 perfume beneath each ear and on her wrists. Picking up a black velvet clutch bag, she was ready.

With two minutes to spare, Helen entered the reception area close to the hotel's dining room and spotted Richard. He took her breath away, handsomely dressed in a black tuxedo, crisp white shirt and bow tie, and was attracting admiring glances from women who walked by on the arms of their partners. She was able to look him up and down while he glanced the other way; yes, he was handsome in his RAF uniform, but dressed as he was now, she could only think of the Hollywood heartthrobs on the silver screen. He reminded her a little of one of the dashing spies played by her favourite actor, Johnny Johnson. She started to imagine that Richard was a spy instead of an RAF police detective, out to discover who had murdered a Member of Parliament. In the movies he would have been dining with the victim's wife, who he thought had committed the crime. A cold chill ran through her as a further thought came to her – that he could indeed be entertaining her under false pretences. She would have to be careful what she said to him this evening. Yes, very careful indeed.

Even in wartime, the hotel pulled out all the stops to make the dining room look as magical as it could. If one ignored the blast tape on the windows and gas masks carried by diners, it was possible to forget about the war and focus instead on a delightful evening. Chandeliers glittered above crisp white linen tablecloths as Helen and Richard walked across the red carpet. Their table was in a corner of the room, by oak-panelled walls in an alcove close to the fireplace. A Christmas tree bedecked with crystal decorations drew the eye, while a small fire burnt brightly in the grate.

'This looks jolly,' Richard said, waiting for Helen to be seated by the waiter before he too sat down. 'Have you stayed here before?'

'Yes, once before. But I've dined here quite often with

my husband,' she said as she accepted a menu from the waiter. 'I'll have the soup and trout,' she decided while watching him peruse his menu. 'How about you?'

'That sounds very good. I'll have the same,' he said, nodding his thanks to the waiter.

Helen couldn't help but smile. 'No, I meant have you stayed here before?'

He smiled back. 'Has anyone told you that you have the most delightful laugh? It is so much better than tears.'

'My husband told me the same on several occasions,' she said, not wishing to attract his appreciation. She hated to lie, as John had never been a man to give compliments – well, not to her, anyway. 'Have you been here before?'

'No, it was recommended to me by Lizzie. I must say she has very good taste.'

'Considering that, to my knowledge, she's hardly visited London, she has very good taste indeed,' Helen said, surprised. She was beginning to feel that someone she called a friend – albeit a very new friend – was helping this man keep tabs on her. Well, if he thought she was going to make a confession, he had another think coming.

She watched as he confidently ordered wine, but she refused it when the waiter brought the bottle to the table. 'I prefer water, please,' she said with a charming smile. They ate their meal while engaging in social chit-chat. He asked about her family, but she told him very little. She asked about his, and he mentioned a sister. Neither discovered much about the other. Both declined dessert before leaving for the theatre, getting into a taxi hailed by the doorman.

The short trip found them talking about London before the war.

'I miss seeing the windows dressed for Christmas,' Helen said. 'I know they've done their best under the circumstances, but when people kept saying the war would be over by Christmas – and here we are three months on, and nothing much has happened – I'm rather confused by it all. When you think back to the Spanish Civil War, with so much death and destruction, it seems as though we've got off lightly in this country.'

'Did your husband not speak to you about the war?' he asked. Even in the dark she knew he was looking at her.

'We didn't really discuss the war as such. I did assist him at the Ministry of Food, of course, but as you must know, his side of the war work did not involve us discussing the ins and outs. Our cleaning lady chatted more to me about the war than he ever did. My husband is . . . was a very private man.'

'But even so, you were married, so surely you shared confidences?'

'We weren't like other couples. I put that down to him being older than me, and being set in his ways before we met and married,' she said. 'But then, it would be a strange world if we were all the same.'

'Do you perhaps wonder whether – if he hadn't died so suddenly – your marriage would have lasted?'

'My goodness, that's rather a personal question.' Helen's hands flew to her neck as she felt heat rise through her body.

Richard reached out and took her hand just for a moment. 'I'm sorry. That was too blunt of me. I suppose I'm still ruminating on all that you've told me: his affair with your good friend . . . the distance between you . . .'

Helen thought for a moment. 'Who knows?' she said, shrugging her shoulders and looking away from him and out of the window. Even though he could hardly see her face she didn't feel confident enough to look his way, just in case he could read her thoughts. She'd like to have replied that she could have walked away from the lonely marriage without even packing a suitcase, but it was too hard to say it out loud and admit the truth to them both. She took a deep breath. 'You may be right.'

They pulled up outside the theatre, and after paying the taxi driver Richard took her arm and led her inside. 'I do hope you enjoy the show. I asked the reception desk at the hotel to book the best seats possible,' he said, passing her a colourful programme.

'I've heard it's a very good show,' she said. 'I do like to visit the theatre, but with many shows closing down at the outbreak of war, as well as my circumstances, it hasn't been possible.'

'I'm sorry, I should have thought: you may not think this is suitable. Would you prefer not to . . .'

'Don't be silly,' she scolded him. 'I intend to enjoy the evening. Thank you for inviting me.'

'I've not laughed so much in a long time,' Helen said as they left the theatre several hours later.

'I'm relieved the government has allowed theatres to open again.'

'I agree. I feel quite thirsty from all the laughing and singing along,' she said. 'Thank you again.'

'It's my pleasure. It's good to see you enjoying yourself. I do know of a small club down by the river; it's not far to walk. We could have a cocktail or two,' he suggested.

She slipped her arm through his. 'Lead the way,' she laughed, thinking that her worries earlier about being alone with Richard had been rather foolish.

Another hour passed as they enjoyed Brandy Alexanders and also a special cocktail the barman created for them alone.

'I shall call it "true love",' he said, placing the two saucer-shaped glasses in front of them. 'Enjoy, and here's to a happy life.'

Helen blushed while Richard grinned and thanked the barman, tipping him generously.

'My goodness, I don't think I should have had that last drink,' she said, reaching for her coat.

'Time to get you home to your bed,' he said before apologizing hastily. 'I didn't mean to put it like that.'

Helen preferred not to comment, instead pointing as they left the bar. 'Look, the Thames is just there – why don't we walk along beside it for a while, and then cross the bridge further down? It's a nice evening for a walk.'

'Are you sure you're not cold?' he asked as he turned to help her button up her coat.

'I'll be fine, as long as we walk briskly and I can hold your arm so I don't trip,' she said, not waiting for an answer as she held out her hand.

He took her hand and tucked it into the large pocket of his overcoat. It felt strangely comforting, she thought, as they covered the few yards to the river and turned right, following the almost empty pavements. 'It's quite soothing, isn't it?' she said.

'What, with the ships all painted battleship grey and the blimps floating overhead?'

'No,' she scoffed. 'I meant the lapping of the river on the shore. But imagine for a moment what has happened here over the centuries as the city has grown. Think what it must have been like when the Tower of London was first built, or the Great Fire destroyed most of the capital . . .'

'That's a lot of history,' he said, leading her towards a wooden bench. 'Shall we sit for a while?'

'Yes, that would be nice,' she said. 'These shoes may look pretty, but they're not really meant for long walks.'

'You should have said. I'd have hailed us a taxi and taken you back to the hotel.'

'No, I wouldn't have missed this for the world,' she said as she slipped off one of the black velvet-covered slippers and started to rub her foot.

'Here, let me,' he murmured as he leant over and took her left foot in his hands, gently rubbing the sole.

Helen felt a shiver run through her body and bit her lip before she sighed out loud.

'Would you like me to rub the other foot?' he asked, moving closer.

'No, no, that's fine,' she said, slipping her shoe on again before facing him, at first not realizing how close he was. She could smell his cologne, which was nothing like her husband's, and the warmth of his body made her wish they could stay like this forever.

He reached out and ran a finger across her cheek before taking her face in both hands and brushing his lips gently against hers.

A low moan came from Helen as she reached out and pulled him even closer. I shouldn't be doing this, she thought, but she didn't try to stop. 'My goodness,' she gasped when at last they broke away from each other. 'That should not have happened.' She pulled away and held a hand to her burning face. 'Do you think perhaps we should call that taxi now?'

Without saying a word, he tilted her head back once more and kissed her forehead. 'Perhaps it's best if we make a move,' he said in a deep voice that almost resembled a growl. 'We may not have meant to let it happen, but I'm pleased it did,' he said, taking her hand and helping her to her feet.

Helen knew she should think otherwise, but at the moment all she could do was savour the last few minutes and try to control her rapidly beating heart.

There was no sign of Richard when she came down to the hotel dining room the following morning.

Not having slept well, with thoughts of his kiss at the forefront of her mind, she had decided at six o'clock to get up, pack and be ready to leave after breakfast. Even then she was early, and sat for twenty minutes in the foyer until a waiter informed her the dining room was open. The menu looked tempting and after some deliberation she chose kedgeree and coffee, knowing she might miss lunch. Chatting to the friendly waiter, she asked how the introduction of rationing would affect the hotel. She had an idea of how businesses would run, as John had been passionate about keeping the nation fed no matter what.

What a loss, she thought again – although there would be many more men ready to step into his shoes in the country's hour of need. She was pleased to hear that although the average housewife would be working with ration books, for now most hotels would still be able to provide meals for their guests.

After finishing a second cup of coffee, she thanked the attentive waiter and headed back to her room to collect her suitcase and coat. Settling her bill, she headed out into the street to find there was a light drizzle in the air, which didn't feel very festive at all considering there were now only three days left before Christmas. She wanted to pick up a few small gifts, so headed to Dickins & Jones on Regent Street. Leaving her suitcase with cloakroom staff, she browsed counters full of tempting gifts and visited the toy department to choose presents for Effie's children, before collecting her case and hurrying outside to hail a taxi to the station. With luck, if she could catch the half past eleven train, she would be back at The Maples in good time to change her clothes and wrap the presents. An idea had come to her during her trip that she wished to write down on the plan she'd made for the double wedding ring quilt, while it was fresh in her mind. She also hoped to have a word with Lizzie before her friend was consumed by plans for Christmas Day.

'For heaven's sake, Helen, you cannot go out on your bicycle in this weather. You'll be soaked to the skin in this freezing rain. I don't want my Christmas spoilt by having to nurse you,' Hillary Davis scolded. She had caught

Helen in the process of leaving the house, dressed in her Mackintosh raincoat and with an unbecoming woolly hat pulled down over her ears.

'I'm sorry, Mother, but I really do need to visit Lizzie this afternoon. It's my last chance to do so, as I'll be too busy here tomorrow.'

'I'll ask your father to drive you, as long as you don't stay there too long. You know we have a function at the golf club this evening. Gavin, being on the committee, is required to be there early.'

Helen looked daggers at her mother. 'You may have forgotten, though I haven't: my father died some years ago. If you mean the man you married, I would prefer to take my chances in the rain. Besides, he may not have the petrol to drive me. There is a war on, you know.'

'There's no need to talk to your mother like that,' Gavin called from the sitting room. 'I'll fetch the Austin from the garage, it will give you time to change into something more becoming of a young lady.' He gave her a look that swept from her head to her toes. 'As for the petrol – let's just say I know a man,' he added with a knowing expression.

Helen knew it was sensible to accept the lift and begrudgingly agreed; the rain really was pelting down. She could be ready in five minutes. She dashed back upstairs to her bedroom. Throwing open the wardrobe, she pulled out a pair of navy-blue wide-legged slacks. Her mother hated them, but they were becoming quite the fashion. The few times Helen had worn them, she'd felt warm and comfortable. With a cream high-necked pullover and a pale-blue silk scarf draped round her shoulders, she felt ready for the journey. She was at the bottom of the staircase putting on her coat and adjusting her navy felt hat when Gavin honked the horn of his Austin 7.

Picking up her bag containing Christmas gifts, she hurried out to the car and climbed into the passenger seat beside her stepfather. As they pulled off, he gave her a quick look and grumbled, 'I wouldn't say trousers on a woman are very becoming, would you?'

'I like them, and no one has ever complained before,' she said, looking away from him to the dreary lane of bare trees and water running freely down the side of the road.

He reached out and patted her knee. 'If you say so,' he muttered, keeping his hand there just a little too long before she pushed it away. He chuckled as she told him to keep his eyes on the road.

Taking the bag from beneath her feet, she placed it on her lap and snarled, 'I don't know why my mother puts up with you.'

'Because, my dear, she can't afford to live without me. It's as simple as that.'

Helen frowned. 'But it's Mother's house. You moved in with us, remember?'

'You need to speak to your mother. Things aren't as straightforward as you believe them to be. And by the way, I'll be expecting you to find somewhere else to live come the new year, unless . . . Let me put it this way, unless you are more friendly towards me.'

Helen moved further away from him, pressing herself against the passenger door. The interior of the vehicle was small at the best of times, but at the moment she felt trapped alongside him. They were halfway down the lane to Lizzie's house when she decided she'd had enough. 'You can stop the car now, this very instant,' she said forcefully. 'Stop right now, I'm walking the rest of the way. And I'll make my own way home,' she added, raising her voice as she opened the door. The vehicle was still moving, but her impulse to get away was too strong to resist.

'You silly little cow, you'll have an accident or kill yourself,' Gavin snarled.

'At least I'll be free of you then,' she shouted back at him. He pulled up sharply as she fled from the vehicle, stomping off down the muddy lane, not caring that the rain was falling harder by the minute. Her smart clothes would be ruined. She recalled somebody once remarking that no one can see you crying in the rain; that was most certainly true, she thought, as she let her anger and distress pour out. 'I'll be having a word with Mother when I get home and find out exactly what he was talking about,' she said aloud as the rain washed away her tears.

Feeling utterly miserable, she entered the gates of Dalton Court and ran up the driveway. As she approached, the main doors opened and Lizzie stepped out to greet her.

'My dear – you're soaked to the skin! You should have phoned. I'd have arranged for you to be collected.'

Helen tried to reply, but could only shake her head before breaking down in tears.

'Oh, my poor love,' Lizzie said, putting an arm around her and coaxing her into the house before calling for Doreen to come and give her a hand. 'I'm taking you straight upstairs to my bathroom. A hot bath and dry clothes will make you feel much better, and then you can tell me what has distressed you so much.'

Helen, still unable to speak, allowed herself to be led up to a sumptuous bathroom on the first floor.

'Leave all your clothes outside the door and Doreen will take them away to dry. You can use my bathrobe that's hanging behind the door. I'll be waiting for you in my workroom, the fire's burning bright and it's warm and cosy. Take your time,' she insisted before giving Helen a kiss on the cheek and pushing her through the door of the bathroom, closing it behind her.

Helen watched as Doreen turned on the tap of the deep bathtub and sprinkled in a generous amount of rose-perfumed bath salts. 'Check the water before you climb in – it tends to run a little hot,' Doreen smiled before leaving her alone.

She peeled off her saturated clothes and climbed in. Leaning back and closing her eyes, she allowed the water to soothe her cold body while wondering what she'd done in life for this all to happen to her. A husband she barely loved, who was unfaithful, a stepfather she hated, a mother who didn't seem to care about her . . . And now Lizzie, who seemed so generous – but was she helping Richard with his investigation? Going by what he had told her in London, that seemed to be the case.

As for Richard himself – her mind was a muddle. The man was investigating her husband's murder. What did it say about her that she allowed him to kiss her, and more to the point, that she enjoyed it so much? Yes, her life was a mess, and she needed to do her utmost to take back control of it.

'You look so much better,' Lizzie said when, thirty minutes later, Helen joined her in the workroom. 'Here, sit yourself down by the fire.' She leant over, tugging on a brass pulley on the wall. 'I hate using this thing, as it seems so decadent to summon a staff member in such a way. I much prefer the telephone, but I'm told by the staff the bell on the wall is much louder. Cook doesn't like to answer the telephone – it frightens her.' She chuckled.

Helen made an effort to join in with the laughter, but she was thinking that the world Lizzie lived in was so different to her own. Here was a friend who could billet members of the RAF, host sewing groups and still have more than enough room to swing a cat; meanwhile, in just over a week, Helen would be homeless. Even if she wanted to, she couldn't move back to London without a steady income. No job she was qualified to do would pay enough for the rent on a suitable home in the city.

'You seem troubled, my dear,' Lizzie said as she watched Helen closely. 'I'm a good listener, if you want to talk.'

Helen didn't know what to say. Lizzie was clearly a decent sort. Perhaps she was wrong – perhaps it wasn't her friend who'd told Richard where she was staying, and which train she was catching? Taking a deep breath, she decided to ask her.

'I was quite surprised to bump into Richard on my train, when I hadn't told him what time I would be travelling. Then for him to be staying at the same hotel as me, when there are so many available in London, was quite a shock. I did wonder if a little dickie bird had whispered in his ear?' she said, forcing herself to smile and speak lightly as if she found it funny.

Lizzie raised both hands in the air in surrender. 'I confess – it was me. I meant nothing by it . . . But then, perhaps I did. I never could resist a little matchmaking. I hope you can forgive me, and hope this hasn't ruined our friendship.'

Helen's thoughts had been of murder, ruined friendships and betrayal. She had not given a moment's thought to the possibility that Lizzie had simply been pushing two acquaintances together, hoping to create a romance. What an idiot she'd been! She laughed ironically before mumbling an apology to Lizzie. 'You're going to think I'm such an ungrateful person.'

'Why would I think that?' Lizzie asked, looking puzzled.

'I thought the reason Richard was on the same train to London, and also booked in to the same hotel was because . . . Well, I thought perhaps you thought I had something to do with my husband's death. And that you had given Richard details of my trip to London so he could keep an eye on me, and perhaps find something out.'

Lizzie nodded slowly as she absorbed this, her expression thoughtful. 'In the short time I've known you and the even shorter time I've known Richard, I came to the conclusion that the pair of you were suited to one another. Please – let me finish,' she said, raising a hand as Helen opened her mouth to protest. 'My daughters and my close friends all know that I'm a bit of a matchmaker. I love nothing more than to put two lonely people together and see what will happen. It should have occurred to me that Richard being involved with the investigation into your husband's death, and you being a suspect – although not for one moment do I think you are responsible – would cause a problem. I hope I didn't cause you too much embarrassment. I would understand if you got up and stormed out of the house. Although in my bathrobe and slippers, and with the rain having got worse outside, I wouldn't recommend it.'

Helen smiled; she couldn't be annoyed with Lizzie for long. 'I'm sure you meant well, although I don't know that I'm ready for a romance at the moment. I've only been widowed for a few months – not that my marriage was a normal one, going by most other people's experiences. Although I would like to enjoy a romance one day,' she said, remembering Richard's kiss. 'And in the end, actually, I was pleased Richard was there, because after my visit to John's office and seeking out Felicity, I needed a shoulder to cry on.'

'And the shoulder of a handsome man helps a lot,' Lizzie said, raising her eyebrows. 'Did he help?'

'Oh yes, very much. In fact . . .' She paused, not knowing whether she should disclose the information, but deciding Lizzie could be trusted. 'I feel my meeting with Felicity has brought about a few questions that I hope he will investigate. If he wants to find the murderer, he should add Felicity to his list of suspects.'

Lizzie was thoughtful. 'Based on the little you've told me, I did wonder if that was a possibility.'

As tea arrived, Helen filled her in on all the details of what had happened during her encounter with Felicity.

Lizzie was sympathetic. 'It must have been difficult to hear her confirm that John was carrying on with her behind your back.'

'I thought about it on the journey home. I was sad – and angry – but now I feel almost pleased that it fills in some of the gaps, as the police need to know what happened leading up to John's death. I'd rather know they were having an affair now than have it come out in court; that would have been horrendous. I want to be able to move on from this, and I can't do so until the person responsible is arrested.'

She reached for her handbag and took out the square of fabric from Felicity's blouse. 'It did make me think about my quilt, and how I could add this particular square,' she said thoughtfully. 'I remembered that traditional idea you told us about – that no quilt is perfect, because only God is perfect. I know it sounds rather like an old wives' tale, but for me it solves a small problem of how to add an imperfection to my own quilt. I'm going to add the one red piece into a corner of the quilt, so it will be out of sight of the main pattern, but still there to show that no marriage is perfect – especially mine.'

'That's a jolly good idea; but might I make an alternative suggestion? Your pattern is one of two intertwined wedding rings. Why not have one ring made from your fabric and one from the fabric taken from John's clothing? Within his ring, you could add that one patch from Felicity's blouse. Why should a cheating husband, and a friend who really isn't a friend, not have their story told in your quilt? Their guilt for all to see.'

'Oh, that is a good idea – I shall do just that. And when I send it as a gift to John's mother, if she asks about the odd colour, I may just tell her . . .'

Lizzie sucked in her breath before bursting out laughing. 'I'll remember never to cross you, Helen Wentworth,' she said. 'What is it they say – revenge is a dish best served cold? But once this project is completed, you can move on with your life. At least for now you can live amongst your family and your new friends and look to the future – hopefully a happy future.'

Helen grimaced. 'My future is not going to be with my family. I do wonder what I've done to deserve all this trouble falling on my shoulders. My stepfather has told me I'm to find somewhere else to live as soon as possible. It seems I'm not welcome at my mother's house.' She shrugged her shoulders. 'I really do want to stay in the area, but goodness knows where that will be.'

'How strange that your stepfather should act as he does. I would love to invite you to live here, but every room is used up at the moment, with my husband entertaining so many servicemen and of course with me running the sewing circles. Perhaps later on, when the groups have moved back to the church hall, I could find room for you?'

'Oh no, Lizzie. I didn't mean for a moment that I was begging for a place to stay. You've been more than kind to me. Even if you had a room available and offered it to me, I would have to refuse – I can't lean on your friend-ship any more than I already have done.' It also occurred to her that living at Dalton Court would bring her far too close to Richard for comfort. She had enjoyed his kisses and would like to see him again, but it was still too soon after John's death – whatever would people think? Apart from that, he was still part of the investigation. It wouldn't be right, however much she was tempted.

'I do need to look for a job,' she continued, taking a sip of her tea, 'so perhaps a live-in position will come up. Anything will do – anything at all to get me away from that odious man.'

Lizzie knew little about Helen's home life; just that she was an only child whose father had died when she was very young, and since then, her mother had married someone whom she now knew Helen despised. She told herself not to ask any more questions. The girl had enough on her plate already.

'I have the local newspaper here – that might help you with your search,' she said, going to where a pile of magazines and newspapers were heaped on the table. 'Ah yes, here it is. It's nearly a week old, but who knows, there may be something in here . . .' She opened it to the 'situations vacant' page. 'How are your cooking skills?' The look on Helen's face spoke volumes. Lizzie picked up a pencil and crossed out all of the advertisements for cooks, live-in or otherwise. 'Hmm . . . how is your shorthand and typing?'

'Rusty. I could probably build up my speed fairly easily, but I've not done much of that in recent years. I've been more of a personal assistant; perhaps I should look for something else . . .'

Lizzie ran her finger down the columns, frowning. 'There is very little here for women, I'm afraid. Had you thought about joining one of the services? So many people are, you know.'

Helen nodded. 'I have thought about it, but to be honest I feel as though until everything is settled with John's death, I can't make a decision as significant as that. I need something to fill the gap. I know for sure I won't return to London to work, unless I'm forced to if nothing else comes up. I wonder if there's any work available at the airfield? There must be female civilian workers there, surely?'

'I'll ask my husband to enquire. You never know, something might crop up. What about this?' Lizzie tapped the bottom of the final column. 'Are you any good with dogs?'

'Well, we had an old collie when I was a child – why do you ask?'

'The kennels up at Stan Trentham's place are looking for someone to help in the kennel business. You need to have bookkeeping knowledge and be prepared to muck in with the kennels. There is a room available as well. It's not far from here, a short cycle ride in fact.'

'I remember the kennels, we visited when I was a child. I bet somebody has grabbed that job,' Helen said, getting up to look over Lizzie's shoulder at the advertisement.

'I have an idea. Stay here and finish your tea and cake. I just need to see someone.'

While Lizzie was gone, Helen wandered over to the worktable where her patchwork quilt was laid out. She removed the few fabric pieces from her handbag and put them in place. It was clear that Lizzie's idea would work; she'd need to do some unpicking, but not very much. The end result would be well worth it. Picking up a small pair of embroidery scissors, she snipped at stitches and parted several of the pieces. She put in the piece from Felicity's blouse between two different-coloured pieces of shirt fabric. 'Perfect,' she said aloud, and pinned the pieces into place.

'Helen, can you spare a moment?' Lizzie said as she came back into the room and spotted Helen, now seated at the sewing machine. 'I have someone here who would like to have a chat with you.'

Helen looked up and smiled a greeting, recognizing one of the women from the knitting group.

'This is Jean Carter; she's popped in this afternoon to help out with the rag rug group. Several of the ladies wanted to finish their rugs in time for Christmas, and although she helps run the knitting section, she's a rug maker as well – that's when she's not the cook up at the kennels . . .'

Helen looked between Lizzie and Jean and thought how fortuitous it was that Lizzie seemed to know everybody in the area. 'It's nice to see you again, Jean. Did Lizzie mention that I'm looking for a live-in position for at least the next few months? Something to tide me over until I know what's going to happen with my life. My husband died recently . . .'

'My condolences,' Jean said. 'Lizzie did mention that I might be able to put a word in with my boss up at The Grange. Can I fill you in a bit more on what the job entails? The women who've replied so far have been unsuitable. One didn't even like dogs.'

Lizzie pointed out the two armchairs, and the women went to sit down. 'I'll leave you to it for a while, I have one or two things to do. And I'll check to see if your clothes are dry.'

Helen thanked Lizzie and turned back to Jean. 'You said The Grange – but I thought the job was at a dog kennels?'

'It is, but Mr Trentham's home is more than just a dog kennels. It's been in the family for donkey's years. He happens to be a champion dog breeder – or at least, he was until the war stopped everything. He was always off showing his dogs all over the country; he judges dogs and is quite an expert, you know.'

'That does sound interesting. My late husband's sister breeds poodles, so I know a little of what goes on, but I'm willing to learn more.'

Jean smiled at Helen's words. 'You wouldn't be expected to get involved with the breeding or anything like that. It's more to sort out Mr Trentham's office and his paperwork. He's such a messy so-and-so. There's paperwork all over the place. He'd rather spend all his time with his dogs than do what he calls boring administration stuff. I would think you'd be required to do some typing and look after his finances as well. Customers pay him, and then he never bothers to go to the bank. Everything is a complete mess,' she added.

'It does sound as though he needs a helping hand. I'm sure I could do the job. I did something similar for my husband when he was alive, although dogs weren't involved. Would that go against me if I applied?'

'I don't think it would, Miss, especially if I put in a word for you. With regard to the dogs, though, he does run a boarding kennels – that's where the money comes from – so there are some long-term lodgers as well as some that just come in for short stays. The long-term ones belong to people in the services. We do lend a hand at feeding times, give the odd bath and so on. For me it's a pleasure to get out of the kitchen for a while and get some fresh air. I have my favourites that I walk. Then, of course, there are the strays . . .'

'The strays! Do you mean he takes in stray dogs?'

'Half the time he has no choice in the matter. A week doesn't pass without dogs being tied to the gates of The Grange. Some people leave a note and others don't.'

Helen frowned. 'I don't understand; why is this happening?'

Jean shrugged her shoulders. 'It's the war. You can blame bloody Hitler. People are worried, you see, that before too long they won't be able to feed their dogs, let alone care for them if the rumours about bombings continue. Because Mr Trentham has a big house and kennels, people believe he can afford to take them all in. The silly old sod has got such a soft heart, he can't say no. So you see, whoever takes on the job will be expected to help out with the strays as well. Granted, you get your bed and board, and if I say so myself, you'll be well fed. But there won't be much money by way of wages. If what you really need is a decent income, don't even think of applying.'

Helen turned to Lizzie, who had just returned with her dry clothing. 'May I have some notepaper? If I write a letter now, perhaps Jean will take it with her. The job sounds perfect.'

10

Christmas Day 1939

On Christmas morning, Helen popped down to the kitchen to hand out gifts to the excited children. She'd put a lot of thought into the items in the two stockings, choosing jigsaw puzzles, books and a box of sugared almonds for each girl. Effie had been overjoyed to open a gift box to find a shell-pink cardigan embroidered with spring flowers around the neckline and down the panelled front. She had scolded Helen good-naturedly for spending far too much money, although Helen could see the joy that the gift had brought to the woman's face. In return, the two girls proudly handed over a gift each to Helen, who was delighted with the homemade calendar and a cross-stitched panel that declared there was 'no place like home'. Effie gave her a knowing smile; they both knew the sentiment was not actually true in Helen's case.

Helen was surprised when Effie handed her a large box, and worried she'd spent too much money. She knew that her mother paid the lowest rates she could possibly get away with for a housekeeper.

'Whatever could this be?' she asked as the three faces watched in anticipation while she slowly opened the present. 'This is a perfect gift,' she exclaimed, and had them all laughing as she pulled a rag rug from the box.

'I had help making it,' Effie explained. 'I wasn't sure I would finish in time for Christmas. You won't find any of the fabric from you-know-who in there,' she added as Helen ran her hand over the pieces of fabric neatly inserted into the sacking back. 'In the rag rug group, we exchanged material to make these special gifts. I hope you'll remember the three of us when you put your feet on it each morning as you climb out of bed.'

'I adore it,' Helen said, kissing each of the girls in turn and giving Effie a huge hug.

She had not yet told Effie that she might be moving out of the house. Jean had promised to let her know as soon as there was news about the letter she'd sent to the owner of The Grange. Until then, she thought it best to keep her plans a secret. 'Have you found somewhere to move to?' she asked Effie.

'Nothing yet; that's why I think it best if I move back home to the East End. It's not perfect, and in fact I'm rather worried about it, but I get the feeling we are no longer welcome here.' She lowered her voice so her daughters didn't hear. By now they were busy opening the sweets and arguing over which jigsaw puzzle to work on first.

'Look, don't do anything rash.' Helen kept her voice low too. 'You never know – something better might come up.'

Effie promised she wouldn't, and then invited Helen to join them for their trip to church for the morning service.

'I would like to have gone to the midnight mass last night, but it wouldn't have been fair on the children. This morning will be just as special. And I have everything prepared for the dinners, so there'll be no complaints,' she said, looking upwards to the ceiling and the floor above, where she knew the dining room was laid out ready for her employer's Christmas meal.

'That's a splendid idea,' Helen said. 'I just need to fetch my coat and hat and I'll be ready. Shall I meet you on the drive in ten minutes?' she asked, knowing that her mother didn't like Effie bringing the children through the house. That way she could use the back entrance that led to their own rooms as well as the basement kitchen.

'Can we make it fifteen minutes, please? I need to run a flannel over the girls' faces and make them look presentable,' Effie said as they both smiled at the sticky mess round the children's mouths.

'I'm going to church,' Helen called out to her mother, who was sitting in the drawing room listening to a service on the wireless. 'Would you like to join me? I'm going with Effie and her daughters.'

'I don't think so. Have you forgotten one doesn't socialize with the staff? You should have learnt that in your position as John's wife. It is especially wrong to be seen in public with them,' Hillary tutted.

'Oh, Mother, try to show some kindness. It's Christmas. And as for my position, it no longer matters. Besides, as a Member of Parliament John did not distinguish between rich or poor, or people of different social standings. In his eyes, every person was equal and treated with respect.'

Hillary Davis shook her head in disbelief. 'That kind

of thinking would never have made him prime minister. A Member of Parliament needs standards to live by. And to think we had such high hopes,' she said, reaching for a handkerchief and sniffing into it in an affected way. 'I do wonder why you didn't go to stay with John's family, as it is their first Christmas without him.'

Helen grimaced. 'For one thing, I wasn't invited – and in any case, all the time I was married we never spent Christmas with them. We entertained in London. Don't you remember? You were invited every year and refused.'

'That was your father refusing, not me,' Hillary hit back at her. 'You know he didn't agree with your husband's politics.'

'Mother, when will you remember that the man who lives here with you is not my father? I would never give him that honour, so please don't keep talking as if we are one happy family, because we aren't. He has no idea how to handle children, he was harsh and intimidating. He was only interested in me once I was a young woman.' Hillary's eyes widened at her words. 'Now, if you are sure you don't wish to join me, I'll be on my way,' Helen finished, heading out of the house and walking down to the gate where Effie and the girls were already waiting. Taking each girl by the hand, they headed off in the chilly morning.

The girls asked all kinds of questions as they hurried along trying to keep warm. Questions about Christmas, Helen's life when she lived in London, and whether she thought Father Christmas was real. Apparently, one of the children with whom they'd been evacuated had told them adamantly that there was no such person.

'He must be real, otherwise you wouldn't have received such lovely gifts,' Effie chided them gently. 'Where do you think Miss Helen got your presents from?'

'Father Christmas?' chimed the youngest girl as the older one shouted, 'London'.

As they arrived at the church they saw from a distance Lizzie and her husband, who were just climbing from their car.

'The petrol ration doesn't seem to worry them,' Effie whispered good-naturedly. 'Considering they are foreigners, I quite like them – and she has a lovely home. It's so full of laughter. The girls are going to look forward to attending school in the barn in the new year. That's if we're here,' she added sadly.

'Think positively,' Helen encouraged her, giving her a quick hug just as they were joined by Jean Carter.

'May I have a quick word?' she asked Helen. Effie took hold of her girls' hands and said she would see Helen inside.

Helen felt as though she had butterflies in her tummy. Was Jean going to give her some news about the job at the kennels?

'I have a reply from Mr Trentham,' Jean said, handing over an envelope with Helen's name on it in fine copperplate handwriting. 'I must go,' she said, waving to where members of the knitting circle were standing together.

Helen quickly opened the envelope and read the contents of the letter, chewing her lip as she did so. Putting the letter into her pocket, she squared her shoulders and hurried inside to join her friends.

*

'You seem to have something on your mind, Helen,' her mother said as she set down her knife and fork after Christmas lunch, picking up the bell to summon Effie for the next course. She looked expectantly at her daughter, waiting for a reply.

Helen put a hand on the pocket of her cardigan, feeling the shape of the envelope. Now is as good a time as any, she thought, as she stacked the plates and left them at the corner of the table ready for Effie to take away.

'I really wish you'd leave that for the girl to do,' Hillary muttered while still waiting for Helen to respond.

As Helen sat down she heard Effie approaching, carrying the plum pudding her mother had made months earlier. No doubt it would be as hard and dry as the ones she'd made in previous years. The pudding reminded her of her mother; there was no sweetness or joy to be had from either.

'I have some news to share,' Helen said, removing the envelope from her pocket. She saw Effie's eyes widen in anticipation. 'I have secured a position and will be leaving home in just over a week.' Effie's shoulders drooped in dismay, while Gavin's eyes bored into Helen.

'You've told your mother nothing about this!' he said, thumping the table with his fist. 'After all we've done for you, taking you in when you were homeless.'

'I was never homeless. I chose to come home and stay here in my mother's house. This was once my home as well, before you arrived on the scene.'

'Helen, really! There is no need to speak to your fa— your stepfather like that.'

'I'll speak to him however I wish, Mother. I'm a grown

woman now. Just because you kow-tow to the man, it doesn't mean I have to. For heaven's sake – this is your house and he moved in. Why does he have this hold over you? I don't think for one moment that it's love, do you?'

Her stepfather got to his feet, his face so red it looked as though he would explode at any moment. 'I'll have you know that if it wasn't for my money, you and your mother would have been out on the street. You and she were left with hardly anything after your father died. In fact, to use one of your quaint East End terms,' he said, nodding towards a dumbfounded Effie, 'you didn't have a pot to piss in.'

Hillary burst into tears. Effie suppressed a grin as she placed the plum pudding in front of Gavin, along with a small bottle of brandy for him to pour over the hot pudding and set alight. He swept it away with one hand, sending plates and cutlery crashing to the floor.

Hillary spat at Effie: 'And you're not helping. I thought I told you – we do not want children in this house. You've had plenty of time to either send them back to the country, or have a member of your family take them in. A condition of your employment was that no child lived under this roof.'

Any flicker of sympathy Helen might have felt for her mother was instantly snuffed out by these words. She watched Hillary's face and realized she knew more than she was letting on. Memories of her early life, when Gavin had married her mother, came flooding back. 'For once, Mother, you are right – no child should live under this roof.' She stared coldly across the table at her stepfather. 'This house was never welcoming to me as a child, and it's really no place for children now.'

Effie looked shocked. 'I've been trying to look for some-where,' she said, as her bottom lip started to tremble.

'There is no need,' Helen said, going to stand beside Effie. 'When I leave in a few days' time, so will you and the girls. My mother and her husband can fend for themselves. Come along, let's go down to the kitchen and enjoy what's left of Christmas with the children. Mother, don't forget, the king will be speaking shortly so you'll need to warm up the wireless set. God forbid I should stand in the way of you having a pleasant Christmas.'

'Shouldn't I at least clean up the mess?' Effie said, but Helen took her arm and led her firmly from the room. Behind them, her mother was calling for Effie to return, but she marched on, pulling Effie all the way back to the kitchen and closing the door behind them. 'Let her stew for now. I'll help you clear up later.'

Effie looked worried. 'What if your mother gives me the sack?'

'It doesn't matter,' Helen replied as she rummaged in the pantry and then one of the many cupboards. 'We are leaving. Here – take a look at this.' She handed over the letter she'd stuffed back into her pocket earlier. She'd meant to show her mother, but the opportunity had passed.

Effie held the letter close to her face and slowly read the words. 'I'm pleased you have found a live-in job, but I don't know how this affects me and the girls? I'd best pack me bags and move back home. My sister might take us in for a while, but it isn't perfect. I'll miss living around here.'

Helen chuckled. 'Jean told me the quarters I'd be given, if I got the job, would be over the old stables that are now

182

used to house the vehicles for the kennel business. The driver-cum-handyman has joined up, so the rooms are available for me to use.'

'Rooms?'

'Yes; two bedrooms with a small sitting area, a bathroom and a kitchen, Effie. You are coming with me. I said as much in my application letter. Now, let's open this bottle of sherry and tuck into the Christmas cake, shall we?' she said, holding both up high with a grin. 'We deserve to celebrate.'

Effie took the cake from her and placed it on the table. 'I'd best take this before you drop it,' she said. 'And before you open the sherry bottle, can you tell me more about the dog kennels? I only ask as I don't want my girls ending up sleeping in a kennel,' she smiled, pointing to a chair for Helen to sit down.

'I suppose I should, considering I'm stealing the three of you away and you don't have an idea about my plans,' Helen laughed.

Effie could see how excited Helen was: joy shone from her face. It was an expression Effie had never seen her new friend wear before.

'It was Lizzie, God bless her, and it's not as if I've known her very long. Look at how she's taking in all the sewing circles and billeted men from the airfield – she's a wonder.'

'Well, I know all of that; but what about us moving?' Effie urged.

'A few days ago, I got soaking wet after I climbed out of Gavin's car in the rain and walked the rest of the way to Lizzie's house. Yes, this is an important part of the story,' she added as she noticed Effie getting impatient.

'Well, after a nice bath and a delicious afternoon tea, I explained to Lizzie that I couldn't live here anymore, and that I needed a job – preferably a live-in job. We looked in the local paper and Lizzie noticed there was a vacancy up at the dog kennels. I did laugh, as I don't really know one end of a dog from another. However, Jean Carter, the cook up at the kennels . . .'

'I know her,' Effie chipped in.

'Well, she was there helping out the knitting circle. Lizzie fetched her, and she explained more of what the job entailed and that it would be a live-in position. It's mainly office work, so I wrote a quick letter and she took it home with her to hand over to the owner of the kennels. Honestly, it happened so quickly. A letter was popped through the letterbox the very next day to go up to the kennels and have a chat. It seems the owner, Mr Trentham, is desperate for help.

'I was up there within two hours. It wasn't too far to cycle and this time I didn't worry too much about the rain, as I wore my Mackintosh and hat. I assured Mr Trentham that I could do the work, it's nothing I haven't done before, and then he took me to show me the living accommodation. It's very large and situated over what was a kind of garage for their vehicles. He told me that years ago, when his dad and his grandfather owned the property, it was where they kept the horses and carriages. His driver-cum-handyman has joined up and the rooms above are now going begging. He did wonder if, being on my own, I'd find the accommodation to be too much. So I explained that I had a very dear friend and her two daughters who would be living with me. I said that currently you had a live-in position as a housekeeper, but the situation was no longer right for you. And I hope you don't mind, but I said you might be available for light housework, if you were allowed to live with me. Honestly, Effie – he jumped at my offer, and didn't even ask to meet you. He said that Jean had put in a good word for me, and that the widow of an MP was more than good enough for him. When she brought in a cup of tea for us, I made a point of saying that Jean knew you and she was thrilled with the idea of having some help around the house. That's about it, really. What do you think?' Helen said, pausing for breath.

Effie reached for the sherry and poured two generous amounts into clean teacups that were on the table. Her hand shook as she took a gulp. 'Blimey. And all this has happened over the past couple of days?'

'Yes, Jean passed me this letter at church this morning. Take a proper look,' Helen said, placing it on the table. 'I intend to reply to him and cycle over tomorrow to drop it through his letterbox. I won't bother him in person, as it'll be Boxing Day and Jean mentioned the hunt are meeting there.'

Effie's eyes shone with happiness. 'It sounds ideal. Cleaning is all I know, along with a bit of cooking, so as long as I'm not treading on Jean's toes, I'm more than glad of the job. That's if you don't mind living with me – what with you being a posh woman, and me being working class?'

Helen got up from her chair and hugged Effie. 'For heaven's sake, I was always a working woman myself – just as working class as you are. Don't start with all that chip on your shoulder business. Why, if it wasn't for you, this house would be in a right state, and my mother would be living in a right mess.'

They looked at each other and simultaneously grimaced. 'God, what is she going to say when she knows she really will be without a housekeeper within days?' Effie bit the inside of her cheek.

Helen chuckled. 'Don't worry. I'll write a letter placing an advertisement in *The Lady* magazine and post it tomorrow. She'll be as happy as Larry to have a new person to dominate.'

Effie gave a big sigh of relief and topped up her cup. 'Talking of tomorrow, would it be all right if me and the girls walked up with you to the kennels? That's if you don't mind walking rather than cycling? It will be a chance to see where we're going to live, and the girls would love to see the dogs and the horses, if the hunt hasn't set off.'

Helen raised her cup. 'It's a deal,' she said, clinking it against Effie's. 'Now, let's have some of this cake to soak up the sherry, or I will be fit for nothing tomorrow.'

Boxing Day morning started with a fine layer of frost on the ground. There was a weak sun in the sky, and Helen wrapped up in a woolly hat, scarf and mittens. She prayed for a dry day as she stepped out of the house to be joined by Effie and the girls, all similarly dressed.

Effie had checked the local newspaper to find that the hunt met quite early in the morning, so they'd decided to leave in time for the girls to see it set off.

'Do you think we'll be allowed to ride a horse when we move to the kennels?' Dorothy asked excitedly.

'I'm not sure if you'll find there are any horses at The Grange, but we can always ask now we're all going to be proper country girls. It will be a good idea to learn as much as we can about country life; what do you say to that?' Helen replied.

'Does that mean we don't have to go to school?' little Jane asked, looking hopeful.

'You don't get out of school that easily,' Effie chuckled. 'In fact, I have a feeling you're actually going to be closer to Lizzie's house and the barn school once we move.'

'I believe you're right,' Helen said. 'It's in a different direction, and there's a footpath that leads across the fields.'

'It would be nicer if you had a car,' the child observed.

'Oh, you lazy so-and-so,' Effie scolded good-naturedly. 'By rights there should be hardly any cars on the road now that the government is getting strict about the allocation of petrol; isn't that right, Helen?'

Helen nodded. 'I did wonder if we could ask for a patch of garden – somewhere we could grow our own vegetables? We can all work together. It could be fun,' she said encouragingly, looking at the children's doubtful faces.

'Will there be worms and slugs?' they asked in unison, looking unsure.

'We can borrow some gardening tools, so you don't have to touch the ground,' Helen assured them.

'They'd better be big ones, then,' Jane said, pulling a face at the thought.

They continued chatting about their new life as they left the main road and climbed over a stile, following a public footpath across some fields.

'Listen,' Helen said, stopping for a moment. 'Can you hear that?'

'Dogs – I can hear dogs,' Dorothy exclaimed. 'It sounds like hundreds of them. Will we have to bathe them all? Is that part of your job?' she asked thoughtfully. 'I think I'd prefer to do that, rather than dig in the garden.'

They continued walking slowly across the furrowed field, both Helen and Effie holding on to the children's hands in case they tripped on the uneven frozen earth. They stopped again as a low rumble that turned into a roar filled the sky with sound.

'It seems to be getting closer,' Effie said. 'Oh, look – over there!'

'Aeroplanes – hundreds of them,' Jane exclaimed. 'Are they Germans?'

'No, silly,' her sister said, 'they are Spitfires. I told you to listen when we had lessons about the aeroplanes at school.'

'That was weeks ago, I've forgotten,' the younger child said, shrugging as she gazed upwards. 'Aren't they noisy!'

It was sad, thought Helen, that youngsters were learning so much about aeroplanes and war when they should have been learning about reading, writing and arithmetic. 'I would think they're approaching Biggin Hill airfield,' she said, and a shudder ran through her. Every day, newspapers brought more information about the German army advancing across Europe towards them. She'd heard there were Polish pilots who had escaped their own country as it was invaded, and now flew with the British air force. More and more, it felt as though the war was changing all of their lives – and not for the better.

They put their fingers in their ears as the Spitfires, with their distinctive engine sound, flew overhead before descending to the airfield below them. The planes taxied to a halt, ground crew rushing out to put blocks under the wheels and assist the pilots.

'They look like ants,' Jane laughed.

'They are all brave men, every one of them,' Effie said, looking sad. 'Come on – let's hurry up if you want to see the hunt setting off. I don't know about you, but I'm freezing. The cold seems to be coming up through my feet.'

They hurried on until they arrived at the border of the land belonging to The Grange. 'We can't just walk through the paddock,' Helen said. 'It seems rather rude. We really ought to go in through the front entrance. Look; there's a pathway heading in the right direction, through those trees.'

'I'm not sure we will be able to cycle from here to get to Lizzie's house when I need to get the girls to school,' Effie said.

'We'll be going in the opposite direction. Jean said she often cycles to Lizzie's house and also to the church. I'll have to ask her for the route, so we don't get lost.'

'Or stuck in a muddy field,' Dorothy giggled.

They headed through the trees, following the widening path until they came out onto a road. Turning left, they walked on until they spotted a gathering of people and horses.

'It looks as though we're here,' Effie said. 'Look at all those dogs milling about; goodness, are these the ones that live here at The Grange?'

'No, these are the hounds that belong to the hunt. They're only meeting here before they set off. Can you see the man in the red jacket, with the horn? Watch when he plays a tune and all the dogs follow. I'm told people follow on foot as well, but that's about as much as I know,' Helen explained. 'It all looks very exciting.'

'Can we follow?' Dorothy asked as they arrived at the gate to The Grange.

'Not this time,' Helen said. 'I believe this hunt is called the North Kent Hounds and there is quite a history surrounding it. We will have to learn more.'

'That's right,' a middle-aged man said as he walked up, holding his hand out. 'Hello, Helen, it's a cold day for you all to be out walking.'

'I wanted to bring the children to see the hunt before it set off. This is Effie and her children, who will be living here with me.'

Stan Trentham shook Effie's hand firmly. 'Pleased to have you on board, and welcome, young ladies. What would you say to a nice hot cup of cocoa? Jean's just gone off to put the kettle on. Let's just wave the last of the stragglers off, and then we can go inside.'

'Oh, I didn't want to put you out,' Helen said. 'We only came up to see the hounds.'

'Nonsense, you must all come inside and rest for a while and warm up. Why, the children's faces are almost blue with the cold. Would you like to see where you're going to live while you're here?' he asked.

'We certainly would, if it's no trouble,' Effie said shyly. 'You have no idea just how grateful I am for your generous offer. I'll work as hard as I can helping Jean.'

'I'm sure you will. It's non-stop here, but we all muck in together to get the work done.'

'We wanted to ask about bathing the dogs,' Dorothy said, while her younger sister asked about growing vegetables.

Stan rubbed his bristly chin, looking at the children's expectant eyes before bursting out laughing. 'We'll have to see about that. Come along, let's get inside out of the cold.'

Jean welcomed them all into the large kitchen and helped take the girls' coats off. 'That's better, at least you'll get the benefit when you put them on to go outside again.'

'That's what my mum says,' Jane commented.

'And so she would, it's a clever thing to say. All mums are very clever, so you listen to her,' Jean smiled, giving a wink to Effie and Helen. 'Now, hands up who wants cocoa. I've got some bacon on the go as well. Would you like a slice between some buttered bread, girls?'

There was a round of agreement as Effie hung her coat over the back of a chair tucked under the large scrubbed wooden table. 'I'll give you a hand. Just tell me where things are, and I'll get on with it.'

'Perhaps you could butter the bread? The bacon will see to itself in the pan, I'll make the cocoa. Stan, why don't you show Helen the office; I hope you don't run away when you see the mess in there! I used to be able to go in and tidy up, but since we've been short-handed it's out of the question. After we've eaten and tidied up, I'll take you over to show you the accommodation. I wish I'd had time to tidy up in there, but you know what it's been like . . .'

Helen waited for Jean to draw breath so she could

speak. 'We'll be fine, don't you worry about a thing. A bit of tidying up never hurt anyone.'

As Helen followed Stan into his office, she was surprised at how large it was.

'I used to have a smaller office out the back. But it made sense to move it to here in the library, where it's warmer,' he said, as she looked around at the wood-panelled walls and the heavy velvet curtains hanging from tall windows. Every conceivable surface was stacked with paperwork, magazines . . . she even spotted a few coloured cards and silk rosettes.

'These are pretty,' she said, picking one up. 'Oh, it's a prize from a dog show.'

'Hardly any of them running anymore. Most shows have closed down for the duration. It's a rum do when the sport of dog showing stops. In fact, we've had a bit of a problem in that some people feel they can't feed their dogs, and are having them put down.'

'Oh, how awful,' Helen said. 'I've heard of such things and read about them in the newspapers, but I really hoped it wasn't true.'

'Every word of it is true. What with women and kids being evacuated and not being able to take their pets with them, and men being called up and not having anyone to care for their dogs; then, of course, there's the worry of how they're going to find enough money to feed them. I'm sorry to say, the general dog-owning public think more of themselves right now than their dogs.'

Helen decided she really liked this man. It was clear that he cared a great deal for the dogs. If only he cared as much about keeping his paperwork straight, she thought as she looked around her. 'When can we move in? I'd really like to get stuck in here and also learn more about the dogs.'

'Would tomorrow be too soon?' he grinned.

It was tempting – but thinking of her mother needing a new housekeeper, and knowing she'd only just dropped a letter to *The Lady* in the postbox at the end of her road, Helen knew it wouldn't be fair. 'One week from today?' she suggested. 'But in that week, we can come over and sort out our accommodation and start to move our things. Speaking for myself, that will take a few trips.'

'There is a car you can use. I take it you can drive?'

'Yes . . . although I've not driven much lately.'

'You'll soon get used to it again. It's like riding a bike: you never forget.'

Helen had never been a confident driver, but didn't feel this was the moment to say so.

'I'll let the local bobby know you have permission to use the vehicle. In the meantime, if anyone asks, you're doing essential work for the war effort on my behalf. I'll leave a bale of hay on the back seat. It'll be all right,' he said, noticing her alarmed expression. 'There'll be no problem. Let's just say I have contacts.' He gave her a crafty wink.

11

Richard stood on the doorstep of The Maples, stamping his feet to keep his circulation moving. Even wearing his RAF uniform and greatcoat, he felt cold. Hopefully Helen would invite him in; then again, when she'd heard what he had to say, she might slam the door in his face.

He looked up as the door opened and Helen's mother stood before him. 'Good afternoon, Mrs Davis. May I have a word with your daughter, please?'

'My daughter is moving out of the house. Goodness knows when, as she never tells me anything these days.'

'Would you be able to give me her new address, and I'll pay her a visit there? I have some news about the investigation into her husband's death that I feel she should know. I'd especially like her to hear it before the information gets into the newspapers.'

Mrs Davis raised her eyebrows, showing interest. 'You may as well come in, as I don't like discussing business on the doorstep. I'm not sure what the neighbours would say.'

He followed her inside, wondering, when the house was a distance from any other property, how anyone would notice. Even if he'd been spotted pulling up in his vehicle, the neighbours would only have seen an RAF officer paying a visit. It never ceased to amaze him how some people's minds worked.

'Please take a seat and warm yourself. I will give my housekeeper a call to bring up a hot drink; it is almost teatime,' she said, making it sound like an accusation. He declined the offer, but even so she rang a rather large bell on the sideboard and seconds later a harassed-looking woman appeared. Richard recognized her from his last visit here. 'Can I help you, Mrs Davis?' she asked, drying her hands on her apron.

'Would you bring tea, and call my husband in. I feel he should hear whatever this man has to say.'

'Yes, ma'am,' Effie said, hurrying away.

Richard wasn't sure he wanted to tell Helen's parents the news without her being present. Although he wasn't giving any secrets away, it didn't feel quite right. 'I wonder, would you give me her address?' he asked for a second time.

Hillary Davis dismissed his question with a wave of the hand. 'It seems my housekeeper knows, as she is moving away with her tomorrow. Goodness knows how I am going to cope,' she said. 'All the applicants so far have been unsuitable. Trust my daughter to not think things through properly. If these final applicants aren't suitable, Effie will just have to stay here. If she insists on going, she will leave without references; that'll show her,' she sniffed.

Richard decided not to comment. He already knew that Helen wasn't happy at home; good luck to her if she'd found somewhere else. However, she had been requested to keep the police informed if she should spend time away from this address. Hopefully he could get the housekeeper to give him an idea before he left.

'Please help yourself to a sandwich,' Mrs Davis said, after Effie placed a tray on an occasional table and bobbed a curtsy to her mistress. She gave him a sideways glance as she left, which he acknowledged with a slight nod. Yes, he would do his best to find out where Helen was by speaking to Effie.

'Oh, finally my husband has honoured us with his company,' Hillary Davis said as a tall man with a slight stoop joined them, giving Richard a puzzled scowl. 'Why is the RAF here, Hillary?' he asked, ignoring Richard.

Richard held up his arm, pointing to the badge of the RAF police. 'I'm on special secondment to Biggin Hill while at the same time continuing my investigations into the death of Mrs Wentworth's husband.'

Gavin Davis piled a plate with sandwiches but did not sit down, much to his wife's annoyance. 'What's there to investigate? Wasn't it a simple case of being in the wrong place at the wrong time – a gas explosion, I believe?'

'I'm sorry, I thought your daughter would have informed you – Mr Wentworth was dead before the explosion. It's a case of foul play,' Richard explained, not wishing to give too many details.

Hillary Davis flinched. 'You mean he was murdered?' She fanned herself with a napkin. 'That all sounds rather unseemly. Who would have done such a thing?'

Richard had summed her up very quickly. 'Would you tell me how well you knew John Wentworth? Did he come here often – or perhaps you visited him in London?'

'Surely you don't have us on the list of suspects?' she sniffed, glancing at her husband, who stuffed another sandwich into his mouth.

'No, I'm merely trying to piece together a picture of the private John Wentworth, rather than the public figure we all know from newspapers and the wireless.'

'You're asking the wrong people,' Gavin Davis snarled. 'Once Helen married, she thought she'd gone up in the world and wanted nothing to do with us. I found him unbearable, a right know-it-all. When he asked for her hand in marriage I told him so, as well.'

'Now, dear – this gentleman doesn't need to know what goes on behind our closed doors. I was pleased for my daughter. She worked hard in her job and made a good marriage. What more could a mother ask for her daughter? There was talk, you know, of him one day being considered for prime minister. I know it was only talk, but as I told my friends, there must be something in it for the rumour to start in the first place. It is such a shame. I had such hopes for my daughter's prospects – and now she's going to the dogs.'

'I'm sorry?'

'The dog kennels. She's going to work at the kennels, of all places.' Mrs Davis flinched, belatedly realizing she'd slipped up: she had clearly known all along where her daughter was moving. 'It is neither here nor there what Helen's up to now. Her prospects are ruined and she'll end up an old maid,' she huffed.

Richard thought for a moment, sipping his tea. 'And what's your line of work, Mr Davis, if I might ask?'

'I've been pensioned off for a few years now.'

'He has suffered with his nerves ever since the first war,' his wife said. 'And not been the same since – although I didn't know Gavin at the time,' she added with a coy smile. 'This is my second marriage.'

'You worked locally?' Richard asked.

'No, my work was in the suburbs of London. I ran a department for one of the councils. My work was quite important.'

'A life well spent, you could say,' Richard said politely, brushing a few crumbs from the front of his jacket. 'Working in London, did you see your daughter very often?'

'As Helen will tell you, I'm only the stepfather, and in her opinion I'm of no importance. She conveniently forgets that if it wasn't for me, there would have been no food on the table when I married her mother. She didn't want to know us once she was mixing with the great and the good of the political world,' he sneered.

Richard got to his feet. 'I must thank you for the refreshments. I'll leave you to finish your correspondence,' he said, nodding towards the six envelopes balanced on the arm of Hillary's chair. 'I'll let myself out,' he said, wishing them good day.

Closing the front door behind him, he walked along the side of the house towards the sound of children playing in the garden. They stopped to look at him. 'Hello there. Is your mummy about?'

'She's in the kitchen. Through that door,' the smaller child said.

He followed to where she was pointing and knocked on the open door. 'Excuse me,' he said, startling Effie, who put her hand to her throat in shock. 'I didn't mean to make you jump. I wondered if you could tell me where Helen is moving to? You may remember me from my last visit here, and from the party at Lizzie Donnington's house – although I was wearing my red outfit at the time,' he grinned, looking over his shoulder to where the two children were watching.

Effie chuckled. 'Yes, I remember – you're the gentleman investigating the death of Miss Helen's husband. Let me write down the address of where we're all moving to. Me and the kids are going with Helen,' she beamed. 'It's a fresh start for all of us.'

'I imagine it must be. I hope you'll be very happy,' he said as he took the slip of paper and bid her good afternoon.

The old car jerked several times as Helen gripped the steering wheel. She'd never been a confident driver, and this old vehicle was testing her nerves to the limit as she made her way down the lane towards her mother's house. 'At least this is the last trip,' she muttered to herself, pulling up close behind her stepfather's Austin. Gavin was standing beside it.

'New job and you can drive the car?' he said, looking down his nose at the mud-spattered vehicle as she got out.

'My new employer lent it to me so we could move our bits and pieces to our new home,' she snapped back. 'This is used for business, that's why I am able to drive it occasionally.' She wasn't going to tell him that it had taken Stan Trentham a little while to get the vehicle running smoothly before siphoning off petrol from the open-back truck used for his business. 'I do sometimes wonder how you manage to run a vehicle, Gavin, when you don't work or help the war effort?'

He stopped and threw the cloth he'd been using to polish his windscreen to the ground. Wagging a finger at Helen, he walked closer. She took a step back. 'Let me tell you . . .' he started to say in a threatening manner, getting even closer. He stopped mid-sentence as the two children came running towards them, both carrying small boxes.

'Can we put these in the car, please?' they both chimed.

'Yes, if you could both get in the car and hold them on your laps because we have a few more things to collect. Then we can go to our new home and settle in,' she said, looking back over her shoulder as Gavin stood watching her.

Locking the girls into the car, she hurried up the side of the house and into the kitchen. 'Do you have much more?'

'I've taken all the bits out of my bedroom,' Effie said, 'and also what was mine from the pantry. I did like you said and packed up some of the older saucepans and crockery. Are you sure your mother won't miss them?'

'My mother only likes the finer things placed in front of her, thanks to Gavin's influence. She will have no idea anything is missing,' Helen said, picking up the larger of the boxes on the table. 'It'll be a tight fit in the car, but I really don't want to make another journey if I can help it. He's poking about, and I can't be bothered to argue with him again.' She shivered.

'You really don't like him, do you?' Effie asked, looking concerned.

'Let's just say I wouldn't trust him further than I could spit – so can we get back out to the car, as the girls are waiting. Come on, let's get cracking. I don't like leaving them sitting in the car while he's about. He's so bad-tempered,' she said.

Effie grabbed the nearest box and hurried out of the house. Was there something Helen wasn't telling her?

Back at The Grange, with the car parked safely in the garage underneath their first-floor rooms, they carried the last of their possessions up the outside staircase and into the large open living area. 'I think we should celebrate,' Effie declared, noting that Helen still looked preoccupied. 'Can you take that tin out of my bag, please, Helen, while I put the kettle on? And I have a bottle of lemonade I made yesterday for you two,' she said, as the girls jumped up and down in excitement.

'This looks nice,' Helen said as she opened the tin to discover a jam-filled sponge cake. 'That looks like black-berry jam, if I'm not mistaken?'

'All made with my own fair hands,' Effie said. 'I picked the blackberries a few months ago and used my own ingredients to make the jam. I've never took anything that doesn't belong to me.'

Helen scolded her. 'I don't imagine for one moment that you would. You never have to explain a thing to me; I trust you one hundred per cent. I'm afraid I can't say the same about myself, though,' she said, reaching into her own bag for a large tinned ham. One by one, she lifted out several more tins of corned beef and Spam, along with some cans of fruit and other tinned goods. 'They were at the back of the pantry. I did purchase some of the items myself, but the others I purloined for the war effort. Our war effort, that is,' she grinned.

'We won't starve, that's for sure,' Effie laughed as she tipped out another bag and vegetables tumbled onto the table.

'It serves Mother right. She didn't deserve to have such a loyal staff member. Why, the children are absolute darlings and have been no trouble at all in the house. By complaining, she lost not only you but me as well. She's had plenty of suitable applicants for your replacement, so if she can't find somebody amongst that lot then she'll just have to roll up her sleeves and do her own housekeeping.'

Effie clapped her hands over her mouth and tittered. 'I'd not have said that myself, but I do agree with every word you've spoken. Oh, I forgot to tell you: that RAF policeman came to find you yesterday afternoon. The poor soul was lumbered with having afternoon tea with your parents and I overheard your mother saying she didn't know where you were moving to. When I went back to the kitchen, I wrote our new address on a piece of paper ready to slip to him. But then he appeared at the kitchen door – he did give me a start, I can tell you. I did do the right thing, didn't I? He's a nice chap, isn't he?'

A jumble of emotions stopped Helen in her tracks while she was digging out plates from one of the boxes. She had such mixed feelings about Richard. She should pull herself together; he was investigating the murder of John, and that was all he meant to her. Then she remembered his kiss and ran her fingers over her lips, deep in thought.

'It's like that, is it?' Effie said, giving her a little grin and a nudge.

'Stop it,' Helen laughed, pushing Effie away. 'I admit he's a nice man, but I'm recently widowed so I can't think of anything else for the moment. All that matters is that we're away from The Maples and my awful stepfather. We are safe here.'

'Safe? That's a funny word to use. If I may say so, your stepfather gives me the creeps – and he has caused you pain, am I right? I won't ask about him again, but I want to say thank you for thinking of me and the girls and getting us away from there.'

'Let's not mention him again. We will be happy here. Come on, let's eat this cake and drink up, then we can go out and investigate our new home,' Helen said as she sliced into the cake with a large knife.

'I'm glad I bumped into you,' Stan said, as the girls ran ahead of the two women down the steps and into the yard at the side of The Grange. 'There was a delivery for you earlier today, and I've also dug out a few more sticks of furniture for your bedroom,' he said to Effie. 'It didn't feel right that there was only one large bed in your room and the three of you sharing in there, so I pulled out two single beds and the mattresses. If you can manage for tonight, we can set them up in the morning.'

Effie was overjoyed. 'We would've been more than comfortable top to toe in that big bed, but I can't thank you enough,' she smiled, her cheeks turning a little pink as he watched her.

'There is a bundle of bedding as well, but it might need a wash or at least airing,' he added. 'Jean sorted them out, so they should be good enough to use.'

Before Effie could thank him once more, he turned to the two girls. 'Now, where are you off to?' he asked.

'We are going to take a look around before it gets too dark,' Dorothy said politely. 'Do you think we could see the dogs?'

'I can do better than that. I can show you some new puppies,' Stan said. 'Follow me, young ladies.'

Helen and Effie laughed as the two children took his hands and skipped along beside him until they reached the first barn, a hundred yards from the house. Pulling open the side door, he ushered them all in and closed it behind them.

'Oh, it's lovely and warm in here,' Helen said, pulling off her woolly hat. 'Do you keep all the dogs in here?'

'Just my own. I breed Old English Sheepdogs,' he said, opening a wooden gate halfway along the barn. Six large, shaggy-coated grey-and-white dogs bounded out, sniffing around the new visitors. At once the girls wrapped their arms around the necks of two of the dogs and hugged them while trying to avoid their long pink tongues.

'They are very big,' Dorothy said, as she stood looking almost face to face with the one who had two black ears.

'That's Johnny, and the one you're stroking is Bert. The other four are Jenny, Florence, Bluebell and Dolly. You will often see them wandering around the yard or in the house; that doesn't bother you, does it?' he asked.

'No, not at all,' both women said as they joined in, stroking the gentle giants.

'I'll just put them behind the gate, and then I'll show you the puppies. They are four weeks old now, and the mum is still in with them. Her name is Holly,' he said, turning to open another gate closer to them. 'Watch the puppies or they will escape. They're at the age now where they are starting to investigate the world around them.'

'My goodness,' Helen exclaimed as eight black-and-white puppies ran up to greet them. 'I've never seen anything so sweet in all my life.'

Effie and the children bent down to stroke the puppies, who ran around their legs making small yelping noises while the mother stood patiently behind them waiting for her turn for a fuss.

'Are people still buying puppies during the war?'

Stan nodded. 'Yes. Elders in each breed registered in this country are monitoring the situation with dog owners carefully. We need to ensure the future of all our breeds, or they will die out, and none of us wish to see a sad future with some breeds lost forever. Old English Sheepdogs, or Bobtails, as they are also called, are a working breed. You will see them on farms herding and guarding cattle. These ones here, all but one, will go off to farms that have always had Bobtails earning their keep on the land. They are biddable dogs who also make perfect family pets – but while this war lasts I won't be allowing any to go to family homes. It's not fair on the dogs, and with the best will in the world I don't feel it's right for the families to have the added worry.'

Helen was impressed by Stan's ethics. 'You say all but

one; why is that?' she asked, watching him lean over and pick up a puppy that stood out because of a black eyepatch and one black leg.

'I like to think this one here is the future of the breed. I plan to always keep one from every litter, not that I have many. That way, come the end of the war – whenever that will be – I'll have stock to keep my bloodlines running, and the breed won't die out.'

'I had no idea so much thought went into dog breeding. When she's older, will you take her to dog shows?' Helen asked, thinking of the pretty rosettes and numerous prize cards she'd seen in his library.

'Owning a pure-bred dog is not all about exhibiting our stock, although you wouldn't think it from some of the young upstarts in the game right now,' he said, shaking his head.

'I'd love to know more,' Helen said. 'Are there any books I could borrow?'

'I'll dig some out for you. I look forward to teaching you all about it, but now I must get on, as the other dogs need feeding.'

Effie stood up and brushed the straw from her knees. 'Other dogs? Are they boarders?'

Stan rubbed his bristly chin as he chose his words. 'In a way, you could say that. These are the ones I've taken on when people can no longer care for them. Do you want to see them?'

'Yes please,' the children chanted together, putting down the puppies they were holding and watching them run over to their mother, who had settled in the straw bedding.

'Follow me, ladies,' he said, closing gates behind them as they left the barn. They walked down a cinder path away from the house to where a long concrete building was set in the corner of a paddock. 'It's likely to be noisy. This crowd aren't as well-mannered as the Bobtails,' he said as he opened the door at one end of the building.

'They certainly are noisy.' Helen put her hands over her ears as a cacophony of high yaps and deep barks filled the air.

'They are shut in for the night. I let them out into the pens through those doors,' he said, waving his hand towards small metal gates in each pen. 'They have the paddock to run free as well, but we have set times for that. I don't like the Bobtails in with them because they keep herding them, and not all of the newer visitors appreciate it,' he grinned.

'You say visitors. Do they still belong to someone?' Effie asked, enchanted by all the expectant faces looking towards Stan. They seemed to adore him, she thought.

He started to point at various dogs before saying, 'Those have been abandoned, tied at the gate. These two belong to someone who has joined the army and has no one to care for them.' He stroked the heads of two adult Saint Bernards. 'I've promised to keep them safe until he returns; if he doesn't, well, it's only two more mouths to feed. They can live out their lives here; they are no trouble at all.'

'They're pretty large mouths,' Jane said in a serious tone.

'Can we help you look after the dogs?' Dorothy asked expectantly.

Stan looked between the pair of them. 'You look old enough to learn a bit about life here at The Grange. As long as your mum says it's okay, you can take on some chores to help with the dogs. I'll give you pocket money for helping out.'

He held his hands up to silence her as Effie started to protest that he'd been more than generous already.

'No, I insist, but be warned we start working early,' he said, giving the girls a stern look. 'After the first chores of the day, you come to the kitchen where Jean gives us all breakfast, every one of us,' he said, looking at Effie, Helen and the children in turn.

'I think we've landed on our feet here,' Effie grinned. 'So much better than where I used to work,' she added, before giving Helen an apologetic look.

'I agree with you,' Helen said. 'It feels as though a new chapter in my life has just begun. Stan seems to have adopted us just like his stray dogs.'

Helen watched as the children helped Stan by scooping out cooked meat from large pans and dividing it out into row upon row of dog bowls before carrying them into each kennel that housed half a dozen small dogs or several larger ones. They watched as the bowls were quickly emptied and heads turned to lap up water from galvanized buckets. Effie collected the empty bowls, taking them to a stone sink at one end of the kennel and washing each one carefully before leaving them to dry on a wooden draining board.

'This must cost you a bomb,' she said to Stan, who'd been distributing fresh straw in the bed area of each kennel. 'However do you cope?'

'Well, friends muck in, and there's also the hunt.'

'The hunt? Haven't they got dogs of their own?' Helen asked, thinking of the various people on horseback that they'd seen at the front of The Grange when they'd visited on Boxing Day. She'd been quite disappointed that the motley crew of people on horseback had looked nothing like the smart prints her mother had hanging on the wall in the dining room. Apart from one man in the traditional red jacket, to her they had looked more like farmers and riders out for a hack, rather than what she'd expected of a hunt.

'It's like this; I let them use my fields to hunt, and in return they keep me in horsemeat. You're not squeamish, are you?'

'I never have been, but it depends what you're going to tell me next.'

'When horses die, they've got to go somewhere. They're not buried in the back garden like a family cat or dog would be. The pack of hounds disposes of most of the horsemeat, although they keep some back for me. The local butcher rides out as well, and I look after his animals and he drops off tripe, offal and the like. It's the way of the countryside,' he said, watching Helen's face closely as she did her best not to grimace. After a moment he let out a large guffaw. 'You'll do,' he said.

They left Effie and the children to clear up, and headed back to the house and into the messy library. As they worked, Helen told Stan a little about her late husband's work for the Ministry of Food and plans he'd mentioned about rationing, as well as about educating the people of Great Britain to grow their own food.

Stan scratched his head. 'That gives me an idea. There's a two-acre patch of ground that stands on its own just up the lane from here. I won it years ago in a game of cards at the pub. I've never gotten round to clearing it. But it might be something we could organize and turn into allotments for locals to use.'

'I see you have an eye for business,' Helen said, admiring the way he'd come up with a solution for the local community.

'Oh, I'll not charge anyone. We could ask for a basket of veg every so often as payment.'

Helen smiled. Stan Trentham was a gem of a man who seemed to think of others much more than himself.

'By the way, there's that box that was delivered here for you earlier,' he said, pointing to a chair close to the side door where the box rested.

'I wonder who it could have come from, and what's inside?'

'You won't find out standing there staring at it,' he laughed. 'Be assured I don't think it's horsemeat or tripe, so you'll be okay. It was delivered here by some young RAF chap who seemed disappointed you weren't here.'

Helen felt her cheeks start to burn and turned away to open the box. Pulling back the flaps, she spotted an envelope on top of parcels wrapped in brown paper. Thinking it must have been Richard who had delivered the box, she opened the envelope and pulled out a single sheet of paper. A few lines inside confirmed her guess. The words stirred butterflies in her stomach as she read them:

*Please accept this gift for you and your friends as
you move into your new home. I would like to call on you
tomorrow at eleven a.m., but will understand if you're
busy. If it's not convenient, please leave a message for me
using this telephone number.*

My fondest regards,
Richard Gladstone

'Going by the colour of your cheeks, I'd say you have an admirer.'

'No, it's nothing like that. I've only been widowed these past three months. I can't even think of such things,' she said as she started to poke amongst the parcels. They were labelled: she could see dried fruit, sugar, flour, and underneath, bottled fruits. 'Oh my goodness,' she whispered as, digging deep, she came across several boxes of sweets and a bar of chocolate. The dear, dear man, she thought to herself – what a considerate gesture.

The next morning started early, as they all tracked off to help out in the kennels. Helen thought it seemed rather too early to go into the office to start work, so decided to give Effie and the girls a hand. They walked down the track towards the orphan dogs, as the children had named them, and spotted Stan already there.

'We're not late, are we?' Effie asked. 'We'll have to try harder tomorrow morning,' she told the children.

'Not at all; I wanted to be here to show you the ropes. You can devise your own routine. As long as the animals are fed, watered and their kennels cleaned out before nine, it doesn't matter what you do first. I'm grateful to have such willing workers. I have this for you, Helen,' he said, reaching into his pocket and pulling out a key. 'It opens the side door in the passage next to the office – that way you can come and go as you please. I have left a contract of sorts on the desk for you to check your hours. If you disagree, we can alter them. As I've said before, I'm an easy-going chap. Just remember that come nine o'clock, Jean expects us all in the kitchen for breakfast.' He glanced from Helen to Effie, who both nodded to show that everything was clear. 'I'll be off now, as I've got the Bobtails to sort out. I'll catch you later.'

Helen continued helping Effie and the girls for another fifteen minutes before heading up to the office, letting herself in by the side door. She decided to sort out the paperwork scattered all over the desk and chair to begin with; at least then she'd have somewhere to sit while she sifted through the rest.

She'd not been there five minutes when Jean came in through the other door. 'I'll just leave this for you, my love,' she said, placing a cup of tea on the corner of the desk. 'Don't forget to come in for breakfast,' she added, before leaving Helen alone.

Helen checked the clock on the wall. She had an hour – it should be possible to wade through quite a bit by then. She reached for a heap of papers, dividing them into one pile for invoices and payment requests, another for letters and enquiries about the housing of dogs, and a third for the personal paperwork that seemed to be left willy-nilly all over the desk. As she came across books, newspapers and magazines, she moved them over to a side table, not knowing where else to put them. 'Stan will have to sort these out for himself,' she muttered. The desk was quite dusty, so after breakfast she would see if Jean had any cleaning materials she could use.

Amongst the piles, she found more of the pretty prize cards that marked the names of dog show societies and the placement of winning dogs. She could see Stan's name was on them, along with some unusual names of the dogs. These must be their pedigree names, she thought as she read a couple aloud: 'Trueblue That's the Ticket Boy . . . Trueblue Mummy's Boy.' Most had the name 'Trueblue' at the beginning of the official titles. 'I'll have to ask Stan what that means. It's obvious I have a lot to learn about the dog world.'

She got up and moved to a bookshelf where there were several books about the breed, pulling out one that had been published twenty years earlier. She was still reading when Jean shouted 'Breakfast's up' from the kitchen. Reluctant to stop halfway through a chapter and also having numerous questions, she slipped it into the pocket of her cardigan and headed through to the large kitchen. Effie and the girls were already seated at the table along with several other people and just then Stan joined them, rubbing his hands together.

'It's getting chillier out there. Make sure you light the fire in the library, Helen, you'll get frozen to the bone sitting still for so long otherwise. Did you happen to look at the contract I left for you?'

'I did and it's very generous; are you sure you don't want me to work longer hours? There's quite a lot for me to do, and I'd also like to learn more about your world,' she said, taking the book from her pocket.

'Ah, you found the Tilley book. It's one of the best. Take it with you, and borrow any others that catch your eye.'

Effie helped Jean carry food to the table and placed plates of fried bread, eggs and sausages in front of everyone.

Stan introduced them to a couple who'd joined him at the table. 'This is Jake and Sarah, they've come to collect one of my boys to take back with them.'

Without thinking, Helen said, 'Oh, how can you bear to give them away, especially the older ones?'

Stan and the couple laughed. 'No, he's only going with them for a couple of weeks,' he explained. He glanced over to the two girls, who'd started eating their food, before whispering, 'It's easier if he goes to stay with them to serve their bitch, rather than bring her here at the moment, as we have so much going on. It should be a good mating, as the bitch also comes from my lines going back a few generations. Their place is a good fifty miles from here, so it makes sense for them to stay over and then leave with the boy after breakfast.'

Helen was embarrassed. 'I have so much to learn,' she said as she looked back at the book where she'd marked several pages with slips of paper. 'Perhaps when you have a little time you can answer some questions and explain about the show world?'

'Oh, he will find time,' Jake said as his wife agreed. 'He's always ready to chat about dogs.'

As talk turned to other subjects, Helen started to eat her meal. 'This is delicious, Jean, thank you, but surely we should be contributing something?'

'Didn't you read your contract properly?' Stan asked, looking up from where he'd been buttering his toast. 'Meals are included in your employment – that includes you, Effie – and of course the children are more than welcome. They've worked hard this morning, don't forget. I'll be giving you pocket money come Friday afternoon,' he reminded them, much to the girls' delight. 'Don't forget to ask Jean for your contract too, Effie.'

'There is no need, sir, I don't usually have one.'

'In this house, no member of my staff works longer than the hours they are supposed to. I do not do it myself and I don't expect anyone else to. Now, Jean tells me that the pair of you take part in the sewing circle down at Dalton Court with that Canadian couple. It would make sense if Jean used the truck to take you, as you're all travelling in the same direction. And you two are going to start at the little school in the barn, I hear?'

Dorothy looked up with egg yolk around her mouth. 'Yes, we're looking forward to it. The teacher is lovely and it's better than being evacuated. We like it here,' she grinned before returning to her meal.

'One of us will drive them down, if you don't have a meeting. We can work it out between us,' he said.

'But I planned to walk them down there,' Effie said.

'And I said I'd collect them in the afternoons,' Helen added.

Stan wouldn't hear of it. 'It's a nice walk in the summer, but at this time of year it's a bit of a bugger.'

The children giggled, but stopped when they saw Effie frown. 'Eat up, girls, then you can go back to our place and read your books until I'm finished helping Jean.'

'There's no need for that,' Jean said. 'The drawing room is warm and cosy, they can go in there for now if they want to read. When I'm done in the kitchen I'm off to feed the chickens and see to the kitchen garden, they can come and help if they want?'

'But . . .' Effie started to say. 'What do you want me to do?'

Jean started to explain about cleaning the bedrooms and the other rooms in the house.

'You've no need to clean the library,' Helen interrupted them. 'If I can take some cleaning items back to the room with me, I can do it as I sort out the paperwork. It won't take long.'

'If you're sure, it will be one less job for us,' Jean grinned, nudging Effie with her elbow.

'Will it be all right if I pop back to our accommodation? Someone is coming to see me at eleven. I'll only be half an hour or so?'

Stan sighed. 'Oh, you women! You seem to worry about so many things. Take all the time you want, I don't care. I know you'll do your jobs, so stop your worrying. There's a war going on outside this house, so let's at least try and stay happy here at The Grange, shall we?'

12

'You're dead on time,' Helen said, opening the door to Richard just as the small clock on the mantelpiece of her new home chimed the hour. She cringed and could have kicked herself for saying 'dead' – it was one of those words people avoided using at funerals, or when they met the recently bereaved and tried to make small talk. For her to use the word would remind him that she was a widow, and possibly remind him of that inappropriate kiss.

She'd had time since leaving the dusty library for a quick wash and change into one of her cotton day dresses. Feeling chilly, she'd pulled on a cardigan, added a dash of lipstick and run a brush through her unruly curls, and she'd been ready to greet him seconds before he knocked on the door.

'It's my RAF training. However hard I try, I can't be early or late, if that makes any sense?'

'It would make more sense,' she said, stepping back to let him in, 'if you could explain to me how you can be a police inspector and in the RAF? Surely the two careers are separate?'

'To a civilian, it may seem so. Every service has its police division. Because of your late husband's position, and also him once serving in the RAF, I was called in to investigate his death. I'm also known to people in the cabinet, so it made sense for me to take on the investigation.'

'That seems sensible when you put it like that. I'm sorry to question you about it, but it has been on my mind for a while,' she said, filling the kettle and placing it on the stove. Opening a small tin, she took out a few biscuits and put them on a plate next to the cups and saucers. 'Please do take a seat,' she added, realizing he was still standing, and nodding to a couple of armchairs placed either side of a log-burning stove. 'Oh, and let me take your coat.' She felt a little flustered, and wondered what had happened to her social skills in the few months since she'd left London. 'I've not long got back in myself,' she continued as she took the coat and hung it on the coat stand beside the door. 'I must thank you for the gift you sent – it was most appreciated, but you really shouldn't have done it.'

'Think nothing of it. Besides, it meant you would have biscuits to offer me when I visited.'

Helen wasn't sure whether offering someone the food they'd recently given as a gift was proper etiquette, but it was too late to worry about that now. 'Next time you visit, I promise to provide something we've made ourselves,' she said before checking herself. What must he think? She had openly assumed that he would be visiting her again.

He smiled and seemed to know what she was thinking. 'I'll look forward to that.'

Helen was saved by the whistle from the kettle, and hurried to make the tea. At least I supplied the tea leaves, she thought to herself as she placed the knitted tea cosy over the brown earthenware teapot. 'It will only be a couple of minutes.' She sat down opposite him.

'How are you enjoying your new home and job, or is it too soon to ask?' He looked around the long room that housed the sitting area and kitchen, with a door leading through to a small bathroom and two bedrooms at one end.

'We like our new home. It's so cosy up here. Stan Trentham seems to be an ideal landlord and employer,' Helen enthused. 'The children simply adore helping out with the dogs, and Effie is in her element working with Jean Carter. I feel as though a load has been removed from my shoulders,' she added without thinking.

He narrowed his eyes. 'I take it you were not happy living with your mother and father . . . ?'

'Stepfather,' she snapped before he could finish his sentence.

'I'm sorry, my mistake. Why is there so much animosity between you? I called the other day while you were out and got the impression all wasn't well between you.'

Helen's laugh was bitter. 'Oh, well, sometimes he likes me far too much, other times he hates me for not liking him.' She rose to fetch the tea.

'How long has he been your stepfather?'

'Since I was ten. My mother had been widowed for six months when Gavin Davis appeared on the scene and swept her off her feet. He didn't have the same success with me,' she added quietly, placing cups, saucers and biscuits onto the tea tray and carrying it back to where they were sitting. Richard took the tray from her while she pulled forward a low table and placed it between them.

'Do you mind if we don't talk about him? He's not what you came here for.' Trying to lighten the mood, she asked if he'd enjoyed his trip to London just before Christmas.

'Yes, most enjoyable,' he smiled, his lips twitching as he spoke. 'I was sorry not to see you at breakfast. I thought we might travel back together.'

She could have kicked herself for mentioning the London trip, but she had been so desperate to turn the conversation away from her stepfather that she hadn't stopped to think; and now she'd dug another hole for herself. She felt as though she was walking over hot coals as she tried to choose the right words. 'I had errands to run. I thought you must have business to attend to, that's why I left so early.'

'My work didn't take long. There were a few things I needed to check out and then I too was heading back. It's that trip that I want to talk to you about.'

Helen felt a flutter in her stomach. So the kiss had meant something to him as well as to her? She regretted her harsh comments about her stepfather; she wasn't usually such a bitter woman, but whenever his name was mentioned . . .

'Are you sure your new employer can spare you for a little while? I feel as though I've imposed myself on you when you should be trying to make a good impression.'

Helen smiled and waved a hand, dismissing his comments. 'Stan is very good, I have quite a flexible contract. I suppose with us all mucking in and helping with the dogs, he's pretty easy-going.'

'I'd like to see the dogs before I leave, if that's possible?' Richard said, checking his watch.

'Why don't we finish this, and then we can walk down to see the puppies?' She felt it was the right thing to do, as he was making a social call.

'I'd like that. You know, your Stan Trentham is quite a name in the dog world.'

'I would think he is. I've been working in his study and I'm quite amazed by all the cards he's won and the champions he has bred. Do you know something about that world?'

'My mother breeds Collies – but on a much smaller scale than your Mr Trentham. When I rang her to ask if she knew of him, she couldn't stop talking about his successes and the standard of his dogs. She told me this place is his life, especially since he lost his wife to the Spanish flu when his son was only a couple of years old.'

Helen refrained from asking why Richard had apparently been checking up on where she was going to live. 'I didn't know any of that. He hasn't mentioned his private life but then he'd have no reason to, as I'm only an employee. I wonder where his son is?'

'Serving in France with the Buffs.'

'Oh, I see. It must be a worry for him, the poor man. Unless you'd like another cup of tea, shall we go down and see the puppies?' she said, getting to her feet.

'After you,' he replied. They both took their coats from the stand and stepped out into the chilly late morning air.

They took the path towards the barn where the Bobtails lived. Sliding the bolt back on the door, Helen pointed

221

towards the area, fenced off, where the puppies were. At once they all woke up and ran towards the couple.

'Who would believe these little bundles of fluff will turn into such big dogs?' Richard said, looking to where the other sheepdogs were leaning over the gate of their pens waiting for their share of the attention. 'Hello there,' he said, picking up one of the puppies.

Helen did the same. 'They are adorable, aren't they? If only they could stay this size.'

'Dogs this size are a big commitment. My mother's dogs are smaller than this and even she has her hands full.'

'I suppose any dog is a commitment,' she replied as she put her puppy back down and stroked the mother, who was patiently watching. 'Look, she's always smiling. She must be so proud of her little brood, bless her.'

'Have you got time to walk a couple of these?' Stan said, coming up behind them. 'One of my volunteers has twisted her ankle. They are no trouble,' he said, taking their silence as agreement. Pulling two leads from the hooks on the wall, he handed them to Richard. 'Take these two – being older, they prefer to dawdle. If you follow the cinder path down past the boarding kennels, you'll reach the first paddock. You can let them off the leads there and give them a good run. Put a couple of these in your pockets, then they will come back when it's time for you to head home,' he said, handing them each a dog biscuit.

'See you later, then,' Helen said to him. She gave Richard a grin. 'I hope you can spare another half hour. If you can't, I'll take them both myself.'

'No, I'm fine for an hour,' he said, looking down at

his overcoat. 'Although I may need to borrow a clothes brush before I leave. I'd also like to have that talk with you.'

'You can do that once we let the dogs out for their run,' she replied, as again her stomach gave a little flip. She'd never felt like this before – not when she met her husband, and not even after she was married. Deep in thought, she watched Richard expertly leading the dog down the cinder path while she was pulled along behind him.

'It looks like there's somewhere we can sit over there,' he said, as they closed the gate to the paddock and let the dogs loose.

They walked over to where a wooden bench was situated under the branches of an oak tree.

'We have a fine view here of the airfield. It's surprising how high up we are.' He looked over the fields below them.

Helen agreed, although she was dying to hear what he had to say. She was on the point of asking him to spit it out when he turned to her and took her hand. 'I don't want to worry you in any way, but we took Felicity Davenport in for questioning after you told me what happened the day you went up to London.'

Helen frowned. This was not what she had been expecting at all. Pulling her hand from his, she tucked it into her coat pocket. 'What did she say?'

'I can't tell you everything word for word. But not only did she deny any involvement with your late husband, she implied that you told her on several occasions how unhappy you were and that you wished you'd never married him.'

'But . . . but that day I saw her, she told me openly that she and John were in a relationship. She was quite rude about it, in fact; I told you what she said. Did she happen to say why her blouse was amongst my husband's clothes, and her scarf was in his pocket?'

'She gave perfectly reasonable answers to everything, and said she had lent the clothing to you. Her explanation for the scarf being in his pocket was that she'd left it behind in the office, and he had picked it up to take home to give to you because you were meeting her that day. She was also strongly implying that you'd killed your husband.'

Helen shook her head, not believing what he'd told her. 'Surely you didn't believe her? Why, that's ludicrous – quite a few people heard what she said to me when I went to the office. For one thing, Bella was there . . .'

Richard nodded. 'Yes, I intend to speak to colleagues of your husband, and to Bella Jones. I just wanted to let you know about your friend and wondered if perhaps in the next few days we could have a formal interview to get some more information about your husband's background. Also, any of your friends that knew him. I'd like to know more about Felicity Davenport as well.'

'Do I have to see you at the police station?' she asked, feeling worried.

'No, not at all. I've been doing some work at Lizzie's house. As long as I have my sergeant in attendance, we can do it there. Perhaps we could find some time when you're next at one of your quilting meetings?'

'I'm going to be there tomorrow afternoon; you know the room where I work with Lizzie. If it's convenient, I'd rather speak to you then and get it out of the way,' she said in a quiet voice.

He pulled a small diary from his pocket and checked. 'That's good for me, I don't have to be anywhere else. I'll have my sergeant available, and he can take notes while we have a formal interview. Now I'm really going to have to leave you,' he said as he checked his watch before standing up and brushing down the front of his coat. 'Will you be able to handle both dogs when you take them back to their kennel?'

'Don't worry about me. I can cope. Did you not want to use a clothes brush?'

'No, I can sort myself out back at the office.' He wished her a good morning and walked briskly away, shooing the dogs back as they tried to follow him through the gate of the paddock. When they saw he was going without them they both ran back to Helen, resting their heads on her lap as she stroked them distractedly.

'Well, lads, that wasn't the conversation I expected. There may not be many more walks with me if I'm arrested.'

'I'm so pleased you've settled into your new home,' Lizzie said after cross-examining Helen at length about her living accommodation and her job, as well as The Grange.

'You must come and visit, have tea with me. I'll give you the whole tour,' Helen said, returning her hug. 'I'm afraid our place is not as grand as yours' – she waved her arms around the workshop – 'but it's homely, and we like it. I do have a little corner for my sewing table, which is nice. I'm sure Stan will let me show you the dogs.'

225

'I'd simply adore that,' Lizzie said. 'We've always been dog owners. In fact, it's only living here in England that we've been without one. We had to leave Trixie behind,' she added, looking sad. 'She now lives with my older daughter and her children. Here, I have a photograph.' She went to a shelf and took down a small framed print. 'That's my Natalie, and the two little ones are Anita and Christine, with Trixie between them. They spoil her rotten, so I'm afraid if ever we're in a position to return home, the dog will stay with the family. I've lost her for good,' she said with a little chuckle.

'Have you considered taking on another dog? Perhaps even two – you have such lovely grounds here that are perfect for dogs. In fact, on the way here Jean was saying Stan is fast running out of space for the rescue dogs. Couldn't we help him by asking people to consider taking on one of the dogs – or if they can't, perhaps donate some money for their upkeep?' Helen suggested. 'What do you think?'

'Now that's an idea. Until you mentioned dogs, I'd not thought about taking on another. Two would be ideal, as they could keep each other company. Can you have a word with your Mr Trentham?'

'I'll speak to him this evening. We've been invited to dinner. I may be asking you for a few more favours after I've spoken to him. It's all to help the dogs, but I need Stan's agreement first.'

'Ask any time. I'll help in any way I can,' Lizzie said. 'Now let's take a look at this patchwork quilt of yours. I've laid it out on the table and I hope you don't mind, but I've stitched a few of the panels together.'

'Not at all. I'm thinking of going back to my mother's house to borrow her sewing machine now I have space. She doesn't use it, and it is still in my bedroom. If I set it up at home – my new home, that is – I can do some work in the evenings, and Effie will be able to use it too.'

'That sounds like an excellent idea. Why don't I take you home this evening and we can collect it on the way?'

Helen grimaced. 'That's good of you, but my mother and my stepfather . . .'

'You've told me enough about them for me to know what to expect, so don't you worry. I'm able to hold my own with many kinds of people; they don't frighten me at all. Your mother can't be all bad, to have turned out a daughter like you.'

'You are far too generous,' Helen chuckled. 'I like to think I take after my father more than my mother, and if anything, my stepfather is the person who taught me I need to be strong and also wary. I'd not wish his kind on anybody.'

Lizzie frowned as they made their way to the large table. She wanted to see this stepfather for herself. The little Helen had said about Gavin Davis had not made her warm to him at all.

'This is coming on a treat,' Helen said as she ran her hands over the pieces of fabric that had already been stitched together.

'I did wonder if you needed to use this?' Lizzie asked, pulling out the satin from the negligee Helen had found gift-wrapped in her husband's trunk.

Helen picked up the fabric, hating the feel of it between her fingers and knowing that it hadn't been purchased for

227

her. She took hold of it with both hands and ripped it several times before dropping it into a wastebasket nearby. 'I already have the reminder I need of Felicity in this project,' she said, stabbing her finger at the small piece of red inserted into one of the rings made from John's clothing. 'I don't need another.'

Lizzie frowned. 'Has something else happened?'

Helen told her about her conversation the day before with Richard Gladstone. 'I think he feels I am still one of the major suspects. In fact, I have to see him here this afternoon to be interviewed and sign my statement. I don't understand why they haven't caught someone yet.'

Lizzie tried to smooth over Helen's worries. 'Please don't feel there is more to this than what he has said. The authorities need to have formal paperwork rather than take notes from a couple of chats. As for it not being the police investigating – my Gerald told me that this is a joint investigation, due to your husband's important position in the government.' As she spoke, she glanced at the torn fabric in the bin and decided she'd better retrieve it and mention it to Richard. It might just add evidence to the case.

Before Helen could ask more, Lizzie turned back to the patchwork on the table. 'Now why don't you tell me more about the fabric in this quilt? I do admire the fine navy-blue woollen fabric, and this pretty green with cherries scattered around is delightful.'

Helen didn't wish Lizzie to feel she was always moaning; perhaps she should keep the investigation to herself in future? She'd hate to spoil a good friendship. 'This is from the suit John wore when we married.'

'It must have looked very smart. I would love to see some photographs; that's if you haven't thrown them away?'

'No, I have a small album in amongst my possessions back at my accommodation. Whatever I've found out since John's death, I should not forget the happy day when I walked down the aisle. When you come to visit, remind me to pull it out and show you.'

'Thank you. I'd like to see them. Was it a local church nearby where you married?'

'No,' Helen said, looking a little embarrassed. 'It was the small church where John is now buried in Oxford. His family have used it for generations, and it was important to him to continue the family tradition.'

'Did your stepfather give you away?'

Helen was aghast. 'Goodness, no; it was a small, intimate affair. A colleague of John's walked me down the aisle. Mother and Gavin were away at the time.'

Lizzie decided not to pursue the conversation. It certainly didn't sound right. She enjoyed reading the society pages and it seemed to her that every person of importance in England, plus those who spoke with a plum in their mouth, had large weddings with everybody who was anybody in attendance. 'What about the green fabric in your own circle of rings?' she asked, running her finger across the cherry pattern.

Helen smiled. 'It was a frock from my childhood. I have memories of wearing it when my father was alive. There was one summer when we caught a train and went to the coast. Mother wasn't keen and didn't even wish to sit on the beach. It couldn't have been long before he went away to serve in the Great War, so although it doesn't directly relate to the wedding bands, it holds a memory for me. I like to think my father made me the person I am today; I'd have loved him to be at my wedding. Does that sound silly?'

Lizzie felt so sad for her young friend, who seemed to have been through an awful lot in her life. 'I think it's admirable that you've included a memory of your father in a quilt that depicts your married life. I do wonder, though . . .' She stopped, not sure whether she should say any more. 'No, never mind.'

'Please do tell me,' Helen urged.

'It's just . . . you said that when this quilt is completed, you would give it to John's mother. But if you do, that will mean you no longer have that memory of your father for yourself.'

'Oh goodness, I hadn't thought of that,' Helen said, looking distraught. 'Would it be too hard to unpick it and put something else there?'

Lizzie turned to the pile of scrap fabric at the end of the table. 'Why don't you make something else for yourself – something drawn only from happy memories of your childhood? It could be a cushion. I see there's more of the green fabric here. Do you have anything else you'd like to add to it?'

'I do; there are some other items back at my mother's house. She's threatened to throw them out or use them for dusters. She doesn't seem to have an ounce of nostalgia in her bones. I could retrieve them and at least put them to one side, ready for my own personal memory piece.' Helen smiled at Lizzie. 'Thank you so much. Wherever do you get all these good ideas from?'

'From years of quilting and creating my own memories. Don't forget, I was brought up by quilters – remember all the quilts I've shown you? They are full of people's memories. And I always feel that even if you're going to give a quilt away, it's worth keeping some record of it. Why not do that? Keep a snippet of each fabric. I'll ask my husband to take a photograph of the finished quilt, and then I want you to write down the memory of each piece – yes, even the red fabric. Then we're going to seal it in an envelope and move on to happier projects.'

Helen hugged her. 'That's a marvellous idea. Now, shall we get cracking and finish piecing the fabric together? I want to move on as soon as possible,' she smiled, wishing it could be as easy to truly move on in her heart.

13

Helen was leaning closely in to the sewing machine, carefully trying to thread the needle, when there was a knock on the door of the workroom.

'Ouch,' she exclaimed, sucking her finger where she had pricked it on the sharp needle.

Lizzie gave her a worried look. 'You haven't bled on the fabric, have you?'

Helen chuckled. 'No, the precious fabric has survived. But I'm not sure this needle is going to – I feel like throwing it out of the window.'

'I'll just see who that is at the door and then I'll help you. I have a secret trick to threading. In fact, if you pull the drawer out at the side of the sewing table you'll see what it is.'

Still sucking her finger, Helen pulled out the drawer and spotted a small magnifying glass. 'Oh, that will help immensely,' she said, snipping off the end of the thread and starting again. She cheered as the thread went through the fine eye of the needle at the first attempt.

She turned to tell Lizzie, and saw a young RAF officer standing there. The smile fell from her face. 'Have you come to collect me?' she asked. 'I wonder, could you give me ten minutes just to finish this?'

'Of course,' he said, nodding his thanks to Lizzie, who was still holding the door open, and stepping back outside.

'I'm dreading this interview,' Helen confessed. 'It feels rather like I've been summoned to the headmistress for some minor misdemeanour. But of course this isn't minor, is it?'

'You are not to worry,' Lizzie told her firmly. 'If you know in your heart of hearts you've done nothing wrong, then everything will be fine. Richard is an understanding man. It could be so much worse. Now, just let me make a phone call and I'll walk you down to Richard's office. You could get lost in this barn of a house.' She chuckled. 'I'll finish this piece for you, and before long you'll be back here and Doreen will bring up something tasty for our afternoon tea to cheer you up. Just give me a couple of ticks . . .' She picked up the internal telephone.

Helen snipped the ends of the threads from the panel she'd been working on and held it up. 'I wonder if women are allowed to sew when they're in prison. I suppose it would be mailbags. I've heard that's where they are produced.'

'For heaven's sake, Helen, don't even jest about such things! Now, come along – put a brush through your hair and reapply your lipstick. Who knows, your appearance might just tip the scales of justice . . . Don't worry, that was a joke.'

Helen was thankful Lizzie was taking her to Richard's interview room. She knew the main rooms of the house – the large lounge, the kitchens and the rooms that had

233

been designated for the women to work on their projects – but when Lizzie opened a door off the main hall and led her down a narrow corridor, she knew she'd have been lost on her own. She heard the sound of typewriters behind several closed doors and wondered what was going on. Was there more happening here than her friend had told her? At the end of the corridor they faced double doors that were slightly ajar. Lizzie tapped before pushing them open and leading Helen into a large room.

'This used to be a garden room in more pleasant times. It has a glorious view, or so I'm told, as so far we've only witnessed the autumn and winter garden. I may be biased, coming from Canada where autumn is so much more splendid. For now, I've lent it out to the RAF,' she smiled. 'Hello, Richard – I see tea has arrived. I'll leave you to it.' Before departing, she gave Helen a quick peck on the cheek.

Richard had risen to his feet when they came in. 'Please do sit down,' he said now, pointing to an armchair next to his place on the sofa. Both looked out through French windows that gave only a glimpse of the view due to a heavy criss-cross of blast tape, along with stacks of sandbags heaped against the lower part. 'Lizzie kindly arranged tea for us. We seem to drink rather a lot of it here, as Lizzie sees it as a British tradition that she needs to uphold single-handed. Thankfully she has supplied biscuits as well, so help yourself – and you, Corporal Jenkins,' he called across the room. 'And bring your notebook with you. We may as well be comfortable, as this could take some time.'

Helen accepted a cup of tea from him and stirred it,

her expression puzzled. 'I really don't have much to say . . . I've told you everything I know already.'

'You've been more than helpful, Helen, but we need to put this down in such a way that anyone else reading it will know exactly what happened. There may also be something you missed out before that didn't seem important, or that you only now remember. Think of this as a time to clarify and consolidate your thoughts.'

'Oh, I see,' she said, declining a biscuit from the plate he held out to her.

'First I'd like to take you back to the day before your husband died. I know this may be distressing, but anything at all you can remember could help us to piece vital details together. You have already told me that you were going to visit Felicity Davenport; do you remember what time you left?'

Helen coughed to clear her throat. 'I was due to meet her around midday . . . no, I think it was half past twelve. I'm so sorry – I don't want to get this wrong,' she said, closing her eyes and trying to think.

'Just take your time. You're not under any pressure,' he assured her.

But I am, she thought to herself before taking a deep breath. 'I was going to meet her at her flat at half past twelve. I was running late. John was working at his desk when the telephone rang; he was annoyed it was Felicity and told her she shouldn't be ringing there, which I felt was very strange, but then he had been disturbed. I hurried over to take the telephone from him before he hung up. John was surprised I was still there and returned to his work. He didn't like to be interrupted, and already I'd irritated him when I rang my mother an hour earlier. I just wanted to ask her what colour necktie she thought I should purchase as a Christmas gift for my stepfather. As it was, Gavin answered the telephone and told me my mother was out but due back in a couple of hours, and I was to ring then. I informed him that I was about to go out for the rest of the day and asked him to tell Mother it would be late before I was home.'

'Go on,' Richard encouraged her as he checked the corporal was keeping up with his notes.

'Felicity told me she had a headache and asked if we could reschedule our lunch for another time. She was aware the table was booked and I also had errands to run that had to be done that afternoon.' She took a deep breath before continuing. 'I told her to rest and that I would call in on her later that afternoon around five o'clock. I placed a call to Bella Jones; she checked to see if she was free to join me, but there was a meeting she couldn't avoid. I mentioned how poorly Felicity was, as she does work in the same office and is known to both of us. Bella asked me to give Felicity her best wishes when I said I would be calling in on her later.

'After that I went to Claridge's and lunched alone, which was rather miserable and the fish dish rather bland; and then I headed off to do my shopping. As I've mentioned before, I did call in to Liberty's and purchased a scarf and tie as Christmas presents. I gave the receipt to the constable who was with you on the day we first met.'

Richard checked his own notes. 'Yes, that does fit in with what you told me before. Is it right that you then went to the haberdashery department?'

'Sir, we do have confirmation that Mrs Wentworth spoke to the sales assistant,' put in the corporal. 'This would have been between four and half past.'

His words took Helen aback. Perhaps it should have been obvious but she hadn't really considered that anyone would be checking up on what she'd said about her movements on that day. It was quite disconcerting.

'Where did you go when you left Liberty's?'

'I hailed a taxicab to go to Felicity's . . . No, wait a moment, I stopped for a coffee in a small hotel. Gosh, now where was it? I know it wasn't far from Liberty's. After that I hailed the taxicab, so got to Felicity's around half past five. I had thought if she was still poorly, I would make her comfortable, see if there was anything I could do to help before going home. If John had finished work by the time I got home, I was hoping we could go out to dine.'

Richard encouraged her to keep talking. 'What stopped you going home that evening?'

'Felicity was in a terrible state. The curtains were drawn – I thought she'd been crying, but she insisted her puffy eyes were because of the headache. She was trembling and a complete mess. I'd never seen her like that before. I wanted to call a doctor, but she refused so instead I convinced her to go to bed and promised to stay there overnight in case she took a turn for the worse . . .' Helen stopped for a moment and frowned. 'There was something else: she'd been drinking. I remember thinking that whisky wasn't really very good for someone who had such a terrible headache. I tidied up, turned on the wireless, keeping the sound low in case it disturbed her, and found a book to read. It was a new one just out that John had also recommended to me. I remember that as I opened it. It was called *How Green Was My Valley*.'

'I've read it myself,' Richard commented. 'Did you not think to speak to your husband to let him know you would not be returning home?'

Helen slapped her hand to her mouth. 'I'm terribly sorry – yes, I did ring him – but I couldn't get through. This would have been around . . . oh dear, I can't remember. I know I had settled Felicity and selected the book when the thought came to me. For some reason I couldn't reach the porter to ask him to put the call through to our apartment. Knowing that John often spoke to his office manager in the evening, I rang Bella Jones to let her know and asked her to pass on the message. If it's any help, Tommy Handley was on the radio at the time I placed that call. I turned the volume as low as it would go, so I could hear Felicity if she called out.'

'*ITMA*, sir,' the corporal said, '*It's That Man Again*, a very good radio show. I'm partial to it myself.'

'Thank you, Corporal. Carry on, please, Mrs Wentworth.'

'Not long after that, I fell asleep. It was a policeman knocking on the door the next morning that woke me with the news of what had happened to my husband. I went to St Thomas' hospital, where he'd been taken, but was informed he was dead.'

'Did the police officer who visited you not inform you that your husband was deceased?'

'Yes. But I didn't believe him. I woke Felicity and told her and she was in such a state she begged me to check, to make sure. That's when we went to the hospital. The policeman tried to dissuade us, but Felicity told me we needed to be certain. She was absolutely insistent.

'We sat for a while at the hospital, but they wouldn't let us see John. The police constable was still with us and encouraged us to go back to Felicity's until he could find out the state of my home. A gas explosion had been mentioned by then, and all sorts of hell was going through my mind. In the end I went to Cadogan Mansions, the porter accompanied me upstairs and that's where I met you. Felicity couldn't face accompanying me, so she went home.'

Richard passed her a fresh cup of tea. She felt shattered as she sipped the cooling liquid; even so, it helped to calm her. She realized her hands were trembling. 'Is there anything else you'd like to know?'

'Nothing else for now,' he answered. 'I had been going to ask you about your husband's acquaintances, but I can see you're tired. I can make a further appointment for another day.'

'Thank you,' she said, finishing her tea and then standing up to go. 'You know where to find me,' she smiled weakly, her hand already on the door handle.

'Just one more thing, Mrs Wentworth. Will you explain to me why you ripped up all your husband's clothing?'

Helen froze, anger surging through her before she spun to face him. 'Perhaps you would like to tell me why you kissed me?' she threw back at him before storming from the room.

'Did it not go well?' Lizzie asked as Helen marched into the workroom and threw herself down in one of the armchairs, arms folded in front of her and cheeks flushed with anger.

'Oh, it went perfectly well – until the very end,' she said, before filling Lizzie in with the details.

'Oh, my lord, he kissed you? But when?'

Helen took a deep breath – she had lost count of how many of those she'd taken today – but avoided Lizzie's inquisitive look. 'It was in London, after he took me to a show. We walked by the side of the Thames in the moonlight.'

'Oh, how romantic,' Lizzie said, momentarily forgetting what had just happened and why Helen was so angry.

'I thought so as well, at the time. But it seems I was wrong. The damned man was just trying to get around me to find out more about me, and no doubt whether I killed my husband or not.'

Lizzie sat down in the armchair opposite Helen's and leant forward to place her elbows on her knees, looking Helen straight in the face. 'Did you have anything to do with your husband's death?'

'And now you don't believe me!' Helen threw back at her. 'Does nobody believe what I say?'

'I do,' Richard said, from the open door of the work-room. 'Lizzie – would you mind giving us a few moments alone?'

Lizzie, without saying a word, got to her feet to leave. Passing Richard, she squeezed his arm gently, then closed the door behind her, leaving the couple alone.

Helen glared at him. 'Have you come here to cross-examine me again? Or perhaps arrest me? How can you say you believe me, after what you said not ten minutes ago?'

Richard stood in front of her. 'Would I kiss somebody I didn't believe?' he asked gently.

'I have no idea. Perhaps you go around kissing everybody you interview. It shouldn't have happened; you took advantage of my vulnerability.'

'If I remember correctly, you were a willing participant. As for me kissing everyone I interview . . . well, I can assure you I'm very choosy. And I chose to kiss just you.'

Helen felt warmth spread through her body, and hoped it didn't show in her face. Of course she had enjoyed his kiss. She'd never experienced such a feeling before and knew that even if she was never kissed again, she would take the memory of it to her grave. Her husband had been patient with her, but for him it was more skill than tenderness. He'd had a few relationships before their marriage that she was aware of, and knew what he wanted in the bedroom; whereas she was a novice where such things were concerned. 'But why ask that question? It was hurtful.'

'I apologize − I had no wish to hurt you. I wanted a reaction that the corporal, who took down the notes, would remember more than your calm responses to my questions.' He took her hand as she stood up to face him. 'Can we talk some more?'

She led him to a sofa set beneath one of the large windows. 'Ask me anything you wish; I have nothing to hide,' she said, feeling herself tremble at the touch of his hand.

They both sat, keeping a little distance between them. 'Tell me again about John's clothing. I appreciate there was anger inside you, but talk me through what happened. For you to do such a thing, you must have been hurting. Remember, in a court of law, what you did in anger could

241

be seen as some form of revenge. Imagine the jury wondering if a wife who cut up her husband's clothing was also capable of murdering him.'

'Oh God, that never crossed my mind. You need to speak to Effie King. She was with me when I sorted the clothes – she knew what we came across.' Helen explained how, while sorting through the garments, they had come across the other items. 'As I mentioned before, that is where I found the red blouse which now forms part of the quilt.' She stood up to fetch the patchwork from the worktable. 'Look, you can see the rings and how they intertwine. That one is made up of John's garments, and this one' – she traced the ring made of the more delicate patterns – 'is made up of fabric from my life. This,' she said, stabbing at the patch of red fabric with a finger, 'is what was hidden from me but connects us both, as it was Felicity's blouse, found in amongst John's possessions. I have no idea how he got hold of it. I didn't pack the trunk; as you know, that was left for others to do. I assume it was somebody from your department, or perhaps it was the porter and his wife. It most definitely isn't my blouse, and Felicity didn't lend it to me. I've seen her wear it on several occasions. In fact, there is a photograph of her wearing it at a garden party to raise funds for a children's charity. Plenty of people would have seen her in it that day; would that be enough proof it belonged to her? Perhaps I did wrong, but I was upset, distraught even, and it's not as if I disposed of the clothing; the rest of the blouse is in the ragbag. Parts of John's suits can now be found in some of the ladies' rag rugs. Nothing is being wasted. But if it is evidence, well, then I'm sorry I damaged it.'

Richard kept quiet and let her continue speaking.

'I suggest you interview Felicity again. I'm not trying to tell you how to do your job, but thinking back to the day I visited her – when she had that headache – she would have had plenty of time to get to Cadogan Mansions to kill John, and be back at her flat before I arrived. And there's something else: Felicity has been known to use the excuse of having a headache to leave work early, or even not come in at all. Speak to her colleagues, if you haven't already. She had plenty of opportunities to conduct her affair with my husband.'

Richard was thoughtful. 'Do you know whether your husband had any other . . .'

'Affairs?'

'If you want to put it that way, yes,' he said, looking uncomfortable.

'Please, Richard,' she said, without noticing that she'd used his first name. 'My husband was very much a man of the world when I married him. There was a large age gap, but it suited me to marry him and give myself a future – a future away from Biggin Hill.' She laughed harshly. 'And look where I am now: back where I started.'

'Did you love your husband?'

'I was truly comfortable with John. Surely that's just as important as love?'

'Not to most people,' he replied as he took her hand. 'You deserve so much more,' he murmured as he moved towards her to pull her closer.

'Please – no,' she said, leaning away from him, although she wanted nothing more than for him to hold her close.

'You can't deny the attraction we have to each other,' Richard said as he let her go.

Helen felt herself weaken at his touch, and had to force herself not to follow her heart and reach out to him. 'I'm sorry, but it's too soon. Whatever John did in the past, he doesn't deserve his wife falling into the arms of another man only three months after his death. It wouldn't be right.'

'After what he's done to you . . . ?'

Helen groaned with frustration. 'I'm turning into my mother, not wanting people to think badly of me. Yes, he was unfaithful to me; perhaps it was naive of me not to realize it much earlier. There were always rumours circulating among the wives of his colleagues. I did ask him once if there was any truth to something I'd heard about him and one particular lady – this was long before Felicity . . .' Her eyes took on a distant look as she thought of that time. 'He laughed at me,' she said, giving Richard a hurt look. 'He laughed at me – can you even begin to understand how that felt? Treating me like a child, when I asked him about the gossip I'd heard regarding his involvement with a cabinet minister's wife? He said the wives of MPs should rise above such things: they are there to be supportive of their husbands.'

'I thought as much. In my line of work, we do hear rumours about people in high office positions. Sometimes it's true and other times, just gossip. Because of my family connections – my father and grandfather served in the police force in investigative duties – my work has always involved investigating any criminal activity surrounding people in prominent positions who are, or have been, associated with the RAF. I'm afraid to say that yes, many wives do turn a blind eye just so they can live a privileged life. I just don't feel that it's true in your case. What made you stay?'

'Oh, believe me, I wanted to run away many times. I felt so inadequate, and at times, rather like a country bumpkin. I thought marrying John would mean I could help him with his constituency work and secretarial duties, and life would continue very much as it had been before I married him. But being his wife meant there were certain social expectations of me and often, when John was in meetings or working late, I went to events alone and had to mix with wives in a similar position. It was something I never enjoyed and gradually I kept away from it, rather than put on a brave face and spend exorbitant amounts of money on gowns and hairdressers. Now I can see that I was out of my depth, and if I'd had any sense I'd have gone home.'

'So why didn't you? Was it the thought of living with your mother again? I know you mentioned the uncomfortable atmosphere at home.'

'It wasn't just that, although it did play a part. It was Felicity. She said I should stick it out, make the most of the situation. I'd not long started helping out with a charity that helped elderly people. With war looming, the older generation seemed so vulnerable. Back then, I thought that was what she meant – now I know differently. Being able to visit me meant she could get closer to John. She certainly had an agenda.'

There was a knock, and Lizzie put her head round the door. 'Excuse me for interrupting – Richard, you are wanted downstairs. A dispatch rider has delivered something that requires a signature. It's one of those "for your eyes only" envelopes,' she said apologetically.

'I'll be there in a minute, Lizzie, thank you,' he said, standing up as Lizzie pulled the door to. He turned to Helen and took her hands. 'Trust me, please? I want the truth to come out. And then, maybe . . .'

Helen kissed his cheek. 'I do too, but please give me time.'

'It will be hell to wait, but I'm prepared to. I want you to know, I've requested I be removed from the case. It doesn't seem right to be overseeing this now . . . well, you know what I mean. However, it may be a while before I have a replacement,' he said before leaving her.

Deep in thought, she returned to the table and straightened out the patchwork. There was one more block to sew before she could think about adding wadding and the backing, then learning how to hand-stitch the intricate quilting pattern. It could then be parcelled up and sent away to John's mother. Perhaps Helen would feel more at peace after that. Running her fingers around the ring pattern, she promised herself to focus on a new quilting project and say goodbye to the quilt that told this chapter of her life. 'And good riddance,' she muttered out loud.

'Oh dear; did your private talk not go well with Richard? I thought you looked quite cosy when I popped my head in just now,' Lizzie said, looking concerned.

'Not completely – but we've ironed out the kinks, so to speak, and have a new understanding.'

Lizzie raised her eyebrows, but said nothing.

The women worked on in companionable silence until sounds from the hallway indicated it was time for the patchwork group to start. Doreen pushed a tea trolley into the room and was followed by a chattering group of women. 'We have two new members for your group,' she said to Lizzie, as Helen helped her bring out the equipment needed for that session's lesson. 'You might know one of the two ladies,' Doreen added, giving Helen a smile. She stepped aside to reveal Hillary Davis standing there.

'Mother? I never had any idea that you were interested in patchwork?'

'I'm not,' said her mother. 'Embroidery is what I prefer, although I'll probably join the knitting group if nothing else interests me. We all have to pull our weight during these uncertain times, and knitting for the troops is much better than playing with fripperies.' She glanced round the room. 'Wouldn't you agree, Mrs Donnington?'

'I'm afraid I wouldn't,' Lizzie said with a charming smile, causing Hillary to raise her eyebrows. 'This group is recycling old fabric to make bedcoverings and other useful items, while next door, ladies are learning about rag rug making. So, no fripperies here, as you see. You might find the rag rug group quite interesting.'

'I don't think so. Rag rugs are not the kind of adornment you will find on the floor of a home like mine,' Hillary said, giving a sniff. 'However, I'm also here to see my daughter. If she won't come to visit me, I've decided to seek her out. What is it they say about the mountain and Mohammed?'

'Why don't you collect your tea and sit with your mother, Helen? There's time for you to chat before I start. Take the two seats over by the window, so that you are able to see the view while you talk,' she added. 'The grounds aren't up to much this time of year, but you'll probably see the deer grazing.' She knew this would impress the woman – either that, or make her jealous. Lizzie instinctively felt that Hillary needed taking down a notch or two.

'I don't understand why you're here, Mother,' Helen said frankly when they had seated themselves. 'We hardly passed the time of day while I was living at home – and now, when I've only been gone a few days, you turn up here. Has something happened I don't know about?'

Hillary sipped tea from her bone china cup. Helen could see her hands were trembling slightly. 'It's your stepfather. I don't know what to do . . .'

Helen almost dropped her own cup and saucer. Had her mother finally realized what Gavin was like? 'What's happened?'

'It's just that I can't cope with the pain of you being at each other's throats. He told me how rude you've been to him – and how you almost caused an accident when you got out of his car and walked away. I know he can be a difficult man, Helen, but you've really got to try and get on with him.'

The hopes Helen had held for a few seconds were dashed. 'Has he sent you here to talk me round?'

'No . . . no, not at all. In fact, things are changing at home. I've taken on a new housekeeper, a woman much older than that Effie – so at least there's no chance of children turning up on the doorstep. Your stepfather really doesn't like them in the house. That's the reason I always complain about them.'

Helen frowned. That wasn't her impression at all. Was her mother really so ignorant that she didn't understand why Helen was unhappy under the same roof as Gavin? 'He's always been awful to me, Mother, ever since I was a youngster when you married him. He's made me feel so uncomfortable and unwanted in the house. Then, as I got older . . .' She trailed off, unable to find the right words to explain.

'The problem is, Helen, your father spoilt you far too much. That is why you've never tried to get along with Gavin. However, if you do decide to come back home, he won't be around the house quite so often, which does mean the two of you shouldn't be at loggerheads so much.'

'Do you mean he will be spending even more time at the golf club?' Helen asked wryly. Gavin already spent a great deal of time playing golf – and even more time sitting in the clubhouse bar.

'No, he's been offered a job at the airfield. When I say a job, I mean he's returning to running a division – he will be in management again. His name was put forward by one of his contacts at the golf club.' Hillary raised her voice a little, glancing round to see if anyone had heard. 'He is hiring a few men for the building work and repairs; one can only assume that with so many men working at the airfield, there will be a lot of maintenance work for him to see to.'

Helen doubted that was the reason at all. It was likely that the airfield would see a lot of action, so Gavin might well find himself having to work very hard indeed. For her mother's sake, she hoped he wouldn't be injured, although for her part she couldn't care less.

'That's good to hear, Mother. I'm pleased for him – please send him my congratulations. However, I have a lovely home and job up at The Grange. Have you ever been there? Do you know it's where the hunt meets, and Mr Trentham is involved with the Kennel Club in the breeding of pedigree dogs?' She knew that mentioning such things to her mother would bring out the snob in her. 'You are welcome to visit me any time you like. But do bring your wellington boots and wear casual clothes, because any visitors are roped in to help walk the dogs.'

'I have heard of Stanley Trentham, and The Grange is quite an impressive property and so much land . . .' Hillary said approvingly. 'Perhaps I will visit, but I'm not so sure about helping to walk dogs . . . perhaps just a small one,' she considered.

Helen jotted down the telephone number and made it very clear to her mother what her hours would be in the office. She didn't want Hillary bothering Stan or Jean, or having them run about carrying messages; that wouldn't do at all, when she'd only just started work there. 'Now, Mother, I don't think sewing patchwork quilts is quite your style – but bring your cup of tea along, and I'll introduce you to Betty Daley. She leads the knitting group and will welcome you with open arms, considering your organizational skills and time spent running committees.'

After only a few minutes, Hillary and Betty were chatting like long-lost friends. It seemed both of their husbands played bowls as well as being members of the golf club.

'Your husband must also have gone on the trip a little while before Christmas, as did my stepfather?' Helen said, feeling as though she should contribute something to the conversation before she could slip away and join Lizzie.

Betty looked puzzled. 'You must be mistaken, my dear. The bowls group haven't made any trips. It was decided when war was declared that all matches would be cancelled for the foreseeable future. Rita Binks can confirm this, as her brother is a member.'

Well, that was interesting – so what had Gavin really been up to? Helen wondered. She glanced at Hillary, but her mother didn't comment and seemed unaffected by this new information. Making her excuses, Helen left the two older women chatting, wondering where her step-father might really have been that day.

14
~

'I do see what you mean about your stepfather,' Lizzie said, as she helped Helen carry out the sewing machine and a couple of bags of her personal bits and pieces from The Maples.

Lizzie had offered Hillary a lift home after the meeting and she'd accepted, sitting in the front seat and completely ignoring Effie and her two children, who squeezed in beside Helen on the back seat.

'He seems to be quite a sour-faced man, but the way he looked me up and down I thought he was imagining undressing me,' Lizzie went on with a wry look.

'I have that feeling all the time,' Helen said. 'I've always wondered what my mother sees in him. He's made it clear that if it hadn't been for him, she and I would have been left destitute. But it's very hard to believe that my father would have left us this house with no money at all to survive on. It just doesn't make sense.'

'These things do happen when a husband dies young. I've experienced it myself,' Lizzie said, looking sad. 'But whatever happened, it's all in the past now. You have to remind yourself that you've moved on – you don't live under his roof and you will have little to do with the man from now on. I do feel sorry for your mother, but she's old enough to look after herself. What's that saying? You've made your bed, and now you must lie in it. I suppose that's true in this case.'

Helen agreed. Deep down, she still wanted to be closer to her mother; however, Hillary would have to make the first step, as Helen had given up trying. 'I've invited her for tea one afternoon, and to look around The Grange,' she said as she climbed into the front seat beside Lizzie. Behind them, she heard Effie groan. 'Don't worry, Effie. I've arranged it at a time when the girls will be at school and you'll be working, or on the way down to collect them. I had a feeling you wouldn't feel comfortable.'

'Thank you, Helen, that might be best. Besides, you'll want some time alone with your mum, won't you? Saying that, I'll make one of my Victoria sponges and use our plum jam for the filling – so you don't have to attempt any baking again,' she giggled. Helen's last attempt to make a cake had not been a success, and Effie had promised to give her some lessons.

'That sounds delightful, thank you. If you make one large enough, we can all celebrate after my mother has gone home,' Helen said, before putting a hand over her mouth and apologizing. 'That didn't sound very nice of me, did it?'

Lizzie laughed. 'It was truly heartfelt, though,' she said as they set off into the darkening afternoon. 'I don't know about the rest of you, but I feel as though there is some snow in the air. You get a sixth sense about that when you've lived in Canada – although the snow here is nothing like what we have,' she said, and went on to entertain the children with stories of deep snowdrifts and the fun and adventures she'd had with her own children while they were growing up.

Listening to her talk, Helen couldn't help comparing Lizzie with her own mother. Lizzie couldn't be much younger than Hillary Davis, but with her sunny disposition and welcoming ways, she was a far cry from the woman who had just watched them depart from her front window at The Maples.

In her hand, Helen held a couple of envelopes: letters that had been sent to her old address. She opened one that had the mark of the Palace of Westminster on its stiff white envelope. 'Oh,' was all she could say, as she pulled out the card from inside.

'Is everything all right?' Lizzie said, glancing quickly sideways and seeing Helen's pale face.

'It's something I'd been expecting,' Helen said, tucking the card into her handbag along with the other envelopes. 'It's the official memorial service for John. With all that's been going on, I'd completely forgotten that Bella had suggested a few dates when I saw her. It seems I'm invited to take somebody along with me.'

'Surely that would be your mother?' Lizzie said, looking both ways before she turned the car up the steep lane towards The Grange.

'Well, no – she didn't want to go to his funeral, and she really doesn't like being in London. She hardly ever visited me when I lived there; it was me who had to travel to Biggin Hill. I wonder, Lizzie, would you accompany me?

I warn you now, you might find me rather weepy, as I've not met many of our colleagues since he died. The funeral was very small, with only a few representatives from government in attendance. This service is to be held in Westminster, in March.'

'I'd be more than glad to. But if it doesn't sound wrong of me, I must warn you I'll be seeing London through the eyes of a tourist, so you'd best be prepared to act as my guide. In fact, why don't we stay over? I hardly ever go anywhere these days – we can make it a treat. That's if you don't think it's wrong, when we should also be paying our respects to your late husband.'

'You both need a treat,' Effie piped up from the back seat. 'Everyone should see London at least once. I've had my fill of it, coming from the East End, but the pair of you should go out and enjoy yourselves. Please do be careful, though – carry your gas masks and make sure you know where all the air-raid shelters are. I keep hearing people talk on the wireless about it being a phoney war and nothing much happening, but something in my water tells me that won't last. That Adolf Hitler is up to something, you mark my words.'

Lizzie gave Helen a small wink. 'We'll make sure to be as safe as we can, Effie, so don't you go worrying about us. Now, girls, are you going to tell me about your school? I just wish I could have joined you; the barn looks so cosy. Do you like your new teacher?'

Dorothy and Jane chatted excitedly about their teacher and how they'd been taken on a nature trail, collecting leaves and foliage to stick into their nature books. 'Tomorrow we're going to take our pencils and paper and draw deer. Dorothy said she spotted some – is that true?' Jane asked.

'Most certainly,' Lizzie said. 'I might just dress up warm and come with you. I can point out the best place to spot them – I often see them from my window, grazing in that large field in front of the house. Do you not see any where you live?'

Dorothy gave an exaggerated sigh. 'All we see are lots of dogs,' she exclaimed, and her sister giggled.

'Then why don't we try and draw dogs as well? I have lots of painting equipment in my workshop. Perhaps as a treat for you, we could all paint together outside of school hours, what do you think?'

The girls were overexcited and wanted to show Lizzie the dogs as soon as they were back at The Grange. They all helped to carry Helen's sewing equipment indoors before setting off down to the kennels.

'It's getting close to feeding time,' Helen explained, 'so I'm afraid you'll probably get roped into helping. Later we take them out, so they can run around the paddock before they're bedded down for the night. If you'd like to stay for tea, you're welcome to help?'

Lizzie chuckled. 'I take it you're desperate for helpers. I'd love to stay.'

'We are very short of helpers. We've put cards on the shop noticeboard asking for volunteers, but I'm afraid we've only had one so far and the lad is still at school. He's due to move further into the country to live with a relative in a couple of weeks.'

'We must try and do something about that. I've heard all about Stan Trentham bringing in stray dogs and caring for them. It infuriates me that so many people have decided to have their dogs put to sleep unnecessarily. In some ways I blame the national press for their scare-mongering. It's not needed at the moment.'

'He's a good man,' Effie said, 'and the best employer I've ever had – no offence meant,' she added, looking towards Helen, who agreed with her.

'You might wish to change your shoes,' Helen said, looking down at the smart court shoes on Lizzie's feet. 'We have a spare pair of wellington boots indoors. Stan gave us some when we moved in. It's all essential fashion around here,' she laughed as she rummaged in the cupboard and pulled out a pair that just about fitted Lizzie, once they'd stuffed the toes with socks.

'Crikey, that's a din,' Lizzie said, putting her fingers to her ears as they entered the kennel block where the stray dogs lived. 'Stan's got a good set-up here, but it looks to me as though he's full to bursting.'

Effie glanced up from where she was already laying out bowls for the dogs' meal. 'He hopes to build another kennel block. We've got most of the materials out the back. He cadges a lot from local farmers and grateful owners. We just need to find the people to do the brick-laying and labouring. It's not something we're very good at, even though I offered to learn.'

Lizzie mucked in, handing out the food and asking about the feeding routine. 'They seem to enjoy tripe,' she said, wrinkling her nose as she dispensed the pale offal.

'Last week it was horsemeat,' Effie said, screwing up her face. 'I try not to think too much about where it came from.'

'Horsemeat is very nutritious,' Lizzie remarked as she stacked bowls on top of each other and headed towards one of the kennels filled with smaller dogs. 'You'd eat it if you were hungry enough,' she called over her shoulder. 'In fact, you've possibly eaten it before and not known about it. I do believe, the way this world is going, that we're going to have to learn not to be so fussy.'

'Blimey,' Effie said to Helen, 'I thought she was going to be as posh as hell, living in that grand house. But she's just like us, isn't she? And a bit of a laugh, too. We'd best hurry up, or she'll have fed all the dogs before we start.'

They needn't have worried, as once Lizzie had distributed the small bowls in the first kennel she stopped to watch the dogs eat, a soft look on her face as she bent to stroke some of their heads.

'Don't start making friends with them, or you'll want to take half a dozen home with you,' Helen called out as she moved on to the next kennel, which held larger dogs. 'What about one of these instead?'

Lizzie looked over the wall dividing the kennels. 'Oh no, I prefer smaller dogs – and I've chosen three already,' she said, pointing to three sandy-coloured terrier-type dogs.

'Would you really take three?' Effie asked. 'And how did you know three of them came in together? It seems the old lady that owned them was moving in with her daughter-in-law, who refused point-blank to take Tom, Dick and Harry. There were floods of tears when they were dropped off here. Stan promised they'd be rehomed together or else live out their days with him.'

'That does it,' Lizzie said. 'I'll have a word with Stan

and see if he'll sell them to me. I could see they were brothers from the way they shared the same bowl and licked each other's faces, bless them.'

'He doesn't want money,' Effie assured her. 'He just wants to find good homes for them.'

'Then I'll make a donation to help with the upkeep of the others. Do you mind if I walk up to the house now and see if I can find him?'

'Is someone looking for me?' a voice said from the door.

Helen introduced Lizzie to Stan and left them to chat while she, Effie and the two girls finished feeding all the dogs, then started stacking bowls in the sink before doing the washing up. Both women draped large aprons around themselves to protect their clothes. Lizzie joined them as they were washing the last of the bowls. 'Shall I start drying up?' she asked, looking for a cloth.

'No, it's all right. We leave them stacked here to dry on their own,' Helen said. 'We'd best start letting the dogs out into the paddock, and then we can clean out the kennel runs.'

The two little girls appeared, each holding a small spade. 'This is the part of the job we don't much like,' Jane said, wrinkling her nose.

'Then let me help you,' Lizzie smiled. She took a spade and went off with the girls to help. Each kennel in turn was emptied of dogs, and they raced and galloped around the paddock.

Helen leant on the edge of the wall, watching the animals. Lizzie might have thought snow was on the way, but there was no sight of it, although the ground was crisp with frost. The dogs revelled in the chill air. 'They do say it's a dog's life.'

'Yeah, but who wants to be one of these?' Effie said. 'It's only luck that they're here and not been put to sleep. I've been wondering if we should take one on, but what with us working so much, it wouldn't really be fair, would it?' she said wistfully.

'Why choose one, when we have so many here to care for? Let's just enjoy all of them for now, shall we?'

Lizzie arrived, her face flushed, holding hands with both the girls. 'That was fun,' she declared.

'Oh, you've not finished yet – there's quite a bit to collect in the paddock.' Helen pointed to where a large spade and bucket were propped against the wall.

'I can see why you need so many volunteers,' Lizzie said, 'but I do have an idea. I'll get on to it once I'm back at the house. But first I've got to find Tom, Dick and Harry and get them ready to come home.'

Once the paddock was clear, everyone helped Lizzie load her three little dogs into her car along with enough leads and equipment to see her through until she'd visited a pet shop. After waving her off, they returned to their own home over the garage.

'I'm going to prepare a spot of tea for the girls, then we'll go over to help Jean for a couple of hours. She's teaching the girls how to knit. They have a bee in their bonnet about knitting blankets for the dogs – God knows how long that will take,' Effie smiled. 'Do you have to return to your work?'

'No, I brought over a few files earlier. I'm going to sit at the kitchen table and enter the paperwork into a ledger,'

Helen said, indicating a bag full of folders. 'First, I'll sort out my bits and pieces we brought from home, then I'll put our dinner on. I thought we could have sausages and mash – I know Jean and Stan said we can eat with them, but sometimes I feel as though we're relying on them a little too much. What do you think?'

'I'm ahead of you,' Effie said, as she went to the small pantry and lifted out a pie. 'I tried one of the recipes from the leaflets supplied by the Ministry of Food. You just need to boil a few spuds and cabbage to go with it. The pie only needs half an hour in the oven to warm through, so you can get on with your own work and not have to worry about cooking a meal.'

When Effie and the girls had gone, Helen settled down to her paperwork. She spread the invoices out on the table and opened the ledger. Putting the paperwork in date order, she picked up a pen and started to enter the details. It was satisfying to be able to concentrate on something other than her personal life.

With the clock gently ticking in the background, an hour passed before she realized. She needed to put on the vegetables and place the pie in the oven, as Effie had instructed. Once everything was under way, she decided not to return to her paperwork just in case she lost track of time and burnt the meal. She wasn't a natural cook, but was determined to learn. Remembering Jean had given her some Ministry of Food leaflets too, showing recipes and helpful hints, she returned to the table to retrieve her handbag where she'd placed them, first putting away the invoices and ledger. She had ten minutes to read the leaflets before she needed to set the table.

Opening her handbag, she came across the envelope with the invitation to the memorial service and remembered there were two other letters yet to be read. Tutting at her forgetfulness, she slipped her finger under the flap of the first and pulled out a short letter from a girl she had been at school with years earlier. She would need to reply, she thought as she read the belated condolence.

The third envelope had a London postmark, and she was surprised when opening the envelope to find that it was from Felicity – the very last person she'd expected to hear from, after their last encounter. As she read what her former friend had written, her heart began to thump with worry. She needed to speak to Richard before it was too late. Quickly slipping on her shoes and coat, she hurried across to The Grange, going in by the kitchen entrance.

'Whatever is wrong?' Effie asked. 'Have you burnt our dinner?'

'Oh God, I forgot about that – and everything is bubbling away on the cooker. I really need to make a telephone call before it's too late,' Helen said urgently, flapping the letter in the air.

'Don't worry. I'll shoot over there right now and check it's all right.' Effie wiped her hands on her apron. 'Get back as soon as you can, will you?'

Helen agreed distractedly and went into the library, where she quickly dialled the operator and gave the telephone number that would put her through to Lizzie's house. She tapped her foot impatiently while someone went to fetch Richard.

'What's the problem?' he asked. 'I was told you were rather agitated.'

'You could say that,' she said. 'I've received a letter from Felicity.' She read out the letter, which told her that Felicity was sorry for everything that had happened and was moving away, where no one would be able to find her. Her grief over what had happened was apparently too much for her to bear. The letter finished with Felicity hoping Helen would forgive her.

There was a short silence as Richard digested this.

'Please say something,' Helen implored. 'She doesn't have any close family, so I'm not sure where she would be going.'

'Something tells me she's not going anywhere,' Richard said in a sombre voice.

'Then why would she write this letter? It doesn't make sense,' Helen said, her voice a little hysterical.

'I believe it is a suicide note.'

'Oh my God,' Helen cried. 'For all that she's done, Felicity was my only friend when I first moved to London. I'd never forgive myself if I didn't go to her in her hour of need. What can we do – should we contact somebody? This is postmarked last post yesterday . . .'

'We should go straight there. I'll take the staff car. I'll be at The Grange to collect you in ten minutes, as soon as I've made a telephone call to the local constabulary. Have a bag packed, in case we need to stay over.' Without saying goodbye he ended the call, leaving Helen holding the receiver to her ear until she realized he'd gone.

Hurrying back to their home over the garage, Helen quickly explained to Effie what had happened. 'I'm sorry to leave you in the lurch like this, but I've got to go. Richard reckons it could be a suicide letter – I hope to

God he's wrong.' She held it out for Effie to read. 'I must hurry and pack a bag, I've no idea how long we'll be gone.'

Effie followed Helen to her bedroom, where she began stuffing clothes into a small suitcase. 'Do you think it's possible she killed your husband?'

Helen paused and closed her eyes for a moment. 'I'll admit I've considered it. It would explain why she was so distressed when I saw her in the evening on the day John died; but would she really have been capable of causing a gas explosion to cover her tracks? I can't think straight,' she said unhappily, closing her suitcase. She sat in front of a small mirror to brush her hair and quickly reapply her make-up. 'That will have to do,' she said as she kissed Effie's cheek. 'Would you please tell Stan I'll make up my time when I get back?'

'Don't you go worrying about any of that.' Effie passed over Helen's gas mask and handbag. 'I'll let everyone know you've had to dash off. That sounds like Richard is just coming into the driveway – you'd best hurry,' she called after her friend, before realizing she was still holding Felicity's letter. She ran after Helen. 'You may need this,' she said, passing it through the open window of the vehicle. 'Godspeed.'

Helen leant back in her seat and let out a long sigh. 'That was a rush.'

'I'm sorry to hurry you, but the sooner we get to London, the sooner we may be able to do something to save her. I've put through a call to the local police station but not said what has happened – only that a life may be in danger.'

Helen shuddered. 'It doesn't seem right that she could

die, but if she survives she will be arrested for attempting suicide.'

'She could be arrested for more than that, if she played a part in John's death.'

'I only hope we'll be there in time.'

'We'll be there in half an hour – as long as this weather doesn't get any worse,' Richard muttered, as a scattering of snowflakes fell across the windscreen.

'What if we're too late?'

'What time is on the postmark?'

Helen peered closely. 'It's smudged, but it looks as though it would have caught the last post yesterday.'

'Anyone who tries to take their own life generally does it very soon after writing a note. Often they're only discovered much later, when someone notices they are missing and breaks into their property. I'm sorry; I didn't mean to upset you,' he said, as Helen gasped in dismay.

'Isn't it possible she's just run away? There again, if she has, does that mean she is guilty? Wouldn't she have just disappeared, rather than write to me?' Helen sighed. 'The more I think about this, the less I understand why she wrote this letter. Perhaps she really is responsible for John's death, as that's the only reason I can think for her to write to me . . . The state she was in on that day, and then her attitude to me later . . . I just don't know. They do say that attack is a form of defence,' Helen said thoughtfully.

'Maybe the letter is just a final aggressive stab at you, before she leaves London.'

'Possibly,' Helen said. 'It's such a conundrum, isn't it? May I ask you something?'

'Fire away,' he said as he peered through the windscreen first, cursing the worsening weather and then apologizing for his language.

Helen gripped the seat. It didn't feel particularly safe to be driving through what was becoming heavy snow, and the wind seemed to have picked up as well. 'I wondered if you could tell me whether you have any other suspects?'

'Apart from you, do you mean?' he said, giving a wry smile as she glanced towards him with a worried look on her face.

'You don't honestly think that I murdered John, do you?'

'Would I have kissed a murderess?' he asked.

'I'm not sure how many you've met,' she replied, wondering if he was just avoiding answering. 'I am serious, Richard.'

He apologized. 'I've spoken to many people who know you, and I've looked into where you were on that day. Very early on, I struck you off my list, and it's an extremely short list. I know now that you'd never hurt a fly. The job John did at the ministry is not something that would have been likely to put him on the radar of the enemy. I must say, it's disconcerting not to have discovered who killed him by now; in some ways, I feel as though I'm failing. I'm also aware that I could be called away on another job at any point – and with resources stretched because of the war effort, we may never find out who murdered John.'

'I'm sure you're doing your best. We live in such uncertain times. Whatever is discovered, I can't bring

John back; the thing that worries me is that his murderer could strike again.'

'I agree with you. But often murder is a one-off – something that happens because someone is aggrieved enough to kill a particular person. Serial killers are not as prolific in life as they seem to be at the pictures, or in novels.'

They fell into silence as Richard manoeuvred the car through the darkening afternoon. What would normally have been a straightforward journey was now complicated by both the weather and the blackout restrictions.

At last, Richard pulled up outside Felicity's address. A policeman stepped forward. 'The building is secure and all exits covered, sir.'

Richard thanked him and led Helen to the flat on the second floor at the rear of the building.

'Are you sure you want to go in? I could go alone.'

'Yes, I'm sure.'

Bending down, she lifted up a doormat that had seen better days and picked up a key beneath it. 'We were terrible at losing keys, so we always kept a spare under the doormat. Thank goodness Felicity has done the same in her new home.' She handed the key to Richard, who slipped it into the keyhole. The door opened with ease.

They both stepped inside, Richard pulling the door closed behind him and flicking the latch to lock it. He put his finger to his lips to remind her to be quiet.

There was an open door into the kitchen; they could see that it was empty. Helen pointed to one of two doors on the other side of the room and they moved silently towards it, Helen hoping that Felicity had not done anything stupid.

As Richard swung open the door, Helen gasped in shock and rushed to the bed, where Felicity lay sprawled across the sheets wearing the skimpiest of underwear. She quickly pulled a sheet over the woman's body to protect her modesty before shaking her shoulder. 'Felicity, Felicity, wake up,' she cried.

Richard gently moved her aside and felt for a pulse at Felicity's throat. 'She's not dead,' he said, 'but going by all of this, she made an attempt.' He held up a whisky bottle with only an inch of alcohol left in the bottom and nodded towards an open pill bottle that had fallen to the floor. White pills were scattered everywhere.

'Will she die?' Helen asked anxiously. 'Is there anything we can do?'

Richard gave Felicity a shake. 'Miss Davenport, wake up,' he said as Felicity groaned and pushed his hand away. Richard propped her up against the pillows. 'Can you get a glass of water, please?' he asked Helen. Felicity's make-up was smudged, her hair in disarray, and from her blotchy cheeks and puffy eyes, it looked as though she'd been crying heavily.

Helen returned with a full cup of water, which Richard held to Felicity's lips, encouraging her to drink. She came to slightly as she gulped at the cold liquid.

'She won't be sick, will she? Should I get a bowl?'

'That might be a good idea,' he said as he kept encouraging Felicity to sip the water. 'Would you mind picking up the pills and putting them back in the bottle, and can you count them? It should hold thirty, going by the label. If we know how many she's taken then we'll know how serious this is. As for the whisky – most of it seems to have been spilt on her bed, going by the smell. Let's hope your friend was more sorry for herself than suicidal.'

'Thank goodness,' Helen said after a moment, holding up the pill bottle, 'only three missing. She's too young to die, whatever she's done . . .'

15

It took half an hour to bring Felicity round enough for her to talk to them in a coherent manner. Helen washed her and put her in nightclothes and a dressing gown before leading her into the sitting room and settling her in front of the fire, which Richard had lit. He pumped coffee into her, ignoring her protests that she was all right. Meanwhile, Helen stripped the bed linen and put it into a bag ready for the wash collection. As there had only been three pills missing from the bottle, they both agreed Felicity's condition must be mainly the result of alcohol consumption and melancholy. Once she'd remade the bed, Helen joined Richard and accepted a cup of coffee from him.

'I'm afraid it's black. The milk was off,' he said, grimacing as he took a mouthful.

'Anything is fine right now,' Helen said. 'I'm just relieved you're all right,' she snapped at Felicity. 'What a bloody stupid thing to do.'

Richard raised a hand for her to calm down. 'I need to ask you some questions, Miss Davenport,' he said, reaching into his pocket for a notebook and pencil. 'Can you explain why you sent this letter to Mrs Wentworth?' He took the envelope from Helen. 'It appears you posted it late yesterday afternoon. Did you intend to take your own life after doing so?'

Felicity shook her head, refusing to speak.

'Please, you've got to tell us the truth,' Helen implored. 'What was so bad that you wanted to kill yourself?'

'It felt like a good idea at the time, but I'm not sure I really wanted to die. When I wrote the letter, I was undecided whether to pack a bag and go away . . . but then it was raining, and I don't have a lot of money left since losing my job. In fact, if I don't find work very soon, I'll not be able to pay my rent either.' She looked over to where Richard had put the almost-empty bottle of whisky and the pills on a side table. 'I couldn't even get that right, could I? I should have taken the pills before drinking the whisky.' She started to cry.

'Miss Davenport, people don't try to commit suicide – which you do realize is a criminal offence? – unless something really terrible has happened in their life. Granted, the war and losing your job could have made you miserable, but there are people you could have spoken to. Why didn't you reach out to a friend for help?'

Helen agreed. 'I'm so upset by your betrayal. We were meant to be close friends! How could you have an affair with my husband?' she blurted out, and then looked at Richard to apologize for the interruption.

Felicity started to cry. 'You have no idea how much I loved him,' she sniffed into her handkerchief. 'It was getting harder and harder to say goodnight to him when he went home to you after pretending to work late. I begged him to tell you so we could make a fresh start together, but he laughed at me,' she sobbed. 'He laughed at me, that last time I saw him. I'd given him an ultimatum: he had to ask you for a divorce, or I'd tell you what we'd been up to. I'm not the first, you know. He only married you because you were the right kind of woman to be his wife and stay loyal for the general public to vote for him. He didn't love you; he only ever loved me – he told me so.'

By rights Helen knew she should have been crying herself, or perhaps even screaming at Felicity, but by now her heart was hardened to the truth. The signs of what was happening had been there for a long time, if only she'd been willing to see. Perhaps she should have tackled John about them, but she hadn't. If she had, she could have started a new life. She wouldn't be mixed up in all this mess.

She was about to reply, but Richard was looking at her and raised his hand slightly to hold her off. Helen stayed silent.

'Miss Davenport, please tell me: when was the last time you saw John Wentworth?'

Felicity shot a new look of pure hatred towards Helen. 'I'd feigned a headache to cancel meeting Helen so that I could see John. I knew we'd be able to have a few hours together before I had to get back to my flat. You were too trusting,' she snarled at Helen, who jerked back in her seat, shocked by her sudden ferocity. 'But then, plans don't always pan out as you expect them to.'

'Did you go to Mr and Mrs Wentworth's apartment?'

'Yes, I did,' Felicity said defiantly.

Helen frowned and turned towards Richard. 'Surely the porter would have mentioned this?'

Felicity laughed. 'That man is a fool. A simple telephone call meant he left the reception desk and went outside to look for a delivery. I slipped in and he was none the wiser.' Her eyes took on a faraway look. 'I'd picked up a new negligee to wear for John. He knew I was coming and he'd left the door on the latch. When I entered the room, I saw him lounging on the sofa. I crept up behind him and slipped my hands round his eyes and said, "Guess who?" – and he slumped to one side. It was then I saw the blood,' she whispered, looking at her hands and turning them over before rubbing them together. 'It was everywhere, and there was the knife and everything was silent apart from the ticking of the clock ... That engraved paper knife you gave him for his birthday, it was ... I couldn't bear to look at him for a moment longer ... I backed away into the bathroom and washed my hands. And then I left as quickly as I could. I heard the lift moving and knew at any moment whoever was coming up to that floor might see me. I was frightened it was you,' she said, looking at Helen, 'and I thought that if you'd killed him, you might just kill me as well ... I was confused because I thought you were in the bedroom. It's strange how one's mind can play tricks at times like that. I could have sworn I heard floorboards creak ...'

'Did you smell any gas?' Richard asked as she started to wipe her hands together once more, mumbling about the blood.

'No. I didn't notice anything like that. I slipped down the staircase and left by the rear entrance in case the porter had returned. I didn't know what to do, so I decided to go home. I thought that way, when you arrived at my flat, I'd be there, and you'd be none the wiser.'

Helen couldn't keep quiet a moment longer. 'But John hated you – he told me to stop being friends with you, and yet all that time you were . . . the two of you . . .'

'It was a game he liked to play to cover himself, in case you ever guessed what he was up to. Goodness, there's been a few times I've wanted to put my hands round his throat and kill him, when he wouldn't agree to leave you . . .' She gasped and looked at Richard. 'But it wasn't me who killed him.'

'Miss Davenport, we need to take you into custody in order to take down your statement.'

'But I didn't . . .'

'You need to be formally interviewed again,' was all Richard said. He crossed to the window and waved down to a police officer who was standing on the pavement.

'So the negligee was yours, then,' Helen said.

'Yes. It cost a fortune, but I knew he'd like it. I was hoping he'd give me the money to pay for it,' Felicity said bitterly. 'I take it you kept it. Not that it would suit your scrawny body.'

'We do have the item of clothing,' Richard said, not looking at Helen, who had thrown it into the waste bin in Lizzie's workroom.

Two police officers came in and stood to one side as Richard spoke quietly to them. They took Felicity's arms to lead her from the room. She turned to look at Helen. 'I meant what I wrote in my letter. But I loved him – and you didn't deserve him,' she said before being led away.

*

'I think I'm still in shock,' Helen said, as she took her case from Richard at the door to her hotel room and placed it on the floor. 'In a way I'm relieved Felicity wasn't the one who killed John, even though I'll never forgive her betrayal; but then, you are no further forward in your investigations, are you?'

'Finding the culprit is never that easy,' he replied. 'However, at least now we know when he died – or at least what time he was found dead. That's if she's telling the truth, but I think she is now – and we can check some of her story.'

'How did you work out what time he died?'

'Felicity said she rushed from the flat around half past four; so whoever killed him did it before then. And she said she didn't smell any gas. My thoughts are the killer was hiding in your bedroom and finished off the job once she left.'

'To think there could have been a second body, if the killer had decided to attack her as well.'

'Which makes me wonder whether, in fact, she intended to kill John, or went there simply to have things out with him. So often, we say we will kill someone without meaning we would actually commit murder.' He shrugged. 'Whatever the reason, we know that the culprit would have been leaving Cadogan Mansions not long after half past four, as by five o'clock the explosion had occurred.'

'So, you are a little way further forward?'

'Just a little. I wish I could give you more information. At least then perhaps that worried expression would leave your face for good.'

Helen put a hand to her cheek. 'I must look an absolute fright.'

'Never to me,' he replied, reaching out and taking her hand from her face and brushing it against his lips.

For a moment, Helen was lost for words. She looked up and searched his face. 'You must be extremely tired, to say such a thing?'

'I've never felt more awake,' he murmured, taking her in his arms and holding her close. 'Ever since our kiss – which I know was most inappropriate, because of your bereavement and my employment – I've had to hold myself back on more than one occasion from doing this . . .' He gently brushed her lips with his own.

'I wish you hadn't held back,' she said as she returned his kiss with more intensity, pulling him into the room and kicking the door closed.

Much later, as she looked up from where she was snuggled against his chest, she chuckled at their clothes scattered from the door to the bed. 'I hope you don't think this is something I've done before?'

'How many years were you married?' he asked, as he kissed the top of her head.

'I'll have you know, never before have I made love with such fervour. My husband and I did not have a demonstrative relationship,' she said, hiding her face in his chest.

'Don't tell me – you lay back and thought of England?'

Helen blushed. She didn't like to admit it, but that was about right. Making love several times in one night was something she'd never really experienced with John. 'I was just the wife. I would think he left more adventurous things for his mistresses.'

'My poor love,' he said, pulling her closer if that was

276

at all possible and running a finger down her naked back, sending shudders of desire through her body.

'Don't feel sorry for me,' she whispered in his ear. 'This has been worth waiting for.'

'You look radiant,' Richard said as he gazed across the breakfast table in the busy hotel dining room. 'Anyone would think you've been entertaining in your bedroom all night.' He grinned as he nonchalantly picked up a knife and cut open a bread roll on a side plate.

'Shush!' she scolded him. 'People might hear.'

'Let them,' he whispered back. 'I want the world to know I spent the night with a woman I could easily fall in love with.'

Helen waved her butter knife at him. 'Could? You ravish a woman in her bed and then can't tell her you're in love with her?' she said warningly.

Richard looked at the knife and then at Helen, who quickly put it down on her plate. There was a brief silence, broken when a waiter appeared beside their table.

'Excuse me, sir – there's an urgent telephone call for you, from your office.'

'Take the number. I'll ring them back,' Richard replied.

'I'm sorry, sir, they insist you come to the telephone now.' Leaning closer, he went on, 'They mentioned national security, sir.'

Richard threw Helen an apologetic look. 'Enjoy your breakfast, don't wait for me. Goodness knows how long this will take.' He followed the waiter out to the foyer of the hotel.

Twenty minutes later, Helen pushed her plate away. She'd tried valiantly to eat the cooked breakfast as she waited for Richard to return, but failed. She had just finished a second cup of tea when she felt his presence by her chair. He was carrying his suitcase, with his overcoat over one arm.

'I'm sorry, but I've got to go; something urgent has cropped up. I've settled our bills and arranged for someone to drive you back to Biggin Hill. They will be here in fifteen minutes.'

'Take care,' she whispered as he turned and left with a serious look on his face.

Helen watched him go, then left the dining room to collect her own case from her room. She wondered how their conversation would have gone if they hadn't been disturbed by the waiter. Something about the look on Richard's face made her think he was wondering if he'd made a mistake by spending the night with her, when she could have been a killer.

'Don't be daft, Helen,' she scolded herself out loud as she touched up her lipstick in the dressing-table mirror. 'You've got to stop questioning yourself. That was just a silly moment at the table. He told you he doesn't suspect you, so you are quite safe.'

Back at The Grange, she left her case in her room and hurried over to the main house, entering through the kitchen door.

'There you are, lovey. Blimey, going by the glow on your face things couldn't have been as bad as what we thought when you dashed off like that,' Jean said.

Effie was busy rolling pastry out on the kitchen table. She looked up and agreed. 'Was it all a scare?'

278

'Yes; Felicity is all right, and the police have it all in hand. I was so tired once I got back to my hotel room, I slept the sleep of the dead,' Helen replied, moving swiftly through to the library and ignoring their raised eyebrows.

Even though Stan had repeatedly said that as long as her work was done, she could do as she pleased, she still felt guilty for having taken so much time off. She got stuck in, sorting out correspondence and updating the boarding kennel ledgers as well as the accounts for Stan's dog breeding business.

There was one ledger that she'd yet to examine. Now would be as good a time as any, she thought, opening it to the first page. Her heart lurched as she looked at the title. It was a log of all the dogs that had been abandoned or taken in since the start of the summer of 1939. As she flicked through the pages, she saw that Stan had not only logged the size and colouring of each dog but had also given each one a name if they'd arrived without one. He'd also listed any health problems and the cost of veterinary treatment; it was this that made Helen flinch. Surely Stan should not have to take on this cost himself? Opening the top drawer of the desk, she took out a folder of bank statements and turned to the most recent. Her worst fears were proved right. Stan's generosity would bankrupt him within months.

Things will have to change, she decided. Putting down her pen, she went back into the kitchen and sat at the table. 'Do you think I could have a private word with you both?' she said. Seeing the serious look on her face, both women sat down to hear what she had to say.

After Helen had explained, Jean dabbed at her eyes

with the hem of her apron. 'He is a silly bugger. Why has he kept this to himself? His problem is he is a soft touch with all those dogs. Do you know, that last litter of Old English Sheepdog puppies that would have brought in a good few pounds to keep the place ticking over – he gave away every single one! He can't survive like that.'

'Can we tell him we don't want our wages?' Effie asked. 'After all, we've got a roof over our heads. We really don't need a wage as well at the moment.'

'Yes, that would save him a few pounds each week,' Helen agreed.

'If you think Stan would accept that – well, you don't know him very well,' Jean said. 'We can be frugal with the meals to save a bit, but it's out there' – she nodded towards the window overlooking the dog kennels – 'where we need to start bringing in the cash. Let me put the kettle on, and we'll start an action plan.'

Helen went back to her desk to fetch a notepad and pencil, and they gathered again at the table.

'So, ladies: what do we think?'

'We could put up a sign asking people not to leave their dogs tied to the gates,' Effie suggested.

'Even if we camped out at the front gate, we couldn't turn some poor little wretch away. They'd end up being drowned in a bucket,' Jean said. 'I'd not be able to sleep at night if that happened. No, we need more money to look after them. They need more room, as well as somewhere strong and safe so that if there is enemy action they can be sheltered. Let's face it, we've got an airfield almost on our doorstep at the bottom of the hill – we are sitting targets. Stan's had some building materials for a long while, but never the time to build extra kennels.'

'What about the allotments he mentioned? That land could be cleared and turned into viable plots for people to grow their own veg.'

'Would people have enough money to rent an allotment, though? I know I'd love one and, in the end, it would save us money on food, but it's paying the rent that will be the problem,' Effie said, starting to look glum. 'This is going to be hard work.'

'I have an idea. What if they pay us in kind?' Jean suggested. 'They get the plot for nothing as long as they help clear the ground, and everything they grow they split fifty–fifty with us.'

'So, no money comes in, but we end up with loads of cabbage and potatoes?' Effie scoffed.

Helen scribbled on her notepad. 'Then what we do is set up a little shop in the shed by the side of the kitchen, selling fruit and veg and anything that will help the locals who aren't able to grow their own.'

Jean beamed. 'I could keep an eye on it from here. We could put a bell on the door.'

'And approach shops to see if they'd like to buy from us. It would be small scale, but anything we make could be handed over for the upkeep of the stray dogs,' Helen smiled.

'We need to make sure everybody knows it's for the abandoned dogs, rather than Stan's Bobtails,' Effie grinned.

'And we can try to find homes for some of them. Look how Lizzie took on Tom, Dick and Harry – we could ask her to speak to people she knows, see if they might be interested in taking on one of the dogs in exchange for a donation. If you like, I'll collect the children from their classes at the barn today and speak to her about all this. I reckon she will come up with a few ideas,' Helen said.

'But will Stan accept money and help from us without arguing?' Effie asked. 'He doesn't seem to me like a man who would take charity.'

'You leave him to me,' Jean said. 'I'll tell him we're setting up a committee to help with the strays. By the time I finish with him, he'll see it as a very good idea.'

'You seem to have a spring in your step,' Lizzie said as she met Helen at the door of Dalton Court. 'It's good to see you with a smile on your face. I heard you went up to London yesterday with Richard. Would that have anything to do with it?'

Helen shrugged. She'd been so enthused about the ideas for fundraising that she'd completely forgotten Lizzie would want to know all about the situation with Richard. 'I suppose I'd best update you,' she said as she followed her through to the drawing room. 'But that's not what I came here for; I'm here to pick up Dorothy and Jane from school.'

'Oh, come off it,' Lizzie said. 'Collecting the children has never put a smile like that on your face before. I want to know everything.'

Helen sat down, and quickly explained what had happened with Felicity. 'I suppose it's all right to tell you – it's not as if I'm breaking any laws or anything – and at the end of the day it seems she didn't kill John, so really we are no further forward.'

Lizzie had been watching her closely as she spoke. 'Well, the investigation may not be any further forward. But I have a feeling your relationship with Richard may be.'

'Oh, for heaven's sake! It's as if I have a piece of paper stuck to my forehead with "Richard and Helen went to bed together"—' Helen said, before slapping a hand to her mouth. 'Blast!'

Lizzie laughed in delight. 'Why, that's wonderful news. I said you were suited to each other. I know it's only been months since you lost your husband; but to be fair, you lost him a long time before that, and you know it. Which is why Richard is so right for you.'

'I'm not sure,' Helen replied, and explained what had happened at breakfast.

'Think nothing of it,' Lizzie said, waving her hand in the air to dismiss Helen's worries. 'Men are not like us. They can switch off their feelings just like that.' She snapped her fingers.

'Time will tell, I suppose,' Helen said thoughtfully. 'But there's something else I need to speak to you about.' She launched into an enthusiastic explanation of the situation up at The Grange, including the plan they'd hatched for the land being turned into allotments and the urgent need to raise funds to help cover Stan's expenses. 'With the way things are, I'm not even sure he could afford to pay a vet to put the dogs to sleep if he couldn't look after them anymore.'

'Good grief! We mustn't let that happen. We need to make a plan.'

'Well, I rather thought I had,' Helen said, showing Lizzie the notebook where she'd listed all their ideas.

'As brilliant as that is, we need to take it further – and I do believe the people who meet under this roof can help out. Leave it with me. We have a meeting here the day after tomorrow, for all the groups. We should throw ourselves on their mercy, and if Doreen plies them with enough scrummy food and endless pots of tea, they won't be able to say no.'

Helen was puzzled. She wasn't sure what Lizzie was up to, but she'd have to trust her for now. 'I really must dash. I need to collect the children before Mrs Binks starts to think we've abandoned them,' she said, kissing Lizzie's cheek.

Helen headed out of the house, following a footpath towards the barn. As she passed a side door, she saw the RAF corporal who'd helped Richard take down her statement. She stopped to say hello, and asked if Richard was about. Surely, she thought, he must be back from London by now.

'I'm sorry, Miss – we won't be seeing him for a while. He's been called away overseas.' The corporal tapped one side of his nose as he dropped a cigarette end to the ground, stubbing it out with his foot. 'It's too big a secret to share.'

16

February 1940

Stan Trentham looked between his three employees and then at Lizzie, who beamed back at him. 'So this is what you've been up to these past few days? Every time I've seen the lot of you, you've had your heads together nattering. I thought you were chatting about your sewing and knitting. Who am I to question, as long as you get your work done?' he grinned back. 'Well, well, well, this is certainly a plan and a half. And you're doing it all for the dogs.' He nodded thoughtfully, looking at the table where Lizzie's copious notes lay in front of him. 'It's the wrong time of the year to start clearing the land for those allotments,' he went on, running his finger down the list, 'but there again, there's been a fair bit of rain this last week, so the ground won't be hardened by frost. We could possibly make a start. Do you have many volunteers?'

Lizzie was quick to reply. 'Just us at the moment, but we have a meeting of the sewing group tomorrow afternoon and I intend to explain everything to them then. I want to make it quite clear that we are not doing it to work for you – this is to help the abandoned dogs. Perhaps we could even set up some kind of charity on behalf of the poor animals?'

'I appreciate it,' Stan said, 'but some of it is heavy work, and not what women should be doing,' he added, seeing three faces suddenly look glum. Only Jean agreed with him, but then, she was slightly older than the others.

'No, we will make it perfectly clear how you've taken on all the stray dogs and it has nothing to do with your business.' Helen said quickly, not wishing him to change his mind.

'I do have some good news,' Lizzie said, getting back to the subject of the stray dogs. 'You have most of the materials here for a new kennel block. I was speaking to my husband, Major Gerald Donnington, and we wondered if we, that is, me and my husband, could sponsor the building of the kennel block? That way, you could leave that side of it to us. Of course, we would pay for any extra materials and manpower.'

Stan looked shocked. 'Why would you do such a thing? It's not as if you're from round here?'

Lizzie chuckled. 'It's more than that. We see this area as our home. We have no plans to go back to Canada any time soon; let's face it, this war's not going to end next week, is it? I love the area and want to put down roots here whenever the war ends, but one thing we miss, apart from our family, is being involved with dogs. That's why I jumped at taking on Tom, Dick and Harry. My husband's family were very involved in the world of dogs back home in Canada: we both miss being able to visit the kennels and helping out, as well as attending the dog shows. It's such a shame there aren't any at the moment. Perhaps one day that will be remedied – once we've won the war.'

'We've got to win it first,' Effie said. 'Going by what my husband says in his letters – and it's not much due to the censor – he's having a pretty bad time of it over there. Not that I know where over there is. I just hope he's keeping himself safe and not doing anything foolish.'

Helen felt sad for Effie. She never said much about her husband, although it sounded like they had a rock-solid marriage; she must miss him terribly. 'We all hope it will be over soon.'

'Your idea about it being over by Christmas didn't come to much,' Stan said, with a look at Jean. 'Or did you mean next Christmas? I sympathize with you worrying about your husband, Effie. My son is over in France, that's all I know. I'm not a man for praying but I've done my fair share since he went off to fight.'

They all echoed their agreement.

'Well, Mrs Donnington, you seem to have found your-self a plan. I know the sooner the dogs are housed in better conditions, the sooner I can sort out the older building ready for more dogs to arrive. I like your idea about the allotments,' he went on, turning back to Helen. 'With gardeners paying with produce, I won't feel as though I'm taking money out of their pockets. But Jean, will it be too much for you if we set up a little shop in the shed outside? I don't want you overdoing it,' he said considerately.

'I'll have a few people here to help me, and no doubt others will follow. We intend to mention it at the meeting. There will be women wanting to have an allotment, or even share one between a few of them, and we think some will volunteer to help out in the farm shop too. We won't be able to pay them wages, but I'll feed anyone who works here and make sure they don't go short of anything.'

'It's February, so if we can get the ground cleared by March and the individual allotments marked out, people will be able to plan their spring planting,' Helen said. 'I don't know much about vegetable gardening, but it always seems to start pretty early on in the year, doesn't it?'

'Then I suggest we get started right away,' Stan said, rubbing his hands together. 'I'll borrow the tractor from the farm over the way.' He picked up a pencil and added it to the end of the list. 'Let me know how you get on at your meeting.'

'But we thought you'd like to come along to the meeting, as it's your land? We don't want any decisions made that you might not like.'

Stan looked rather uncomfortable. 'Women's meetings aren't something I'd go along to. If you don't mind, I'll leave it all to you. I know I can trust you. If any problems crop up, you come along and tell me. I'll see what I can do to help.' He reached out to shake Lizzie's hand. 'Please pass my thanks along to your husband. It is most generous, what you're both offering.' He looked out of the window to the view down the hill, towards the airfield. 'Goodness knows what's going to be happening down there before too long. I know people think I'm daft, worrying about dogs; but we need to have them safe in case there's any enemy action. Speaking of which, can you add to your lists that everybody who is a volunteer here must know where our shelters are? If the airfield sirens go off, they all need to know where to go.'

'I'll make some posters and have them pinned up everywhere our volunteers will be working. But what if somebody is up at the allotments when it starts?'

'I'll find some way to get an Anderson shelter for the allotments as soon as an area is cleared,' he said.

'This is going to be fun,' Effie grinned. 'I can't wait for everyone to do more to help those poor dogs.'

'Poor dogs?' Stan laughed gruffly. 'They lead the life of Riley down there: food, walks, a warm bed. I reckon that's why we have so many turn up. The word is out it's a great place to live.'

'I'll second that,' Helen said, and meant it.

She and Lizzie linked arms as they walked out to the car. 'That seemed to go very well. I was rather worried Stan would resent us trying to take over his affairs.'

'Me too, but now we're all systems go. I can't wait for the sewing circle get-together tomorrow. Doreen has been instructed to lay on a delicious afternoon tea so that we have everybody in the right frame of mind before we call on them for their help. They say the way to a man's heart is through his stomach; I'm hoping the same applies to women's generosity,' Lizzie said as they reached her car and she opened the door.

'It will be expensive,' Helen said, concerned. 'You shouldn't really be expected to lay on food for over thirty women – and surely the children in the school will expect something as well?'

'My darling, don't worry about it. Gerald is supplying most of the provisions. Let's just say that along with the dog kennels, the Canadian air force will also be sponsoring tomorrow afternoon's tea,' Lizzie said, giving a broad wink. 'It's a shame you can't come back with me right now – we could get on with your quilt. It's coming along beautifully.'

'I'm getting rather nervous about it now that the wadding and the backing is stitched in place. It seems so final to be starting the quilting. Then of course it will be finished, and I'll have to think of something else to make.'

'I have an idea about that as well, but I'll bring it up tomorrow at the meeting.'

'Gosh, Lizzie, you're so full of ideas and energy. I don't know where you get it all from!'

'Well, I have more time on my hands than you do. What is it they say about the devil making work for idle hands?' She chuckled. 'Now, there's something else I wanted to ask you before I go: will your mother be coming tomorrow afternoon?'

'I don't know. She's been much friendlier since she's attended some of the sewing and knitting circles; she enjoys teaching some of the newer members how to turn a heel correctly. She's coming here to tea this afternoon, so I'll ask her then.'

'She's coming to tea? I'm full of admiration for you, offering an olive branch. I take it the stepfather won't be coming?'

'No – it seems he has something on. But I don't want him here anyway. It's going to be hard enough work with Mother on her own.'

Lizzie reached through the open car window and took Helen's hand, giving it a squeeze. 'I know you don't get on with your stepfather, but I can't help feeling there is something more to it; something that lies much deeper.

I'm not asking you what it is. I'll just say that if ever you want to chat about it, I'll be here to listen to you.'

Helen mumbled her thanks and kissed Lizzie's cheek before standing back as she started the engine. She waved as her friend's little car left The Grange. Lizzie was so kind, but it would take a lot for Helen to open her heart and share the fears and worries that had been with her for so long.

She headed to the office to get on with her work. She had a lot to do before she packed up for the day to go back to their rooms and prepare to entertain Hillary Davis. Although her mother had softened towards her in recent weeks, Helen still found that she was hard work. Even so, she intended to play the dutiful daughter and try not to allow her mother to upset her.

Helen spent a couple of hours with her head down, completing monthly accounts and typing up a few letters to suppliers before checking the library was spick and span. Since she'd started working for Stan Trentham she had overhauled the whole room. One wall of shelves held his books on dogs and animal welfare, a smaller bookcase was home to the leather-bound classics, and old filing cabinets filled with paperwork lined a third wall. The desk was now highly polished and the rugs that covered the parquet flooring had been beaten over a washing line to remove all the dust. The low winter sun shone through the clean windows and made Helen smile as it warmed her face. She loved her work here and hoped that when she showed her mother around later, Hillary would be impressed with The Grange.

There was a tap on the door and Jean stuck her head

round. 'Sorry to bother you, Helen – but I had time to make a few bits and bobs for you to take back with you. I know you're a bit nervous about your mother visiting later today, so I wanted to play my part.' She held out a large tin that held a sausage-meat plait. 'You can serve it cold, in slices.'

'Gosh, that's impressive! Thank you so much, Jean. I wonder, would you like to join us?'

Jean's face showed clearly what she thought about sitting down to tea with Hillary Davis. 'I've got the ironing to be getting on with, if you don't mind. I want to be up to date so I can go off with a clear conscience to the meeting tomorrow. There's also a half-knitted balaclava helmet that needs finishing for me to hand over when I go. I do hope you have a good time and I want to hear all about your mother's visit. Don't forget to walk her round the grounds and show her the dogs as well.'

'I intend to show her as much as possible,' Helen said. 'In fact, I'm going to do that before we have our tea, so that we don't lose the light. God forbid I get lost with her in the dark.'

Jean chuckled. 'Don't worry. Just shout and we will send out a search party,' she said, bidding Helen a good afternoon.

When Helen arrived back at their rooms, she saw that Effie had been very busy. 'There was no need for all this, honestly.'

'Well, I'm not giving Mrs Davis any excuse to pick holes in where we live. I've collected every toy belonging to the children and packed them away in our bedroom, and I'll be out of your hair for a few hours as I'm going to walk down to the shop before jumping on the bus to go and collect the girls when they finish school. They love it there so much, and Mrs Binks is such a darling. They were full of how they've learnt their numbers this week. It seems she had them playing bingo, but to be honest, it worked. Both of the girls are getting much better at recognizing numbers, although I wish they wouldn't keep saying *two little ducks* and *legs eleven.*' She giggled. 'We will be late back because the Brownie meeting is going to be held in the barn and the girls have been invited to attend. It will be lots of fun for them.'

'I must say, the barn has come into its own, hasn't it? I'm not sure many people will want to move back to the church hall once the repairs and rebuilding are complete. That's going to upset Tish.'

Effie took her coat from the coat stand and picked up a bag. 'I hope it all goes well,' she said, giving Helen a quick hug and checking her watch. 'I'll be scooting off before she arrives. By the way – how was she getting here?'

'A bus to the end of the lane, and she's walking up the rest of the way.'

'In that case I'll take the footpath across the field.' Effie giggled again and hurried off.

Helen sat at her sewing machine, carefully piecing together strips of colourful fabric while keeping one eye on the clock. This is worse than waiting to sit an exam at school, she thought to herself, as she got up and wandered around the room, straightening cushions and pictures that were already straight. Wondering if her mother could be lost, she slipped her coat around her shoulders and stepped out to the top of the steps that led down to the driveway in front of The Grange. She could call out if she saw her mother arriving. Already the February afternoon was turning darker. She'd be glad when spring arrived and with it the lighter evenings, but there again, was she being selfish – would this affect the pilots at the airfield? Lighter nights meant the enemy could cause problems, bombing the airfield.

A cold shudder ran through her. She tried to imagine what it must be like down there, preparing and waiting, wondering if or when the enemy would strike. She'd read of several attacks on the country, and accounts of trouble in Europe were in the newspapers and on the wireless every day. She made a promise to herself to try to find out more about the war news; she'd been too bound up with her own problems of late and selfishly ignored world news.

Noticing a movement at the front of The Grange, she walked down a couple of steps to see more clearly. It seemed her mother had arrived and was chatting to Stan Trentham. 'Oh, please don't say she knocked on the front door of the main house . . .' Helen muttered to herself as she hurried down the steps to join them.

'Here she is,' Stan said as he turned to greet Helen. 'I was just about to walk your mother over to your place; I'm afraid I stopped her to chat. I had no idea you were Hillary Davis's daughter. I went to school with your dad,' he explained.

Helen's heart leapt; it had been so long since someone mentioned her dad, as her mother refused to speak about him. 'What a small world,' was all she could say, eyeing Hillary nervously to see if she would change the subject or snap at Stan. But her mother looked as if butter wouldn't melt in her mouth, and smiled so charmingly that for a moment, Helen wondered if it was even really her standing there.

'I'll leave you to enjoy one another's company,' Stan said. 'You have a good daughter – I don't know what I'd do without her here. And Helen, you must remind me to dig out my old photograph album to show you. I'm surprised you've not come across them in the library. There are a couple of photographs in there of me and your dad together,' he said, bidding them good afternoon.

'I had no idea Dad was friends with Stan Trentham,' Helen said cautiously as she led Hillary back towards her home. She was wary of her mother's reaction, but even so, this new information had put a spring in her step.

'It was a long time ago, and some things are best left to memories rather than always bringing them up,' Hillary said, returning to form as she looked around her. 'Stan certainly has an impressive home,' she commented approvingly. 'I wonder why you don't live in the house? It looks large enough.'

Helen directed her to the stairs that ran up the outside of the building. 'Because I'm staff, Mother, and The Grange is his home. Only Jean lives in, and that's because the cook's rooms are close to the kitchen. This used to be the stable block and these days it's where Stan keep his vehicles. We like living here, it's cosy – and there's a beautiful view down the hill from the window in our living room.'

Hillary didn't reply. Instead she stepped in through the door and stood looking around. The scent of lavender furniture polish greeted them, and Helen was thankful for Effie's elbow grease.

'It does look cosy,' Hillary said, watching as Helen switched on lamps to give the room a warm glow. 'I do like what you've done with the place.' She looked at one of Effie's rag rugs, which decorated the hearth. Although Helen had encouraged her to use the colourful rugs for her own bedroom, Effie had wanted to use them for the shared living area.

Helen placed the kettle on the stove and checked she didn't need to add another piece of wood to keep it going. 'We have a sausage loaf warming in the oven,' she said. 'I thought it would be more filling than sandwiches, and it should be ready in half an hour. I'll make our tea, and perhaps you'd like a slice of cake with it? Jean Carter is the cook here; you know her from Lizzie's groups.'

'A delightful woman,' Hillary said, 'and I also approve of your friend Lizzie. It's good to see that you're keeping up your social contacts, even though you've decided to live with a housekeeper.'

Helen ignored this barb, choosing to focus on her mother's more pleasant comments. 'I like Lizzie, and her husband is very nice too. I'll introduce you to him when we're next at one of her groups. Are you going tomorrow afternoon? It's going to be a very special meeting. There are some new projects being announced that will benefit the dogs here at The Grange.'

'I wasn't planning to attend, but if something special is happening my services may be required. Especially if it has something to do with Stan's business. Is he still breeding his pedigree dogs?'

Helen raised her eyebrows. Of course her mother would attend if it helped her climb the social ladder. 'Yes, he is – in fact, he has some puppies at the moment. Most of the pedigree dog showing has stopped until the end of the war, but Stan and people like him are doing their utmost to keep their breeds going. If you like, I could show you round before we eat. It's quite a set-up. Lizzie and her husband are going to sponsor a new kennel block.'

'Are they indeed?' Hillary said approvingly. 'I am impressed.'

Helen left her mother warming herself by the fire as she poured hot water into the warmed teapot and covered it with a knitted cosy, made by Jean as a moving-in gift. It was quite a jolly thing that looked like a large red strawberry. Taking the tea over to her mother, she went on to explain about the many stray dogs Stan had taken in and how it was becoming a problem. Hillary didn't seem interested until Helen mentioned that Lizzie was organizing fundraising events, expecting local newspapers to become involved – and that Gerald Donnington would announce a special fundraising event the following day.

Hillary's eyes lit up. 'Perhaps I would be able to devote some of my time to help with the fundraising. After all, my organizational skills are in much demand up at the golf club. This is why you are so good at your job; you've inherited it from me,' she said, preening.

'That's good to know, Mother,' Helen said politely, filing this remark away to share with Lizzie later. 'If you've finished your tea, perhaps you'd like to take a stroll before it gets too dark? I have a spare pair of wellington boots, if you'd like to borrow them. I'd hate your shoes to get messy.' She didn't expect her mother to accept, but Hillary did, and noticed Helen's raised eyebrows.

'I wasn't always so refined, you know, my dear. I was a country girl long before you were born. I used to ride out with the hunt at one time. You needn't look so shocked – you were too young to remember when your father was alive, and we did such things together.'

'I'd no idea.' But then, Hillary had never spoken about the past, so how was Helen to know? She was aware that her memory of being a young child could be selective. If she'd ever been involved with her parents and their pursuits, those memories had long since slipped beneath the surface. It comforted her to know her mother was at last able to speak of her father. Even if it's only when Gavin is not around, she thought as she pulled out the boots for Hillary to wear.

Hillary wobbled slightly as she put her foot into the rubber boot, and reached out to grab the back of a nearby chair. At the same time, Helen caught hold of her arm, not wanting to see her fall. Hillary cried out in pain.

'I'm sorry – did I hurt you?' Helen apologized.

'No, it's an old injury, I'm fine,' Hillary said as she rubbed her upper arm.

'I don't think you are fine,' Helen said gently, concerned by the pained expression on her mother's face. Without asking for permission she slipped Hillary's cardigan from her shoulder and cried out in dismay as she saw a large purple bruise around the uppermost part of her arm. She could see the imprint of fingers.

'How did this happen?'

'It's nothing. I walked into the edge of the door, that's all,' her mother said, pulling her cardigan back on.

'Then it's strange, because I've had a similar bruise on my arm and I most definitely did not walk into a door. I think perhaps we need to have a talk, don't you? Here, let me help you on with your coat. We can talk while we walk around the grounds.'

Helen took Hillary's other arm, as they walked down towards the kennels housing the Old English Sheepdogs. She pointed out the paddocks, and the area further up the lane that would be cleared for allotments. Hillary showed interest, and when the shop was mentioned she offered to put in a few hours a week.

'Don't look at me like that, Helen. I'm perfectly capable of working,' she insisted.

'Even with a badly bruised arm?' Helen asked pointedly.

'Good heavens, it won't be for a while and this bruise will go down very quickly. I may be getting on in years but I am still capable of healing.'

'Until the next bruise?'

Hillary stopped and turned to face her daughter. 'What are you talking about?'

'I too have had bruises like this – not only when I was a child, but after I came back to live at The Maples. Gavin is quite a violent man, isn't he?'

'He's a good man. He took us both on when we had nothing apart from the house. I don't know what I would have done without him. I would have become an old and lonely woman, worrying about her future,' Hillary answered with a catch in her voice. 'We should be grateful.'

'Grateful? For a man who acts like a thug? He's abusive, Mother, you must understand that. I'm fearful that one day he will go too far and really injure you . . .' Helen couldn't go on, as memories of what she'd endured as a child with Gavin's harsh words and punches came back to her. Then as she turned into a young woman, his behaviour had changed . . . 'I did try to tell you . . . but you wouldn't listen. I thought you would believe him over me. Then he told me if I ever spoke to anyone about it, he would leave us both destitute . . .'

'He's changed,' Hillary insisted in a strained voice. 'He's been offered work over at the airfield. He will be in charge of men doing repairs, very much like he was when he worked for the council. He had such a responsible job,' she said, for once not bragging. 'He's also suggested we put The Maples up for sale and find somewhere smaller, now it's only the two of us in the house. The money would come in handy. I owe it to Gavin to pay him back for all he's invested in our lives.'

Helen was horrified. 'Pay him back! Was this his suggestion?' she asked, grimacing when her mother confirmed her fears.

'I hate the thought of leaving the house, but if Gavin says it's for the best then so be it.'

'But Dad left the house to us. You were supposed to live out your days in the family home,' Helen replied, suddenly feeling close to tears.

'You have to remember that for all his faults, Gavin means well. I do think he's changed.'

'If he's changed so much, why did you want Effie to get the children out of the house as quickly as possible?

As far as I can see, he is still a bully. And that bruise on your arm is proof of that.'

'I don't want to talk about it . . . I just want a quiet life. Please don't ask me any more.' Hillary started to cry.

'I don't want to upset you, Mother, but I'm fearful for your safety. No woman should have to endure such things. I blame myself for not doing more to stop him.'

'You've got to believe me. Gavin is so much better now it's just us in the house, and Daisy.'

'Who?'

'Our new housekeeper.'

'Oh, I see. But Mother, a leopard can't change its spots. He's always been the same.'

'But he's like a different man at the golf club – he is so involved in everything there and now he's going to be working again, it's like I have the old Gavin back. Things will be much better, I promise.'

Helen couldn't believe what she was hearing. Why was Hillary ignoring what this man had done, and was still doing, going by that bruise? 'There is something I've always wondered, and you've never really answered me when I've asked. Why did he leave his job, if he was so important overseeing the works department?'

'He told me there had been a change in management. He couldn't cope with the bullies who made his life unbearable. That's why he left.'

'But surely he could have gone to somebody for help? What with him being such a valued employee?'

'I don't know. Please – just stop asking me these questions,' Hillary said. 'I came here to look around and settle in my mind that you are happy where you are now living. I always used to feel that although you had married well, you were unhappy.'

Helen stopped in her tracks. Had it been that obvious – even to her mother, who could not accept that she had an abusive husband under her own roof? She gave an ironic laugh as she tucked her arm through Hillary's. 'We're a right pair, aren't we? I think it's time we started looking after each other, don't you?'

'I'd like that, dear,' Hillary said, and did something Helen could not remember her ever doing before. She turned to her daughter and kissed her cheek.

17

Helen slipped into one of the rooms Lizzie had designated for the craftswomen. What she saw made her put a hand to her mouth to stifle a gasp. So it was true: her mother really was helping to teach women how to sew.

Helen had only ever known Hillary to sit with partly completed embroidery on her lap. She'd thought it was mainly there to impress visitors, rather than because Hillary had any intention of creating something beautiful. Yet here she was, showing women how to repair a frayed cuff on a man's shirt.

Hillary moved around the circle of women, bending over shoulders to point out errors or to praise the seamstress. She was surprised to see Helen and stopped to speak with her. 'I'd have invited you to join us, but I thought you preferred to cut up shirts rather than repair them,' she smiled.

Helen was taken back. For once there was no malice in her mother's words. 'I came to remind the ladies that afternoon tea is to be taken in the barn today, as Lizzie has some announcements to make. I didn't expect to see you taking a class.'

'Rita Binks was going to do it originally, but her arthritis is playing up, so I offered to help. I've quite enjoyed myself so I will suggest to Lizzie that I run a few more classes on repairing clothing. I fear in the years ahead we will all have to think about taking more care of our clothing. I'd even thought of starting a clothing exchange group for mothers. Children grow so quickly . . .' she murmured, looking round the room with a smile. 'It is nice to feel needed.'

Who is this woman in front of me? Helen thought, as a warmth spread through her. I like her very much.

'You are very much needed, Mother. Now gather your brood together and let us go hear what Lizzie has to say.'

'I'd like to introduce you all to Tom, Dick and Harry,' Lizzie said proudly as she walked into the crowded barn with her three little terriers on matching leather leads.

Cries of delight could be heard rippling through the room, with several women stooping to pick up the dogs to give them a cuddle. The dogs loved the attention and were soon begging for titbits.

'Please don't give them too much cake,' Lizzie said. 'I dread to think of the consequences. Now, ladies, my reason for bringing these little visitors to you today, and for us to be enjoying our tea in the barn, is that I need to speak to you all together. And such is the success of the craft circles that we can't all fit into one of the craft rooms.' She clapped her hands to gain attention as a buzz of chatter started towards the rear of the barn. 'Please, ladies, this won't take long, and then you can get back to your tea and cake. Some of you will know a house called The Grange, which is owned by Stan Trentham. Stan is a breeder of pedigree dogs. You may have seen his beautiful Old English Sheepdogs being walked – some of them even work on farms around here. Well, Stan has a lot on his hands keeping his breed alive during this war and running his boarding kennels, which are full to overflowing with dogs being cared for at special rates because their owners are serving away from home.'

Helen, who was watching from the side of the barn, was touched by the women's reaction to this; there was even a round of applause for Stan.

'Now, Stan is no spring chicken, and his own son is away serving in France – but he has another problem. I'm afraid word of his kennels has spread far and wide. Sadly, as so many people are worried about the upkeep of their pets during God knows what we will all be facing, they've started to leave their dogs outside his premises. There have been many people too embarrassed to speak to Stan, who have simply tied their dog's lead to his fence and left.'

'Shame on them,' someone shouted.

'What else can they do, apart from have them put down?' another woman responded, causing an argument to break out.

Once everyone had calmed down, Lizzie continued. 'I hate to think what I'd do if I found myself faced with a choice between relying on a stranger's charity and having my three dogs put to sleep.'

A rumble of agreement echoed through the barn.

'But thanks to Stan, all of these dogs have a good home.

He refuses to have any put down. Now, it's a big commitment to have all these extra dogs cared for, and although he has staff who volunteer in their own time to feed and exercise them, it's a big expense. There is a new kennel block being built, along with an Anderson shelter, and the costs of all that are covered, but Stan needs help with the additional costs of caring for these animals. We're all local – some of you know Stan, some went to school with his son. Some of you may even have been at school with Stan himself. I've met a few of you who have purchased dogs from him, and mighty fine animals they are too. I could go on; but you get the picture?'

'We do!' was the response.

'Good!' Lizzie shouted back. 'Because this is where all of you ladies can start to help Stan out. A few of us have made some tentative plans and run them past Stan, the idea being that we establish a charity that will hopefully help the abandoned dogs live a happy life. What do you say?'

'I hope you don't want us to take any dogs in. My husband won't stand for that,' one woman called out.

'No, that's not what we mean at all. First of all, Stan is signing over a field up the lane just past his house to be divided into allotments, so that anybody can have one to grow their own vegetables. His idea is to put a shelter up there for any of you who don't feel safe out in the open at the moment. For that, he's asking a payment of fifty per cent of your crops.'

'I thought there'd be a catch,' another woman called out.

'No, it's not a catch. Please do listen,' Lizzie said as the woman got up to leave. 'We are going to set up a small shop at The Grange. Jean here, and Effie, and I believe Helen's mother Hillary, have offered to help run the shop. We will sell the produce. Any money that's made will go to the upkeep of the dogs.'

There was a loud cheer, and the few people who'd made negative comments looked down at their laps in shame.

'That's splendid,' Tish called out supportively.

'But it's not enough,' Lizzie added. 'We need to do more. We need those of you who can offer an hour or two a week to sign up to go up to The Grange to help out: walking a dog, cleaning out a kennel or just doing general jobs. It's nothing technical, you don't need to handle a large dog if you don't like large dogs – we are just asking that you show friendship to the animals, and Stan will be eternally grateful.'

'And there will also be more of this cake, and gallons of tea,' Jean called out. 'Anyone who comes to help out will leave with a slice of cake.'

'Where do we sign?' a couple of women in the front row asked. Effie, who was standing with Helen, held up a clipboard ready to collect names.

'But that's not all,' Lizzie laughed, looking at the expectant faces of the women. 'Some of you don't enjoy the outdoors. Perhaps you're not fit enough to help with dogs? But there are other ways you can help. This next idea will bring the community together. I'm going to invite my husband over. Please welcome Major Donnington.'

Gerald stepped forward and said hello to the women waiting for him to speak. He looked embarrassed as they clapped and cheered.

'I won't speak for long, ladies. I know you want to get back to your handiwork, but I've had a word with the people over at the airfield, and there are many men and women who are away from home right now, who would like some home comforts, or gifts to send to their loved ones. This is where you all come in. We thought a display of your work could be set up where the airfield personnel can see it, along with tables full of knitted goods, your rugs, patchwork and anything else you can think of to sell. All the profits will go to supporting the dogs. I'll sort out a date to give you all plenty of notice.'

'What about baked goods, as long as someone can supply the ingredients?' Jean suggested.

Gerald smiled. 'Consider it done. We can come to an arrangement, ma'am. I'm going to leave it there and let you all get on. I will speak to my wife about dates. Let's work together, and do some good. Don't forget, all the profits go up to The Grange to help support the stray dogs.'

'Are there any questions?' Lizzie asked, and worked her way through simple questions like, 'I can't knit very fast but I'd like to make a pair of gloves,' and other comments like, 'How much should we charge for items?'

'We can work all of this out, ladies, please don't worry. What I suggest you do now is volunteer to go up to the kennels to help out as much as you can, if you can. Please leave your name and details with Effie King.' She pointed to where Effie was waving her clipboard in the air again. 'And anyone who would like to get involved in handiwork sales, please see Helen Wentworth,' she added, pointing to Helen, who also had a clipboard.

Jean stood up and shouted: 'If anyone wants to help bake and make things that people might buy to eat, which we can sell in the farm shop when it's up and running, please come and see me.'

'Oh, I almost forgot about the allotments,' Lizzie said. 'If anyone would like to put their name down for an allotment, please can you see Mrs Tish Green and Mrs Rita Binks, who will make a list of names. The ground needs clearing, and we've had a few volunteers from the RAF boys; but if you feel up to rolling up your sleeves and helping out, or perhaps you've got a lad still at home that can help, then please ask them. The sooner we get the allotments up and running, the sooner there will be more vegetables for your own kitchens and money to go into the pot for the dogs.'

'You can put me down to carry the baked goods and vegetables in my shop. I'll pay the going rate, as well,' the lady from the corner shop shouted out.

'Please speak to Jean, and thank you,' Lizzie called back to her over the hubbub. 'If there's nothing else, ladies, please help yourself to another cup of tea – and I do believe there is a little cake left,' she said as her speech ended.

'There is something else,' Helen piped up. Lizzie gave her a puzzled look, but she carried on. 'We'd like to thank Major and Mrs Donnington for giving up their home for our groups, and also for their generosity, because it's the Donningtons who have sponsored the new kennels for the stray dogs up at The Grange. I had a word with Stan before we left and he has decided that the kennels, when finished, will be called the Donnington Block.'

Loud claps and cheers were heard as an embarrassed Lizzie and Gerald took a bow.

'Phew, I think that went well,' Lizzie said as she joined Helen, Effie and Hillary. 'I'm glad you could join us today, Hillary,' she added, aware that mother and daughter had made great strides towards getting along better.

'I've enjoyed it,' Hillary said. 'I'd like to echo my thanks along with everybody else. I'll put my thinking cap on to see what I can do to help. I have lots of time on my hands these days.'

'Are you not going to the golf club so much, Mother?'

'No, I prefer to go when Gavin is also available, and he is rather busy.' She turned to Lizzie. 'He's managing a team doing maintenance work over on the airfield. It's quite an important position, and very similar to what he did when he ran a department for a London council.'

Lizzie showed interest. 'You must be very proud of him, Hillary. I hope to see you at more of our groups – and by all means, if you can think of anything that we can do to raise funds, then please mention it to Helen and we can add it to our list.'

'She can help me with my bingo,' Rita Binks said as she joined them. Hillary looked aghast and Helen tried not to laugh.

'Bingo – what's this?' Lizzie asked, raising her eyebrows.

'I've had a word with the vicar's wife, and because the church hall's still out of action we thought we could use the barn one evening a week. Everyone loves to play bingo, and it's bound to raise some money. I've got all the equipment because I've run it up at the old folks' home,' Rita said proudly. 'You can help me by being a caller – you've got a nice loud voice,' she added, turning to Hillary.

'We'll have to see about that,' Hillary replied.

Lizzie thanked them. 'Helen, I need to have a word with you,' she said, and the two of them went back to the house and into the drawing room.

'Is there a problem?' Helen asked, looking slightly worried. 'I thought it all went splendidly. If anything, we'll probably end up with too many volunteers.'

'Never turn down a volunteer. I'll make sure every name is entered before they leave today – and also make a list of those that haven't volunteered, and see if we can twist their arm at a later date,' Lizzie laughed.

'Then why did you want to see me? Have I made a mistake on my quilt again? It's taking quite a while. I'm not very good at the hand stitching when I can't get to my machine. Why, I stabbed my finger with a needle yesterday and almost bled over part of the quilting.'

'You've also cried over it a few times, so that's blood and tears. Don't worry about it; it'll all come out in the wash, as they say. What I wanted to speak to you about was your husband's memorial service. A while back, you invited me to attend with you, and I wanted to tell you that I mentioned it to Richard Gladstone. It was only in passing, and I didn't want you to think that I've been telling tales out of school.'

Helen felt uncomfortable. She had once accused Lizzie of tittle-tattle, telling Richard something when it hadn't been true.

'I thought he was still away? One of his men told me he was working overseas. I did wonder if the investigation was any further forward, what with him not being in the country.'

'Then perhaps you could ask him yourself? I do believe he is back today.'

Helen looked around, half expecting Richard to walk into the room. 'I will when I see him next.'

'The thing is,' Lizzie said, looking uncomfortable, 'when I mentioned the memorial service, he offered to drive us both. He's going in an official capacity, you see.'

Helen didn't know what to think. Part of her wouldn't know how to react when she saw Richard, and another part of her wanted to know why weeks had passed without him making any contact. There hadn't even been a letter. It troubled her that he'd gone so silent, especially after the night they'd spent together.

'I really don't mind – at least that will mean we don't have to travel on the train in our best clothes. But I thought we were going to stay over and take in a show? That was our original plan.'

'I do feel, with all that's going on here, that perhaps we shouldn't stay over after all. And if Richard is driving us then we can get back, even if it's late evening. Do you mind very much?'

'No, I don't mind at all. In fact, I'd prefer to have a couple of friendly faces by my side. I feel it's going to be something of an ordeal meeting colleagues as well as all the important VIP guests; and of course John's family, too. Do you think Felicity will have the nerve to turn up?'

'After all you've told me, that wouldn't surprise me at all. I reckon she will arrive looking like the scarlet woman she is,' Lizzie said darkly.

Helen chuckled, 'Who's been watching too many spy films at the cinema?'

'If only I had the time. Perhaps we ought to think about treating ourselves? It would be fun!'

'If you want fun, we will have to wait until Mrs Binks's bingo evenings start. We're far too busy in the meantime, my dear. Besides, with my mother being one of the callers, it should be entertaining,' Helen laughed.

Lizzie stopped laughing and looked at Helen. 'I've had an idea.'

'Another one? You need to sit down and rest.'

Lizzie shushed her good-naturedly. 'If we are using the barn for one evening of entertainment, why not use it for more events?'

'More bingo?'

'No, I thought we could hold a dance. People always enjoy getting dressed up and going out.'

'That's not a bad idea,' Helen said. 'Locals normally have to go into town for that kind of thing. Let's add it to the list of ideas.'

'What are you women planning now?' Gerald Donnington asked as he joined them along with Richard Gladstone. 'I turn my back for a minute and you're up to all kinds of things. If I'm not careful, my home will be taken over as a house of ill repute.'

'In your dreams, my love, in your dreams,' Lizzie chuckled.

'We were making some more plans to fundraise for the stray dogs up at The Grange,' Helen explained, flustered by Richard's sudden appearance, but smiling at Lizzie's interaction with her husband. It must be wonderful to be so at ease with the person you loved.

Lizzie looked towards Richard. 'I was speaking with Helen about your kind offer to drive us to Westminster for the memorial service.'

'It's very generous of you,' Helen said, not making eye contact with him, as memories of their night together came flooding back and she felt her face start to burn. She knew her thoughts must be obvious, as Lizzie was giving her a strange look.

'What about your mother? Does Hillary not wish to join us? She seems to have mellowed lately. I've noticed quite a difference in her disposition,' Lizzie said.

'I do believe she would like to – especially as we're travelling up together, and she doesn't have to bother with trains. You're right, Mother has changed; you have no idea how pleased I am.'

'What about your stepfather?' Richard asked. 'I appreciate you don't get on; I hope I'm not speaking out of turn here.'

'No, it's fine, say what you want,' Helen assured him. 'I've never got on with him,' she explained to Lizzie's husband. 'I doubt he would want to come, and to be honest I would prefer not to invite him. In any case, Mother informs me that he is now working over at the airfield, managing a team of workers.'

'Is he now?' Richard asked. 'Would you be able to spare me a few minutes, Helen? I just need to ask you a couple of questions, as something has cropped up.'

'Of course. I'll see you back upstairs in the patchwork room later,' Helen said to Lizzie, as she and Richard left the room and wandered down the hallway to his office.

'Take a seat,' he said, nodding towards an armchair. 'This isn't a formal interview or anything like that.'

'I'm relieved to hear it, because I really don't have anything else to tell you.'

Richard picked up a few sheets of paper from his desk and shuffled them before clearing his throat. 'I want to apologize to you first . . .'

'Whatever for?'

'I feel as though I loved you and left you.' He looked uncomfortable. 'It was urgent that I went over to France, and I've only just got back.'

'It must have been important. I hope you weren't in danger?'

'I was well taken care of,' he said, adding with a small smile, 'You've no need to worry about me.'

But I do! she wanted to say, but instead kept her feelings in check. It came as a shock to her at that moment to realize that she loved Richard, and although the thought was exhilarating, she was also keenly aware that her husband had been dead not six months. She felt disloyal to John's memory, and for a moment dwelt on how her mother would wonder what everyone would say. Giving herself a mental shake, she smiled gently. 'I worry about all my friends.'

'I'm glad we can be friends, and you forgive me,' he answered, although there was a sadness around his eyes.

'What was it you wanted to speak to me about?'

'Gavin Davis.'

Helen shook her head. 'I've nothing to say about that man, apart from the fact I find him detestable.'

'Would you be able to tell me why? I don't know much about him.'

'I'd rather not. Do I have to?' She gave him a desperate look. 'Speak to my mother instead, she knows more about him than I do . . .'

'Would it help if I spoke to both of you together?'

'I really don't know. She may resent the fact that I've asked you to speak to her. Look, Richard . . . I'm only just starting to build bridges with my mother. We've never been close. She is not an affectionate woman at the best of times. When my father died, I was a young child; she took it badly, and blamed him for leaving us alone. She saw Gavin as a lifesaver. He was able to pay the bills and keep a roof over our heads after my father's investments had come to nothing. The house belonged to Mother, but Gavin found out we were in dire straits and came to Mother's rescue.' She gave a harsh laugh. 'Mother called him her knight in shining armour. She always took his side whatever he did, and she would never listen to me. I've already told you that I left home as soon as I could – and I don't think he's changed one little bit since then,' she finished, her voice wavering.

'I'm sorry,' Richard said sincerely. 'I didn't mean to upset you.'

'No, it's fine – you need to know the truth about him. Ask Mother about the bruises on her arm; ask why he lied to her, saying he'd been on bowls club trips that turned out never to have happened. I think he is carrying on with another woman, and if so, that's his least serious crime against our family. He's a nasty bully and made my life hell as a child. I have reason to know that he is still nasty to my mother, but please don't tell her I said so.'

'Of course; he doesn't sound a pleasant chap. I'll do

what I can. You do understand that I need to speak to everyone who knew John, don't you?'

'I understand completely. I take it you've spoken to John's family? No, there's no need to answer my question. I shouldn't have asked; your investigation is private.' She held up a hand in an attempt to stop him speaking.

'I can tell you that his mother and sisters were distressed, but had nothing to add to my enquiries,' he replied. But he had started to shuffle his paperwork again, and wasn't making eye contact.

Noticing his discomfort, she tried to reassure him. 'They've never liked me. Perhaps if I'd given John an heir it might have been different, but as far as his mother was concerned, I'm some kind of gold-digger. If only she'd known the truth.'

'The truth?'

'John needed the voting public to think of him as a family man with an agreeable and dutiful wife. Working in his office, he spotted me and decided I fitted the bill. I was fool enough, after my miserable childhood, to believe he cared for me. Just like Mother, I thought I'd found my knight in shining armour,' she said bitterly.

'The man was a fool,' Richard muttered angrily before composing himself. 'Can you tell me anything else about Gavin?'

'There is something. I was going to look into this myself – more out of curiosity than anything else. He may well tell you that he was some big noise working for a London council, but it seems he left suddenly and never explained why. Knowing that he's lied to my mother about the bowls club trip, I've been wondering if he could be hiding something darker? But this has nothing to do with John's death; it's just something that has been bothering me.'

'It would be good to get to the bottom of it,' Richard agreed, 'if only for your peace of mind. I'd like to help, but first I'll have a word with him. I'll not say anything that makes him turn on your mother, or you. I'll just have a general chat about things. I can catch him at the airfield, and later I'll let you know what he has to say.'

'Thank you, Richard, I appreciate your help. If that's all – I must get back to my group,' she said, hoping for one fleeting moment that he would kiss her.

'Any time,' he said as he watched her leave the room. He wanted to tell her that he would move heaven and earth to see her happy; but perhaps it was far too soon to declare himself.

Richard wasn't one to let the grass grow under his feet, and as he had an appointment at the airfield the next morning, he decided to seek out Gavin Davis and have that little chat.

Poking his head around the door of the administration block, he asked if he could be pointed to Gavin's office.

The WAAF behind the desk laughed. 'Do you mean that chap who's running one of the maintenance teams? He doesn't have an office, but you'll find him down the end of the field. There's a problem with one of the drains. If he's skiving, which does happen quite often, he'll be in the hut where the tools are stored. He enjoys a cup of tea in there.'

Richard gave the girl a wink and thanked her before

318

taking the footpath around the perimeter of the airfield in the direction she'd pointed out. He stopped occasionally to talk with people he knew. Mostly it was to say hello and ask after the staff he'd worked with on previous cases. It made him think about the number of cases he'd investigated, and whether he saw this as a career to take him into middle age. He'd been headhunted by Scotland Yard; perhaps after the war was over, he would reconsider his future. For some reason, Helen Wentworth came to mind. He'd very much like her to be part of his future too, but first he needed to sort out Gavin Davis.

Up ahead, he could see some men standing around a freshly dug hole. This must be him, he thought to himself as he approached the first of the men, who was leaning on a spade.

'Excuse me, I'm looking for your supervisor – Mr Davis?'

'Supervisor, you say? Next he'll be calling himself the prime minister,' the man chuckled, with several of his nearby companions joining in.

'So he's not in charge of the team, then?'

'Well, he's probably more experienced than some of us, but I wouldn't say he was the boss around here. We answer to one of the suits back at the office,' the man explained, indicating the building Richard had just visited on the other side of the airfield.

'Does that mean he's not here?'

'It's his turn to brew the tea. You'll find him over there in the hut.'

Richard thanked them and knocked on the door of the hut before stepping through the door. Gavin Davis was sitting on a bench reading a newspaper while a kettle steamed away on a single gas ring. He looked up and did a double take. 'Aren't you the chap that came to our house looking for Helen?' he asked.

'I am. But this time, I'm here to speak to you.'

Gavin frowned. 'Why would you need to see me? I am working, you know.'

'Yes, I'm aware of that. I want to talk to you about Helen and her late husband. I am the investigating officer working on the case. Is there anything you can tell me about John Wentworth?'

'She changed, you know, after she met him in London. Never had any time for her mother or me. After all I did for her when she was younger,' Gavin snarled.

'Can you elaborate?' Richard pulled out a notebook and pencil.

'I did everything for that girl when I took on her and her mother. Every time I reached out to her she was rude and nasty. They are the only words I can think of for her. In fact, she's such a bad influence in the house that I eventually had to ask her to leave. She's moved on somewhere, mucking out at a dog kennels I was told. A bit of a comedown for the young madam, isn't it?'

'Did you ever meet John Wentworth?'

'He once came to the house to ask my wife for the girl's hand in marriage. My wife? I told him he should've asked me. I gave him what for, I can tell you, jumped-up little Hitler.' Gavin laughed viciously. 'In fact, the way people talked about him being prime minister material, he could well have been our equivalent of Hitler.' He roared with laughter at his own weak joke. Richard merely clenched his teeth and kept writing.

'Did you ever visit Helen and John's home?'

'I wouldn't have been welcome,' he answered quickly.

Richard paused and looked up from his note-taking with a questioning frown. Something wasn't right. 'Is it not true that you tried to get to see John Wentworth a few times and were shown the door?'

Gavin's eyes narrowed. 'I did have trouble getting past that snotty-nosed porter, just because I was in my work clothes.'

'So it wasn't a family visit?'

'No. I called in on the off chance to see his nibs. It was business,' he added, clearly trying to impress Richard.

'How so?'

'I was planning to run my own business. I'd left my previous job as I wanted to set up on my own, but I needed some financial assistance. I thought after all I'd done bringing up Helen, I could ask her old man for a loan.'

'How long ago was this?'

He thought for a moment. 'Must be six or seven months ago now.'

'And did Mr Wentworth help you?'

'He told me to come back with some figures,' Gavin scoffed. 'Figures – I ask you! I work with my hands. I'm a qualified, time-served craftsman, I'll have you know.'

'I was under the impression you were in management at the council,' Richard said mildly.

Gavin shrugged, but he looked angry. 'Are you trying to catch me out or something? I worked my way up through the ranks. They lost a good worker when I left.'

Richard looked back down at his notes, pencil poised. 'Did you argue with John Wentworth at any time?'

'If you mean did I give him a piece of my mind, yes, I did. Then she returned to the flat and they nigh-on kicked me out. I told him I'd come back some time when she wasn't there, and I'd be telling her mother what a little mare she was.'

One of the men stuck his head in the door and called out for his tea.

Seeing Richard frown, Gavin was quick to explain. 'I'm not normally the tea boy, we're just short-staffed today. Rather than have one of them pack up work, I'm making it so they carry on working and don't skive off.'

Richard understood. 'That makes sense; so what is it you're laying out there?'

Gavin stood up to pour the boiling water into a large enamel teapot. 'We're running a new water pipe across to one of the hangars.'

'So your time served was in plumbing, was it?'

Gavin laughed. 'No, no, no, my trade is gas work. I was indentured as a lad and served a full apprenticeship. That's what took me up in the world; if you've got a gas problem, I'm your man,' he bragged. 'Would you like a cuppa?'

Alarm bells started to ring in Richard's mind. He thought back to the hours his team had spent dusting for prints, checking gas records, the two autopsies and knocking on doors in Cadogan Mansions, even though not every resident had been home. 'No, thanks. I've got to be on my way. If you can think of anything about Helen and John that would help my investigation, please let me know,' he said, leaving a card on the edge of the bench where the tea was being brewed. 'Thank you for your time.'

18

28th March 1940

'It is so kind of you to transport us to John's memorial service,' Hillary Davis said as she took the front passenger seat of Richard's vehicle. 'I fear it will be a very difficult day for me, thinking of my late son-in-law and what might have become of him and his career had he lived. How very sad that an explosion brought an end to such an important career.'

Lizzie, who was sitting in the back seat alongside Helen, whispered, 'Have you not told her what really happened?'

'No; the opportunity never arose. To be honest, I couldn't face dealing with her tears and consoling her.'

'Surely she should have been the one consoling you?'

Helen laughed quietly. 'One would think so; but I'm afraid my mother is one of those people who needs to be the centre of attention. You must have met people like her?'

'Oh yes, most certainly. A distant relative who came to visit me once while I was in hospital. It was nothing serious,' Lizzie added, seeing the concern on Helen's face.

'But this woman arrived and declared she felt faint because she didn't like hospitals – so there was I, hopping out of my bed in my best nightdress to fetch her a glass of water and fan her with a knitting pattern.'

'A knitting pattern?'

'It was on my bed. I'd been knitting before she arrived.'

'Gosh,' was all Helen could say.

Richard raised his voice so that they could hear him in the back seat. 'I know there is a small reception after the service, but I wondered if I could take you ladies out to dinner afterwards? I have booked a table, but if it's inconvenient I can easily cancel.'

Helen felt a little dismayed. She'd hoped to slip away after the reception and pay a visit to the offices of Lambeth Council. She wanted to find out more about her stepfather and his time working there, supposedly in the important job of overseeing a department. This little investigation wasn't something she wanted to tell her mother about – or Lizzie, come to that – but she simply couldn't shake her suspicion that Gavin wasn't telling the truth about his past life. The thought had crossed her mind that he might have a mistress, or even another wife. She wanted to find out, for her mother's sake.

'What do you say?' Hillary called out loudly. 'It's so kind of Mr Gladstone to treat us to dinner, don't you think?'

Lizzie looked at Helen's face. 'Is there a problem? If you're thinking of all the work we've got to go back to, well, we can always work harder tomorrow.'

Helen realized she had to make a decision. Not wanting to disappoint anyone, she smiled and said that would be wonderful. 'Thank you very much, Richard. Are you sure we're not putting you out?'

'Not at all,' he said. 'I only have a desk full of paperwork to get back to, and I wasn't looking forward to it. I would rather spend the evening with three delightful women.'

Hillary gave a girlish giggle which had Helen and Lizzie trying hard not to laugh out loud themselves.

'I hope this awful weather doesn't spoil the day,' Hillary said, leaning forward to peer through the windscreen. 'It must be a challenge to drive in these conditions.'

Richard assured her he was fine, and went on to tell her about driving overseas on mountain passes. Hillary soon changed the subject.

'Have you attended this church before?' she called out to Helen, who noted that her mother seemed to be putting on a posh voice just because she was going to the Palace of Westminster.

'Yes, Mother, I have, but sadly that was also a memorial service.'

'I'm led to believe that it's a great honour for a Member of Parliament to be remembered in such a way,' Richard said. 'The Chapel of St Mary Undercroft is rarely used.'

'That's right,' Helen replied, leaning forward and resting her arm on the back of her mother's seat. 'John's colleague, who organized the service, had to put forward his request to Black Rod and also the dean of Westminster Abbey. It was quite complicated in the end. That's why I was happy to step back and let those who know the ropes organize the service.'

Lizzie was fascinated. 'We have nothing like this back

home. Was this allowed because John was a Member of Parliament, or are his family part of the landed gentry?'

'Ha! His mother would like to think so. John wasn't one to speak of his ancestors, but I understood there were a few important people among them. His mother liked to remind me they were a special family. You'd get on with her well, Mother,' she couldn't help saying.

'I only met her once, at your wedding. She didn't seem very interested in chatting, and left soon after the service. It will be pleasant to have a proper conversation with her today and pay my condolences.'

Helen leant back in her seat. At one time, it would have irked her that her mother displayed emotion to other people but never to her. Of late, however, she'd started to see a softer side to Hillary, and she liked that person very much. Consequently, she'd made a promise to herself not to argue and just let whatever her mother said wash over her.

'I must thank you for all your hard work in arranging the sale of works at the airfield, Hillary,' Lizzie said. 'It has been a great weight off my mind knowing somebody who can organize such things is in our circle.'

'It's my pleasure,' Hillary said, almost preening. 'I have had to chase up some of the ladies, as they've been rather slow completing their items for sale. But hopefully everything will be all right on the day, as they say. I'm so pleased to be able to help the poor animals up at The Grange.'

Lizzie thought of the women who had come to her complaining about Hillary's heavy-handedness. 'Oh well, another few weeks and it will all be done and dusted, and you can take a rest.' She smiled politely.

Helen was looking out the window quietly, and Lizzie

touched her hand. 'I thought these might help you stay calm,' she said, passing over several pieces of cut fabric and paper shapes. 'I find small tasks like this so therapeutic during long journeys.'

Helen thanked her, and started to tack scraps of pink patterned cotton to the paper shapes. 'What are you making with these?'

'A pram cover, to go into the shop when it's open.'

'I've been showing Effie's girls how to cut the shapes and tack them together. They have both decided they're making quilts for their beds, bless them. I suggested they start with a smaller project, so we are all making pot-holders and tea cosies. Effie is going to show me how to make a rag rug, which will be fun. To think that only six months ago, I had no idea how soothing hand stitching could be.'

As Richard's car approached the capital, Helen fell silent and gazed out the window again. Today was about John and his work in government. For all his shortcomings, he'd done much to ease the lives of the population as war started. Each day when announcements were made, information distributed guiding people on how to eat and how to cope with rationing, she knew that he had been behind it. Soon she would be meeting his colleagues and the people who had stepped into his shoes, and listening to glowing eulogies of him as a Member of Parliament for the area of Oxfordshire he represented. It would be hard, remembering their life together and knowing he was such a loss to the country even though they'd been living a lie. Her emotions were bittersweet.

She'd been sent a seating plan, so she knew that she

would be seated in a prominent position close to John's family. Hillary would be with her, but Lizzie and Richard were placed elsewhere. She wished both of them could have been closer, as their presence made her feel stronger, but today protocol had to be observed. Now was the time to think of her past – the future could wait for another day.

'Oh my,' Lizzie sighed as she sat down at the dining table. 'I hope there won't be an air-raid warning, because I've kicked my shoes off under the table and may have to scramble on my hands and knees to find them.'

Hillary chuckled. 'I was thinking of doing the same. It's all very well dressing smartly, but my feet have suffered too,' she said as she also removed her shoes. 'Thank goodness the tablecloth is almost to the floor,' she added. 'How are your feet, Helen? You were on the go for most of the afternoon, after the service finished; you must be exhausted.'

Helen looked up and caught Richard's eye. Was he thinking of another time she'd removed her shoes because of her aching feet? Or the night at the hotel when they had both removed so much more? 'I'm all right at the moment, thank you. But who knows, I may join the pair of you before we finish our meal.'

'I felt it went very well,' Lizzie said. 'I have to confess to not knowing much about your late husband previously, but I feel as though I know him inside out now after such glowing words. His death is a great loss to the country.'

'Did you meet his mother today, Lizzie?' Hillary asked

as she picked up the menu. 'I found her quite an obnoxious woman, and such a snob.'

'Mother, please!' Helen hissed, looking around to make sure no one had overheard. Hillary's voice was known to travel.

'Thankfully, we won't have to meet her again. I found the way she spoke to you, and about you, quite appalling. I put her right, I can tell you. I told her my daughter has a very responsible job at the moment and has carried on regardless of what her husband got up to.'

Helen was puzzled. What was Hillary talking about? At no time had she ever mentioned John and Felicity to her mother – and thankfully Felicity had not shown her face today. Could it be something to do with her striking Felicity's name through on the seating plan before she sent it back? 'I'm not sure what you mean?'

'I visited the ladies' room during the reception after the service, and overheard that woman wearing the atrocious fox fur talking about John carrying on with other women behind your back. You don't look that surprised, Helen?'

Helen took a deep breath. She wasn't sure a busy restaurant was the right place to explain to her mother about her married life. 'There have been many rumours, Mother. John had a job that kept him in the public eye, and inevitably stories would be fabricated from time to time. Some people do like to gossip.'

'Oh no, this woman sounded sure of what she was talking about. They mentioned somebody called Felicity. I can't recollect the surname, but would that have been the girl who was your bridesmaid?'

'I have no idea, Mother,' Helen said, noticing Lizzie and Richard's sympathetic glances. 'Would you mind if we didn't talk about this just now? It's not as if John is here to defend himself,' she said, her last words causing bile to rise in her throat. Why was she sticking up for him?

At that moment the wine waiter appeared. Richard took control and ordered champagne. 'I know it may not seem like the natural thing to drink after such an occasion. However, I want to toast you ladies and all you are doing for the dogs up at The Grange.' When the waiter re-appeared and opened the bottle, Richard raised his glass. 'Being a stray myself who has benefited from your care and generosity, I can say that the county is very lucky to have you. I thank you.'

All three women chuckled and raised their glasses.

The meal was a great success and enjoyed in relaxed company. Once the tricky subject of John's infidelity was out of the way, Helen thought she'd never seen her mother on such good form. They ate, drank champagne and took no notice of the time.

'What is next on the cards for the fundraising, apart from the sale of goods at the airfield?' Richard asked.

Lizzie spoke up before Hillary could open her mouth. 'I've had a word with Gerald and we have both agreed the event should be in May,' she said, trying not to meet Hillary's eye. 'Given the extra time, there will be more goods prepared by the ladies without us harassing them to hurry up. In the meantime, Rita Binks has been doing a marvellous job with the bingo evenings, they've become very popular; and again, thank you, Hillary, for helping out.'

'Someone had to,' Hillary said as she finished her

champagne and held her glass out for a top-up. 'The barn is rather on the large side, and some of the people sitting towards the back could not hear the vicar's wife calling out the numbers.'

Lizzie, who had stuck her head in that night to see how the evening was going, had been surprised at how far Hillary's voice travelled. 'Your voice projects extremely well.'

'Thank you,' Hillary smiled. 'I'll be offering my services again in future, so the fundraising continues to succeed.'

'That's so kind of you,' Lizzie murmured, not knowing what else to say. 'I'm just going to nip out to the ladies' room before we set off; does anyone wish to join me?'

'I'll come with you,' Hillary said as she got up and followed after retrieving her shoes.

'A coffee while we're waiting?' Richard asked Helen.

'Not for me, otherwise I'll have to join the other two,' Helen smiled.

He got up and moved around the table to sit next to her. 'I know it's been a big day for you. You've had a lot to contend with; but I've sensed another sadness. Is there something else worrying you?'

Helen sighed. She knew she could trust Richard, but even so, it seemed rather petty after his generous offer of dinner. 'It is so silly, but I'd planned to do something today . . . something I've thought about for quite a while. It has nothing to do with John. It's just – well, it's Gavin. As you know, he's been an absolute beast to my mother, but thankfully he's got his important job at the airfield to keep him busy at the moment, which means Mother comes to The Grange to help out. And you've heard that she's joined in with our fundraising events at Lizzie's place. I thought after the reception this afternoon, I would get a cab over to the council office and see if anyone could give me some information about him. He's a terrible man, but I think I'll need proof before Mother will truly see that.'

'I can see why you want to do it, but I doubt very much whether the council authority would speak to someone outside the department and give away personal details. So, you'd have made the journey for nothing,' he said, trying to help her see sense.

She shrugged her shoulders. 'Oh well, I suppose you're right; it was just a thought. It's just that I know he's lied to Mother.'

'In what way?'

'Only what I already told you when we last spoke about him. It may not seem like much, but I can't get his deceit about that bowling club trip out of my mind. I was going to ask if anyone knew why he left the council job. If he is cheating on Mother, I want to find out. Perhaps it was someone he used to work with, and it meant he got fired? Am I putting two and two together and making five?'

Richard didn't feel it was the right moment to tell her about his talk with Gavin; Hillary and Lizzie might return to the table at any moment. Besides, he wanted to investigate a little more. 'Please leave it with me. If I find anything out, I'll tell you. At least it will put your mind at ease and a smile back on your face. I hate to see you so sad.' He reached out and took her hand.

'Thank you for listening to me. Even if you can't find out anything, at least I know I have a friend who cares.'

'I care a lot,' he said, and was starting to lean forward

to kiss her cheek when across the dining room he spotted Lizzie and Hillary returning. Letting go of her hand in case they noticed, he asked, 'Do you happen to remember when this bowling club trip was supposed to be?'

'I can't remember the exact date. I feel it would have been just before I returned home after John died; I recall Mother mentioning that Gavin hadn't brought her a gift. That's something he's always done when going away on trips with the bowls team. At the time I could only just function after the shock of John's death, and felt she was being selfish.'

'It's understandable,' he sympathized, 'you've had a lot to think about.'

'Perhaps you could ask some of the women when they come along to Lizzie's house? Rita Binks may be able to help you. I'm sure her brother is one of the team.'

'I'll do that,' he smiled as the waiter brought over their coats and he helped Helen into hers, giving her shoulders a gentle squeeze as he did so. He was keen to know what Gavin was up to, and if it also put Helen's mind at rest, that was all for the good.

'Thank you,' she whispered.

19

30th April 1940

On the day of the grand opening of the new kennel block, the spring sun shone down on visitors to The Grange. Jean had dug out some old bunting not used since the coronation, and with Dorothy and Jane's help she had draped it around bushes and trees close to the paddock where guests had assembled.

Invitations had been sent out far and wide, to owners of Stan's Bobtails as well as the ladies from the sewing circles and their families. There was also a scattering of men in uniform, predominantly RAF working out of Biggin Hill airfield. Stan personally welcomed everyone who came in through the large gates of The Grange, shaking hands and pointing out the way to go for the proceedings. A little while later he stepped into the roped-off grass area to make a short speech before inviting Lizzie to cut the red ribbon draped across the main entrance of the new block.

'I now declare these kennels open,' Lizzie announced with great aplomb as she cut the ribbon, waving her best dressmaking scissors in the air and almost knocking off her wide-brimmed hat.

'She's had one too many sherries,' Effie chuckled as she stood behind a long table full of refreshments, helping Jean serve.

'Perhaps give her a cup of tea when she's finished speaking?' Jean suggested. 'We don't want her falling flat on her nose in her best clothes. I will say she's dressed the part; that's such a smart suit. Not everybody can wear green. As for that hat, draped in netting – it could be used for beekeeping.'

Effie giggled. 'You are funny. I really do like Lizzie and her husband. People have told me that Americans can be quite loud and brash, but those two are nice.'

'You need to go and look in the children's atlas in the library,' Jean scolded her. 'The Donningtons are Canadian, and very different from Americans – and wait until you meet a few of those, too, before you start judging them.' She nudged Effie with a grin.

'Oh, silly me. I'm not thinking straight, of course they are,' she giggled.

Lizzie finished her speech and Helen stepped forward, looking nervous. 'I've been called upon to thank Lizzie and her husband Gerald for their generosity in arranging for this kennel block to be built. You are welcome to take a look around, but could we do it in groups, please, because some of the dogs are a little timid. There are collection buckets placed in prominent spots, so please be generous, because we are still desperate for money. All these dogs need feeding and caring for, as well as veterinary fees for those who are poorly. We would also like to thank the ladies who supplied this delicious buffet today, and – I know he will hate me naming him, but Stan Trentham is the man behind saving all of these dogs, and also helping our small community. If anyone hasn't seen the allotments, I suggest you take a walk up the lane and look around. They're a sight to behold. Six months ago the field was scrubland, and nothing like it is now.' She looked at her notes. 'Thank you also to the men from the airfield who set out the allotments, cleared the ground, and in some cases helped to build a few sheds out of old doors and planks of wood. It's quite miraculous what has been achieved.'

Effie's elder daughter, Dorothy, went over and tugged at Helen's sleeve. She bent down to listen, and the little girl whispered in her ear.

'I've been reminded that we also need to thank the husbands and sons of the members of our craft circles for digging the area over and building an air-raid shelter close to the allotments, so we can safely grow our produce and feed our community'. She coughed nervously and looked at her notes again. 'When you've had your fill of the delicious refreshments, may I suggest you walk over towards the house, where we've set up a farm shop? It's a little sparse at the moment as we await our first crops, but the ladies who are members of our craft circles held at Mrs Donnington's home have used the shelves to display items that they have made. Some are for sale, so please dig deep into your pockets, as all profits go to the upkeep of the dogs in the Donnington kennel block. I've almost finished speaking, you'll be glad to hear,' she chuckled. 'We will have, with the help of Major Gerald Donnington, a sale of work, which will be held at the airfield on the fourteenth of May over three days, again with proceeds going towards the stray dog fund.'

She waited until the applause stopped before turning over her page of notes. 'Finally, we thought it would be fun to hold our own dog show. As you know, Stan Trentham is a top dog show contestant, and as proper dog shows aren't running during the war, we thought, with the kennel full of cute-looking dogs, those who wished could rent a dog for the next hour and enter it into our fun classes. There will be rosettes presented to the winners of the classes, made especially for the event by our Mrs Rita Binks. Rita – stand up and take a bow.'

Everybody cheered and clapped as the popular Rita Binks took a curtsy and headed to one side of the roped-off area where Helen was standing.

'Rita will be our judge for the afternoon. There will be four classes. One will be for the scruffiest dog, another for the dog with the biggest smile, the third for the dog with the waggiest tail and the fourth for the dog who can sit down for the longest time without moving. If you would like to register to be a handler, you can go over to where Mrs Green is in charge of handing over the dogs. Just one thing . . .' she called out, as most of the visitors started to move toward the kennels. 'If you don't want to give the dog back at the end of the day, please speak to us about adoption!' she laughed. 'We'd be grateful if anyone could give a dog a good home.'

Leaving the roped-off area after stopping to thank Rita, she accepted the glass of lemonade Effie handed to her.

'You wouldn't catch me standing up and talking in front

of so many people,' Effie commented. 'For one thing, I could never wear a hat; I'm so short I look rather like a mushroom in anything that has a brim, whereas you look so elegant,' she said, admiring Helen's floral dress and pale-green straw hat.

'But then I can't bake such delicious cakes, or concoct fancy fillings out of nothing for the sandwiches. Considering what we had to hand, you've created a miracle.'

'Oh, it's nothing,' Effie said. 'Look, take this tea over to Lizzie; we think she needs it.'

'You could be right; her nerves got the better of her. She was worried about cutting the ribbon and speaking in front of all these people. It's wonderful how many have turned out to support us. This is something really special.'

'It helps having a nice warm day,' Jean said as she added a dash of milk to the tea. 'You'd best go before it gets cold, and mind how you carry it as we don't want tea spilling down that pretty frock of yours.'

Helen carried the cups and saucers over to the grassy area Stan had carefully nurtured over the past few weeks, in readiness for today. She stopped for a moment to watch as people began to enter the ring for the dog show. Stan was in charge of the ring today and was handing out a number to each participant, which was pinned to their chest. He looked resplendent in his best tweed suit and cap.

'This is for you,' she said, handing a cup of tea to Lizzie, who was standing with her husband and Richard Gladstone.

'Oh, thank you. I don't think I could stomach another sherry.'

'Neither do we,' Gerald said, giving Helen a cheeky wink.

'Would either of you gentlemen like a drink?'

'Not for me, thank you,' Gerald said. 'I've had my fill for today. What is it with you English drinking so much tea?'

'It's our favourite pastime,' Helen smiled. 'How about you, Richard?'

'Not for me, thank you. But I wondered if I might have a quick word with you, Helen? That's if you weren't planning to enter the dog show?'

'Goodness no, not me. I see enough of the dogs every day. Let someone else have the fun! I've given Dorothy and Jane a few coppers each so they can enter on my behalf,' she said as he took her arm and they walked away from the crowd. They made small talk until they were alone on the other side of the house, where Richard pointed to a garden bench and they sat down.

Her hands shook with nerves. 'I always feel as though when we are alone you tell me news I don't want to hear; so, unless something new has happened, can we talk about the weather or something instead?' she asked as she straightened the full skirt of her frock, trying not to think of the intimacy they'd shared and how since then he'd kept his distance. She'd not seen a lot of him at Lizzie's house, and felt that clearly he didn't love her as much as she now knew she loved him. 'What is it this time?'

'First, I want to tell you how much I've missed you. It feels as though every time I make plans to return to Dalton Court, I'm called away on another assignment.'

'I had no idea you weren't there. Lizzie never said.'

'She wasn't allowed to say anything. Gerald had to make sure she kept quiet. You have no idea what it's been like,' he said, giving her a desperate look.

'You could have written a letter,' Helen pointed out. She wanted so badly to find a crack in his armour, something to show that he really didn't care for her. Then she could move on and forget him. As she lay awake at night thinking of him, she had decided that if he couldn't declare his love to her – and mean it – then it was best to make a clean break. Her heart ached at the thought.

Richard shook his head. 'It wasn't possible to write. If I had, the censors would have stopped the letters. You have to remember, we are at war,' he said, looking at her desperately, 'and my line of work means at times I will not be here, and I can't speak of what I'm doing.'

Helen frowned. She wanted to believe him. 'So, what you're saying is it's rather like a detective doing undercover work?'

'Yes, in a way it is, but if you factor in the military and overseas it will be easier to understand.'

'I do want to believe you. It's just that with everything that's happened in my life . . . I don't want to be let down again. You may think it's selfish of me, but it's the only way I can stay strong,' she said, her expression imploring him to understand.

He took her hand and tenderly squeezed it. 'I don't want to let you down, that's the last thing on my mind. I love you desperately, and never want to see you looking sad. If you can't understand that at times I'm going to have to disappear, and it has nothing to do with you, then perhaps you should tell me now that you no longer want to see me.'

Helen gasped. 'I can't face the world without you,' she told him. 'I know there will be times I'll worry when you aren't here, but when you are home, my heart will sing. So please try not to leave me too often – but when you do, I'll understand. I'll also pray for the end of the war to come soon, so that hopefully we can be together forever.'

'Oh, my love,' Richard said as he crushed her in his arms and kissed her until she could hardly breathe. They were both brought back to earth when they heard the giggling of young children.

'I told you they hadn't gone to look in the shop,' Effie's younger daughter said.

'We'd better creep away before they hear us,' the older one replied. 'We can show Helen our rosettes later.'

Richard released Helen from his arms, and they laughed as they watched the two little ones disappearing between a row of hedges.

'So much for me trying to find somewhere private to speak to you,' he said as he stroked her cheek.

'It was perfect for the few minutes we were alone. What did you want to tell me, though? Please don't say you're going away again?'

'I have some news for you,' he said, not replying to her question.

'You've arrested Felicity?'

'No. Although she's been no friend to you, she's not guilty of the murder. I'm sorry she let you down so much, but hopefully you won't have to see her again. The last I heard, she'd taken a position in Scotland.'

'She's certainly put a few miles between us,' Helen said cynically. 'But then, what is this news? Do you have a new suspect?'

'Well, I've managed to follow up what you told me about Gavin Davis leaving his job in Lambeth, and your feeling that it was rather a mystery.'

Helen's eyes lit up. 'What happened? Please do tell me!'

'I spoke to his former boss, who informed me that Gavin had been invited to leave.'

'Invited?'

'Yes. There'd been more than one misdemeanour, apparently, and it was felt that he couldn't continue to work for them.'

'Did his boss say what kind of misdemeanours they were?'

'He was very reluctant to give me the details, but I did manage to find out more. First of all, Gavin has been lying about his status as a manager. He did have a couple of staff reporting to him in the department where he worked, but he was not part of the management.'

'Why am I not surprised?' Helen sighed. 'But then, how could he have afforded to keep up the care and maintenance of The Maples and also run a car – let alone have membership at the golf club? None of that is cheap.'

'That's a good point. Perhaps he has savings? Has he mentioned anything like that?'

'No, and I'm sure he'd brag about it. He likes to brag. What else did you learn?'

'As I was leaving the office, a secretary followed me out into the corridor and asked if we could have a word. She kept looking over her shoulder, so I suggested we meet at lunchtime at a pub just down the road, where we could talk without her looking so jittery. What she told me made a great deal of sense, and it answers some of the questions you've had about your own home life.'

'Crikey! Whatever did she tell you?' Helen was intrigued.

'It seems that part of Gavin's job was to go out and make site inspections after a job or repair had been completed. On more than one occasion, there were complaints.'

'Oh my God,' Helen said. 'Did he rough-handle female customers, like he has me and Mother?'

'This woman – she spoke to me in confidence and asked me not to reveal her name – gave me a few examples of his rudeness. There was something else.'

'Oh no.' Helen put a hand to her mouth, eyes wide. 'He didn't badly hurt anyone, did he?' she asked, as unhappy memories came flooding back.

'No,' Richard reassured her. 'It's more a case of money going missing from one of the properties he visited.'

'But why wasn't he arrested? Why has something like that been kept quiet?'

'The secretary was all for informing the police, but the family involved didn't want their name to get into the newspapers. It seems it wouldn't have sat well with their church, and with their eldest daughter about to be married, they preferred to sweep it under the carpet. If only one of them had spoken out, you and your mother would have been free of Gavin and he wouldn't have continued his nasty ways. It crossed my mind that he might well have had his fingers in the till at the golf club, too. What with his bullying tendencies and arrogant manner, I imagine he'd feel able to talk his way out of most situations.'

Helen shook her head in disbelief. 'I need to get my mother away from him. I suppose the police can't do anything?'

'I returned to the council office to ask a few questions. I wanted to know if there'd been any documentation of these accusations, but Gavin's former boss told me there hadn't been. I got the impression he found it all too distasteful to write down. Getting rid of Gavin was enough for him.'

'But why did that secretary want to tell you all this, if we can't do anything about it?'

'Well, she gave me the name of one of the tenants . . .'

'And?'

'I went to visit the family. The wife was almost hysterical, begging me not to say anything. Her husband is now in the army and would be upset if anyone felt he'd been fool enough to let someone steal money from his home. Even though she has experienced Gavin's rough ways, she was prepared to stay silent.'

Helen sank back against the bench with a sigh. 'I'm prepared to give a statement if need be, but in my case, I wonder if my mother would be able to cope with the outcome? I'm as bad as everybody else, aren't I? This is why people like him so often get away with things. So, are we supposed to just leave it there?'

'I'm loath to – for starters, because your mother still lives with him. I'm thinking of having a word with him, to let him know we are aware of what has gone on in the past.'

'You mean, imply that someone's going to report him?'

'I'm saying a word in his ear may work. If he knows he's being watched, it might just do the trick.'

'Thank you. It would give me some kind of closure. Even so, I want my mother to leave him – but only I can solve that problem.' She stood up. 'There is one other thing that I need to do before I lock that door on the past. Come with me,' she said, taking his hand. 'I have something to show you.'

She led him to the shed close to the house.

'They've done a good job here,' Richard said, taking in the new windows and bright paint. The shelves that had been put up ready to sell vegetable crops were now being used to display handiwork from the sewing groups, including their brightly coloured rag rugs. 'And what's this?' he enquired with a grin as he noticed something displayed against one wall. It was Helen's quilt.

'It's finally finished,' she said with a smile, 'and I thought we'd put it on display just to show what can be done with some old, unwanted fabric. It's going on display down at the airfield as well, after which I'm packing it up and sending it off to John's mother. I've decided not to tell her about the red patch that reflects his deceit, but I will tell her that the rings are made from the fabric that made up our life. Then I can finally say goodbye to my patchwork life.'

Richard pushed the door to and kissed her. 'My patchwork girl,' he murmured.

'I'll be going up to London the week after next to visit our old apartment. Apparently the repairs have been completed and the decorating finished. I'd like to take one final look around before I close that door too. I spoke to the porter on the telephone, and he said if I visit before the new tenants move in I'll be able to have a moment on my own to make my goodbyes to that part of my life. But I'm not sad about it,' she assured him. 'I have so much to look forward to now.'

'Are you certain?'

'I am. Please do have that word with Gavin. Make it clear to him that a lot of people know what he's done, but don't put your own career in danger. He will be quick to complain if he thinks this is a personal vendetta. I've decided that before too long I'll be moving out of The Grange, so that Effie and the children can have the rooms to themselves. When her husband comes home on leave, I'd like her to be able to show him a proper home. It will use up my meagre savings, but if I can find my own place I'll make sure there's room for my mother. I'm sure we will manage even if we have to tighten our belts.' She smiled. 'As we are growing closer, I hope she will agree to join me. I can only hope she will accept what I tell her about Gavin.'

20

12th May 1940

'Thank you for coming with me, Mother,' Helen said as she paid the taxi driver and they stood looking up at the red brick facade of Cadogan Mansions. 'Come on – let's get this over with.'

They stepped into the foyer. 'Good afternoon. This is my mother,' Helen said as Hillary nodded politely to the porter.

'I must thank you for looking after my daughter while she lived here,' Hillary told him.

'It was a pleasure,' he replied. 'The Wentworths were perfect tenants.'

Apart from the philandering, murder and a gas explosion that almost wrecked the building, Helen thought wryly.

'I'll leave you to visit your rooms on your own,' the porter said, handing over a set of keys. 'Take as long as you wish.'

Thanking him, they went up in the lift and stepped out into the corridor that led to the four apartments on that floor.

'They've done a good job with the new paintwork,' Helen said, opening the door and stepping over the threshold into the now-empty rooms. Even on close inspection, there was no evidence at all of what had happened before.

'Do you think the letting company will inform the new tenants that someone was murdered here?' Hillary asked. 'I'm not sure I would like to move into an apartment where someone had met a violent end.'

'I'd feel the same,' Helen agreed. She'd only recently told her mother that John had been dead before the explosion, and the police were yet to discover who had killed him. It had brought the women closer together as Helen confided in Hillary. 'It doesn't feel like my home now,' she said, moving on to check the bedroom and bathroom.

'It's happy memories that make a home, and one's personal possessions. I don't know whether you have any good memories left now, but as for possessions, you do need to decide what to do with your remaining furniture in storage.'

'I'm not sure I want it anymore. When I set up my new home, I'd rather like to start afresh. I may ask the porter to contact an auction house. The money can go to the fundraising at The Grange. Have you given any more thought to my invitation? I'd love you to live with me when I set up my place.'

'My love, with all that has happened, and how awful Gavin has been to you, I still feel that if I move away he will find me and cause trouble. I don't wish trouble to follow you to your new home. I do promise you that if things become unbearable, I will tell you immediately, so please will you keep the invitation to move in with you open? However, if in the meantime you marry Richard, then of course you'll not want me. The poor man doesn't need his mother-in-law living with him, does he?' she chuckled.

Helen hugged her mother. If only something could be done about Gavin. She'd yet to hear from Richard, but hoped that soon he would have a word with her stepfather. With luck, Gavin might simply disappear for good. 'Mother, there will always be a place for you in my home.'

'That's enough of that,' Hillary said, straightening her hat. 'I feel quite tearful.' She reached for a handkerchief and dabbed at her eyes. 'Come on, I'll treat you to a meal.'

'At the Ritz?'

'No, it's the Lyons Corner House for us from now on, my dear. Times have changed – and for the better. I will be providing for myself rather than have Gavin spending money we don't have. I'm going to look for employment and let Daisy go.'

They paused in the corridor while Helen checked the door was locked, chuckling as Hillary chatted about the possibility of applying to work as a Nippy. As they were turning to go, somebody called Helen's name from down the corridor.

'I'm so pleased I caught you, Mrs Wentworth. I wanted to pay my condolences,' an elderly woman said, stepping into the corridor from two doors away. 'It must have been so awful for you. Are you moving back in?'

Helen remembered the woman but couldn't recall her

name; only that she liked to gossip, just like the porter's wife. 'Thank you very much. No, I won't be moving back. This is my mother, Mrs Hillary Davis . . .' she said, trying in vain to remember the woman's name. Her mind remained a blank.

'I'm Davina Bostock-Smythe,' the woman said, offering her hand to Hillary. 'Would you care to come in for coffee?'

'That's very kind of you, but we are already running a little late,' Helen said, smiling politely. 'I do hope the building work and the explosion didn't inconvenience you too much?'

'Not at all. I went to stay with my niece that very evening and only moved back in the other day. It's such a shame that gasman didn't do his job properly. I hope action is being taken against his company.'

'Gasman?' Hillary and Helen echoed at the same time.

'Yes – I spotted him coming out of your apartment only minutes before the explosion. I was just leaving at the time, and he walked past my door to go down the stairs at the back of the building. I wished him good evening, but he didn't even acknowledge me. He looked very grumpy.'

'Did he say he was the gasman?' Helen asked.

'Well, no, but I assumed he must have been. After all, the story we read in the newspapers was that it was a gas explosion. I'm just thankful it didn't damage my flat, apart from some broken windows. He did have the name of the council and department printed on the back of his over-alls. If he'd not knocked me with his toolbox I'd not have looked back and spotted the words. It was strange really, because Cadogan Mansions is not situated in the Lambeth council area. I just hope he got the sack for his negligence.'

Helen looked at her mother as a thought suddenly dawned on her. 'Mother . . . do you still have that photograph of Gavin in your purse?'

'I think it's somewhere in here,' Hillary said, taking the purse out of her handbag and pulling out the small image. 'But why . . . ?'

Helen said nothing, but looked at the photograph of Gavin staring down the lens of the camera. She held it out to her former neighbour. 'Do you recognize this man?' she asked.

'Why, yes, it's the gasman. Whyever would you have a photograph of him in your handbag?' Davina asked, looking perplexed.

Helen didn't answer. Instead, she led Hillary by the elbow and directed her towards the lift. They travelled down to the foyer in tense silence. Handing back the keys with perfunctory thanks, they left the building.

'I need to make a telephone call to Richard,' Helen said as they stopped at the end of the road.

'I have some change,' Hillary replied, opening her purse and handing Helen a pile of coppers. 'I'll stand outside the telephone box. Knock on the windowpane if you run out of money. I'm told they eat coins up like no one's business.'

Helen chewed her fingernail as she waited for Richard to come to the telephone. She couldn't believe Gavin had caused the explosion. But why? As thoughts tumbled in her mind, she heard footsteps approaching and the receiver was picked up.

'Mrs Wentworth? I'm sorry, but you've missed him. He's been called away on urgent business. He will be back on the fourteenth. Can I take a message?'

'Are you able to ask him to contact me? It really is urgent.'

'I'm sorry, we have no way of doing that. Can someone else help you?'

Helen knew it was only Richard that she could speak to, as she had no idea who else to confide in. Richard knew the most intimate details of the situation and only he could help them right now. She would have to do the best she could until his return. 'I'm afraid not, but please tell Inspector Gladstone to get in touch with Helen Wentworth as soon as possible.'

'May I make a note of your problem?'

'Just tell him that I have an update on Cadogan Mansions.'

There were only a few coins left, but she decided to place a call to Lizzie as well. Thankfully her friend answered straight away. 'Lizzie – it's me, Helen. Can I ask you a huge favour?'

'Of course, you can, my love, any time at all.'

'Can I bring Mother to stay with you for a few days? Things have taken a turn for the worse. I don't want to worry her too much – I can look after myself, but I'll sleep much better knowing she's there with you and a house full of RAF officers.'

'But what about clothes? She can't stay here for days with nothing to wear . . . I'll have a couple of the lads escort me to The Maples and pack a case after first checking Gavin is at work. Oh, drat – I don't have a key to the house.'

'Daisy, the housekeeper, may be there, but if not Mother hides one in the garden. If you walk down the side of the house, you'll find it hanging in the potting shed.'

'Gotcha. Don't worry about a thing. By the way, where are you?'

'Down the road from my old apartment in London. We're going to have something to eat and then we'll catch the train back.'

'So you'll be arriving around two hours from now? I'll be at the station to collect you both, and don't worry, I'll have somebody with me. Are you sure you don't want to stay with me as well?'

'No, thanks all the same. I'm going to go back to The Grange. I can't abandon Effie and the children.'

'You're not to worry. I have no idea what's happened, but I can assure you that there are people here who will take care of you both,' Lizzie promised.

Helen joined her mother on the pavement. 'Come on – let's go to the Corner House. I'm hungry,' she said.

Once they'd been served scrambled egg on toast, Helen explained her plan. 'That's why it's so important that until Richard is back, you don't go home . . . No, please, no arguments,' she said as Hillary started to object. 'I've spoken to Lizzie and you're going to stay with her, and have your own bodyguards. Don't tell me you won't like that; all those handsome men at your beck and call?' She forced a smile. Looking at her mother's pale, anxious face, she knew for the first time that she loved her dearly and would protect her until her last breath.

'What about my clothes? I can't just vanish and live in what I'm wearing now.'

'Lizzie has arranged to collect some things for you; but you're not to go back there, even with her, do you understand? Think of what Gavin's done to you in the past. I'm pretty certain it's been more than a few bruises, Mother; I'm not stupid. Not to mention what he's done to others. If he gets an inkling that he's been rumbled, God knows how he will react.'

'Won't he suspect something when I don't go home?'

'Lizzie is going to scribble a note and leave on the table where he will see it.'

'But what excuse can she give?'

'It will say Lizzie is poorly, and you've volunteered to look after her for a couple of days. That should do it.'

'All right. I'll do as you say.' Hillary reached across the table and took her daughter's hand. 'I'm afraid for you, Helen. If Gavin has an inkling that we have discovered he caused the explosion, then goodness knows what he will do.'

'Don't worry about me. If he knows you're at Lizzie's, he may assume I'm there as well, but I don't think with your reasonable explanation that the penny will drop. We've just got to carry on as normal with you being out of harm's way until Richard comes back. We only have a couple of days to wait. As for me – well, we have a lock on the door, and Stan can lend us a couple of the loudest and largest of his dogs. You've met those Old English Sheepdogs; they've got one hell of a bark on them. They're the softest dogs going until they are protecting someone they love. I like to think I get on pretty well with them, so they will look after me,' she chuckled, trying to reassure Hillary despite her own fears.

'I've just thought,' Hillary said. 'If Richard is back in a few days that will be the day we start our exhibition and sale of work, at the airfield. Should we stay away?'

'No, I think we must carry on as normal. We have special permission to set up in the mess hall, and there will be plenty of people about; so again I'd say don't worry, Mother. Those RAF lads are protecting our country, so protecting a couple of women shouldn't be a problem! Now come on, tuck into your food before it gets cold. I may very well have the spotted dick and custard after this.'

'So you see, I've got it all arranged,' Lizzie said as they approached The Grange in her car. She had collected Helen and Hillary from the station, and hadn't batted an eyelid as Helen explained everything that had happened – although her knuckles had turned white as she gripped the steering wheel. 'I've spoken to Stan, and you, Effie and the girls are moving into the main house, where you will have him and Jean for company. More importantly, he has a telephone, so if there is a problem – which I doubt there will be – one of you can call us here. We will be with you quicker than the local police.'

'I don't like putting everybody to all this trouble,' Hillary said anxiously.

'I feel the same as you, Mother, but it's for the best. And it will only be for a few days.'

'How will I know that you're all right?' her mother said, sounding tearful.

Lizzie cleared her throat and interrupted the conversation. 'Because you are going to use my telephone twice a day to speak to your daughter, do you understand?'

Hillary pulled herself together and thanked Lizzie.

'Have you noticed something?' Lizzie asked them. 'We have a car following us.'

'Oh my God – who is it?' Helen exclaimed.

'Don't worry. There are three airmen in that car. Gerald has given them orders to follow us everywhere. One of them will be staying at The Grange. Now, are you both happy with that?'

'We can't argue, can we, Mother?' Helen said, thanking her lucky stars that they had such a generous and caring friend in Lizzie.

The two days that followed felt like an eternity, even though they continued with their craft work and preparations for the fundraising event at the airfield. There was no word from Richard, which made Helen's life feel empty, so it was best she had plenty to do.

Stan brought in two of his largest dogs at night, with one, Johnny, insisting on sleeping in Helen's bedroom. She'd fallen in love with the large, affable dog, even though he snored and had a tendency to break wind, and was planning to ask Stan if she could adopt him. As for Gavin, it was just as she'd predicted to Lizzie during one of their many telephone conversations. The man's life seemed to carry on as before, working at the airfield and going home to The Maples each evening. It was everyone else who was looking over their shoulders and worrying about what might happen . . .

21

14th May 1940

'I really admire that Winston Churchill,' Rita Binks exclaimed as she helped Hillary set out knitwear on one of the trestle tables allotted to the women in the mess room at the airfield. 'He will be a breath of fresh air after that last shower. I reckon we will win the war with him leading us. In fact, I can feel it in my water. What was it he said in his speech yesterday?'

'I have nothing to offer but blood, toil, tears and sweat,' Effie said as she joined them. 'It gave me goosebumps when I read it in Stan's newspaper. Well, he must mean business, as I've never heard so many planes taking off as this morning. I could kiss the man!'

'It's a shame you don't toil a little harder. Those balaclava helmets aren't displayed very well at all, and you've not yet cut up the ribbon to decorate the tables,' Hillary said, sliding Lizzie's dressmaking scissors across the table. 'I could have done it myself,' she muttered as she turned her back on them.

'What's wrong with her?' Rita murmured.

'I may as well tell you, as it will be common knowledge before too long,' Effie said, and she filled the older woman in on why her friends were so jittery.

'Well, no wonder she's worse than usual. I feel the same now you've told me. Fancy that! If you want any help with the situation, you only need to shout. I may be getting a bit long in the tooth, but I can still handle any man who causes trouble,' Rita said, hurrying off to speak to Tish Green.

Effie wondered if she'd done right by telling Rita. There again, she was a kindly soul and a good friend to one and all.

'Ladies!' Lizzie clapped her hands together for attention. 'Would you man your tables, please? You should all have a copy of your rota for today. Any questions, please do speak to the team leader on your table,' she said before joining Helen. 'I don't know what I'm more nervous about – selling our wares, or your Richard arriving and sorting out you-know-what.'

'I couldn't eat this morning, I was so nervous. Jean wanted to pack me up a bacon sandwich, but the very thought made me dash to the toilet.'

Lizzie gave her an old-fashioned look. 'Are you sure it's just your nerves?'

Helen's chin almost hit the ground as what Lizzie hinted at hit home. 'Goodness . . . you don't think . . . ?'

'It's a good thing, if it is what we are thinking,' Lizzie said, giving her a hug. 'Richard's not the sort of chap to not step up to the plate, if you are . . .'

Helen looked around in case any of the women had overheard. Plenty were chatting amongst themselves and looking in their direction, but . . . Surely not, she thought to herself, and turned back to Lizzie.

'I'm not sure I want a man to think of me as an obligation,' Helen said. 'I want romance and roses, and to live happily ever after. But then, a baby would be lovely . . .'

'My dear, you are about to have your dreams come true,' Lizzie said, as Richard appeared at the door.

He looked nervously around before striding purposefully towards her, holding a large box and a bunch of roses.

Helen was oblivious to everyone around her as he placed the box on one of the tables and handed her the roses. 'I thought you'd never come,' she told him. 'Did you receive my message?'

He frowned for a moment. 'I've not heard a thing, but then, I've been working all the hours possible to get back to you. I've also had confirmation that I've been taken off the investigation into John's death. I told my boss some time ago that I was too close to someone involved,' he said, watching a delicious blush flood Helen's face. 'Here,' he said, taking the roses from her and passing over the box. 'You've been through this before, but for me it's the first time, so I hope I got it right,' he added, looking nervous as she undid the ribbon fastening and pulled off the lid.

'Oh, Richard,' she sighed, as the women pushed forward to watch what was happening. 'Fabric, lots of new fabric – how wonderful.'

The quilters around her echoed her sighs of appreciation, while the knitters lost interest.

'You need to unpack it all,' he urged her. 'Lizzie helped me with the quantities for the quilt.'

'Quilt?' she questioned as she took each colourful layer out of the box and placed it onto the table. 'Such beautiful colours – but I've only just finished a quilt,' she said, looking to where the double wedding band quilt was displayed on the wall behind them.

'That quilt has too many bad memories for you. I want this one to have nothing but happy memories, as it's part of your new life . . .'

'New life?'

Richard reached into the bottom of the box and lifted out a ring box. Opening it, he held out a solitaire diamond ring as he got down on one knee. 'Helen Wentworth, would you do me the honour of making me the happiest man in the world? But only after you've finished the quilt for our wedding bed . . .'

'Oh, Richard,' was all Helen could say as he slipped the ring on to her finger. Since she'd found out about John's betrayal, she'd taken to not wearing her wedding band. 'I'll sew as fast as I can. But there's something I have to tell you . . .'

He took in her serious expression. 'I'm sorry, my darling – no one told me about your message,' he said as he drew her over to a quiet corner of the room. Lizzie ushered the women back to work.

'. . . So you see, it was Gavin,' Helen said a few minutes later as she finished explaining what had happened. 'He is still working here on the airfield, and Mother has been kept safe at Lizzie's house. He's not aware we've found out his secret. I've been waiting for your return for another reason – I wasn't expecting your proposal . . .'

'Instead of being here to protect you and your mother, and pulling in Gavin, I've left you in danger. I'm sorry.'

'Oh, Richard, your work is important – and everyone has made sure that we've been safe. Gerald and his men have cared for Mother, and I have Johnny on my bed every night.'

'Johnny?'

'I'll explain later,' she said, nudging his elbow. He followed her look towards the door, where Gavin stood, looking angry. 'I'm going to keep Mother company. Will you be able to deal with him?'

'I have enough to take him in for questioning,' he said, kissing her cheek and striding across the room towards Gavin Davis – but Rita Binks beat him to it.

'You utter bounder,' she said, thumping Gavin on the chest with both fists. 'I've heard about you and your games. How anyone could kill a future prime minister, I don't know. You deserve to be locked up and the key thrown away!'

Helen could have cried. Richard would have taken Gavin away quietly, and before he knew what was happening. She had to remove Rita from the situation before things got even worse – if that was possible. She ran past Richard, and heard him call her back, but ignored him as she took Rita by the hand, pulling the older woman away from Gavin before he could hurt her.

'What's this?' he hissed, grabbing her hand with the diamond ring shining brightly on her finger. 'You make me sick – running after another man when your first is not cold in his grave. If your husband had been a little more sympathetic to my request, he'd still be here now,

361

rather than six foot under. And my money problems would be over . . .'

Helen gasped and hit out at him, but Gavin was faster, ducking past Richard and grabbing her arm tightly, at the same time snatching up the scissors. As she screamed for help he dragged her away and out of the door, holding the open scissors at her throat. In the busy room, Richard fought to reach them, but women got in his way, congratulating him on the surprise proposal, unaware of what was unfolding.

'Oh no, madam, no other man is going to have you,' Gavin said. 'I tried to tell your husband how you threw yourself at me before running away to London, but he wouldn't listen – just as he wouldn't listen when I invited him to invest in my business plans.'

'It's all in your mind,' Helen cried out, doing her utmost to free herself.

'Oh, I know you will deny it, but we know the truth, don't we, my little beauty? Now you want to move on to pastures new. What will it take for me to stop you, eh?'

'Please let me go. You've got this all wrong,' she pleaded, trying to keep up with him without falling. 'I'll not say anything.'

'It's too late,' he hissed, thrusting Lizzie's scissors closer to her throat. 'Now stop struggling,' he growled as he fled across the airfield. Helen struggled to stay on her feet as he pulled her along. If she slipped, so could the scissors.

'Be careful,' she cried as the draught from a Spitfire landing within yards of them almost blew her off her feet. 'It's too dangerous out here. Let me go – and I'll make sure you are able to escape before Richard catches up with us,' she begged, knowing the man she loved as much as life itself would be following them. She eyed the scissors in Gavin's hand, and prayed Richard wouldn't do anything to put his own life in danger.

They'd passed the last of the hangars now and were out in the middle of the runway. Helen kept begging Gavin in the hope it would distract him from observing the people who were following, ready to rescue her. They were holding back from tackling him while he still held the scissors close enough to severely injure her.

'Keep back,' he shouted over his shoulder. 'I swear I'll kill her if you get any closer.'

'Free her,' Richard called, holding out his hand to Gavin as he moved ever closer. 'We can talk about this, but don't hurt her, I beg you.'

Another fighter plane screeched close by, causing Helen to stumble. She screamed, thinking Gavin would be bound to stab her. At that moment there was flash of movement as someone leapt onto Gavin and brought him down. It was Rita Binks, closely followed by Effie, who had cut through a nearby hangar in order to get closer to Helen.

'Get the scissors off him,' Rita screamed as Gavin waved them about wildly. There was a spurt of blood and she collapsed, holding her arm. Gavin struggled free just as Richard and other officers caught them up.

'Put the scissors down,' Richard said slowly and calmly. 'You can't escape now, we have you surrounded.'

Gavin looked wildly around before diving through a gap where Effie was tending to Rita. 'You'll never get me,' he shouted, his words turning to a scream as he ran straight into the propellers of a Spitfire landing close by.

Richard pulled Helen into his arms and turned her face away from the scene while his colleagues helped Rita and Effie to their feet.

The bells of ambulances and fire engines filled the air as the subdued group headed away from the scene.

'Is it all over?' Helen whispered.

'It's all over and you are safe, my love. I'll never let anything happen to you ever again.'

Epilogue

Christmas Eve 1940

'I don't want to cause a fuss,' Helen said as her mother tucked blankets tightly around her.

'If I can't take care of my own daughter at a time like this, what kind of mother would that make me?' Hillary admonished as she stood back from the bed, hands on hips, raising a finger that she wagged at Helen. 'I want you to rest. You must promise me not to move a muscle for at least three hours, and try to get some sleep. At least the Luftwaffe won't disturb you down here. They seem to be targeting towns up north at the moment,' she added, chewing her lip and looking worried before folding a newspaper and moving it away from where Helen lay.

'There's no need to hide it away, Mother. I'm able to read the news,' Helen smiled, thinking her mother was wrapping her in cotton wool. 'Those poor, poor people.'

'I thought it bad enough what we went through here. I truly imagined we'd be killed in our beds, with the airfield taking such a pounding.'

'Apart from the fact we were using the Anderson shelter at the time,' Helen replied. She had been so worried about Hillary living alone at The Maples that she'd changed her plans to find her own home and moved back in with her mother. Despite her trepidation about such a move, they'd got on admirably well.

'I must say, Richard has done a good job turning the cellar into our own shelter,' Hillary said as she looked around the long room that ran below the length of the house. 'Who'd have thought it could be so cosy? And at least you can recover in comfort. Now, I must leave you for a little while and prepare lunch. Remember, you can use the bell if you need me,' she said, pointing to a small brass bell on the bedside table.

'I'll be fine, Mother. I'll take the chance to close my eyes for a while. You have no need to worry about me.' Helen snuggled down under the cover a little more and yawned.

'But I do worry,' Hillary said, leaning over and kissing her cheek. 'I have a lot to thank you for.'

Helen closed her eyes and allowed her mind to wander back to the early summer and the awful situation culminating in Gavin's death. It had been apparent straight away that Hillary should not be left to live on her own, and Richard had agreed at once that after their wedding they would make their home at The Maples. Hillary had purpose in life now: to care for her daughter and son-in-law, but also to help out with the embroidery group and up at the kennels, where she had taken on an allotment as well as helping out in the shop. Throughout the devastating bombings, the women's knitting and sewing groups had battled on, doing all they could for friends and neighbours.

Helen sighed as she thought of how decent her friends had been over her quick marriage to Richard, enveloping them with love and warmth – just like the beautiful quilts they'd continued to work on whenever possible. A smile flitted over her face as she thought about how much happier her life had become in the course of just over a year. Her hand reached out to run her fingers over the quilt her friends had helped make in time for the wedding, with the fabric Richard had given her on the day they became engaged . . .

'Hello, sleepyhead,' Richard said as he sat on the edge of the bed. 'This little lady has been crying for her mummy.'

Helen propped herself up and reached out to take their daughter. 'I can see you have your daddy wrapped around your tiny fingers,' she murmured into the baby's ear as she hugged her close.

'After only a week, she is the boss in this house. Does she remind you of anyone?'

Helen chuckled. 'Perhaps naming her Elizabeth after our good friend means our little darling has inherited her feisty nature as well.'

'I thought she was a miniature version of her mummy,' Richard said, leaning in to put an arm around his wife and daughter.

Helen smiled. 'This little bundle of joy and many like her are our future. I for one look forward to peace – whenever that may be – and hope that everyone can experience the happiness we've found with each other. My life feels complete, with everything coming together . . . just like this quilt,' she said, running her hand over the colourful bedcover. 'Pieced together with love.'

Acknowledgements

Although it may feel it at times, an author is never actually alone while writing a book. This is yet another of my books written during lockdown. Hopefully, by the time it is in the shops, we will be looking back at these times perhaps not in fondness, but with a heightened knowledge of how we have all participated in beating this awful pandemic into submission just by staying at home. A book created while staying home and 'just writing' is hard for any historical author, however we do have our memories to fall back on of people who are like our characters – a useful tool for any writer. We also have books and research material to hand that can be used instead of going out to visit archives and attend talks – we can always purchase more! Therefore, I must acknowledge not only booksellers, archivists and libraries, but the wonderful delivery services who supplied me with so many books and documents during these horrendous times. To be able to place an order and have it delivered the next day is a dream come true for any author.

Libraries have been a godsend, promoting authors on social media and ensuring readers manage to get hold of

369

their favourite authors' books whether by a special collection service or via digital download. Who'd have thought that library talks would turn into Zoom talks? I know I'm not alone in being dragged kicking and screaming to my laptop to talk to readers. Standing in front of a roomful of people is one thing, to be up close on Zoom is something else completely!

What about all those events we attend that have now gone virtual? A big thank you to the literary organizations who have fought to bring events to members. Thank you to the Society of Women Writers and Journalists, the Romantic Novelists' Association, the Society of Authors, and the Crime Writers' Association for their continued service for us authors.

I also have to thank my agent, Caroline Sheldon, who has been there for me all the way through lockdown, albeit working from home, and a big thank you to the whole team at Pan Macmillan for your continuing to produce my books. I can look at each of my books and recall what was happening in my life during the writing process. *The Patchwork Girls* is my third 'lockdown publication' and I pray it is the last and life gets back to some semblance of normality very soon.

To my loyal readers. We may not have been able to meet in libraries and book groups for a chat, but we've got together on my Facebook author page, via Twitter, Messenger, email and reading groups. As you know I love to chat so please do keep in touch.

Finally, my husband, Michael, who listens to my moans, chats about plot lines, and searches eBay for suitable research books and memorabilia. Thank you for being part of my writing life and reading my early drafts.

A Letter from Elaine

Dear Reader,

How are you?

We've all been through a lot together these past eighteen months. One thing is for sure: we have read a lot more books than usual! What about new hobbies? My attempt to crochet a blanket has been well documented and I promise to persevere, although it may take some time. I should have started with a smaller project – perhaps a crocheted tea cosy? While planning and indeed during the writing of *The Patchwork Girls,* I immersed myself in the world of patchwork quilts, which meant buying even more books and watching YouTube videos showing the craft. I've always sewn, having been taught by my mum and having an aunt who was a dressmaker by profession. One of my favourite lessons at school was sewing; in fact, if it had been allowed, I'd have liked to have taken dress design up as a profession. Like many women my age I made my bridesmaids' dresses and my own clothing. Back in the late sixties it was a way to create the latest fashions on a shoestring budget. I did make my own patchwork quilt, which sadly suffered after our house fire. I do intend to make another – perhaps it will be the double wedding ring design as features in *The Patchwork Girls*, but without the memories of the fabric like Helen's.

There was a time I had a business making dog coats for show dogs. If you spotted an Old English Sheepdog on the TV going into Crufts wearing a colourful waterproof all-in-one rain suit, it was probably mine. I must have been the only exhibitor who attended dog shows carrying a tape measure, colour swatches and notebooks. It was a very happy time in my life. Mentioning sheepdogs brings me neatly round to the other subject in this book – dogs and their care during World War Two. I so loved writing about my favourite breed – the second is the Polish Lowland Sheepdog, like our current dog, Henry. Although the kennel in *The Patchwork Girls* is pure fiction, I created it from the many stories, memories and wonderful people I've known since my involvement with the breed, which started way back in 1972. Our many lovely dogs may have gone to Rainbow Bridge, but friendships remain. For that I am truly blessed.

Why not visit my Facebook Author Page (Elaine Everest Author) and tell me about your lockdown crafts and your pets? You can also sign up for my newsletter via my website www.elaineeverest.com, where Henry runs the occasional competition and where you can follow my blog posts.

Please stay safe.

Until next time,

Elaine xx